MW01103861

Dark Secrets

P.L. Reed-Wallinger

PublishAmerica
Baltimore

© 2005 by P.L. Reed-Wallinger.

All rights reserved. No part of this book may be reproduced, stored in a retrieval system or transmitted in any form or by any means without the prior written permission of the publishers, except by a reviewer who may quote brief passages in a review to be printed in a newspaper, magazine or journal.

At the specific preference of the author, PublishAmerica allowed this work to remain exactly as the author intended, verbatim, without editorial input.

First printing

ISBN: 1-4137-7831-3
PUBLISHED BY PUBLISHAMERICA, LLLP
www.publishamerica.com
Baltimore

Printed in the United States of America

Dedication

I would like to dedicate this book to my family and friends. Your support and encouragement gave me the audacity to pursue a long-time dream. I would like to thank Dwayne Johnson, alias 'The Rock' as well. Although I don't know him personally, he did inspire the hero of this book, Beau Hawkins.

P.L.Reed-Wallinger

Acknowledgements

I would like to thank my brother, Bill Reed, for his advice, tutoring, editing, emails, and support. I would have been lost without you, Bro, and I am a better writer because of your expertise and talent. I would also like to thank my friend Carol for being my first and most enthusiastic reader, and catching all of the more blatant blunders. Thanks to Carmen for being there, and to Earl for help with research.

Special thanks to Jan Schlieman, my wonderful critique partner. Also, thanks go to Deputy Sheriff Gary Bergmeier for patiently answering my questions on law enforcement procedures.

P.L.R-W

Disclaimer

This book is a work of fiction. Names, characters, and incidents are all products of the author's imagination, or are used fictitiously. The setting is *loosely* based on southeastern Nebraska, and the town of Humboldt, but the author has taken literary license with that, as well. Any resemblance to actual events or persons, living or dead, is purely coincidental.

1

A late afternoon breeze bit at his windshield, as Hawk turned his pickup into Lake Park. Fall was his favorite season, but the brilliant colors of autumn were nearly gone now. By the end of November, they'd be little more than a memory. He weaved his way among the twisting roads of the park, wondering just how much longer they'd have until the snow started flying. Rolling down his window, he inhaled deeply. It smelled like snow in the air today. Man, I love this time of year!

Suddenly, Hawk stiffened, tipping his head to pick up the ghost of sound wafting in on the breeze. There it was again—music. He heard the faint sound of guitar picking, and an even fainter voice, singing accompaniment.

He turned his pickup toward the sound. Despite the numerous camping sites in the park, no one—as far as he could remember—ever came to Humboldt, Nebraska in November, to camp. Hell, there'd be snow on the ground by week's end, he was sure of it. Hawk spotted the wood smoke first, and then a small camper tucked into one of the last stalls. The trees surrounding it nearly concealed the place.

Maybe that's the intention, the thought touched the periphery of his mind, leaving a disquieting suggestion.

Light, and shadows of movement, attested to life inside the camper, but his attention focused on the lone guitarist sitting near a glowing chiminea.

The musician looked up as Hawk pulled the truck to a stop and turned off the engine. Judging by the expression on her face, a cop was the last person she wanted to see.

"Sheriff," she said, standing and setting the guitar down before walking toward his vehicle.

As she moved, she reached into a coat pocket. Hawk tensed. His right hand hovering above the Glock he kept on the console. When her groping revealed nothing but a slip of paper, he relaxed.

The stranger held up a receipt. "I've paid to camp here for the week," she said, her voice low and throaty. Gray eyes, fringed with long, blackened lashes, watched him. Hawk noted the cold-induced pink in her cheeks, and dark, arched brows, but he wasn't able to identify a hair color under the stocking cap covering her head.

"It's not our usual tourist season." Though he tried to curb it, there was the barest nuance of cynicism in his tone.

The woman's only response was a somewhat lopsided smile, and half-hearted shrug.

Removing his shades, Hawk took the receipt she proffered and examined it. "Joanne Kenning," he read the name aloud. "All the way from Fort Lauderdale." Whistling softly, he said, "That's a chunk of drivin'."

"Yeah, I guess so." Joanne Kenning ducked her head, not quite meeting Hawk's eyes. When he made no reply, she looked up and continued, as if compelled to explain, "I...I went through a bad divorce, and then got laid off."

Hawk remained silent, waiting for her to elaborate.

She did.

"Ah, not much in the way of jobs there right now, so I decided to make a new start," Joanne blurted the words out, rushing them together. Her obvious unease seemed disproportional to Hawk.

The gray in her eyes reminded him of a soft fog on a fall day, touching the tops of a Nebraska cornfield. Like the fog, they seemed to be hiding something.

"Nebraska isn't the place most people would choose for startin' over," he said in a conversational tone. "There are lots of small towns, but not many jobs." He smiled amiably, showing even white teeth.

"I...I know," the woman with gray eyes replied. "The kids wanted to see the Heartland." Shrugging, she offered Hawk a tentative smile in return. "They said it sounded like the right place for us—wholesome, or something like that."

"The kids?" Hawk couldn't hide his surprise. The camper looked too small to accommodate a family.

"I...I have three children." Joanne nodded toward the camper.

Hawk followed her gaze, noting for the first time the faces pressed against one of the windows. His eyes returned to the woman's countenance. Choosing to say nothing, he watched the play of emotions she clearly struggled to control.

A breeze pulled at the leaves on the ground, burnt red and toasted brown, scurrying a few into the crisp air, then dying away as quickly as it had come.

Nebraska was like that. Changeable. Unpredictable.

Joanne shivered.

From the breeze—or nerves? Hawk wondered, though he remained mute, intentionally keeping his face inscrutable. That very silence seemed to goad the woman into speaking.

"We've been driving and checking out different places, and we made a pro-and-con list for every town we stopped in."

Waiting for several calculated moments of silence, Hawk finally responded in a soft, curious voice, "So, how does Humboldt stack up?"

"Well, we like it better than any place we've been so far," Joanne replied. "I...I guess finding a place to live and a job of some sort, wouldn't hurt."

"No, I guess it wouldn't," Hawk responded with a chuckle. "The last time I checked the paper there were a few places available for rent, and a couple jobs listed."

Joanne nodded, volunteering a tentative, half-hearted smile.

"There's also Auburn or Falls City, both are a comfortable driving distance from here. We have a lot of residents that commute." Hawk leaned over and retrieved a newspaper from the passenger's seat, offering it to Joanne. "This might help your searching a bit."

Joanne's voice was scarcely more than a hoarse whisper. "Ah…thanks."

Hawk nodded to where the woman's guitar sat propped against a tree trunk. "Nice voice," he said.

"Oh." Joanne ducked her head again, blushing as if the compliment embarrassed her. "I was just passing the time. It's a bit crowded in the trailer."

At her words, Hawk's eyes strayed to the camper again. The faces at the window were gone. As if on cue, the door creaked open and the children spilled out.

The oldest was a girl of about sixteen. She had dark auburn hair, and eyes that looked to be close to the same shade of gray as her mother's eyes. The boy was at least ten, with sandy hair and a nose full of freckles. He watched Hawk warily from light, blue-gray eyes, unease detectable in the tenseness around his mouth, and the rigidity of his small frame.

The youngest of Joanne's three children looked to be barely more than a toddler. Four, or five, at the most. Like a curious midget, she hopped onto Hawk's running board and poked her head in the open window.

"Dooda," she exclaimed, bright eyes surveying the police gadgets and gear inside. "Cool twuck."

"Thanks." Hawk was amused at the look of awe and fascination on the child's face. Wow, what a heart melter, he thought. Short, auburn hair curled in soft wisps about her face, and sapphire-blue eyes regarded him frankly from beneath a dark fringe of lashes. Cotton-candy pink cheeks, reminded Hawk of a picture he'd seen once, with a painting of a cherub.

Smiling at the child he asked, "What's your name?"

"Jennifaw," the girl eyed him with the utmost seriousness, "but evweebody just calls me, Jenny. What's youwa name?"

Before Hawk could answer, Joanne lifted her daughter from the running board and sat her gently on the ground. "Let's not keep the Sheriff from his rounds," she said, sounding anxious to end the unexpected encounter.

"No, it's all right." Hawk grinned and winked at Jenny. "My name is Beau Hawkins, but everybody just calls me, Hawk."

"Like the biwad?"

"Yeah, just like the bird."

Jenny clambered back onto the running board, ignoring her mother's frown of annoyance. "Whoa," she squealed again, her eyes coming to rest on Hawk's revolver. "Big gun!"

Joanne's cheeks flamed. Hawk pretended to ignore her embarrassment. "I save that for the bad guys," he told Jenny. Looking over the child's head, he winked at Joanne in an attempt to ease her discomfort.

"Come on, Jen," Joanne's son pulled his sister away from the truck, hitching her small frame onto his hip. He flashed a furtive glance Hawk's way.

Gut instincts stirred again. What did he sense? Apprehension? Fear, maybe.

Hawk kept his face and voice composed and pleasant, giving no hint that he doubted the legitimacy of the Kennings' presence in Lake Park.

"Well, Joanne Kenning," he handed the woman her campsite receipt through the open window of his truck. "I hope you find Humboldt to your liking."

The woman corrected Hawk automatically. "Jo," she said, and then quickly dropped her gaze, her face suffusing with red.

Hawk arched a single, dark eyebrow. "Jo?"

"Ah, yeah, well…ah, most people just call me, Jo."

Her eyes and voice told Hawk far more than her words ever would. She was scared! Of what, him? Or the law?

"Jo, it is then," he replied, masking his misgivings with a grin.

Fully cognizant of how his smile affected most women, Hawk knew he could count on a second glance or an indrawn breath, and at the very least, a pleased blush. More often than not, coy flirtation followed that initial response.

Jo proved no exception.

Meeting his eyes, she studied his face closely for several intense seconds, and then returned a shy smile, the color in her face heightening perceptibly. With obvious discomfiture, she dropped her gaze to the ground, apparently developing an avid interest in her sneakers.

"An officer usually drives through here at least once a day," Hawk informed her. "So, if you need somethin', just holler." He wondered how long she planned on staying.

Joanne Kenning nodded, her face still flushed.

Slipping on his dark glasses, Hawk touched two fingertips to his forehead in an informal gesture of respect, and then started his pick-up. Pulling onto the road, he automatically glanced in the rear view mirror, catching a look of intense relief on Joanne Kenning's face.

Interesting, he thought, very interesting.

Why didn't she introduce her children? That omission seemed anomalous to Hawk. The whole family was on pins and needles—with the exception of Jenny. So, the question of the day was: Why?

Damned odd behavior.

Every gut instinct he had was firing off alarms.

They're hiding something!

~ ~ ~

"You think he's suspects anything?" Delaney shut the door to the camper. Her cheeks were bright pink from the cold.

Jo's eyes lifted to regard her eldest daughter, but she didn't say anything, she couldn't. Her mind was racing a mile a minute. Why did he stop? Was he suspicious?

"No way, Jose," Casey answered his sister's question as he plopped Jenny onto a bench seat next to the kitchen table.

The table itself, jutted from the wall. Its dull yellow, Formica top was old and peeling. The bench didn't look to be in much better shape, but the children didn't seem to mind the shabbiness of their surroundings.

Casey stifled a sneeze. "He's just a clueless cop."

"Maybe not so clueless," Jo said softly, sitting down at the table and pulling off her stocking cap. She tucked the cap into the pocket of the jacket she was still wearing.

Catching and holding a lower lip between her teeth, Jo's eyes strayed to the small window above the table. The Nebraska wind flung a leaf against the camper window, along with a snowflake. Then another. Despite the closeness of her children, Jo suddenly felt very cold, and very alone.

"He was just out patrollin', Mom. It's no biggie." The reassurance in Delaney's words did little to ease Jo's disquiet.

Sighing with resolve, she made an effort to put on a brave front. "You're probably right." She smiled with as much optimism as she could muster.

"Good thing your new name's pretty much the same as the old one," Casey blurted tactlessly in a misplaced effort to add something positive to the conversation.

Delaney wrinkled her face into a comedic pose and said, "Well you can call me Joanne, or you can all me Jocelyn, or you can call me Jo. Just don't call me Billy Jo Butthead Junior!"

Casey laughed. So did Jenny.

Jo simply shook her head, a grin tugging at the corner of her mouth. "Very funny, Laney," she said," but I don't think I'm in the mood for humor right now."

"Don't worry so much, Mom," Delaney urged. "He's just a cop doing his thing, and being friendly to some newcomers. This is a small town. People are sociable and law abiding, and they think everybody else is too."

"Yeah, *right*," Casey's sarcasm was scathing.

"Shut up, Case!" Delaney snapped.

Casey stuck out his tongue, making what he obviously hoped was a completely disgusting face.

Ignoring her brother, Delaney turned back to Jo. "We're gonna be fine here, Mom. You'll see." She spoke with bright enthusiasm, but Jo didn't feel convinced.

"I know, Honey," Jo's eyes strayed to the kitchen window again. "It's just…well, it's just that everything makes me nervous." She turned worried eyes toward her daughter. "I don't think that's gonna change until…"

Stepping close to her mother, Delaney put a comforting arm around her shoulders. "I know, Mom, it'll be all right," she soothed. "Nobody's gonna find us here."

Jo nodded at her daughter's words, forcing herself to shake off the apprehension that seemed to dog every waking moment these days. She picked up her guitar and tucked it into the storage closet near the camper door, then slipped out of her jacket, hanging it on a peg inside the closet.

Delaney's face brightened. "Hey, Mom," she said with sudden enthusiasm. "I know tomorrow's Sunday, but maybe on Monday, we can check out some of the houses around town. I dunno, I sorta like this place."

Casey looked thoughtful for a moment. "It's kinda small," he added, "and there are too many smelly cows and too much open space, but hey, I guess I could get used to that."

Smiling, Jo felt her mood lighten a little.

Jenny looked up, her face perfectly serious. "I like Hawk bestest," she sighed, resting an elbow on the tabletop and plopping her chin onto an open palm.

Jo tried to stifle a giggle, but when Casey and Delaney nearly lost control of their bladders, she joined in the laughter.

Jenny eyed them all with wounded indignation.

Wiping at her eyes, Jo affectionately ruffled Jenny's curls. "You're a little flirt," she teased. Jenny smiled up at her mother, and then scooted close to

Casey, engrossing herself in the colorbook and crayons he'd pulled from a kitchen drawer.

The quiet chatter of her children filled the cramped space with comforting, familiar sounds. Moving to a tiny stove tucked next to the kitchen sink, Jo began pulling out pots and pans. They were going to have hot dogs and baked beans—again. As she busied herself with the meal, Jo let her thoughts wander.

The carefree joviality felt good. It had been too long since she'd laughed like that—since she'd laughed at all. Inhaling deeply, Jo forced her mind away from that train of thought. There was nothing but pain and terror in those memories.

It was time to find somewhere to land, she realized. They'd been on the road far too long. Her children needed something solid and secure, and so did she. Besides, Humboldt, Nebraska certainly seemed remote enough. No one in their right mind would figure they'd settled in an out-of-the-way location like this.

NEBRASKA, of all places! Jo shook her head in mild amazement. Never in her wildest dreams had she imagined herself in a town like this.

Maybe Delaney's right, she assured herself, nobody will ever find us here!

11

"It's a damn strange thing, is what it is," Hawk said, talking about his meeting with the Kennings the previous evening. He sat at his mother's immaculate breakfast counter, filling up on pancakes and sausage.

"Perhaps for small towns like Humboldt, but I don't suppose it's so unusual, really," his mother replied, setting three more hotcakes on his plate.

"Enough already, Mom," Hawk protested the food being laid in front of him, and then grinned and dived in as if he hadn't eaten a thing in days.

"Yeah, *right,*" his mother scoffed.

She fed him breakfast most mornings, and he hadn't reached his ten-pancake limit yet. Hawk was a big man, running close to 255 pounds. Over the years, he'd augmented his naturally muscular physique with weight lifting and martial arts training. Filling up his six-foot-five frame took some doing.

Hawk's mother furled her brow as she fussed with a carton of milk. "I'm worried about that woman out there all alone, with kids to care for, and living in a camper for Heaven's sake. How can four people live in a contraption like that, in this kind of weather?"

"Hell, Mom," Hawk replied with exaggerated patience, "she chose to come here in the thing, and at this time of year. She had to know Nebraska gets snow, and sleet, and hail, and all kinds of crappy shit in the winter."

"Watch your mouth, Beauregard," his mother chided, though there was little reprimand in the words. Carol Hawkins understood her son all too well—she knew he cared. The two of them had always had a close relationship, but they'd become even closer after the death of Hawk's father, four years earlier, in a farming accident.

~ ~ ~

"I'll do my best to keep an eye on 'em," Hawk assured his mother, but his face and voice were noncommittal. He, too, had been wondering just how Joanne Kenning would manage, and if she'd choose to move on or stay. This time of year could be risky traveling if the weather turned nasty, and Nebraska was about as predictable as a woman's moods!

Hawk glanced out the patio doors of the kitchen, eyeing the sky. It was leaden gray this morning. Thick, pregnant clouds hung low, obscuring all but the barest glimpse of a rising sun. Iridescent pinks and lavenders softened the undersides of those clouds with the kiss of a new dawn, but rough weather was inevitable.

A light blanket of snow covered the ground, picking up and reflecting the sunrise with soft, pastel beauty. Hawk inhaled deeply, savoring the perfection that always seemed new and fresh to him. He loved this time of day best. Nature was lifting sleepy eyelids to greet a world that was, momentarily, gentled and quiet. It wouldn't last long. That realization drew a deep sigh.

"We've got the cottage back behind the barn," Carol considered the possibility aloud. "Maybe this gal would agree to fix it up. Then she could live there with her kids—at least until she decides what she's gonna do."

One of Hawk's dark eyebrows arched upwards. "Now don't go gettin' all charitable on me, Mom," he said firmly. "We don't even know these people. To tell the truth, there's just something wrong with that whole scene, and this Joanne woman seemed way too damned worried."

Hawk poured a generous helping of cream into his coffee and stirred it, eyeing his mother as she sipped on her own mug of brew. Carol seemed impervious to his warning. He could almost hear the wheels churning. Studying his mother's intense expression, he leaned back on his bar stool, grinning. Carol was certainly a force to reckon with when she made up her mind about something.

It was a constant source of amazement to him, that his mother's diminutive build had produced sons that all towered well over six feet. Despite the fact that she barely measured in at five-foot-six, she had a spitfire personality that could put the fear of God into all three of her boys.

Indian heritage was evident in dark hair and eyes, and the coppery overtones in her complexion. She kept her stick-straight hair cropped short and sporty, a style that fit her temperament rather well. She was still a damned good-looking woman, Hawk mused, watching her with surprised awareness.

"I love you, Mom," he said with a smile.

She raised a distrustful countenance, scrutinizing him with narrowed eyes. "You're trying to side-track me, aren't you?"

"No, Ma," Hawk answered honestly. "I'm just suggestin' caution. There's absolutely no reason for that gal to be as jittery and nervous as she was. It just makes me a little suspicious."

His mother unhesitatingly defended the unknown woman. "Well, for

Pete's sake. A mother alone, with kids to protect, can't be too careful, Beau." She'd obviously made up her mind that the woman couldn't possibly be a threat to anyone.

Hawk frowned with exasperation. "Cautious is one thing, Ma, but scared spitless is quite another. Shit, they were damn near peein' their pants!"

"Beauregard!" His mother's tone brimmed to overflowing, with unyielding reproach.

Hawk threw up one hand in agitated frustration. "I'm a fuckin' cop, for Christ's sake," he snapped. "What's there to be scared of?"

"Beauregard James!" Carol glared at her son, her hands fisted on her hips.

"Sorry," Hawk pacified, grinning and winking. "You could call me Hawk, Mom, like the rest of the world." There was a cajoling note in his voice. "That just might improve my temper, and quite possibly my foul tongue, too."

"Hawk isn't a name, it's a bird."

"It works for me."

"No, what it does is give a whole new meaning to the term, Big Bird. It's embarrassing, Beau," Carol said, as she cleared away his breakfast dishes.

"Well, Ma, it don't embarrass me none. But Beauregard? Now, there's a handle and a-half!"

"I named you Beau, not Hawk. Besides, someone needs to keep you humble."

"That's a damned nasty job for such a sweet, old lady."

His mother's eyes narrowed as she faced him. "Excuse me, did you say…old?"

Hawk winked, his grin widening, though he was wise enough to keep his mouth shut.

Rolling her eyes, Carol took another sip of coffee. It was obvious her mind was still wrapped around the problem of a lone woman with children, living in Lake Park in the middle of a cold, Nebraska November. Hawk could almost see the words *Good Samaritan* flashing above her head, like the neon Coors sign down at the Longbranch Saloon.

"Beau, you can't let her stay out there, freezing to death." His mother sounded as though she'd made up both of their minds. It was something Hawk was used to.

"Well, she's gonna stay put for a few days, anyway." Hawk sat his empty mug down and rose to leave. "I wanna do some checking first, but I'll keep a close eye on our Little Miss Hobo for a day or two, okay?"

"You mean to *spy* on her, don't you?" his mother had that 'don't you even dare' look on her face. "Really, Beauregard!"

Hawk smiled sweetly. "Maybe, if you'd stop calling me Beauregard, I'd reconsider," he teased as he kissed the top of his mother's head.

Carol glared at him, but he managed to slip out the backdoor before she had time to come up with an appropriately scathing retort.

~ ~ ~

Hawk wasn't sure why, but he decided to take an unmarked patrol car the next morning, as he made his way around the twisting lanes of Lake Park. The last of the fading reds, oranges, and gold of autumn littered the narrow, blacktopped roads. Leaves danced and swayed in the arms of the wind, scattering impishly before the tires of his vehicle.

The dark, lacey arms of deciduous trees reached out with spindly fingers toward a crisply blue sky, and once-thriving shrub and low-lying brush. looked dry and lifeless. Everything in Mother Nature's world was changing into the browns, taupe, and ochre of winter.

Nebraska was a land of stark contrasts, but that very quality was the inherent beauty of the place. The world around him was turning dormant—waiting—for the long, cold winter to play itself out, but ultimately, for the blood of new life to pulse through it again.

This morning, Hawk felt the need to be inconspicuous. The dark color of the car he'd chosen to drive would blend well with the foliage of the park. Pausing at a bend in the road that gave him a clear view of the campsite, he watched and waited, quietly sipping on a thermal mug of cream-laced coffee.

Surprisingly enough, Jo was outside. It was 7:00 AM, and all of thirty degrees! Most people weren't even up unless they had to be—and certainly not outside.

Her hair was visible today, Hawk noted. Deep, reddish-brown tresses fell to just below her shoulders, and she was dressed in loose-fitting gi pants. That was a martial arts garment Hawk was more than familiar with. In place of the uniform jacket however, she wore a body hugging, long-sleeved, thermal top. Jo moved into an open area to stretch, and then started in on some basic kata movements.

She's a martial artist! Hawk sat up a little straighter. Damn, that's interesting, he thought. He'd never have guessed it.

Joanne Kenning moved through the choreographed fighting drills with practiced ease. She wasn't wearing a colored belt of any kind, Hawk noticed. He had no clue what ability level she'd worked her way up to, but every move was precise, comfortable, and well executed. He was impressed. As the workout ended, he drove on, coming around a corner and into clear view from the camper. Pulling to a stop near Jo's parked SUV, he turned off the ignition and got out.

"Mornin'," Jo said, showing no surprise at all.

Hawk had the fleeting impression she'd known he was nearby—known he was watching.

~ ~ ~

Jo wiped at her face and neck with a towel, leaving it hanging around her shoulders as she watched the Sheriff approach. He was unusually tall, she noted. Broad shoulders and upper torso tapered into powerful hips, and the brown uniform pants he wore didn't in the least, diminish the fluid grace of his gait. It tugged at something primitive in her gut.

Damn, he's a good-looking man. That realization slipped into Jo's head unbidden, drawing a frown of irritation at her lack of control. Holy shit, she reined in her wayward thoughts, don't even go there, Girl!

With an effort of will, she composed herself and forced a smile to her lips. She'd been well aware that Sheriff Hawkins warched her earlier. In fact, she'd sensed his presence from the moment he'd entered the park.

So, Jo wondered with trepidation, what did he want? What did he suspect?

"Early riser," Hawk commented, leaning casually against a picnic table set close to the camper. He removed his sunglasses, hanging them on the unfastened throat of his uniform shirt. A brown, Sheriff's jacket hung open, sporting the usual smattering of patches and insignia. Jo noticed the man's head was bare and wondered distractedly, if his hat were in the car.

Her eyes took in every detail, black brows arched above dark eyes, and black hair cropped close to the scalp. A wide forehead and slightly receding hairline didn't even begin to detract from the man's charismatic good looks. If anything, it enhanced them.

Jo, shook herself with a mental warning, *he's a cop*!

"You, too, it seems," she replied, forcing her mind away from its present train of thought, and wondering if he was aware of her unease.

Hawk grinned and replied, "I usually get stuck with the early rounds."

Returning the smile, Jo chose to saying nothing.

"My mother insisted I make a delivery," Hawk continued in a relaxed, conversational tone of voice. "I was supposed to leave this on the picnic table as a surprise, but since you're up, you might as well offer me one," he said, holding up a large Tupperware container.

"You haven't eaten breakfast yet?" Jo asked, tipping up the lid and peeking inside.

"Of course I have," Hawk assured her. "I eat at Mom's most mornings. Let's see," he said, ticking off the items one by one on the digits of his hand, "I've had orange juice, five eggs, eight pancakes, at least a half-pound of sausage, and five cups of coffee."

Hawk looked as if he were trying to keep his expression matter-of-fact, but couldn't quite prevent the corner of his mouth from twitching.

Jo knew she'd stared at him with open-mouthed astonishment, but he'd listed off enough food to feed her family for a week—and that was just one meal.

She shook her head and returned his grin. "Good, Lord, you can't possibly be hungry."

"Well, a man can always make room for desert," Hawk grinned. "Carol baked those cinnamon rolls while I was eating this morning, and wouldn't let me have even one."

"Carol?" A wife? Jo's glance slipped to the bare ring-finger of his left hand.

"My mother," Hawk supplied.

Jo nodded. "Well, please tell Carol she's an angel. These look and smell like pure heaven, and when the kids wake up, they'll be ecstatic." Jo set the container on the table next to him. "Help yourself, Sheriff."

"Hawk, just call me Hawk," he said, grinning with obvious delight as he pulled a huge gooey roll from the tub and licked icing off his fingers.

Jo couldn't help but laugh at the man's antics. "Hold on, Big Guy, I'll get some napkins and coffee," she said, heading inside the camper. She returned with two steaming mugs and several paper towels, not a bit surprised that the Sheriff had his roll gone already and was once again licking sticky fingers.

~ ~ ~

"How long you been at it?" Hawk nodded toward Jo's gi pants as he casually wiped his hands and took the mug of coffee she held out to him.

The woman seemed suddenly flustered. "Oh, well," she cleared her throat, taking a sip of coffee before continuing. "My father taught Martial Arts. I was pretty much indoctrinated from the time I could walk."

"Whoa, you must be good."

Jo didn't meet Hawk's eyes. "I'm...okay...for a woman."

He had the distinct impression she didn't want him to know just how good she might be.

"What style does he teach?" he asked, not missing the fact that Jo's eyes seemed to dart about, searching for—an escape? A plausible answer? What?

Jo paused longer than necessary before replying, as though carefully formulating her response. "He doesn't, ah, teach...I mean..."

Perplexed, Hawk raised his brows in mute question, waiting patiently for her to elaborate.

"Ah, well, not anymore, he's…he's deceased." Jo couldn't look him in the eyes. She's lying! Surprised by that realization, Hawk managed to keep his features composed and pleasant.

Jo rushed on, as though she felt compelled to clarify what she'd just said. "He teaches…ah, he used to teach, Shotokan, but I haven't trained with him for more than a decade." She looked up, meeting Hawk's eyes.

"That's an impressive style," he said. "One I've admired, though never learned." his tone turned markedly sympathetic. "I'm sorry about your dad, Jo," he offered, his face and voice conveying a sincere condolence.

The woman didn't respond. She just nodded, keeping her eyes downcast, while a deep blush colored her cheeks.

She looks damned uncomfortable, Hawk thought, his mind racing. If he could keep the conversation light, she might relax a little—possibly enough to open up, maybe even make a mistake. She was too tense, and definitely on edge. Hawk could damn near taste the fear and apprehension.

"You know about Karate?" Jo asked.

He nodded. "I took Tai-kwon-do lessons as a child, and then learned an eclectic form of Combat Karate in the service. I've got a studio in town, and give lessons a couple nights a week." He met Jo's eyes and grinned. "If you stay, you'll have to come show us a thing or two."

"NO…I mean, ah," Jo cleared her throat. "I'm not that good," she finished lamely.

"Somehow, I rather doubt that," Hawk winked at her.

Responding with an off-handed shrug and tentative smile, she said, "Maybe I can come by for a workout, at least. I really need to get into a dojo again and exchange some punches."

Hawk contemplated her words. His martial arts school was small, but he had enough students to warrant three teachers. He wondered what the assistant instructors, Dave and Eric, would think of Jo. He was pretty sure they'd love to have her come down to the dojo—for any reason she wanted to. That thought brought an amused smile to his lips.

"You're welcome anytime, Jo," he said. Setting his empty mug on the picnic table, he pushed himself to a standing position. "Well, I still have the early morning rounds to finish up, so I'd best get hoppin'. It was nice visitin' with you." He flashed his infamous smile.

Hawk watched Jo's face suffuse with gentle color, noticing her cheekbones were high and angular, and her eyes an intriguing mixture of misty gray and amethyst. Her mouth was full and delicately carved. The outline of her upper lip reminded him of a bird in flight, and a faint dimple in her right cheek peeked out whenever she smiled.

Jo's nose was straight, with slightly flared nostrils, and her jaw line square and firm. There was strength in this woman, Hawk determined. More than the casual observer would ever guess. He filed that knowledge away for future reference.

Under different circumstances, he'd be physically responding about now, but he couldn't allow that to happen—not until he had more to go on. Despite her obvious charms, something was wrong—something he couldn't quite put his finger on. It stirred his gut instincts to thrumming awareness.

At direct odds with his restless thoughts, his voice was calm and casual, "I'll be by later to fetch the Tupperware. Knowing my mother," he rolled his eyes, "she'll have somethin' else for you."

"Oh," Jo looked and sounded nervous again.

Flashing a smile, Hawk went on, "She's worried sick about a mother and three children, roughing it in this kind of weather."

"She doesn't need to worry…I mean, really, we're all right." Jo's words were rushed and apologetic, but some of the tension seemed to slip away.

Hawk responded with laughter in his voice. "*I* know that, and *YOU* know that, but Carol would argue the point. Just relax and enjoy, Jo." He winked at her as he headed toward his patrol car. "It makes my mother feel all *Good Samaritany*, and besides, it keeps her out of worse mischief," he said over his shoulder, drawing a smile from Jo.

III

"You think she's found anything?" B.J. asked as he stuffed another bite of hamburger into his mouth.

Hawk sat opposite his brother at the Main Street Cafe, idly munching his fries as he scanned a teletype he'd received that morning. He asked absently, "Who?"

"That gal from the park you been tellin' me 'bout." B.J. tossed a fry at Hawk's head, causing his younger brother to peer over the top of the correspondence he'd been holding in front of his face.

Hawk raised a dark eyebrow. "I have absolutely no idea, Beejah," he replied. "You know as well as I do there's precious little around here for sale, let alone for rent."

"Yeah, Dooley's place is the only one worth buyin', and that's hardly more 'n a cracker box," B.J. said as he took another bite of hamburger.

It would not have been difficult for a stranger to pair these two men as brothers. They shared Carol's dark coloring, and their father's height and muscular build. Despite the fact that B.J. was three years Hawk's senior, they'd always been close companions.

"I'm not even sure the lady plans to stay, Beejah, so don't be stirrin' up gossip and speculation." Hawk spoke slowly and distinctly, leveling his brother with his famous *or else* glare.

B.J. wasn't one to let a bone go until he'd cracked it and sucked out all the marrow. "Ma said you been visitin' out there," he pressed.

Hawk sighed heavily as he folded the communiqué he'd been reading and slipped it into a shirt pocket. "I found her on a routine drive through the park last Saturday afternoon, Beejah. I stopped to assess the situation, and we talked. Then I left." Hawk shifted his weight, leaning one elbow on the edge of the table. "I made the mistake of tellin' Ma, and she's all worked up about it. She baked some rolls this mornin', which I was *commanded* to deliver, and that's about it. There ain't no more n' that, Bro." Hawk finished off his coffee, and then leaned his chair back, regarding his brother. An amused half-smile playing about his lips.

"You weren't even curious enough to go out yesterday?" B.J. sounded incredulous. "What's wrong with you, Hawk?"

"It was my day off, thank you very much."

"The whole damn town's buzzin' with speculation, and you gotta shoe-in and not the curiosity God gave a piss ant!"

"It was Cramer's patrol." Hawk smiled a lazy grin, knowing it would irritate B.J. even more. "I told him to make a drive by the place, but let 'em be. Wouldn't wanna go harassin' good folk."

"So, you were there this mornin'," B.J. latched onto that piece of information, "what're they plannin'? You think the gal's gonna stay?"

"I didn't ask."

"Good God, Hawk, you didn't even ask?" B.J. finished off his hamburger, chasing it with the last of his soda. "What the hell's wrong with you? I thought cops were naturally snoopy."

"Give it a rest, Beejah, you're givin' me a migraine," Hawk said as he rose to leave. "You can pick up the tab and the tip."

"Whoa," B.J. protested, though he was already reaching for his wallet.

"That'll teach you to go givin' people headaches," Hawk shot back.

B.J. grinned. There was absolutely no contrition on his face.

"See ya, Marge," Hawk waved at the proprietress as he headed out the door. B.J. didn't need to know he was keepin' his eye on the Kennings in his own way. In fact, the fax he'd been trying to read pertained to them, though it hadn't given him anything to go on. As far as law enforcement in Fort Lauderdale was concerned, there was no record of a Joanne Kenning, or her children—absolutely nothing!

~ ~ ~

It was late afternoon when Hawk found himself pulling into Lake Park again. The day had started out almost warm, but a chilled breeze picked up shortly after lunch. It was tossing dry, dead leaves into the air with reckless abandon.

Two warm cake pans were sitting on the seat beside him. One was filled with his mother's famous spaghetti casserole, and the other with apple-pie bars—a personal favorite of Hawk's. He had tried to argue with Carol, but after a fruitless half-hour, he'd given up and agreed to *feed the hungry*.

His knock caused a flurry of movement within, but it was only a moment before Jenny opened the door. As soon as her eyes lit on Hawk, she squealed and pushed open the screen.

"It's Hawk!" she shouted needlessly, leaping into his arms and wrapping tiny appendages around his neck. Then she planted a loud kiss on his cheek.

Joanne looked as if she wanted to climb into a hole somewhere and not come out for several weeks. Her cheeks were bright pink, and her expression one of complete mortification. The older children however, were laughing, completely amused by their sister's antics. From what Hawk could tell, they'd been engaged in a hot game of cards, all scrunched around a small table that jutted from the wall of the camper.

Hawk returned Jenny's kiss, and then set her down gently. "Looks like you're keepin' busy," he commented casually as Jo came out of the camper, pulling on a jacket.

His sharp eyes noted the faded Levi jeans, off-white cable knit sweater, and scuffed sneakers. She'd pulled her dark red hair into a messy ponytail, but curling tendrils escaped, falling around her face and neck with heedless abandon. It made her appear younger and more vulnerable than she probably was, Hawk surmised.

"Well, there's not much room, and the kids get bored easily. It's a break from TV, at any rate," Jo replied, smiling.

Raising his brows in mild surprise, Hawk asked, "You get reception here?"

"No, but we have this TV-Video thing, and lots of tapes," Jo explained. "To tell the truth, I'm more than a little sick of most of those videos."

Hawk grinned at Jo's uncharacteristically frank response. Usually, she tended to be guarded and reserved around him. Reaching down, he affectionately rumpled Jenny's hair, acknowledging the fact that she was clinging to his leg.

Jo's eyes followed his. "Jenny, go get a coat on," she instructed her daughter.

"But Hawk'll be gone then," Jenny wailed, tightening her hold on his leg.

Smiling down at the child with genuine affection, Hawk assured her, "Nah, I'll talk to your mom awhile, it'll be okay."

Jo's older offspring had followed them outside, but they stood back, watching from the steps of the trailer.

Jo cleared her throat. "These are my children, Sheriff...ah...Hawk," she corrected herself as she motioned with one hand. "Delaney and Casey."

Hawk nodded in their direction, touching the brim of his hat. "Pleased to meet you both," he greeted them genially.

"Laney, go get Hawk's Tupperware, will you?" Jo asked.

Delaney nodded, and then popped back inside the camper.

Casey eyed Hawk intently. "You play pro football or somethin'?" he asked suddenly.

"Casey Robert!" Jo's tone was a reprimand in-and-of itself.

Casey's face reddened and he ducked his head in apology.

Throwing back his head, Hawk laughed, more at Jo's appalled response than Casey's innocent question. "Your mama sounds exactly like mine," he told the boy.

His reward was a bright smile.

"Naw," Hawk continued, answering Casey's question, "not pro, but I did play college ball for the University of Nebraska."

"Really?" Casey was duly impressed.

Hawk nodded.

"Awesome! What position?" The boy was definitely enthralled. He hadn't moved any closer, but his thin body was leaning into the conversation when his sisters rejoined them. Delaney carried the Tupperware, and Jenny had donned a coat and stocking cap.

"Defensive tackle," Hawk replied.

"*Dude*!"

Hawk grinned at Casey's awe. He was accustomed to a reaction. Anyone, who ever played football for the Cornhuskers, was practically a celebrity in this state. Ah, the price of fame.

"Hey," Hawk turned to Jo as he spoke. "I can't stay long, I'm on duty, but Mom sent another care package." He walked to his pick-up and, opening the passenger door, removed the pans, careful to keep the hot pads in place. "Casserole and dessert," he announced with a slight flourish.

"Oh, Hawk, no. It's…it's just too much, really." Jo seemed genuinely touched. Her eyes filled with unshed tears, and one hand covered her mouth.

Hawk smiled as he carefully set the pans on the picnic table. "If you knew my mom, you'd know she loves taking care of people and helping them out."

"But that's just the point, Hawk. We don't know her, and she doesn't know us. We're not her concern." Jo looked embarrassed. "Please, tell your mother not to bother with us," she whispered, her voice a little choked.

Hawk held up two hands in a defensive gesture, a smile tugging at his lips. "*YOU* tell her," he shot back, "*I* ain't goin' there! No one tells Mamma what she is or isn't gonna do. Believe me, 'cause I've been tryin' a *long* time." He winked at Jo, flashing a grin.

~ ~ ~

Hawk's dazzlingly white smile caught Jo off-guard. Her heart fluttered almost painfully. Damn, his charisma was almost overwhelming! Judas Priest, the thought leapt to her brain unbidden, this guy's *hot*!

Suddenly, she was painfully aware of her own appearance. Why hadn't she put on make-up? And her *hair*! A flush of utter chagrin colored Jo's cheeks as she nodded in response to Hawk's statement. What could she say?

"Just enjoy it, Jo," Hawk said with sincerity, pulling Jenny up to sit on his hip as he spoke. “Mom gets a lot of satisfaction out of doin’ for others.”

Jenny reached over and grasped Hawk’s face between two little hands, forcing him to look her in the eyes. “We looked faw a house today,” she volunteered excitedly. “An’ mama saw my teachaw.

“You’ve been a busy little beaver,” he commented.

“I ain’t no beavwah!” she retorted, drawing a deep rumble of laughter from Hawk.

Grinning, Jo shook her head, mildly exasperated with her daughter’s effusive tendencies. “Jenny, why don’t you go back inside with Casey and Laney?” she suggested. “Hawk’s too busy to visit today.”

“Nooooo,” Jenny wrapped her arms around Hawk’s neck again, pulling him into a tight embrace. “Hawk’s gonna take me faw a wide in his police twuck,” she wailed against Hawk’s shoulder. Then, almost as an afterthought, the child pulled her head up and looked Hawk in the eye, “Wight?”

~ ~ ~

Laughing, Hawk hugged the girl. “Not today, Sweetie,” he said. “Your mama’s right, I’m workin’. But tomorrow’s my day off, so maybe then, okay?”

“Okay, tomowwow.” Jenny had Hawk’s face between her palms again. “Pwomise?”

“Yeah, Sweetheart, it’s a promise,” Hawk replied kissing the tip of Jenny’s nose and then setting her down. “Now go on back inside like your momma asked you to.”

Raising his head, Hawk smiled at Delaney and Casey. “Nice meetin’ you kids,” he said.

“See ya, Hawk,” Casey waved.

“Bye,” Delaney’s voice was soft and throaty, just like her mother’s voice.

Hawk noticed she had Jo’s dark auburn hair and gray eyes, as well. Quite a looker. Nate’d be impressed. As the thought crossed his mind, he wondered just what his son would think of these people. Why haven’t I mentioned them to Nate? It was a good question—why hadn’t he?

“Well, how’d your house shoppin’ go?” he asked as the camper door closed.

The woman shrugged. “Not much to rent around here, is there?”

Hawk grinned. “No, a few for sale though. See any that took your fancy?”

Jo made a face. “None in my price range,” she confessed, “but I visited both the elementary and high school. They looked wonderful.”

“Sounds like you’re intendin’ to stay awhile.” Hawk kept his voice matter-of-fact.

"Well, maybe through the winter at least." Jo nodded toward the camper. "This old thing'll barely keep snow out, and winter can be rough-travelin'. Besides, my kids need to be in school."

"Sounds like a plan to me," Hawk agreed casually, reaching for his sunglasses and sliding them on while he spoke.

"Please thank your mother for me, Hawk," Jo said. Her voice and expression seemed sincere as she followed him to his vehicle.

Hawk nodded, and then stopped suddenly. "Hey, I promised Jenny I'd take her for a ride tomorrow," he said. "Why don't all of you come along?"

Jo looked dubious.

"I'll drive to Mom's, and you can thank her yourself," Hawk continued, climbing into his truck.

"Well, maybe. We'll see." Jo was obviously reluctant to commit herself.

"Good enough." Hawk didn't press. He was certain, given time and proximity, she'd loosen up with him. The more she relaxed, the more likely it was she'd give him something solid to trace.

Suddenly, the need to run down anything on Joanne Kenning seemed absurd. She was a lone woman, with three kids—why was he so leery? But the wariness remained, incessantly niggling at the back of his mind. It wasn't something he could have explained rationally—just a hunch, a gut instinct—and Hawk always ran with his hunches.

IV

"Beau renovated the barn about five years ago," Carol said conversationally. "I guess he just couldn't stay in the cottage after Allison took off." She leaned close to Jo and whispered in a loud aside, "That was his wife."

Jo looked at Hawk. Heightened color suffused his copper complexion. He briefly closed his eyes, ever so slightly shaking his head with mild vexation. Carol's confidences obviously embarrassed him.

"Mom, I love you dearly," he said, sounding more exasperated than angry, "but your biggest fault is that non-stop tongue of yours."

"Meaning*?*" Hands on hips, Carol eyed Hawk over the top of her glasses, one dark brow raised in perfect imitation of her son's famous glare.

"Meaning, you don't know when to be quiet," Hawk retorted, though Jo was certain there was no real ire behind the words. Her guess was confirmed a second later. Hawk winked at her and grinned.

Carol didn't see the silent exchange. "Nonsense," she chided, "I'm quiet in church and when I sleep. If God meant for us to be any quieter than that, he wouldn't have given us tongues."

Hawk didn't argue. How did you refute logic like that anyway, Jo wondered, suppressing an urge to laugh.

Rolling his eyes at Jo, Hawk seemed to be silently beseeching her to endure his mother's eccentricities.

Taking Hawk up on his offer had been a good idea, Jo decided. They'd all needed the excursion and besides, it was a beautiful, crisp, autumn day. The kids were romping around the farm with Hawk's son, Nate, as guide. Hawk had given permission for Nate to get the four-wheeler out, and that was all it had taken. Any plans she'd had for a brief visit had ended at that moment.

Jo's mind paused on a mental image of Hawk's son. She'd liked the boy immediately. His handsome face was a study of planes and angles, and like his father, he was tall. He had the same dark hair and eyes too, except that Nate wore his tresses long enough to fall in casual, tousled curls around his face and shirt collar. Like Hawk, he had a full mouth that was quick to smile, and exceptionally white teeth. Jo guessed Nate to be about Delaney's age, sixteen or seventeen maybe.

"You should really see that barn." Carol's words brought Jo back to the present. "Beau and his dad remodeled the whole thing. It's simply a work of art." Carol chatted on amicably, refilling Jo's coffee cup and pushing a plate of homemade oatmeal cookies closer.

"I'd love to," Jo said politely, though she really thought it would be best for them to leave. Even this insignificantly small overture of familiarity was somewhat unnerving. It left her feeling vulnerable.

Carol eyed her son, a somewhat smug look on her face. "*See*, I told you so, Beau! She'd love to."

Hawk apparently knew his protests were futile, but he tried anyway. "Mother—"

"Beauregard James," Carol cut him off at the pass. "I would hate to think my son was being rude to a guest in my home."

Hawk threw up his hands in resignation. "You're a damned stubborn woman, Ma."

"One of my finer qualities, if I do say so myself," Carol rebutted, grinning unrepentantly. Leaning close to Jo, she confided, "He'd be lost without me, really he would."

Jo smiled, saying nothing, but deciding she definitely liked Hawk's mother.

"You two go on," Carol instructed. "Show her the barn AND the cottage, Beau."

Her son just rolled his eyes, lifting his coffee cup to his mouth in an obvious attempt to hide a grin.

Carol chattered on, oblivious to her son's response. "Beau built the cottage too, pretty much by himself," she boasted, clearly filled with pride.

Hawk groaned as he pushed himself up from the bar stool he'd been perched on. "We might as well get it over with, Jo, my mother doesn't take no for an answer." He smiled good-naturedly as he held the door open for Jo.

Once they were outside, he was quick to apologize. "Mom means well," he said. "She just gets overly zealous about stuff." Hawk leaned over and absently stroked the head of a Golden Lab that ran up to greet him.

Laughing, Jo said, "Nonsense, Hawk, she's a dear." It would take a hell-of-a woman to corral this man, and there was absolutely no question that Carol had him in-hand.

"What's his name?" Jo asked, nodding toward the dog.

"Jax," Hawk replied. The dog seemed to adore him.

Good sign, she thought. Dogs have excellent instincts about people. She knew that assumption was irrational, but it made her relax a little, none-the-less.

Covertly glancing at the big man walking quietly beside her, Jo couldn't help but admire the way he looked in casual attire. Hawk's dark red sweater fit snuggly, both defining and emphasizing the muscular bulk in his arms and chest. She could literally see the corded physique rippling under its surface, and it was enough to take her breath away if she allowed herself to dwell on it. And his ass in those Levi's was—*good grief*! Jo was horrified at the direction her libido had suddenly taken her.

Generic thoughts, generic thoughts, generic thoughts! The warning repeated in her head as they walked in silence, toward a huge red barn behind Carol's house. Jo could feel herself blushing and hoped Hawk wouldn't be astute enough to notice—or speculate on the reason why.

He didn't appear to as he led her through the large, rolling barn door. Once inside, he turned almost immediately to the right, climbing up a flight of stairs, Jo close on his heels.

"Watch yourself here," he cautioned, opening a door when they reached the top.

Following him inside, Jo gasped at her first view of Hawk's home. The room was huge. Afternoon light streamed in through a sliding glass door at the opposite end of the room from where she stood, and a skylight above her head contributed to the sensation of a bright, sweeping expanse.

Directly ahead of her, on the right side of the room, was a grouping of chairs and a couch, in shades of taupe and cream. The heavy oak construction of the furnishings gave the vastness of the room a sense of warmth and charm.

A smattering of throw pillows added color, their bright red, yellow, and hunter green hues exquisitely captured in an Olaf Wieghorst painting hanging on the wall. Jo walked to stand in front of the artwork, ehchanted with the western scene of an Indian warrior on horseback.

"You familiar with Wieghort's work?" Hawk asked.

"Yeah," she replied softly. "Yeah, I am." Of course she was, she'd lived in the west her entire life, but she didn't share that bit of information.

Jo let her eyes return to surveying the room. Tucked in the corner was a large, wood burning stove, and an open bar area with a grouping of oak stools, looked through to the kitchen.

"Wow," Jo breathed the word out on a sigh of awe.

Hawk grinned. "We'll start with Nate's room," he said casually, walking to the left.

As Jo turned to look in that direction, she noticed a section portioned off and filled with workout equipment. Directly behind that, she followed Hawk into a bedroom.

It was surprisingly neat. The black and white quilt covering the double bed had splashes of red on it, as if a painter had dipped a huge brush into the vibrant color and repeatedly flung it against the material. Posters of famous football and baseball players plastered the walls, and a large window, directly above Nate's bed, looked toward the front of the property.

"*Next*," Hawk's voice took on the mimed tones of a tour-guide, "we have the laundry room and bath."

Jo made a face, drawing a grin from her guide as he led her around a corner and into a huge room. Behind the door stood a washer and dryer, and the room boasted both a shower and a tub. Light filtered through an octagonal window above the sink, and more sunlight found its way into the room through a skylight in the ceiling.

Jo sighed inwardly, remembering a time when her own world had been replete with similar luxuries. "I'm impressed," she smiled up at Hawk as she spoke, her voice sounding wistful, even to her own ears.

Hawk nodded. "We'll tackle the kitchen next," he informed her. "I'm told it's a woman's favorite place in the house."

Jo gave him a look capable of freezing water, but the only response it drew was another bright grin. Neither of them said any more as Hawk led the way into an open dining area, fronted by the sliding doors Jo had seen when she'd first walked in. Tucked into the corner of the room was a small, round, oak table, with four straight-backed chairs. An oak hutch housed collections of china and glasses, as well as a wine rack filled with a variety of vintages. Jo noticed the glass doors led to a deck, but her attention shifted almost immediately to the right of the dining room.

The kitchen was immaculate and impressive. A large window above the double sinks allowed sunlight to flood the room, and oak cabinets with paned, glass fronts, perched above dark gray, granite counters. The appliances were black.

"It's beautiful, Hawk," Jo breathed on a sigh. "You've done a magnificent job here."

"Thanks," he replied, flashing a lop-sided grin. "We'll finish with the master bedroom." He turned, leading the way as they retraced their steps across the expanse of open room. Opening a door, Hawk ushered her into his bedroom saying, "Come into my parlor said the spider to the fly."

Jo grinned, but her attention was almost instantly absorbed as she stepped into another huge room. It wasn't, in the least, daunted by the king-sized bed and heavy, walnut furnishings. Sliding glass doors opened onto a deck, directly in front of her. On her right, two over-stuffed, cream-colored chairs sat on either side of a walnut table, topped with a heavy pottery lamp.

Another Wieghorst hung above the bed, and the patchwork quilt covering that piece of furniture, was a medley of geometric shapes in shades of green, from sage to dark hunter. Intermingled with the greens were strips of cream, and varying tones of brown.

"That's a gorgeous quilt," Jo exclaimed. "Did your mother make it?"

Hawk nodded. "Yeah, she's quite accomplished at it."

Jo ran an appreciative hand across the top of the quilt, relishing the variety of textures that ranged from velvet to silk.

"Last but not least," Hawk announced, "is my favorite spot of all, the deck." Sliding open the glass door he stepped out.

Jo followed, catching her breath at the view. To the right was a dense grove of fruit trees, nearly bare of leaves, but still impressive. On the left was, what could only be, the cottage Carol had mentioned. Behind the quaint, two-storied, white house, Jo could see dense pine and a variety of deciduous trees in varying stages of nudity. The barest glimmer of water was visible beyond the trees.

"Is that a pond?" she asked, turning to Hawk and nodding in the general direction of the glinting water.

"Yeah."

Jo inhaled deeply, relishing the fresh crispness of the autumn air. "It's...it's just...perfect," she whispered.

Hawk looked as if he completely understood her reaction to the place.

Did he ever tire of this view, she wondered, turning in first one direction and then another. She knew, with certainty, she never would. This was what she'd always dreamed of—as a child—marrying her prince charming and coming to live in a place like this. Close to nature—a life that was simple, honest, and real.

Shaking her head, Jo tried to dislodge that train of thought. Don't go there. The warning was loud and incessant in her brain. Too much pain. Too much humiliation. Too much horror. Forcing her eyes to scan the property she could see from this vantage, Jo resolutely refused to allow her past to dampen the pleasure she was finding in this moment.

In front of the cottage, she noted the large expanse of what, in spring and summer, would be a beautifully green lawn. It was dotted with oak, cottonwood, fire maple, and dogwood.

"What a great place, Hawk." Jo's face and voice reflected her appreciation as she turned to meet his eyes.

Hawk shrugged. "It's home," he replied modestly.

"That's what makes it so special." The words carried a hint of longing.

Hawk's eyes had been taking in the panorama, but they immediately returned to regard her face. She blushed under the scrutiny, rushing to fill the uncomfortable silence with words. "No, really…you…you're very blessed, you know, to have…to live in a place like this." Jo stammered out the words, uneasy with Hawk's perusal.

He looked as if he wanted to probe, but he didn't. "I tell myself that everyday," he said in a soft, reflective voice. "Wanna see the cottage?"

"Yeah," Jo responded with unaffected enthusiasm.

Hawk nodded, and then led her to a steep, wooden stairway that descended, in split sections, to the ground. It was a short walk across the yard to a small patio. Pulling a key from his pocket, Hawk unlocked a French door, letting them both into the house.

Jo found herself in a bedroom. It was bare of everything but a queen-sized, brass bed, complete with a bare box spring and mattress. The floors were polished hardwood, but a powdering of dust gave mute testimony to long disuse. The walls, though peeling in several places, had once been a soft, glowing yellow, and a large window looked into the backyard.

Catching her breath, Jo moved about the room as if in a daze, turning this way and that, to take in every detail. Peering out the window, she recognized the skeletal remains of clematis, honeysuckle, and lilac bushes. A Russian olive sat close enough to offer its sweet, musky fragrance in the spring, and welcome shade in the summer. Not far beyond the olive, Jo recognized the purple twigs and gray trunk bark of several dogwoods.

Hawk watched her expression, amusement clearly discernible on his handsome face.

Neither of them spoke as he led Jo out of the room, stepping immediately into the living room. Next to a side door, a massive stone fireplace covered the left wall. Straight ahead of her, facing the front yard, a large, plate glass window was banked on either side by rollouts. The front door sat to the left of the windows.

"Oh," Jo caught her breath at the view, blushing furiously when Hawk's eyes, once again scrutinized her face.

Straight to the right of the bedroom door was the bathroom. Jo poked her head in. Large squares of cream-colored tile covered the floor, and a sunken tub nestled under a huge window directly in front of her. Jo could easily picture a variety of potted plants and candles, adorning the tiered ledge above the tub. Its tiled surface was a mosaic of cream and taupe. A double-sink vanity sat on Jo's right, and a storage closet on her left.

"This is so nice, Hawk."

"Yeah." He didn't elaborate, but the smile that played about his lips, reassured Jo he was enjoying her pleasure in the house. Earlier, she'd had the distinct impression this hadn't been an easy thing for him to do. She wondered how long it had been since he'd ventured inside the place. Carol said he'd remodeled the barn after his wife left. So, this house had to be the one he'd built for her, Jo speculated.

Following her guide to the right of the bathroom, she stepped through an archway and into an open dining room. Jo stood for a moment, taking it in. The room was small and cozy, with hardwood floors, oak trim, crown molding, and built-in oak cabinets, as well as a glass-fronted hutch. A large, bowed window looked out onto the front porch, and between the dining room and kitchen, Hawk had installed sliding glass doors that led to a cement patio.

Turning to her right, Jo admired the kitchen. The counters were dark gray slate, flecked with a myriad of non-descript colors, and the appliances were off-white. Wainscoting on the walls had once been a soft, dove-gray, but again, time and weather had done some damage.

Jo noticed a back door led to a large enclosed porch. Investigating, she found a washer and dryer, and a screen door leading to the backyard. Overall, she was utterly impressed with Hawk's cottage. To look at the man, you'd think he was all muscle and manly irreverence, but there had to be a deeply sensitive side to him, if he could put this much thought and care into the design of a house.

"There's an upstairs, if you're game," he offered.

Jo nodded, following her escort up a flight of steps off the kitchen.

The pitched angle of the roof was evident here, and she found herself wondering how that influenced headroom in the bedrooms. At the top of the stairs, they turned to the left and stepped into a long, narrow room with two dormer windows, looking out toward the west side of the house. Like all the others, this room was bare, except for a headless double bed pushed against one wall. The wallpaper, which at some point had been a blue and white pinstripe, was faded and peeling in several places, and a light layer of dust covered the hardwood floor.

Leaving the room, they walked straight east and into a large, airy bedroom, which once again sported dormer windows and hardwood floors. Pushed together into the middle of the room stood two single beds with whitewashed, wooden headboards.

"It's a pity such a place is unused, Hawk," Jo commented after a long silence. "It's a beautiful home."

"I guess," His reply was terse, but Jo sensed the irritation wasn't directed at her. "Ready to head back?" he asked. "The kids should be coming in soon, I imagine. I told Nate no later than five. It gets dark earlier now."

"Sure," Jo said, following as Hawk retraced their steps, and then closed and locked the French doors they'd entered through. The Lab immediately appeared beside him, wagging its tail, and panting in excited anticipation of attention.

"Hey, Jax," Hawk spoke to the animal, his voice soft and loving as he rubbed the dog's head.

They walked in silence most of the way toward Carol's house before Jo asked tentatively, "Carol said you did this work with your dad?"

"Yeah," Hawk acknowledged. His face was inscrutable, and his eyes roamed the landscape around them.

"I'd like to meet him," Jo continued, hoping she'd found neutral ground.

"He died four years ago." His tone was stoic, betraying little of what was going on inside his head.

"Oh." Taken aback Jo said, "I'm so sorry, Hawk." She felt awful. So, she thought, that's why he's having such a hard time. First his wife leaves, and then his dad dies. Two painful memories, tied to one beautiful home.

"No wonder you didn't want to show the place," she said, her voice hushed and her eyes downcast.

Hawk stopped walking and turned to look at her. "No, Jo, it's not your fault," he said earnestly. "I'm sorry if I came across that way."

Jo looked up at him, saying nothing. She, of all people, understood grief—and recognized duplicity.

~ ~ ~

The late afternoon sun fired Jo's hair to a deep, vibrant copper, catching Hawk somewhat by surprise. As he studied her more carefully, her eyes captivated him. They looked like two, huge pools of clear, violet-gray water. There was an incredible depth of life mirrored there—and pain.

Joanne Kenning was nothing like the soft, voluptuous women he usually went for. Her body wasn't heavy—but it wasn't slender either. She had the lithe, agile build of an athlete. A gradually fading tan was evident, and her skin looked soft—touchable.

She's beautiful. The thought was sudden and unnerving. Hawk felt his groin tighten with unexpected desire. Holy shit, you can't go there! The reservations and suspicions he'd had about Jo and her presence in Humboldt, Nebraska, seemed surprisingly trivial and ungrounded at the moment. She's alone—with three kids for God's sake—what harm can she possibly do? Hawk prided himself on his ability to read people, and Jo was a decent person—a good woman. He could feel it in his bones, in his heart—and one other place at this particular moment.

Hawk felt a dull flush creep up his cheeks, and he cleared his throat in an effort to distract his rampant thoughts, and regain some measure of control. "Mom is always telling me I need to grow up, you know, get over the past." He turned away while he spoke, walking slowly in the general direction of

Carol's house. The dog was back, trotting affectionately at his side.

"That sounds easy, doesn't it?" Jo responded, the question obviously rhetorical. "How can something that sounds that simple, be so difficult?" Her voice was reflective, as if she struggled with a similar pain.

A strong breeze danced around them, and clouds scuttled in again. It wouldn't be long before the sun sank behind the rolling hills along the horizon.

Hawk's eyes looked off into the distance. "I've moved on, for the most part," he said. "It just comes back now and again at unexpected times, and in unexpected places."

Jo was silent for several moments, enjoying the openness of the world around her. It was relaxing here. Hawk was easy to talk to—a comfortable person to be around.

When she spoke at last, her voice was far away, as if her mind were somewhere else. "I've been there," she whispered in a pensive voice. A humorless half smile touched her lips as she met Hawk's eyes.

He returned the grin. "So've most people," he said. "Life's like that. Shit happens."

Jo nodded. "Yeah," she agreed. "Shit happens."

V

Jo was startled to find Hawk knocking at her door at 7:12 AM. It's definitely a little too early for a casual, social call, she decided. Nearly a week had passed since the excursion to the farm, and he hadn't come by to see her —*them*—not even once. Jo's quickening pulse at the very sight of the man was both a surprise and a shock.

"Jo, can we talk alone for a moment?" Hawk asked. He obviously had something important on his mind.

What's wrong? Jo's mind raced with possibilities—all of them distressing. He looked somber. She felt her heart begin to race. Had he tracked something down on her? What does he know?

"Su...sure," she answered, disconcerted by mounting apprehension.

The children were still asleep. Jo pulled on a jacket and stepped outside the camper. Falling into step beside Hawk, she waited for him to break the silence that grew between them.

The sky was clear, but the wind had a bite to it. A soft, lavender-gray fog hung low to the ground, wrapping the morning in a quiet, dreamlike facade. There'd been no true sunrise this morning, only a gradual lightening of the world around her as the black of night slipped into an overcast dawn.

They walked down one of the paved streets that wound its way around the park. Still saying nothing, Hawk guided Jo onto a hiking path. She felt her insides twist with nervous anxiety, wondering what in the name of God he could possibly want—and why didn't he just come to the point?

"I love this park," he said at last, looking around. The deciduous trees were nearly bare now, but the skeletal starkness of their forms had a strange appeal, intermingled as they were with the wide variety of conifers. The fog softened everything, giving it an aura of surrealism.

Hawk's hand came out suddenly, grasping Jo's arm and pulling her to a stop. A forefinger at his lips, warned her to silence. Pulling her with him, he moved forward slowly, crouching and pointing to a small patch of grass.

Jo caught her breath. A doe lay in a draw, looking as if she were asleep, or resting.

"She's beautiful," Jo said, on a whisper of breath.

Hawk didn't say anything but he put one arm around her shoulders and gently turned her, ever so slightly, and then he pointed. Just behind the doe, possibly ten or fifteen feet, lay a huge buck. His tan coloring made him all but invisible against the muted russets of the brush. Now that she'd seen him, Jo could make out his features, and the enormous rack of antlers.

At her startled gasp, the doe's ears pricked and she came to her feet in one fluid motion. Then she leaped off into the brush, the buck following close on her heels.

"Oh my, God," Jo squeaked. "I've never seen anything so wonderful."

Hawk grinned.

"Are they like, mates or something?" she asked as Hawk led her back to one of the paved roadways.

"No," he chuckled. "A dominant buck like that will chase dozens of females during rutting season, but he'll stay with that doe until he breeds her."

"Oh."

He grinned at her expression, cupping her elbow to guide her over a fallen branch, and then continued, "A big buck can travel up to three or four miles chasing a doe, and this time of year is the peak of rutting season. If a doe doesn't conceive now, she'll come back into heat about mid-December."

"When are the fawns born?" Jo asked.

"Usually, the first part of May," Hawk replied, his hand still on her elbow. "They'll stay with their mother until next fall, when she starts pushing them away so she can breed again. Afterwards, she'll find her young and they'll stay with her until right before she gives birth that spring."

"Was he like, protecting her?"

"The buck?"

Jo nodded.

Hawk laughed outright. "That's a woman's romantic perspective, I guess," he replied. "Actually, he's staking a claim. More or less protecting his prize, until he mounts her."

Jo's face suffused with red. She could feel it burning clear up to her hairline. "Oh," she mumbled.

Hawk grinned, but continued with his explanation, as if he wanted to give her time to compose herself. "He'll chase after her, almost like playing tag or something, but the bucks can get pretty rough. I've seen 'em knock a doe clean off her feet."

"Really?" Jo was fascinated, despite the momentary discomfiture.

"Really," Hawk replied. "A white-tail buck can be damned aggressive. The urge to mate is so powerful, that I don't think they realize just how physical they are. A buck will single out a doe and chase her down—wear her down, actually. When she's ready, she'll lift her tail, and he'll breed her."

"Oh." Jo didn't say any more than that. Hawk didn't either, as they walked on in silence.

After several moments, he brought up the topic he'd apparently come to discuss. "Have you found a place to rent yet, Jo?"

She stumbled, taken aback by his directness. Hawk's hand shot out, grabbing her arm and steadying her. "I…I'm still looking, I guess,"Jo said.

Hawk stopped walking and turned to search her face with his dark, intense gaze. "Mom would like to offer you the cottage, if you'll have it."

Jo's reaction ran the gamut from disbelief, to shock, and then settled on a flicker of hope. She knew it wouldn't take a great deal of astuteness to read those emotions on her face, but she couldn't control her reactions. Turning her back, she tried to conceal the fact that her eyes had suddenly filled with spontaneous tears.

"Whoa," Hawk said, stepping up behind her and gently turning her around. "It's only an offer, Jo, and not a great one at that. The place is a hell-of-a mess." Large hands cupped her face, and his thumbs wiped at the tears still trickling down her cheeks.

She shivered, realizing with a start of surprise, that she wasn't cold. Her response was a physical reaction to Hawk's nearness—to his touch. Oh, dear God, don't let me go there—*please*!

"Damn it, Jo, if you cry out here, the tears are gonna freeze on your cheeks or somethin'," Hawk admonished her in a lighthearted attempt to win a smile. It worked.

Jo's mouth pulled up on one side.

"Well?" he asked, tenseness creeping into his stance and voice.

"I…we…would be thrilled to rent the cottage." Jo whispered the words so softly, Hawk leaned close to catch them all.

"Great," he responded on an exhalation of breath. "You and Carol can work out all the details."

"I thought," Jo paused, wondering if she were treading private soil, and then deciding to risk it. "Isn't the house yours, Hawk? Carol said you built it for your wife."

"Ex-wife!" Hawk was quick to point out, his voice suddenly harsh. He ducked his head almost immediatley, a look of contrition on his face. "Sorry," he apologized.

"It's okay," Jo said with unmistakable empathy.

Hawk met her eyes for several heart-pounding moments before he responded. "Yeah, I built it, but on Mom's property. At the time, I was working to take over the farm and I wanted to be close to home." He paused, looking toward the sky for a few seconds before continuing. "After she left, I decided I really didn't have the heart to farm anymore. So, I went into training to become a State Trooper, and my dad helped me remodel the barn. I deeded the house to the folks." Hawk looked at Jo with his near-black eyes, saying nothing more.

"So, how did you become Sheriff?"

"Shortly after dad passed away, the job came open, and I ran for office. Been at it ever since." Hawk smiled wanly.

Jo was silent, absorbing his words, processing them. If anyone understood the obvious suffering and humiliation she could read in Hawk's eyes, she did. That kind of anguish didn't ever disappear—not completely. It was always an indelible part of the soul.

"Shit happens," she said at last.

Hawk threw back his head and laughed. "Yeah," he responded, "shit happens."

~ ~ ~

"It's a little run down," Carol said, following Jo as she once again moved through the rooms of the cottage.

"It's beautiful," Jo said under her breath. The kids must have felt the same way. They raced wildly from room to room, their shouts carrying down the stairs as they called dibs on the bedroom of their choice.

"Well, I took the liberty of contacting the utility companies and having things turned on, in the hopes you'd agree." Carol blushed. "Hawk said he could take a few days leave and help get most of the rooms in decent enough repair to survive the winter."

"No, Carol," Jo protested. "That's too much to ask. I'm not working right now. I can get the place cleaned up without help, really."

"Don't be a ninny," Carol grinned. "It's good for Hawk. He needs to exorcise old memories, and besides, he's definitely the best one for the job. I want him to make sure all the shingles are secure, and the pipes functioning, and…oh hell, just don't argue."

Jo tried to keep a straight face, but it wasn't easy. "Okay, I guess. We need to talk about rent, though."

"Yeah, we can do that, after the place is fixed."

"No, Carol. We do it now, and I give you a deposit and money to cover the connection fees, too." Jo stopped walking and turned to front Hawk's mother.

"Really, Jo, if you're doing the cleaning and fixing, you shouldn't be botherin' with payin' rent, too," Carol protested.

Jo said nothing. She just stood in Carol's path, her hands on her hips and an obstinate expression hardening her features.

"Oh, okay," Carol conceded, obviously vexed at losing this point. "But I buy all the supplies!"

"DEAL!" Jo held out her hand, grinning.

~ ~ ~

The next week was hectic. Jo enrolled the kids in school, discovered the bus picked them up at the end of their lane, and visited with the local priest about attending mass. She also stopped by the bank to open a checking and savings account, and then she went shopping.

Carol drove her to a town called Beatrice, pronounced Bee-AT'-triss, she was adamantly informed, where the local WalMart proved an invaluable source of low-cost necessities. Jo lacked so much—small things. Things that made a house a home. Money was tight, but she allowed herself to splurge a little, finding more pleasure in the purchases than she would have imagined. Linens, curtains, dishes, lamps, and cookware were a primary concern right now, as well as the fundamentals such as cleaning supplies and toiletries. She even purchased an inexpensive vacuum cleaner.

Perusing the paper Carol brought over daily, Jo found precious little to apply for in the way of a job. It was something that weighed heavily on her mind, but she kept her hopes up. She had enough money, for a while at least. She'd made sure of that before—NO, don't go there, don't remember. It's over—dead—past. Let it go! The silent words sounded brave, but there was still a hollow place in her gut where the dread resided, refusing all her efforts to purge it.

Fixing up her own bedroom, however, gave Jo an exquisite pleasure—something that surprised her. She painted the walls a soft, glowing white, and hung white lace curtains at the north window. Opting to leave the French doors bare of adornment, Jo wondered if Hawk could see into the room from the sliding doors of his bedroom, or perhaps from his deck. It was a possibility, she decided, but she squashed the concern almost before it started. He'd definitely need binoculars or a telescope, and if he was that desperate, *let him look*!

The quilt she purchased for her bed was thick, with a pinstriped pattern in Dresden blue running through it. Digging through her basement, Carol managed to come up with some old, whitewashed, wooden end tables and a wicker rocker, which Jo added to the room as well.

The house was taking shape, slowly but surely. Jo found every day an adventure as she tore into one room after the next, and Hawk was always there. They spent several days painting, papering, sweeping, vacuuming, and polishing. Once she'd hung towels in the bathroom, tossed a few area rugs on the floors, set out candles and potted plants, and hung a picture or two, the cottage felt like home—her home—a new beginning for them all.

"Looks clean and ready to live in, but a little bare," Hawk commented the day he helped Jo and her children officially move in.

"Yeah, I know," she replied. "I'm going shopping with your mother tomorrow for a few more pieces of furniture, and a few nick-knacks to soften the place up a bit. We're going to scour the second hand stores all over this town, and several others, I'm told, not to mention the auction she's dragging me to."

Hawk rolled his eyes expressively. "OOOooooo, sounds like…*fun*." There was definitely the bite of sarcasm in his tone.

Jo snapped the towel she'd been drying her hands on, in his general direction. "Oh yeah? Well, I happen to be looking forward to it, Smart-Ass."

"What*?*" Hawk raised his arms in helpless appeal. "I didn't say anything."

"No? Well you certainly *implied* something." She grinned at his feigned innocence, and then fell quiet, her thoughts pensive as she watched him putter at the last touches in the kitchen.

"Hey, Hawk…"

Completely absorbed in what he was doing, he wasn't looking at her as he replied, "Yeah?"

"Thanks." Jo's voice broke. She felt instant chagrin as Hawk's hands stilled and his eyes lifted to meet hers.

Never, in her entire life, had a near stranger gone so far out of their way to help her. It touched a raw, emotional spot deep inside. Jo turned away, embarrassed at her weakness, polishing a little too aggressively at the windowpanes she was cleaning.

"My pleasure," Hawk said softly. "My pleasure.

VI

"This is yours?" Jo asked in an awed voice as she entered Hawk's dojo, bowing respectfully toward the front of the room. Both her tone and expression said she was more than a little surprised at finding a martial arts training house in a town like Humboldt, Nebraska.

"Yeah, pretty simple," Hawk replied, watching her reactions with interest. "I run two shorter classes on Monday nights, and a longer one on Wednesdays. Occasionally I'll have an open practice session on Saturdays." Hawk had decided they both needed a respite from the stress of house renovating, and insisted on a workout.

"It's wonderful, really." Jo removed her shoes and stepped out onto the training mat.

Hawk grinned at her eagerness.

"So," she asked, a teasing half-smile playing about her lips, "do I call you *Sensei* Hawkins?"

Chuckling, he replied, "Not unless you officially sign up as one of my students."

Nodding, Jo acknowledged her awareness of that fact. "Man," she said with emphasis, "I've missed this, so much." She breathed in deeply, as if savoring the pungent odors of sweat and cleaning products.

"You in for some sparring?" Hawk challenged. He was leaning casually against the doorframe, twirling his keys on one finger.

Jo turned and looked at him with raised brows, a half-smile twitching her lips. "I might..." the words died on her lips as two men came to the door, talking loudly.

"Hey, Hawk!" One of the visitors exclaimed, slapping him on the back.

"Hey, Guys," Hawk responded. "Comin' in for a workout?"

"Yeah, Dave's helping me get ready for that next test," the taller, sandy-haired man replied. "So, who's the looker?"

Hawk felt himself color slightly, but Jo just grinned, taking the initiative. "Jo," she said aggressively, extending her hand as she walked to where the three men stood near the door. "Joanne Kenning."

"These yahoos are my assistant instructors, Jo." Hawk introduced his friends. "Dave Sinclair, and Eric Westermann."

"Pleased to meet you." The two men responded at the same time, almost in unison, shaking her hand in turns.

Jo returned the greetings.

"New to town, are ya?" Dave asked. He was the shorter of the two, but his build suggested a well-muscled, professional linebacker.

Managing to maintain a look of utter sincerity and artlessness, Jo said, "Yeah, Beauregard is being decent enough to escort me around town, and point out the highlights."

The two men looked stupefied for a moment, and then burst into laughter.

"*BEAUREGARD*?" Eric chortled. "He *LETS* you call him that?"

Jo nodded with guileless innocence.

"Oh, *Beauregard*," Dave cooed in a high-pitched, nasal voice, "what a total *sweetie* you are." The lisp he injected into his speech, and the message it was intended to imply, were easily understood. His words drew a heartfelt guffaw from Eric. Even Jo grinned.

Hawk scowled. "Put a sock in it, guys, 'cause it'll hurt like hell if I do it for you," he snarled, but he wasn't really angry. He was used to these friends, and their penchant for teasing. He turned to glare at Jo over his shoulder, his brows lifting in mute question as he mouthed, *'Beauregard?'*

She smiled sweetly.

"You thinkin' about lessons?" Dave asked Jo conversationally, his eyes taking in her assets with obvious appreciation—something Hawk noted with a touch of resentment.

"Why, you needing some?" she asked.

His friends disintegrated into laughter again.

"Whoa, Buddy," Eric breathed in a loud confidence to Hawk, "you're gonna have your hands full with *this* one."

"I'm beginning to realize that," Hawk replied, somewhat taken aback at this uncharacteristic side of Joanne Kenning's personality. He'd seen glimpses of a fiery quality from time to time, but he was more familiar with the quiet, sensitive, nervous woman.

Meeting Jo's eyes, he saw her mouth the words, '*THIS* one?'

Grinning, he informed his buddies, "We were just discussing a sparring match." There was the barest hint of challenge in the words. He kept his eyes on Jo, smiling.

"I definitely wanna see *that*," Eric remarked.

"I'll lay five on Jo," Dave said, grinning pleasantly at Hawk's raised eyebrow.

"Not a smart bet, David," Hawk drawled, "'cause you an' I both know it just ain't happenin'." His eyes never left Jo's face. At her narrow-eyed glare, he stretched his lips into a condescending grin.

"You're looking just a little too haughty there, Big Guy." She said in a soft voice.

"Well, it IS my dojo, and I have you by a foot, and at least a hundred and fifty pounds," Hawk pointed out.

"A hundred," Jo corrected.

"*Okay*, a hundred," he conceded, feeling almost smug. "Of course, I'm expecting you to decline gracefully—to save face and all," he continued.

Hawk could hear his friends guffaws and amused comments. They were carrying on so much, he felt tempted to challenge *them* to a match, but Jo didn't seem to mind. In fact, when she turned to face him, they could have been the only two in the room.

Laughing aloud with hard, feigned amusement, she sobered suddenly and said, "Not likely, Big Guy." Her tone was defiant, though a slight twitch pulled at the corner of her mouth, touching off a dimple.

Once again, Eric and Dave disintegrated into laughter.

"I'll take five on the Lady, too, Hawk," Eric called out, his goading tone intended to rub the wrong way.

Hawk turned a withering look Eric's way, but his attention immediately refocused on Jo. "Okay, Little Girl," he challenged. "The money's on the table, let's get 'er done."

~ ~ ~

Jo's expression became quite serious. "Bring it on, Candy Ass." She knew perfectly well she'd just thrown down a gauntlet no man could refuse—and still live with himself. The guffaws coming from Eric and Dave—and Hawk's reactions to them—were laughable.

"*Excuse me*?" Hawk feigned indignation. "*CANDY*—Ass? Is that *NICE*?"

"I reserve nice for Sunday School, and lady's social gatherings," Jo rebutted. "I don't do *nice,* in a dojo."

"*Dude,*" Dave laughed. "Sounds like you're due for an ass-kickin'."

"You might want to back down, *to save face and all,*" Eric taunted, throwing Hawk's earlier words back in his face.

"Oh, *right*, and you'd never tell a friggin' soul, would you?" Hawk growled low in his chest, and then turned to face Jo. "All right, Bruce Lee, bring it on. There's an extra gi hanging in the dressing room." He winked at her, smiling.

She returned a Cheshire cat grin. The sudden look of wariness on Hawk's face was almost comical. Jo could all but see the wheels turning—he was trying to figure out just what she had up her sleeve.

"Ready?" Dave asked fifteen minutes later, as he settled a padded headpiece on her head, and helped her tie on the second glove. Jo believed the sparring equipment, donned purely for precautionary measures, was a little excessive, but it had saved her from serious injury more than once.

"I was born ready." The smack rolled a little too easily off her tongue. She grimaced inwardly. Judas, she chided herself, I'm probably gonna get my ass kicked, but good. Oh well, she'd leave a bruise or two! Taking a deep breath she taunted, "Come and get it."

Taking in Hawk's appearance in his gi, she had to admit, he was one impressive sight. The jacket gaped open slightly, revealing a heavily muscled chest that was free of hair. The golden brown color of that flesh looked as though he frequented the local tanning salon, which Jo was certain he didn't.

Damn, he looks good! she acknowledged, and then reined in her wayward thoughts. Get your head in the game! The censure was stern. Whether this little sparring match was in jest or not, she fully intended to win—or at least make a good accounting of herself.

Allowing herself a moment or two, Jo relished the feel of the equipment and the mat under her feet. It had been so long—too long! Why had she given up something she'd loved, to try to keep harmony in a house that could never know peace? It was the ultimate case-in-point of satirical injustice.

"Come on, Little Girl," Hawk coaxed playfully, dancing in quick, bouncing movements from side to side, his gloved hands raised and ready.

"I'm here, Candy Ass," she retorted, grinning mirthlessly.

"You're startin' to piss me off, Little Girl," Hawk rebutted, throwing a roundhouse punch to the jaw that Jo parried easily. She pushed him in the direction of the blow and sidestepped.

Dave and Eric tossed out amused comments here and there, obviously enjoying the spectacle unfolding before their eyes, but Jo was barely even aware of their presence. Her entire attention centered on Hawk.

She nearly caught him with a lightening kick to the kidneys, but he knocked her leg down—hard enough to leave a significant bruise.

"Ooooo," she mocked. "You've got a little more muscle than that flabby body might lead one to expect." Jo smiled wickedly at the wide-eyed look of manufactured anger on Hawk's face.

One of his dark brows rose in mute reproof. "Flabby?"

"Sorry, Candy Ass. The truth bites, don't it?" Her body moved easily, and her eyes kept Hawk's upper shoulders in the periphery of her vision. Any attach he launched, would start there.

Hawk smiled, but his expression was unfathomable. Motioning with one hand, he gave Jo a 'come and get it' invitation.

Back and forth, they went—thrust and parry, kick and block. It was a cat and mouse testing of abilities. The only sounds were their kiai's—the striking yells—and the subdued comments of Eric and Dave.

Hawk seemed hesitant to put too much into his attack, but Jo wasn't surprised. Men usually assumed they needed to protect her from her own rashness, and it was a weakness she had no qualms exploiting. He'd learn—or suffer the consequences. Her father had *never* let up for her!

After nearly fifteen minutes of exchanging blocked punches and kicks, Jo unexpectedly dropped to the ground, one hand supporting her body weight as a single leg swept outward in a circular motion, much like a gymnast on a pommel horse.

The move surprised Hawk, taking his feet from under him, and dropping him onto his back. In mere seconds, Jo was on top of him, one hand at his throat and the other poised to execute a death-strike. "Check," she quipped.

Showing a speed and agility at direct odds with his build and bulk, Hawk trapped Jo's body with his legs, and rolled her over and under him, pinning her hands above her head.

"Check mate," he countered, whispering the words close to her ear.

"Im-*press*-ive," Jo said, drawing the word out and pitching her voice to a low, sultry murmur. Her expression softened, and the slightest of moans hung on the air between them. Dropping her eyelids to half mast, she allowed a sultry smile to tug at one corner of her mouth. Then she began moving her body, undulating her hips and shoulders in a provocative, suggestive manner. A tongue-tip flickered across her lips, very slowly, and with carefully calculated effect. She felt Hawk's body respond almost immediately to the mute invitation, and knew, the instant his eyes dilated and his breath caught in his throat, she had the advantage she needed.

"Or not," she quipped, executing an abrupt counter that toppled Hawk head over heels. Straddling him in one, fluid motion, her right hand shot out in a back fist, connecting with the side of his face, followed by a palm heel to the throat. Stopping just a fraction of an inch from his Adam's apple, Jo modified the strike and clipped his chin instead.

As she kiaied, her arm continued its forward thrust, catching Hawk's jaw with an elbow. The return stroke caught his face from the opposite side—a double-tap of elbow, and then palm heel, followed by another kiai. Before the sound of the striking yell had a chance to die, she rotated her striking hand behind her block, landing a back fist on the bridge of Hawk's nose, and then reversed the rotating block-strike, ending with a two-knuckled strike at the base of his throat, her death yell a mere guttural hiss of deadly intent.

It happened fast. That was Jo's biggest asset—her quickness and speed.

Her father had drilled that lesson into her almost from the moment she'd first walked onto a mat. Women didn't have the physical strength or stamina to go toe-to-toe with a man over time—and most especially in a grappling match. *'Get in and out, Jo. In and out. Don't play games. Block, stun, kill.'* Nothing less was acceptable. Hell, anything less and, without fail, she'd paid a *very* painful price!

In less time than it would take to blink, Jo propelled her body away from Hawk, executing a back roll that brought her to her feet, and a crouched, fighting stance.

Eric whistled. "Whoa, Sweetcakes! That was like, totally awesome."

"*Damn*, you're dead," Dave informed Hawk.

Hawk lay where he was, eyeing Jo with an appreciative smile playing about the corners of his mouth. "Nice move," he approved. "A little unorthodox, but damned sweet," he said, winking.

"Thanks," Jo replied, bowing respectfully, her right fist pressed against the open palm of her left hand.

"You don't like followin' the game plan in the ol' play book, do ya?" Eric queried with a narrow-eyed, contemplative look on his face.

Jo smiled. "I was taught never to play by a man's rules," she said softly.

Hawk leapt to his feet in a single, lithe movement, and returned the bow. "And exactly why is that?" he asked, looking as if he already knew what her answer would be.

Jo was certain it was something he probably taught his female students. In a man's world, women had to use whatever advantages their skills—and God—gave them. Their sexuality was definitely a potent weapon, when used properly.

"Men's rules suck!" Jo's face and tone were perfectly serious, but a smile teased at her lips.

"You constantly surprise me, Little Girl," Hawk said in a soft, inscrutable voice. He returned her grin, with an enigmatic one of his own.

"You surprise me too, Big Guy," Jo said evenly. "I would never have guessed a man of your size, and muscular build, to be such a *wuss*."

Hawk made a dive for her.

Giggling, Jo darted to the dressing room for sanctuary.

"You're mine, Little Girl," Hawk called after her, laughing.

She could hear Dave and Eric's amused responses. The deep rumble of male voices wafted into the dressing room from the dojo, causing Jo to smile. It was comforting in a way, familiar and pleasant. She slipped out of the gi and into a shower.

Jo hoped she hadn't bruised Hawk's ego too much, but then again, he hadn't looked like he was going to suffer permanent trauma. What are they saying? she wondered. She would have given a considerable sum of money for the answer to that question, but she closed her eyes instead, reliving the feel of Hawk's body on top of hers. It had felt—*oh God*—she was doing it again!

No, no, no, no. *No way*! Don't be deceived again.

He's a cop—he can only hurt you and the kids!

VII

"Mom says you're to come for dinner," Ellie bubbled happily.

Jo had met Hawk's sister-in-law the day she and Carol had gone shopping for furniture. They'd picked her up on their way out of town, and Jo found the woman to be exuberant and friendly. That Ellie was sitting at her kitchen table this morning, nursing a mug of coffee and munching on a cookie, was something Jo was coming to expect. Ellie seemed to have adopted Jo, finding every opportunity she could to drop over and visit.

"What are you talking about?" Jo asked, her nose deep in the 'help wanted' section of the newspaper.

"Thanksgiving, what else? It's this Thursday, you know," Ellie chirped.

Jo lowered the paper slowly, watching Ellie eat the top off an Oreo cookie before licking the frosting off the other half, and then popping it into her mouth. She was a cute, perky blonde, with naturally curly hair bobbed close around her face. Her two most arresting features were huge, clear, green eyes, and a well-defined mouth that was quick to smile.

Jo found she enjoyed having Ellie bop in and out of her house from time to time. She was light-hearted and warm with her friendship, and though she played the part of an airy blonde to perfection, Jo suspected Ellie was deeper than she let on. Wife to Hawk's older brother, B.J., she proved to be someone Jo took an instant liking to. The couple had two sons, Mark and William, though Jo had yet to meet either of the boys.

"Thanksgiving, already?" Jo had completely lost track of the days. Wow, *Thanksgiving*!

A sudden melancholy settled over Jo as her thoughts strayed to the parents and siblings left behind. She'd run without contacting them, though they had to have known she would do it eventually.

How are they coping? she wondered. It had to be hard on them, not knowing where she was, or how she and the children fared. Were they okay? Safe? Devin wouldn't dare hurt them—*would he*?

Jo shook herself mentally. Don't go there, she warned herself. It was nothing but guesswork—painful, agonizing speculation. She couldn't allow that to happen.

"Yup," Ellie was rambling on. "Turkey, dressing, pies, and belly aches. You know, that Pilgrim thing everybody gets worked up over?"

Jo smiled at her new friend, setting her gloomy thoughts aside.

"Hey, look at this," Ellie exclaimed. She'd been thumbing through a Penney's sale catalog. "This is exactly what you need for the living room."

Jo raised her brows, a doubtful expression on her face as she sipped her coffee.

Sticking her nose close to the ad, Ellie started reading, "Closeout. Solid oak accent tables with antique distressed plank top and classic tapered leg design." Ellie met Jo's eyes and grinned. "Look, Jo, they're on *sale.* They are *soooo* you, Girlfriend." Folding back one of the pages, she pushed the ad toward Jo.

"The bottom line is cost, Ellie." Jo chuckled at the woman's enthusiasm, but she *was* impressed with the look of the furnishings, and she did need *something* to go with the overstuffed sofa and chair she'd found at a second hand store.

"Have you met Bert and Sarah yet?" Ellie digressed, changing the subject as she got up and helped herself to another cup of coffee.

"That's Hawk's younger brother?" Jo asked.

"Yup. They live a couple sections over. He farms, and works part-time at the Co-op in town."

"No, I haven't met them." Jo went back to surveying the want ads.

"Well, they'll all be at Carol's for Thanksgiving."

Jo eyed Ellie over the top of the newspaper, her brows furrowed.

"Come on, Jo," Ellie urged. "You know you want to, and besides, Hawk'll be there." Ellie's face and tone were just a little too neutral.

Lowering the paper slowly, Jo fixed the girl with a narrow-eyed glare. "You aren't playing match-maker, are you, Ellie?" she asked softly.

"Well, you have to admit the man's a long, cool, glass of water, on a death-valley day." Ellie giggled, "And, he's shown more interest in you these past few weeks, then he has any woman, in quite a long time."

Jo's mind slipped back to the last time she'd seen Hawk—at the dojo. What was it, not quite a week ago? Even now, her heart seemed to shift into fifth gear at the mere thought of the man's body on top of hers. She forced herself to set those treacherous emotions aside. It was an impossible relationship—utterly impossible!

"Trust me, Ellie. I'm not in the market to be hitched to anyone right now. Hawk's a nice man, but that's all. It ends there. We're just friends." Jo rose to her feet and started hunting around for her purse. "Hey, I need some clothes, and so do the kids, and a few items for the house, too. Let's drive to that Wal-Mart store in Beatrice, okay? Jo knew the promise of shopping would catch Ellie's attention. With any luck, she could reroute the woman's matchmaking efforts.

Ellie's face brightened predictably. "Oh *good*, shopping," she bubbled. "You definitely need some slip covers for that couch and chair you dug up at The Pink Elephant."

Jo giggled, finding she agreed with Ellie on that point. The faded browns, olives, and oranges were definitely not her taste in décor. "Picky, picky, picky," she kidded.

"I'll drive," Ellie volunteered.

Jo accepted gratefully, watching Ellie fumble distractedly in her purse.

"Drat!" the woman wailed after several minutes of fruitless searching. "I had to have keys, or I couldn't have gotten here, right?" She looked up suddenly, her face stricken. "I didn't lock them in the car—*again*! I'm always doin' that."

Ellie looked so pathetic Jo couldn't refrain from giggling. "They're on the front porch, silly. Right where you dropped them," she supplied.

Suddenly the color drained from Jo's face. She could feel it! A cold clamminess moved slowly from her hairline toward her neck, and down her body.

As soon as the words left her lips, she realized the error.

Oh God! The silent plea was instinctive. What did I just say?

Her response to Ellie had been automatic—unplanned. A picture formed in her head—she couldn't help it, it was just there. She just *knew*. And without thinking, she supplied the information.

Ellie caught the lapse immediately. "Whoa, *Dude*! That's like...how do you *know* that?" She eyed Jo with something close to awe.

"I ah...I thought...I sort of...saw something there earlier. I must have spaced it off, and just now put two and two together." Jo knew she was rushing her words together, but she couldn't help herself. The lie was hard to get past her lips. She could only hope it was substantial enough for Ellie to buy.

"Boy, you had me wondering there. That was like, major weird," Elli's chatter was as lively and vivacious as ever.

Jo watched the woman retrace her steps in search of the keys.

She bought it, Jo assured herself with a deep sigh of relief. The hoped- for reprieve made Jo's knees feel weak and wobbly. Thank you, dear God. It had been close—too damned close!

~ ~ ~

"Mom, if Jo doesn't want to come for Thanksgiving, just give it a rest." Hawk shoveled down a forkful of hash browns. "She's probably sick of us over there all the time, and wants a friggin' break," he said, twitching the newspaper, and then burying his nose in one of the articles.

"Beau, sometimes you are so crass," his mother replied, her tone biting. "I can hardly believe you're my child."

Hawk looked up."Crass? *I'm* crass. You're callin' *me* crass?" Hawk sounded mortally wounded. "What about Bert?" He jerked his chin toward his younger brother, sitting next to him at his mother's breakfast counter.

Bert looked properly affronted. "I take offense at that."

He was four years Hawk's junior, and looked less like his father than either Hawk or B.J. Bert's dark coloring was the only visible tie to his brothers. Standing at only six-three, and weighing in at a mere two hundred-ten pounds, put him at a definite disadvantage when it came to a head butting contest, but Bert seldom acted like it bothered him.

His body was well-proportioned, but he didn't have the powerful muscularity his brothers sported, though his wiry athleticism was certainly apparent. Bert wore his hair short over the ears but longer and spiked out on top, and his dark, doe eyes, seemed to win him more than his share of females in high school. The fact that he'd married the prettiest of those groupies was something Hawk and B.J. enjoyed ribbing him about—endlessly.

"Oh, both of you shut up and help me think of a way to talk that girl into joining us." Carol furrowed her brows in frustration. Hawk knew perfectly well, when his mother had a plan in her head, of how she wanted things to flow, it wasn't advisable to buck it.

"Well, I for one am anxious as hell to meet her," Bert said.

Hawk raised one dark brow in questioning amusement. "She's right next door. You could've dropped by anytime, Little Bro," he replied, winking mischievously.

"Well, that's a *great* idea," Carol beamed.

"*Oh, God*," Bert and Hawk groaned in unison.

Carol didn't acknowledge their response. "Just take your brother on over and introduce him, Beau. If you both invite her, she might reconsider." Carol grinned from ear to ear, obviously more than pleased with herself.

"Mother," Hawk knew it was futile to argue, but he couldn't stop himself from trying. "Jo obviously wants to be with her kids on Thanksgiving, and not us. Why can't you just let it go at that?"

Carol leveled Hawk with a withering scowl. "You have absolutely no comprehension of how a woman's mind works," she snapped.

"Well, I sure as hell don't understand *yours*, Ma," Hawk retorted.

Bert ducked his head to keep his mother from seeing the grin on his face.

Hawk could almost read his brother's thoughts. There was no way Bert was going to tangle with his mother on this issue.

~ ~ ~

"She's been the topic of a conversation or two around town," Bert informed Hawk as they made their way across the driveway toward the cottage.

Hawk looked disgusted. "That's just small town twitter. Hell, a guy can't shit around here, without everyone analyzin' it," he growled. "Since when did you start listenin' to that crap, anyway?"

"It never hurts to keep one's ear to the ground, Hawk."

"Did it ever occur to you, Bert, that if your ear's on the ground you probably got your ass in the air?" Hawk snarled. "It just might get kicked one of these days."

Bert laughed, apparently not fazed in the least by Hawk's foul mood. "You need to get yourself a life, Bro. You're startin' to turn as cranky and cantankerous as old Millie Jessup."

"Oh, *thank you very much*!" Hawk couldn't quite keep the grin off his face. "Talk about low blows."

"So, how're you handlin' the house an' all?" Bert asked, his eyes narrowing. His expression turned sober, and his full lips pursed in thought.

Glancing at his brother, Hawk noted heavy black brows furrowed above dark, thoughtful eyes. Though he seldom showed that side of his nature, Bert had always been the more introspective of the three brothers.

"I'm dealin' with it. Somehow, it's a lot easier than I'd thought it would be," Hawk replied, choosing not to elaborate any more than that.

"It's long past time to let it go, Bro." Bert said the words softly, his eyes turning to peruse his brother's face.

Hawk knew Bert meant well, and he was right. The past was just that—over and done. He was moving on, but it was at his own, slow pace, and in his own good time.

When Hawk didn't respond, Bert felt obliged to lighten the mood. "Well, I image a pretty little red-head buzzing 'round in there, don't hurt none. You just needed the right salve to heal those old wounds."

Hawk was suddenly surly again. "Shut the fuck up."

Bert laughed, throwing a simulated punch at his brother's arm, in perfect imitation of a boxer's right hook. "Get over it, Bro," he teased as they knocked at the front door of the cottage.

When there was no answer, Hawk knocked again. "She's gotta be here," he surmised aloud. "Her SUV's parked in front of the shed."

"Come in." They heard Jo's faint reply from inside.

Hawk turned the handle and opened the door, cautioning Bert, "Just don't push this Thanksgiv—."

He stopped dead in his tracks at Jo's gasp of surprise.

The shocked silence in the room was palpable.

Jo stood transfixed between the bathroom and bedroom, a towel her only covering. Hawk could see the outline of bare hip, tantalizing visible around the edges of the covering she clutched across her bosom. He felt himself harden, a tight, hot tug pulling at his gut.

"Ah…sorry, Jo," Hawk was flustered. "I thought you said to come in."

Jo's hands worked to wrap the towel more securely around her body. "I SAID, '*comin'*,'" she pointed out, a hint of scorn in the tone.

For the position she was standing in, Hawk thought she looked more exasperated than embarrassed. He was having a hard time controlling an urge to laugh, but—damn it—he couldn't help it. Jo looked like a wet kitten, helpless and vulnerable, yet still imbued with enough spirit to be spitting and hissing. Tousled hair fell in damp ringlets around her face, and it was obvious, she'd not had time to dry off. Water flowed in runnels down wet extremities, pooling in a small puddle at her feet.

"Well, since you're in, make yourselves at home, by all means." She hitched her towel a little tighter as she addressed the men sweetly. "I'll only be a minute."

Hawk wondered if Jo recognized his brother from the photos Carol kept on every table, shelf, and wall, in her house. If he hadn't been so shocked himself, he'd probably be rolling on the ground right now, at the look on Bert's face.

It was priceless!

He'd barely breathed, let alone moved. Still raised in astonishment, thick, dark brows capped rounded eyes, and Bert's mouth gaped half-open as he watched Jo back into her bedroom.

"Damn!" he exclaimed under his breath as soon as she closed the door. "You didn't tell me she was *that* good-lookin'. Hell, I was practically prayin' for a tornado wind to come sweepin' through here." Bert grinned impishly.

"You and me both, Little Brother," Hawk returned Bert's smile, leading the way into the kitchen. "You and me both."

~ ~ ~

"So, to what do I owe this, *pleasure,* gentlemen?" Jo inquired as she walked into the kitchen. Her hair was still wet, but the ringlets were a little more orderly now. She'd pulled on jeans and a white sweatshirt, but her feet were bare.

Hawk and Bert had been talking farming over a cup of coffee. Both men rose to their feet respectfully, waiting for her to sit down before they did likewise. Jo was impressed.

"Mom thought it was high time you met her baby boy," Hawk said irreverently, pouring Jo a cup of coffee and setting it on the table.

"You're just jealous 'cause Mom always liked me best," Bert retorted, grinning. "Can't blame her, though," he continued, leaning toward Jo, his eyes eating her alive. "I'm the only one that inherited her incredible charm and grace."

Jo laughed at Bert's obvious flirtation. "I can see that," she responded with insincere earnestness. "You're not full of nearly as much shit as your brother."

Bert grinned from ear to ear. "I *like* this girl," he said, not taking his eyes off her.

"You like any girl, Bert. It's a wonder Sarah hasn't kicked your ass into the next county by now." Hawk sipped his coffee, for all the world, appearing to be piqued at Bert's ardent wooing, and her obvious response to it.

"Jealous, are we?" Bert quipped, winking and grinning at Jo.

Hawk just grunted.

"*Soooo*," Jo said softly, leaning toward Bert and settling her chin on her hand. "To what do I owe the pleasure of *your* company, Bert Hawkins?" Her voice was sultry. If Bert wanted unabashed flirtation, she was more than willing to oblige.

"Well, I don't know about my surly brother," Bert teased, "but I heard there was a towel modelin' event goin' on here. I jus' couldn't stay away."

Jo giggled. "Well, the towels are in the bathroom, handsome," she bantered. "Feel free to model as many as you like, and don't forget to throw a butt shot in, to keep the crowd buyin' drinks."

Bert threw back his head and laughed.

She noted the man had incredibly white teeth and a wide, full mouth, just like his brother. They were attractive men—too damned attractive for her peace of mind. The last thing she needed was a pretty face luring her into an emotional commitment, that would break her heart and jeopardize her safety—or more importantly, the safety of her children!

"Personally, I think we should just model them as a couple," Bert was saying. "You know, matched sets and all."

"Oh, for the love of God," Hawk snarled irritably. "You two wanna pull your faces out of each other's personal space for a minute or two, and come up for air?"

"Not particularly," Bert replied, still holding Jo's eyes with a scorching, dark gaze.

"I could *definitely* learn to like you, Bert Hawkins," Jo purred, well aware that Hawk watched them, with what looked damned close to covetous anger on his face. She felt a thrill of pleasure at that knowledge, though she refused to analyze why his jealousy elicited that response in her.

VIII

Jo couldn't remember a time, in the recent past, when she'd had this much fun.

It almost scared her.

Seated on the floor of Carol's living room, she and Hawk had their guitars in their laps. They'd been strumming and singing for nearly an hour now, going over every folk, country, and light rock song they could think of. Their styles were similar, and Jo's clear, strong alto, was a pleasant contrast to Hawk's rich baritone.

With the dishes done, and turkey on the serving buffet for snackers, Carol's family flopped in chairs, sprawled on sofas, or relaxed on the floor, singing along. Carol seemed inordinately than pleased Jo and her children were with them, and Hawk's siblings and their families had been warm and welcoming.

Jo was surprised to discover Bert's wife, Sarah, was four months pregnant with her first child. Bert had to be at in his early thirties—why wait so long to start their family. Then again, why did it matter?

Sarah seemed very much Jo's kind of woman. Her spunky personality and quick wit entertained everyone, and more likely than not, kept Bert enchanted. When Sarah was around, he had eyes for no one else—and that was exactly the way God intended it to be, Jo mused.

"Proud Mary!" B.J. hollered suddenly.

A look of disgust contorted Hawk's face. "I am *not* playin' *Proud Mary*. You want that damned song every time we get out a guitar, and once is never good enough," he snapped, rolling his eyes at Jo.

"*Proud Mary*," B.J. and Bert chanted in unison. "*Proud Mary. Proud Mary. Proud Mary.*"

"For the love of *God*, Hawk," Jo laughed, "just *do* it." Her words earned a cheer from the chanting brothers.

"Okay, but you're playin' too," Hawk insisted. "You know it?"

"Sort of, but I'm real good at fakin' it," Jo followed Hawk's lead as he started strumming an 'E' chord, ignoring his suggestive smile and raised eyebrow.

"Left a good job in the city…." he started singing.

Jo let him get a couple bars into the song, giving herself a chance to catch onto the chord changes, and then she started harmonizing in a clear, well-pitched voice. B.J. and Bert were singing as well. B.J. added a deep bass rumble while Bert's clear, strong tenor capped it off.

When the song ended, Hawk set his guitar aside and leaned back, stretching. "I can't believe I actually sang the whole damned thing," he moaned. "I hate that song!"

Bert and B.J. grinned from ear to ear.

Jo smiled to herself. This was how a family was supposed to be—sharing, laughing, arguing, and teasing. Yet under it all, there was a strong, warm, loving loyalty—a bond that nothing could weaken or destroy. Sudden emotion welled up inside her, filling her eyes with tears. She blinked hard several times, forcing her features back under control.

What I wouldn't have given for a life this normal and happy, she thought. What went wrong? How did her life—her marriage—get so out of hand? It started like a fairy tale, perfect and charmed, and ended with—no. NO! Jo shook her head in an unconscious effort to dislodge the nightmare that threatened to overwhelm her. It was over—part of the past. It was never going to touch this world—this life. Never!

Suddenly someone hollered 'football', and the men crowded themselves around the television, beers in hand, talking sports and bantering. Once again, Jo's mind slipped back to the past. She loved football. No holiday dinner would have been complete until she'd curled up with her father to watch a game or two.

Was he watching the games today? she wondered. Was he missing her?

Her eyes strayed longingly toward the living room and the memories the scene evoked. It was exactly what her family would be doing—what she'd be doing—had she been with them. Blinking rapidly in an effort to control the tears that threatened again, Jo forced her attention back to the here and now.

She sensed eyes on her, and turned, meeting Carol's steady, contemplative gaze. The woman smiled warmly. Had her thoughts been mirrored on her face? Jo wondered. She prayed ardently that they hadn't, as she returned Carol's smile.

"Come on," Sarah invited. "The ladies get to eat pie and gossip at the kitchen counter."

Jo nodded, resigning herself to an afternoon of inane chatter.

"Not right now, Sarah honey," Carol interrupted, walking up to Jo and putting an arm around her waist. "Jo promised to watch some football with me." She winked at Jo conspiratorially.

Sarah looked surprised.

Ellie started to protest, "But, Mom, you don't even li—"

Carol interrupted her daughter-in-law. "Go on now, you gals have enough to talk about, to keep yourselves entertained for an hour or so." And then Carol steered Jo toward the living room TV.

~ ~ ~

"Dad," Nate hollered at his father, as soon as he heard him come into the house.

"Yeah?" Hawk was dead tired. It was just over a week since Thanksgiving. A week from hell, he thought, scrubbing a hand over his face that ended with two fingers massaging the bridge of his nose. He slumped onto the couch with the newspaper, wanting nothing more than to strip down to his skivvies and park himself in front of the television, with a bottle of beer in one hand and the remote control in the other.

Nate came right to the point. "Can I have thirty bucks?" .

Hawk leveled his son with a dark, probing gaze. "For what?" he asked finally.

"Well, I sort of...I asked...Laney and me are goin' to get a burger, and then see a movie," Nate finished in a rush.

"Yeowzer!" Hawk perused his son with a more thorough appraisal. "That's a hell-of-a catch."

He really hadn't taken the time to appreciate how much the boy had matured this past year, Hawk realized. Nate was growing up right before his eyes, and he hadn't even noticed. He stood close to six-one now, and though he was still wiry and slender, his body was bulking out with taunt, hard muscle.

Nate had Hawk's dark hair, though he wore it cut longer, in the current style. Thick, straight, dark brows, capped black eyes that had the same intense, piercing quality Hawk's did. Like his father's, Nate's chin was square, his nose straight and flared at the nostrils, his lips full and expressive.

He's a mini-me, Hawk thought with something close to amazement. When did that happen?

"You and Laney becomin' an item?" Hawk ribbed as he pulled two twenties from his wallet.

"I hope so," Nate beamed.

Hawk winked at his son, handing him the bills. "Keep the change."

"Thanks, Dad."

"Sure," Hawk responded, "but it's not a handout. You owe me one, spotlessly clean, pick-up." It was a lesson Hawk's father had taught him—nothing's free. If it was worth having, it was worth working for. Hawk had done his best over the years, to instill that same sense of responsibility in his son.

Nate made a face, but agreed readily enough. "Yeah, okay. I figured as much." He grinned at his father.

Hawk smiled back. "Got your cell?" he asked as he watched Nate grab up his keys and head for the door.

"Yeah, Dad."

"Midnight, Son," Hawk called after the boy, setting a curfew.

Nate grinned, winking at his father as he slipped out the door.

God help me get through these next few years, Hawk prayed, smiling to himself.

Images of Allison slipped into his head. Where was she, he wondered, what was she doing? Did she have any clue what she was missing? Nate was growing into a handsome, well-mannered, responsible young man. The worst of the pain and anger were gone, Hawk realized with surprised relief. There was only detached regret now, a sad kind of longing for a different ending to the story.

He sighed as the phone rang shrilly. "Yeah," he barked into the receiver.

"Quit your snappin' and get your skinny little butt over here," his mother greeted him without preamble.

"What?" Hawk really wanted a hot shower and an early bed. It was Friday, and the entire week had been nightmarish—he needed a friggin' break.

"You promised you'd help teach Jo how to play pinochle. Bert and Sarah are here, and Jo'll be here in less than thirty minutes," Carol informed her son.

"Okay, okay. Give me ten to shower and change."

Hawk felt an unexpected surge of adrenalin. It was odd, he thought, suddenly a night of pinochle sounded damn good.

~ ~ ~

"How familiar are you with playin' cards?" Bert asked Jo as they sat down at Carol's kitchen table.

"I've played all my life. Pitch, blackjack, poker, hearts, spades, rummy, you name it," Jo replied.

Bert scratched his head. "But not pinochle," he observed.

Grimacing, Jo replied, "Well, actually, I've never even heard of it before."

Hawk took the initiative. "Okay, no problem. You have your trump, like hearts or spades. The only difference is the ten comes right after the ace in power, not after the jack. And there's no card lower than a nine."

"How weird is that?" Jo mumbled to herself, watching Hawk as he laid cards out to show her.

"There's also two of everything. Two aces of hearts, two tens of hearts, etcetera, etcetera," Bert contributed.

"Got it so far," Jo acknowledged.

Hawk and Bert went on to explain the ins and outs of meld, which Jo wasn't sure she caught on to entirely.

"I'm gonna write out a cheat sheet for the meld," Sarah insisted, grabbing up the score pad and a pen. Jo was surprised to find she was paired with Bert, opposite Hawk and Carol. She suddenly felt bad—why wasn't Sarah playing?

Jo turned to Bert's wife, concern on her face. "I don't want to run you off. I should sit out and watch."

"No way!" Sarah said emphatically. Bert promised me a night in the recliner, and I ain't givin' it up for anybody. Not even you, Jo." At the look of consternation on Jo's face, Sarah rushed on to explain, "It's all right. I don't like cards much anyway. I just play so they can have a warm body in the fourth chair."

"Well, that's about all I'll be, I'm afraid," Jo was scanning the meld list Sarah had copied out.

"Don't worry," Sarah assured her. "I'll sit next to you and help out for a hand or two, but then I'm latching onto a hot cup of tea and that warm, cozy recliner I was promised."

"Yeah, she's gonna need all the help she can get," Hawk taunted.

"Sure, leave me to fend for myself against Carol and Hawk," Jo rolled her eyes. "Isn't that kinda like throwing a lamb to the wolves?"

Sarah giggled, "You got a point there."

Once started, Jo found she really liked the game and the strategies involved. Sarah didn't waste any time snatching up a chair by the fireplace, and Casey and Jenny seemed oblivious to everything but the action video Carol had rented for them.

Jo sighed, relishing the normalcy of it all—the warm comfort of friends, family, and home. Home! The thought startled her. She was already thinking of Humboldt, Nebraska as her home. It was disquieting, in a way. Could she ever have a home again? Could she put down roots here? Did she dare believe in this new life?

"You wanna cut?" Hawk asked, bringing Jo's mind back to the here and now. He finished shuffling the cards and set them in front of Jo.

"Cut bulls don't breed," Jo said automatically, repeating an aphorism her father had said a hundred times or better.

"Hot damn," Bert exclaimed, "I *love* this woman!"

Jo found she caught on quickly, so quickly in fact, that she and Bert were usually on top of the dog heap at game's end.

As they were nearing the end of the sixth game, Jo made a bid. "Thirty," she said with confidence.

"Thirty-one," Hawk countered.

"Forty." Jo leveled Hawk with a challenging raise of the brows.

"What the hell you think you're holdin', Little Girl?" he asked, clearly exasperated.

Jo's retort was sugar sweet. "Wouldn't *you* like to know, Candy Ass."

"Now, there ya go, Ma, see? I *told* you she picks on me. An' you're just sittin' there lettin' her insult me like that. Hell, you're even smilin'."

Carol chuckled at Hawk's aggrieved expression and tone. "Stop whining, Son, it's unbecoming," she said, sipping at her coffee and adjusting the cards in her hand.

Hawk rolled his eyes with manufactured exasperation.

"Well, you got the balls to bid higher'n that, Bro?" Bert challenged.

Hawk leaned back in his chair, sipping on a bottle of beer. "Naw, I think I'll just set yo' ugly ass," he said with relish.

Bert laughed, looking expectantly across the table at Jo.

"Spades," she announced, naming trump, and then laid down a double marriage and double pinochle.

Bert exploded with glee. "HA!" Raising his hand in the air, he slapped palms with her. "Sixty meld! Count 'em and weep, Brother of Mine."

"Shit!" Hawk tossed his cards down, looking aggrieved, though a smile teased at the corner of his mouth.

"Oh, good grief, what a hand," Carol beamed at Jo, pleased she had enjoyed the game and done so well.

"Damn, we just can't win for losing, Mom," Hawk conceded. "I think we'd better call it a night."

"You boys ready for some pie?" Carol asked, rising.

"I was born ready for pie," Hawk replied, putting the cards back in their box and setting them on the counter.

"Maybe afterwards we can find a game to play that you'd have a chance at winning," Bert teased.

Hawk raised a dark brow, a look of disdain crossing his face as he eyed his brother.

Bert was wise enough to keep his mouth shut, but he did wiggle his eyebrows up and down several times, a smug smile on his face.

Jo wasn't in the least intimidated, however. She couldn't seem to stop herself from rubbing it in. "How 'bout tidally-winks," she suggested helpfully.

Bert guffawed.

Hawk turned a wide-eyed glare Jo's way, but she just disciplined her face to an expression of angelic innocence.

Breaking into a wide grin, he shook his head in resignation.

Jo giggled, one hand covering her mouth, and then she followed Carol into the kitchen to help dish up desert. She knew Hawk watched her, she could feel his eyes on her, but the peek she'd had of his face gave her no clue to his thoughts. It was completely unreadable.

Let him look, she told herself with a modicum of defiance. I ain't got nothin' to hide. Then suddenly, her hands stilled—that wasn't true. She did have something to hide, and she could only pray to God, he never found out about her dark secrets.

IX

"Mom?" Laney called out as she came into the kitchen the next morning.

Jo was making pancakes. "Yeah, Honey?"

Jenny bounced around the kitchen and dining room, squealing about the light layer of powdery snow that covered the ground. She was certain there was enough for a sledding party.

"What are we gonna do about Christmas?" Laney asked, looking somewhat despondent.

"What do you mean, Laney?" It suddenly dawned on Jo—it was only three weeks until that holiday.

Oh, Lord, how could I forget Christmas?

"Well, it snowed last night," Laney's face almost glowed. "It looks like Christmas, but we don't have any presents for anyone. We don't even have a tree!"

"I see your point." Jo dished up the last of the hot cakes and set the platter on the table. When they'd all parked around the table and said grace, she broached the topic. "Laney thinks we need a tree and some presents for Christmas."

"Dude," Casey responded with enthusiasm.

"Huwway," Jenny jumped up and ran to hug her mother. "I love pwesents!"

"Well, Honey, we aren't having a big Christmas this year, but we'll manage something, how would that be?"

"Awesome," Casey agreed. Laney nodded.

"Can I see Santa?" Jenny's eyes were big, a look of awed hopefulness on her face.

Tears threatened to fill Jo's eyes. She'd forgotten Jenny still needed the little traditions and beliefs—she'd forgotten about Christmas morning, and a visit from Santa.

"Of course," Jo whispered, pulling Jenny into a hug.

Jenny's arms wrapped around her mother's neck in a vice-like grip, and then she was off, bouncing around the room singing her favorite carol. "Woodolph the wed-nose waindeewa, oh woodolph the wed-nose waindeewa, I love you."

Jo shook her head, smiling at the looks of patient exasperation on Casey and Laney's faces. Jenny never could get the words or melody quite right.

"Okay, enough already!" Casey hollered at his sister as she disappeared up the stairs to get dressed for the outing.

"What about the Hawkins?" Laney asked tentatively. "We should get them something for all they've done."

Jo thought a moment before replying. "Laney, remember those fleece tie blankets Grandma made you kids last Christmas?" she asked.

Laney nodded.

"Yeah, we left them behind." Casey reminded her.

Jo nodded, acknowledging her son's comment. "Let's drive into Lincoln today," she offered . "We'll stop at a fabric store and get some fleece, and then make blankets for gifts this year."

"Cool," Casey agreed. "You could make me another one, too."

Jo smiled, "Okay, maybe."

"Can I make one for Nate?" Laney asked ducking her head as her cheeks flushed.

Jo looked at her daughter for a moment or two. Nate had taken Laney to the movies again last night. Just how serious is this relationship? she wondered. How hard is it going to be on Laney, if we have to leave?

"Sure." Jo had no sooner spoken than the phone rang. She managed to pick up on the second ring. "Hello?"

"Hey." It was Hawk on the other end. "You and the kids in for a road trip this mornin'?" he asked cheerfully.

"Road trip?" Jo had a queasy feeling in her gut. The coincidence was just too unlikey.

"Yeah," Hawk replied. "Nate and I are headed to Lincoln for some shoppin'. We're gonna eat lunch at the Olive Garden, and then stop at Granger's Tree Farm on the way home and pick out our tree. You guys could get one, too. I'll drive over tomorrow and fetch the trees in my truck. Sound like fun?"

Jo could hardly believe her ears. The parallel in their plans was eerie—but then again, she should be used to that by now.

"We were just talking about a trip to Lincoln today for Christmas shopping," she said in a voice that quavered only slightly.

"Great, then you'll go?"

Jo wanted to say no, but for some reason, the word wouldn't manifest itself. "Yeah," she murmured, "sure. We'd love to go along."

~ ~ ~

It was late Sunday night, well past midnight, and Jo was finding it impossible to sleep. She sat curled up in an over-stuffed chair in her living room, looking at the beautiful pine centered in the middle of the front window. The room was dark except for the twinkling of the tree, and a fire snapping and dancing in the fireplace.

Cupping a mug of herb tea heavily laced with honey, Jo admired their tree-raising efforts. There weren't many decorations, but it was a warm, homey tree. She had purchased two boxes of ornaments and some garland. Above the fireplace hung three bright red and green stockings, and Jenny had even talked her into some lights for the outside of the house. Jo and Laney had found the fleece they wanted, stashing it in a closet in her room.

The trip to Lincoln had been fun—exciting. The light snow on the ground made little impact on driving, but it had added an element of excited anticipation to the air.

Bright, mood-lifting decorations were everywhere—along the streets, in front yards. The mall had impressed Jo—the Christmas trappings, the vendors set up down the middle of the wide aisles, and of course, the carols playing nonstop. Jenny had clung to Hawk's hand most of the day, skipping along and singing under her breath. When they'd found Santa, sitting on a huge red, white, and gold chair, Jenny had jumped up and down, squealing.

She'd had fun, too, Jo admitted. She'd gotten caught up in uplifting conversation, laughed, teased, even sung along with the carols the children belted out on the way home. Overall, it had been a wonderful weekend.

This is exactly what family memories are built on, Jo thought, and then suddenly became pensive. How were her folks doing? Her brother and sister? Jo's thoughts focused on her older brother, Kurt. Was he getting on with his life? He'd always tried to protect her—and it had nearly cost him his life!

The memories brought her no comfort—only guilt and misery, and a deep stab of sorrow. Don't go there, she warned herself. Just live each day—here and now.

Padding barefoot into her bedroom, she stood at the French doors peering across the yard at Hawk's windows. She could see a dim light on in his bedroom.

Must be reading or something, she conjectured. What would he do if he found out about them? she wondered. About her?

He'll hate me! The thought slipped unbidden into Jo's conscious mind. What are you DOING? The silent question was frantic. She was settling in—forming relationships—*bonding*, for Christ's sake. It was it a mistake! She knew that. With every instinct in her, she knew her emotions would betray her if she allowed them to.

And then, the optimistic voice in her head spoke up. Could they rebuild a normal life here? Have normal, healthy relationships? It's possible, she insisted, overriding her negativism. Her children desperately needed somewhere to call home—some measure of normalcy and security. And there it was again—security! Could she keep them safe here? Keep them away from—

Turning from the window, Jo abruptly made her way back to the living room. Curling up in her favorite over-stuffed chair again, she pulled a blanket over her lap. You're safe here, she assured herself, suppressing an urge to shudder. Let the past go, her brain cautioned. Yeah, that's what she had to do—let go of the past. Live again—love again. Jo trembled as she pulled the blanket more securely around her body.

Glancing at the phone, she wondered what Hawk was doing. Why was his light on so late at night, anyway? Couldn't he sleep, either?

He's awake, call him. The thought seemed to lodge in her brain and clamor for acknowledgement.

No, it's too late, or early—whatever. I can't.

The impetuous part of her goaded, *Yes, you can.*

It's too forward. The rational part of Jo's mind seemed to be a separate entity within her, arguing with the impulsiveness.

You really need to thank him.

Tomorrow.

Tonight.

No, it's too late.

He's awake. He won't mind.

Jo's hand hovered above the phone a second or two before she snatched it up and dialed Hawk's number.

"Yo." His voice sounded sleepy, though he answered on the first ring.

Jo was immediately embarrassed and contrite. "Did I wake you?"

She heard the deep rumble of a chuckle before Hawk answered, "*Weeeellll,*" he drawled, "it IS one, AM."

"Twelve forty-six," Jo corrected, although the disputed fourteen minutes didn't make her feel any less guilty about the call.

Hawk laughed softly. "Okay, Little Girl, twelve forty-six."

"Sorry," Jo apologized. "I saw your light and thought you were up."

"You...*saw* my...*light*?" Pregnant with unspoken innuendo, the silence that followed Hawk's question was damned close to uncomfortable.

"I...well, ah, I couldn't sleep. I just...sorta saw the light from my room... and ah, I....ah..." Jo stumbled to a halt, completely humiliated by her rash decision. "I'm sorry, Hawk, you're right, it's too late to be calling anyone."

Hawk chuckled. “Actually, I was reading and dozed off,” he said, his voice almost sultry.

The deep, resonant sound of his laughter triggered unexpected heat and hunger in Jo’s gut. “Oh,” she said, suddenly wishing she’d listened to the rational voice.

“And just why are you still up, Little Girl?” Hawk’s tone had a caressing quality to it. “Thinkin’ bout me, weren’t you? Go on, admit it.”

Jo giggled. “Don’t even take it there, Candy Ass,” she warned, surprised that she actually wanted him to ignore her admonition.

Hawk chuckled again. “So, why did you call, neighbor?”

“I…I…well, I’m not sure,” Jo stammered, suddenly tongue-tied again, and wondering just why she had called.

“Mmmmm, impulsive. A quality I’ve always admired in a woman,” he teased.

Jo cleared her throat. “I…I was sitting by the fire, admiring my tree, and it occurred to me, we have you to thank for a great weekend,” she said hesitantly, finding the feat of putting her feelings into words harder than she’d anticipated.

“Yeah?”

“Yeah,” Her reply was barely audible.

“What are you wearin’?” Hawk surprised Jo with the question.

“WHAT?” She laughed nervously, caught off guard.

“What are you wearin’? I’m tryin’ to picture you sittin’ by the fire, watchin’ Christmas lights on a tree,” Hawk said, his voice husky and suggestive.

“A flannel nightshirt,” Jo replied.

“Anything underneath?”

Jo giggled, and then purred out an answer, “Bare-assed naked.”

God,” Hawk groaned. “I’ll never get to sleep now.”

Jo’s voice dripped pure innocence, “Why’s that?”

“Why don’t I mosey on over and show you why not,” Hawk offered.

“Mmmmm,” Jo cooed, “I’m almost wishin’ I could take you up on that offer, Big Guy. Somehow, I’m thinkin’ I might toss and turn a bit myself, if I let you.”

Hawk groaned again.

Jo giggled, and then her voice turned suddenly serious, “Hey, Hawk?”

“Yeah?”

“Thanks,” she whispered. “It’s…it’s really hard…being away from family on a holiday like this.” Jo felt tears welling up in her eyes as an all too familiar pain burned inside her belly. “You and your family have made it bearable.”

"You're welcome, Little Girl."

Jo detected something in Hawk's tone, something that filled her with a desire so fierce she had to bite hard on her lower lip to control it.

"I live but to serve," he continued, his words heavily laced with double meaning.

Her groin clenched and unclenched unexpectedly, aching with a craving she hadn't felt in a long, long time. "I'll keep that in mind, Candy Ass," she whispered, and then hung up the phone. Her hand was shaking.

Lord Almighty, what am I doing? Just friends, just friends, just friends, she repeated the warning to herself, an adamant reminder that she was not free to get any more involved than that—especially with a cop!

~ ~ ~

"I found you a job," Ellie bounced into Jo's kitchen the next morning, exuberant.

"Really?" Jo was instantly attentive. "Where?"

"Right here in town, at The Humboldt Standard News." Ellie literally glowed.

"The what?"

"Oh, it's the local newspaper," she explained. "I already talked with Jack."

"Jack?"

"Jack Hollings, the editor."

"Oh."

Ellie continued, obviously more than pleased with her find. "Six people work there, besides Jack, and one of them is Harriet Niedfelgen." She took several sips of coffee before continuing, knowing Jo was hanging on every word. "Well, Harriet and her husband Bob are heading to Arizona for four or five months, so Jack's lookin' for a temp. Isn't that just perfect?"

Jo looked confused. "Ellie, that's only four or five months. I need something a little more permanent than that."

"And you'll find it," Ellie assure Jo, "but until you do, at least you'll have *some* cash comin' in. Jack said he'd pay seven bucks an hour, and it's only about twenty or twenty-five hours a week."

Seven dollars an hour? Jo was surprised at the low wage, but then again, this was a rural Nebraska town, not Los Angeles. Life—and economics—were different here. Ellie sounded as if she thought the pay exceptional, and maybe it was, for part-time work.

"Well, it doesn't sound too bad, for now," Jo mused aloud. "So, what do I do? Just go in and talk to this Jack guy?"

"Well, pretty much, yeah. I told him about you and that you'd come by.

You can thank me later. Come on, you gotta hurry and get ready."

"Well, can I finish my coffee first? I had a late night," Jo growled good-naturedly.

"Dare I ask doing what, or with whom?" Ellie inquired, her voice slightly taunting.

"No dear, you daren't!" Jo rebutted firmly.

~ ~ ~

"I've never worked at a newspaper before, Mr. Hollings, but I've been a receptionist and I'm good with computers." Jo sat primly on the edge of a straight-backed chair.

Jack Hollings was sitting behind a gray, metal desk, the top of which was buried beneath a pile of unorganized paperwork, newspapers, receipts, and correspondence. Jo guessed him to be in his fifties, at the very least.

Standing at no more than five seven or eight, dark gray, thinning hair, and thick-framed, pop-bottle-bottom glasses, made him appear unyielding and unapproachable. Jo hoped that wasn't the case. Though his build was small, he carried weight in a protruding beer belly, and a bushy Hitler-type mustache twitched beneath a large, bulbous nose.

Ellie had informed Jo, that Jack Hollings needed someone to edit articles, set format in the computer, and answer the phone in the mornings. Some filing and errand running were involved as well, but for the most part, Jo was certain she could handle the work.

Jack eyed her speculatively. "I don't see any references on your application, and no previous address," he commented.

"No, well, I haven't worked in over a decade, sir. My husband wanted me home with the children," Jo lied. "I've only recently divorced and moved here, to try and start over."

Jack nodded his understanding of her explanation. "Did Ellie tell you 'bout the requirements?"

"Yes, sir," Jo replied.

"Just, Jack. None of this *sir* stuff."

"Okay, *Just Jack*, whatever you say." Jo's face was the picture of innocence when Jack's gaze locked on hers.

He laughed. "Well, you do have spunk, don't you, girl? Ellie said you did."

Jo smiled.

Looking thoughtful for a moment or two, Jack asked, "You available to start the week after Christmas? Harriet'll be here `til the first of the year, but I'm thinkin' you could work with her for a few days, and get the hang of things."

"I'd love to." Jo could barely contain her elation.

A job. An income. Thank you, thank you, thank you.

She had some money, but she'd used quite a bit just surviving these past six months. She also had three kids to raise. The fact that she'd cleaned out the savings and checking accounts before taking off, was something Devin would hate her for—hurt her for—but with any luck, she'd never see him again.

"Great, I'll call around the 26th and set up a time for you to come in and start training with Harriett." Jack stood, extending his hand and ending the interview.

~ ~ ~

The day was cold and blustery. Jo pulled her coat tightly about her ears as she left the newspaper office. Crossing the cobbled street, she stepped through an arch and onto a sidewalk that bisected the park. On the opposite side of the town-square sat the Country Cookin' Café. Its bright green trim and door were easily detectable from where she stood.

The park, which sat in the heart of that square, was brown and desolate looking now, its trees stretching bare, emaciated fingers skyward. Jo walked along the sidewalk, passing playground equipment on her left. The east-west sidewalk crossed a north-south one, intersecting under a whitewashed, arched structure that had no apparent purpose other than architectural appeal. On her right sat a whitewashed bandstand, that had obviously seen better days. She wondered briefly, if people used in the summer months.

As Jo stepped into the café, she saw Ellie waving wildly from a booth near the back.

"Looks like more snow," Ellie commented as Jo slid into the seat across from her, shivering.

"Yeah, I guess," Jo, responded. "Hey, I got the job, Ellie," she beamed.

"I knew you would. I told Jack he'd better hire you or I'd start gossiping about him behind his back." Ellie giggled. "Blackmail works every time, trust me."

"Thanks, Ellie," Jo said with feeling, "for everything."

Ellie grinned with delight. "Wanna go shopping for work clothes? I'm tired of looking at denim jeans and Kmart sweatshirts, and you only have three of those—black, gray, and white, for Pete's sake. Not the most exciting wardrobe on the block." Ellie smiled sweetly, too sweetly.

"Well, thank you very much!" Frowning, Jo looked down at her straight black skirt, white turtleneck, and black pumps. Even her formal clothes lacked personality. "I didn't know I needed to dress to impress you, Miss

Ellie," she sighed, her tone pensive.

"Not me, *Dodo*, Hawk!" Ellie winked conspiratorially. "Buy somethin' that shows some cleavage. You know, somethin' that fits a little *too* snug. He's a *big* boob man," Ellie supplied helpfully.

"Good grief," Jo moaned, rolling her eyes. "Give me a friggin' break."

Ellie didn't look the least bit contrite. "I ordered for you already," she said, "and for Hawk and B.J., too."

Jo leveled her friend with a reproving glare, asking, "*Hawk*, and B.J.?"

"Oh, didn't I tell you?"

Jo shook her head, amazed at Ellie's composure. The woman looked almost angelic.

"They're joining us for lunch."

"How...*convenient*," Jo's tone was sarcastic, but she wasn't angry. "So, just what AM I having for lunch?"

"The special, of course, liver and onions," Ellie said, managing to keep a straight face.

Jo groaned. "*PLEASE* tell me you're joking."

X

Laney eyed her mother skeptically. "Is this a date?" she asked, brows drawing together with disapproval.

"No, Honey," Jo replied, her tone almost sad. "I can't get involved with anyone, you know that."

"I want to go," Jenny, pleaded. "I love movies! Is it Disneys?"

"Not tonight, Sweetie." Jo dabbed at her eye shadow. "It's a grown-up night this time," she said, smiling at her daughter.

Jo had mixed feelings about the evening. A part of her wished Jenny could go along, but another part felt excitement at the prospect of going somewhere, without the kids tagging along. It was just casual—not an official date—she'd emphasized that point when Hawk asked her out. So then, why had she'd taken an inordinate amount of time preparing for a *just friends* night at the movies?

"What're we gonna do all night?" Casey whined, flopping down on Jo's bed and tossing one of her shoes in the air before catching it, and then tossing it again. "We don't even have a TV that works."

Jo stopped what she was doing and turned to look at her son. "Well, Carol said you could go over to her place. She's got that big screen TV and some videos, and she said to tell you she's pulled out the board games, and cards, and even ordered pizza."

"*Dude*!" Casey seemed suddenly appeased and more than a little excited at the turn the evening had taken.

Even Jenny seemed assuaged. "*Gwait*," she chirped, bouncing around the room.

"And Nate's gonna be there," Laney volunteered, her face radiant.

Jo smiled a knowing smile. Watching the reactions on her children's faces, she was relieved to see they were not only excited, but eager to go to Carol's place. The woman was replacing grandparents they no longer had. That thought left her feeling downhearted again, but she shook it off determinedly. This was their life now, and it was working. It *had* to work!

Casey and Jenny dashed from the room, anxious to get ready and go.

"Be careful, Mom," Laney cautioned as she started after her siblings. "Remember, he's a cop."

Jo cringed inwardly at her daughter's words. They were equivalent to cold water, dashed on the one carefree night she'd had in—she couldn't even remember a time when she wasn't running scared.

Just the thought of Hawk made her stomach flutter and her pulses quicken. Oh, Lord. Just friends, she told herself repeatedly as she finished brushing her hair and adjusted the snug-fitting, V-necked sweater she'd donned for the evening. Ellie had helped her pick it out, insisting the soft lavender mohair brought out the violet in her eyes, and warmed her skin tones.

Jo's heart leapt into her throat at the sound of the doorbell. This can't be right, she chided herself scornfully. She was pretty sure a *just friends* kinda escort, wasn't supposed to make you hyperventilate, or give you butterflies!

~ ~ ~

Sitting across from Hawk at his kitchen table later that night, Jo twirled a glass of chardonnay in one hand, taking a sip now and again. Hawk was talking about different people, and their histories in Humboldt, filling her in and helping her learn about the town and its populace. His handsome face looked relaxed and animated, and his eyes were exceptionally expressive.

"Thanks, Hawk," she said at a pause in the narrative.

"For what, Little Girl?" his voice was throaty as he leaned forward on one elbow, tipping a bottle of beer up to take a swig. His eyes watched her, waiting for the response.

Jo blushed. "Oh, I don't know, just…thanks. I haven't…it's been a really long time since I was able to relax and laugh and not be scar—" She stopped abruptly. Clearing her throat, Jo finished the sentence quickly, the words rushing together, "ah, worried all the time."

Lowering her eyes, she studied the drink in her hand far too intently. Did Hawk catch the slip? Probably, he caught everything! But for whatever reasons, he let it pass.

"Tell me about yourself, Joanne Kenning," Hawk said softly, sipping on his beer. His eyes watched Jo with dark, probing awareness.

"I….there's not much to tell." She stood and moved toward the living room, trying to dodge the inevitable. Hawk was behind her almost immediately. Turning her around to face him, he took her drink and carefully set it on a nearby table. His hands held her shoulders, effectively forcing her to look him in the eye.

"Why do you do that?" he asked in a soft, concerned voice.

Jo's response sounded defensive, even to her own ears. "Do what?"

"Run?" Hawk replied.

"I'm not running," she retorted, unable to meet Hawk's dark gaze. He just sees too much, damn the man!

His forefinger tipped her chin up, until her eyes met his. "Aren't you?" he asked, his voice a throaty whisper.

All of a sudden, she felt trapped—caged in. The wall was unyielding at her back, and Hawk stood in front of her. The questions seemed to hang in the air between them, waiting for answers she couldn't give. And yet, Jo realized with something close to wonder, she wasn't afraid of this man—not like she'd been of Devin!

"I…I'm not…" she fumbled, looking for the lie that would appease. "There's too much to forget." Okay, that was true, at least. "I…I don't want to remember anything, and I definitely don't want to talk about it," Jo finished lamely, looking down again.

Hawk was just too close.

Leaning forward, his hands pressed on the wall, supporting his weight, one on either side of her head. He asked, "What about your childhood, Jo? Parents? Siblings? Hometown?"

Jo met near-black eyes with firm determination. "Over. Dead. None. Chicago. *Happy*?" she snapped, not sure why his questions made her angry. It was normal for him to be curious. The inquiries were relatively harmless—*for anyone else*. Damn, I hate lying to him!

"Immensely," Hawk said, his voice caressing. Bending his head, he claiming her mouth in tentative exploration. It was the barest of contacts—a feathering across her lips.

Suddenly, Jo's knees went weak. She'd have fallen if she hadn't grabbed onto the front of Hawk's shirt with both hands. His mouth covered hers again, no longer tentative, but demanding now. Jo found she desperately hoped he'd pull her into his arms—hold her against his body.

She wasn't sure if it was his groan she heard, or her own. In fact, the only thing she knew with any certainty was that she raised her mouth toward him, eager and hungry—desperately wanting more.

~ ~ ~

Jo loved the silence and serenity of an empty dojo. She carefully laid her gi jacket on a chair, tossing her car keys on top of it. She'd left her purse in the car—just that much less to worry about.

She'd arranged to clean Hawk's dojo, in exchange for workout time. For her, it was an ideal situation. Cleaning didn't take long, and she had plenty of time for her own pursuits.

Walking onto the mat, she moved her feet in the familiar, ground-hugging steps she'd had drilled into her nearly all her life. She worked through a warm-up, and then began her workout with the Kihon, the basic techniques of Shotokan. The stances, blocks, strikes, and kicks were familiar rote exercise, but it felt good.

Time seemed to loose significance, a few minutes slipping easily into an hour. At last, she decided she was ready for the Kata, her favorite part of any workout. Kata were prearranged forms, sequences of attacks and defense that a Shotokan practitioner executed, following a basic line of movement. Still, Jo had always felt they were more like dancing than choreographed fighting. Her invisible adversaries, or partners, always moved with her—familiar friends—giving her a point of focus.

Tonight she chose her favorite, the first kata she'd ever learned, the Heian Shodan. The room was still—quiet but for the gentle shuffle of her feet, and an occasional kiai. There were no distractions, not even from the street. No horns, no screeching tires, no thrum of incessant traffic—nothing—just the blissful sounds of silence.

"You're good." Eric's deep voice startled Jo. She turned sharply, dropping into a crouched defensive stance, her hands raised to strike.

"Good, Lord," she breathed on a sigh of relief, relaxing a little. "Didn't your mother ever warn you not to sneak up on people like that?"

"Yeah, but I've never been accused of being a good listener," Eric chuckled, running his tongue across thin lips. "What was that you were working on, Sweetcakes?"

"The kata, you mean?"

"Yeah, where'd you learn that? Your form and technique are solid. It's impressive to watch."

Eric's enthusiasm made Jo chuckle. She studied him as he spoke. He wore his sandy hair in a style that was longer than most men his age might opt for. It fell in abandoned disarray around a face that had just a trace of freckles across the nose. Straight brows nearly hid pale blue eyes, and he sported a full, thick, mustache. Eric was a big man, probably close to six-two. Jo was certain he weighed in at well over two hundred pounds, and despite his obvious dedication to the martial arts, he had a bit of a beer belly on him.

She smiled at his complement. "Thanks, Eric. It's just one of the Peaceful Mind katas," she answered his question. "The first one taught to a white belt, actually."

"Peaceful Mind?"

"Heian Shodan is what that one's called," Jo replied.

"I'm sorry, Jo, but it didn't look peaceful to me," he said with emphasis, his tongue wetting his lips again.

Jo laughed. She'd often thought the same thing.

"Hey, I'm sorry," she apologized. "I didn't know the dojo was in use tonight. I made a deal with Hawk to clean on Tuesday evenings, in exchange for some workout time." She was feeling a little uncomfortable in her gi pants and sports bra. Reaching for her uniform top, she slipped it on, but didn't bother to tie it. After all, she was leaving. "I can come back later," she offered.

"No, really," Eric stopped her with his words. "I was just comin' in for some extra practice time myself. Hawk'll be here shortly too, but you're more than welcome to stay."

"Thanks, Eric, but I need to get home. I've been here a couple hours already." Jo moved to pass him on her way to the dressing room.

"Come on, Jo," Eric reached for her arm, pulling her to a gentle stop. "I don't wanna run you off."

It was the briefest of contacts.

Almost nothing—and yet, enough!

When the vision came, it took Jo completely by surprise. She'd almost begun to hope they were gone—ended with the turmoil of her old life. With a gasp, she crumpled to the mat. The images invaded her head—a movie rolling behind her tightly closed eyelids.

There was a child, nine, maybe. She was outside, playing with dolls and a tea set. Odd, Jo thought, the girl looks familiar. A thick mass of sandy hair, bright blue eyes, and a freckled face reminded her of someone, but it was peripheral awareness only. Jo was certain the girl was someone she didn't know.

The day was bright and sunny, light reflecting off gently rolling water behind the child—until the shadow came. It darkened the day, and the girl looked up in fear. Jo couldn't hear the silent scream, but she saw the opened mouth and a terror-contorted face. She saw the raised arms and cringing posture.

A baseball bat came out of nowhere, swung with a viciousness that sent the girl sprawling. Suddenly, a male body leapt on the prone child. Jo couldn't see a face, his back was to her, but she was certain the attacker was relatively young—not yet a full-grown man, but close. He tore at the girl's clothing, and then his hips pumped. There was no misunderstanding what occurred.

It was a frenzied, angry act. Jo could feel the hate and rage with such intensity, it made her gut twist. When he finished, he pushed himself up and looked down at the girl. She was whimpering, curling into a fetal position.

Calmly, the faceless attacker reached for the bat.

Jo wanted to look away—to close her eyes and stop the images—but there was no escape. Her eyes were already squeezed together. She couldn't shut out the sight of that bat swinging, the bloodied surface rising and falling—again and again.

"Noooo!" The horrified cry felt torn from somewhere deep in Jo's gut.

Suddenly, hard, demanding hands grabbed her shoulders, shaking. "Jo?" Eric's voice was close to her ear, worried and insistent. "Jo, what's the matter? You all right?"

Her eyes were wild as she looked up at the man. She couldn't seem to find a voice, only the choking tears. The shock of what she'd seen was too fresh in her mind.

"Jesus H. Christ!" Eric pulled Jo into his arms, trying to offer comfort. "It's okay, Jo. Just take some deep breaths."

She pulled away enough to look up at him, finding a shaky voice at last. "I didn't...I didn't know," she whimpered, her voice dazed "She...she's dead...I—"

"WH—what?" Eric interrupted Jo's incoherent ramblings. He dropped his hands and stepped away, all but staggering, his expression wary.

"I...I'm, so sorry, Eric." Jo's voice trembled. Her gut quivered and her knees shook uncontrollably, but somehow she managed to pull herself to her feet, grabbing onto the back of a chair for support. "I...I don't feel well." She wasn't lying. All of a sudden, Jo was very nauseated, and her limbs felt weak and useless. It was an all too familiar reaction to one of her psychic visions.

The look on Eric's face said it all. Repugnance didn't even come close to describing it. A mixture of anger, disbelief, and alarm furrowed his brow, and glazed his wide-eyed stare.

Damn! What have you said? What have you *done*? Jo felt her own personal brand of terror, settling into the pit of her stomach.

"I didn't mean to startle you like that," she rushed to mend the damage, swallowing convulsively in an effort to keep the nausea at bay.

He can't figure this out. No one can know!

Jo was desperate to leave. Pushing herself to her feet, she grabbed up her car keys and headed for the door. She was vaguely aware of bumping into Hawk as she made her way out, but her mind didn't register that fact until later.

She had to get away. She had to be alone.

What had she seen?

What, in the name of God, did I just see?

~ ~ ~

"Did she talk about it?" Bert's expression was serious as he sipped a mug of coffee the next morning. He and Hawk were at Carol's for breakfast, a common morning routine for Hawk and one, if not both, brothers.

"No." Hawk looked confused and angry. "She just insisted she didn't feel well and dashed home. She wouldn't answer the phone, and when I stopped by the cottage, Laney wouldn't let me see her."

Bert looked worried. "What did Laney say?" he asked, grabbing up several more pieces of bacon, and stuffing one into his mouth.

"Not much," Hawk replied, "just said Jo was asleep, or somethin' like that." Hawk shook his head, unable to make sense of what he'd witnessed. He could still see her in his mind's eye, crouching on the floor with her eyes screwed shut and hands over her ears, as if she saw and heard something no one else could—or would ever want to. If one judged by the look on her face, whatever she'd experienced had been traumatic.

Hawk raised bewildered eyes to his brother. "It was weird, Bert. Even Laney acted strange."

"You two!" their mother snapped. "Give that child a break." Carol turned to level her sons with a stern glare as she dried her dishwater-wet hands on a kitchen towel. "Do you have to pick at and analyze everything she says and does?"

"Mom, you weren't there! You didn't see her face…hear her." Hawk scowled at his mug of coffee, the breakfast in front of him virtually untouched. "It was freakin' weird!"

"Maybe something triggered a bad memory, and she just over-reacted," Carol supplied, attempting to come up with a reasonable explanation. "People do that, you know."

"What kinda memory could do that to a person?" Hawk's voice was skeptical.

Carol scoffed, "Maybe you haven't noticed, Mr. Know-It-All, but that girl is carrying some pretty ugly emotional scars." She was adamant in her defense of the woman.

"Emotional scars are one thing, Ma, reactin' the way she did—*damn*!" Hawk shook his head again, poking at scrambled eggs with the prongs of his fork. "I mean, she was cringin' and shakin', and cryin' out. That's some seriously weird shit, Ma"

Carol's face softened suddenly, her tone cajoling,"She's a decent person, Beau. I just know she is." Carol laid a gentle hand on top of Hawk's, rubbing her thumb along his clenched knuckles. "You have to give her a chance."

Bert took a bite out of his toast, chasing it with coffee "Well, I sure can't see her as a villain," he said. "There's probably some logical explanation we're all overlookin'."

Hawk shook his head from side to side. "There was absolutely nothin' logical about what I saw, Bert."

Bert met Hawk's gaze, his face and voice, about as staid as he ever allowed them to be. "You and I both know, Bro, that the eye can be deceived. Ma's right, you need to let Jo have a chance at explaining this, 'cause your speculations are based on nothin' but your interpretation of what you saw—not on fact."

Carol nodded.

"Since when did you get so damn philosophical?" Hawk snapped, uncertainty making his voice harsher than he'd intended.

"Since about sixty seconds ago," Bert quipped, showing even, white teeth in a parody of a smile.

"Beau," Carol interjected, "we both know she's running from something in her past, that's hurt and frightened her."

Carol paused at Hawk's incredulous expression, and then continuing with a touch of exasperation, "*Well*, if you haven't figured *that* out, you're an obtuse blockhead!"

"Even *I'd* figured *that* out," Bert added, grinning mischievously at his brother's squint-eyed glare.

"Shut up, Asshole," Hawk growled.

"Beauregard James!" Carol glared at her son. "Don't make me smack your mouth, Son," she warned, snapping her dishtowel in his direction.

Bert took Carol's side. "I think Ma's right, Hawk, he said, rising to refill his coffee cup, "Something Eric said or did must have triggered a bad memory, and she just relived it, or somethin' like that."

"See!" Carol latched onto Bert's proposed theory. "I told you so, and it's a perfectly logical explanation."

Hawk raised a single, skeptical brow, though he chose not to argue.

When he didn't respond, Carol seemed to conclude she needed to push her point."The bottom line is, you don't know, do you? You can't condemn her without proof, and all you got is speculation and hunches—and frankly, your hunches suck *shit*." Carol stood with her hands on her hips, glaring at Hawk.

He stared at his mother in open-mouthed amazement, but Bert threw back his head and laughed, until tears rolled down his face.

"Oh, close your mouth," Carol waved an exasperated hand at Hawk, moving to the refrigerator to put away a carton of milk.

Recovering, Hawk grinned mischievously as he pointed out, "You'd slap me silly if I talked like that, Ma."

"Damned straight I would," Carol snapped. "This is still my house, and I get to call all the shots here." Her tone was fierce, but Hawk saw the twinkle in her eyes. "I can say whatever I damned well please. YOU, on the other hand, need to learn some manners."

"Ma, you never cease to amaze me," Hawk smiled with affection.

"I never cease trying to," his mother replied, earning herself a bear hug and a kiss.

~ ~ ~

"You gonna try talkin' to her?" Bert's face was serious as the two brothers left their mother's place, each headed to their own vehicles and eventually, to separate places of employment.

"Do I have a choice?"

Bert shook his head. "Nope, but it ain't gonna be easy."

"Holy understatement, Batman."The sarcasm in Hawk's tone was palpable.

"Ya know, Hawk, people can have really bad things happen to them. Sometimes they just keep it bottled up inside, but when the memories finally surface, it can seem…I don't know…" Bert's explanation died away as he stopped walking and turned to level his brother with a thoughtful frown on his face.

"So, what're you sayin', Bert?"

"I'm sayin', I agree with Ma. This girl ain't a bad person, Hawk. She may not act—or *react*—to things the way we expect, but it don't make her weird, or bad, or suspicious."

"*Shit!*" Hawk was disgusted, but whether it was with himself, the situation, or his brother's defense of Jo, was a toss-up.

"So?" Bert pressed.

"I'll talk to her."

Bert grinned. "You got the *hots* for her, don't you?"

Hawk turned a withering, dark-eyed glare his brother's way, "Bert?"

"Yeah, Bro?"

"Shut the *fuck* up!"

XI

"Forgive me, Father, for I have sinned," Jo began, as she sat across from the Priest, Father Patrick Montgomery. "It's been over a year since my last confession," she said in a quiet, hesitant voice, and then stopped, unsure of what to say next.

A year!

She could hardly believe she'd let her faith suffer so much neglect. Wringing her hands, Jo was quiet for a long time, wrestling with just how much to say and how much to withhold.

Oh great, she thought caustically, there ya go! It's not a real confession, if you withhold the bad stuff!

She wanted to rid herself of the guilt she was carrying, but did she dare speak of it? Surely, a Priest couldn't disclose information gleaned in a confession—*could he*?

Father Pat placed a calming hand over her fidgeting ones, and Jo looked, regarding him with an evaluative eye. He was a young man for such a weighty responsibility—probably in his late thirties or early forties, she guessed.

He stood close to six feet tall, and though wide through the shoulders, he had a slender build, and his features were even and strong. Dark brown hair was graying at the temples, and thinning on the crown of his head. His face was pleasant enough, but his eyes were his most compelling attribute. Fringed in long, dark lashes, they regarded her now from beneath heavy, straight brows. Their deep, aquamarine color was like looking into a clear, bottomless lagoon. A round, rosy-cheeked face, gave him an angelic look that was strangely comforting.

"It'll be okay, Jo," he said with gentle assurance, "just tell me what you can."

"I'm not even sure where to begin anymore, Father," she whispered. "I feel like such a pathetic failure, on so many levels." She could feel the emotion welling up—all the hurt and pain she'd so determinedly held in check for such a terribly long time. Jo worked at controlling an urge to cry.

The priest said nothing, just waited for her to go on.

"I live a lie," she whispered, her voice barely audible. "I mean about who I am, and...and what I've done. I'm not even sure I can confess and be absolved, because I can't stop the lying—not yet, anyway." She looked up with pleading eyes, hoping he had an answer, and yet knowing there wasn't one. God didn't paint in grays. He only had two colors on his palette—black, and white.

"Well, why don't we start at the beginning, Jo, and work through this together," Father Pat said in a calm voice. It was deep and warm, with absolutely no hint of accusation or recrimination. Just the sound of it eased her heart.

Jo took a deep, steadying breath, and then began,"I ran away from my husband about six months ago." She paused to wet suddenly dry lips with a tongue tip, not sure she had the courage to go on. Somehow, she managed. "I just went to the bank and cleaned out as much money as I could get my hands on, took the children out of school one day, and...ran." Dropping her gaze to her lap, Jo interlaced her fingers, moving her hands in a nervous, twisting motion.

She couldn't bring herself to look up, but one of Father Pat's hands reached out and covered hers, effectively stilling them. "Go on," he said.

"I...I left behind my parents and siblings, and I changed my name. The kids and I traveled all over—until we landed here and decided to risk staying." Jo kept her head bent as she spoke, still unable to look the priest in the eye.

"There must have been tremendous need, to force you to make such a drastic choice." Oddly enough, he didn't sound surprised—or angry.

Jo nodded. "I'd do it again, if I had to." That attitude just might exclude her from any possibility of absolution, she thought, but she'd already decided to be as honest as she possibly could. She was sick of the lies and deceit.

"So, why did you leave?" The priest prompted after several moments of silence.

Shrugging, Jo dropped her gaze back to her lap. "My husband is a wealthy, powerful attorney. When I married him, he was one of my father's star martial arts pupils, working toward his second-degree black belt." Jo repressed a shudder as the memories began rushing back. "His strength and power were magnetic," she continued. "I fell in love without really getting to know the man." She cleared her throat, and her hands started twisting again.

Father Pat waited, saying nothing.

"The first years of our marriage were fine. He was critical and demanding, but he never hurt me, and he was a good father to our daughter." Jo wet her lips again, her eyes still focused on her twisting fingers. "A few years after Casey was born, things began to change. He started drinking heavily, and became more verbally and emotionally abusive. He was gone a lot, and I was almost certain he was having an affair—or several actually."

This is unbelievably humiliating, Jo thought. Too embarrassing to share, even with a Priest. She struggled with herself, knowing she needed to continue, but dreading what she knew needed saying.

The silence slipped in, but it wasn't long before Father Pat urged her to pick up the story again. "Go on, Jo, you're doing fine."

She raised apprehensive eyes, meeting his tranquil gaze, and then inhaled and started again, "I tried hard to be what he wanted me to be, but just when I thought I was, he'd change the criteria. By the time Casey was five, Devin had become physically abusive with me. At first it was just a slap in the face now and again, but before long slaps turned to punches, and punches into beatings." Jo closed her eyes, surprised at how hard it was to get the words out of her mouth. They were only memories now, but the pain and humiliation were still as fresh as they'd ever been.

"Did you report this? Get help?" Father Pat asked.

"*Oh yeah,*" Jo closed her eyes against the recollections. She'd gone to the authorities all right, but Devin was too powerful. His hand was in everything—things no civilized man had a right to delve into. "The authorities believed Devin's version of the story—not mine," she explained. "When they were gone, he…ah…he," Jo faltered, and then continued, her hands twisting again. "He threatened to hurt the children if I called the police again."

Father Pat's expression was grave as he nodded. He looked as if he knew that she'd been about to tell him something else, and asked, "Did he hurt you?"

Jo nodded, her eyes filling with tears and her throat constricting. Yeah, he'd beat the shit outta her! "After that, I made up my mind to tough it out, and just try to avoid Devin as much as possible. But then one night…" her words choked to a stop and her breathing came in short, agonized gasps. Her eyes darted anywhere and everywhere—she couldn't bear to look at the priest.

I can't *do* this! she railed silently, furious with herself. What idiotic weakness made her think she could tell anyone about her past?

~ ~ ~

Pat remained silent, somehow guessing what Jo needed to say, but wanting her to get it out on her own. Experience taught him that quiet patience was the best lubricant for words that didn't want voicing.

Jo stood abruptly. "I'm sorry, Father, I shouldn't have come here."

He remained seated as his eyes lifted to hers. "Why?" he asked simply.

Jo began pacing. "I can't...I shouldn't...I mean, I don't want to talk about it anymore. It's over with, now. There's no use dredging up painful memories." It sounded like an excuse she'd used often—a safe explanation for the reticence.

"Did your husband force you to have sex?" Pat knew the words were blunt, but he also knew it took brusqueness to reach some people.

Jo froze in place, her mouth partially open, as if she'd suddenly turned to stone. Her eyes riveted on him, wide and shocked, though she didn't respond.

"It happens, Jo," Father Pat continued in a soft, empathetic voice. "You might be surprised to know just how often."

A pink tongue tip slipped out, darting across her lips. Jo found her chair again and sat down as if her knees were suddenly too weak to support her weight.

"Yeah," she whispered. "Yeah, he did." She squeezed her eyes shut, her hands turning white on the arms of the chair.

Pat waited a few moments more, before encouraging her to go on. "And?"

Jo didn't open her eyes, but the tongue tip was back. She swallowed hard several times, working up the nerve to continue. "He was...really angry with me for making him force the issue. He got violent, afterwards."

Pat could tell Jo wasn't going to elaborate. He knew she had to purge the demons that festered within her—get it out and begin a healing process. He placed a warm hand on her shoulder, but said nothing, waiting for her to continue—to tell him what she would.

After several long, silent minutes, he decided to take the initiative. "He abused you, Jo. It wasn't your fault."

"Yeah, *sure*." Bitter self-recrimination edged the tone of her words.

"You don't believe that, why?" he asked.

Jo's gaze met and held his for several moments before she replied. "I could have stopped him," she said. "I let it happen. I'm not sure that's officially considered *physical abuse*."

"You...*let* your husband beat you?" Pat was confused. "Exactly what choices do you think you had?"

"I'm trained in the martial arts, Father." Jo's voice dropped to a monotone. There wasn't even the slightest inflection of emotion now. "I had choices." She looked down at her hands, clenched tightly together in her lap.

"Your husband was trained in the martial arts as well, wasn't he?" Pat asked.

"Yeah."

"Is that why you didn't fight back?"

"No," she sighed. The sound came from somewhere deep inside her, and then her tone changed, turning hard and cold. "I didn't fight because I was afraid I might get lucky, and kill the son-of-a-bitch."

Pat wasn't sure he understood her reasoning, but he didn't say anything. He wanted to give her time to work through her thoughts—to get past the anger.

"Three months later," she continued, "I discovered I was pregnant again. I felt I had to try harder to make things work, to be a good wife. For a time, Devin was actually civil. He seemed to want this child, and I actually thought we might just pick up the pieces and paste it all together."

"I'm assuming it didn't work out," Pat said.

Jo turned her head slightly, eying him with a bitter half-smile twisting her lips. "Jenny was nearly four when the drinking and beatings started again," she said. "I made up my mind I was going to leave. I even worked up the courage to ask for a divorce." She paused, as if she wasn't sure she could continue, her gaze dropping back to her lap.

Pat could see her jaw clench and unclench. "So, you're divorced?" he asked, knowing what her answer would be.

Suddenly, Jo started laughing. It was a bitter, humorless sound. "No," she replied at last, lifting dark gray eyes to look at him. "I asked, but..." her words trailed off, and her gaze shifted back to her lap. When she finally summoned the courage to continue, her voice was hard and cold again. "I asked, but my answer was a two week hospital stay, and a vow that if I ever left him, he'd kill me."

Pat gasped, stunned. It took him a moment to find his voice. "Surely, you told the police. They'd have to believe *that* kind of evidence," he said with conviction.

"Like I said before, Father, Devin had the power to manipulate the police. He's what...what some people might call a crime boss, and he has people everywhere. I didn't talk, because I didn't know who to trust," Jo replied, meeting his eyes again.

"What about your family, Jo? Where were they?"

"My brother tried to help," Jo's voice was flat and lifeless, though Pat noticed that her hands were shaking. "He tried to talk to Devin—reason with him. Devin had his hired thugs shut Kurt up."

"Kurt?" Pat queried.

"My brother," Jo clarified. "They used a tire iron to convince him he didn't want to interfere. He...he nearly died." Her voice choked to a stop.

"Oh, Lord." The response emanated from somewhere deep inside him. It was inconceivable that such things could happen, and yet he was well aware they did.

"He threatened me, then," Jo continued, her voice emotionless again, "me and my family. The kids, too. Told me he'd hunt me down and kill me if I ever left him."

Pat didn't know what to say. The enormity of what she was sharing left him speechless.

"I was scared, Father."Jo whispered the words, obviously not expecting a response. "I started secretively making plans to leave, but...but I just never had the courage to act on them."

"Well," Pat reasoned, "you obviously left. What pushed you to that point?" As if the violence and intimidation wasn't enough, he thought.

She closed her eyes.

Pat could see her trembling again, but he remained silent, waiting. It was a hard choice, but he knew his silence would prompt her to go on—and she needed to talk! He knew the best medicine was simply getting it out, one way or another. Like detoxification for an alcoholic, it was painful and traumatic, but necessary. Eventually, she had to come to terms with her anger and hatred.

"I came home one day and found—" Jo's voice broke. A shaky hand came up to rub distractedly at her forehead, as if it throbbed painfully.

"Found?" Father Pat pressed in a gentle voice.

"I...I found Devin beating Laney with his belt." The words were an angst-ridden whisper, her eyes staring at a far corner of the room, as if seeing the horror again.

"Oh,, my God!" Pat couldn't keep shock from coloring his response. "He beat your daughter?" Her words shook him to his core, and he prayed for God's help to say the words that would ease this woman's suffering.

Jo nodded, swiping at her face with the back of one hand. "She'd lied about something at school to protect a friend, and gotten in trouble with the principal. It...it was a minor issue. Nothing that warranted serious reprimands. But Devin was *furious*. He just flipped out of control, yelling and screaming about how embarrassed he'd been to get the phone call." Jo shook her head in remembered disbelief. "He was so violent, and seemed to derive some kind of perverse pleasure from what he was doing." Her expression changed from grief to utter hate. "GOD!" the expletive exploded from her.

Father Pat overlooked the fact that she'd just used the Lord's name in vain. He watched her with sad eyes as she stood with sudden agitation and started pacing—like a caged tiger—feral and restless.

"I went crazy," Jo clenched and unclenched her fists, as if reliving that moment in time—reliving her reactions. "I lost it," she said, staring at nothing, but obviously seeing the past. "I just...I snapped. I attacked him."

Walking to the far wall and leaning against it, Jo stared out the window. It was dark out, she couldn't have seen anything—there wasn't anything to see, except perhaps a distorted reflection of her face, and the room behind her.

"I'm a black belt, Father, several times over," Jo said in an apathetic voice, as if she'd accepted the fact that there could never be any hope for her soul. She turned her head, just enough to meet his eyes. "I didn't hold anything back," she whispered. "I intended to kill him."

~ ~ ~

The words were out! She'd finally admitted a truth that had haunted her for a long, long time.

The priest didn't say anything. Jo knew he was having a hard time with her revelations. Hell, who wouldn't? These kinds of things didn't happen in a normal, sane world! But then, nothing about her life with Devin had been either of those things.

To Jo, every sound in the room seemed magnified, as if assuming an exaggerated significance. She could hear a dog bark in the distance, and the overly loud ticking of the clock on the wall. Even her own breathing echoed strangely in her ears. The silence seemed to close in again, but it wasn't a hard silence. This was the silence of the Lamb—peaceful, forgiving, healing.

At last, Father Pat asked the question that was burning to be voiced, "So, did you?" His tone was gentle. There was no reproach, no accusation, and no revulsion.

He should hate me, Jo thought irrationally. *I* hate me! I tried to kill someone. *No, not someone*—I tried to kill the father of my children! She stood with outstretched arms, her hands flat against the wall to support her weight, and her head sagging between aching shoulder blades.

"I came so close to killing him," she grated the words out. "I had his head in my arms, with every intention of snapping his neck. All I could think about was sending him to hell!" She pushed herself to a standing position, her eyes meeting Father Pat's deep blue gaze.

"You didn't kill him, Jo." The priest's words were firm, as if trying to force an obtuse child to see reason.

She shook her head, dropping her eyes to stare at the toe of her sneaker. "I would have if Laney hadn't started screaming. She threw herself on me, begging…" Jo's knees gave out and she sank to the carpet, suddenly feeling weak and drained.

Father Pat was beside her immediately. He sat down cross-legged next to her and reached out to clasp one of her hands with his, holding on with firm assurance. "Life can push us all to the edge, Jo, but it's what we do when we get there that truly counts. You didn't kill him." He said the words with firm conviction, his voice strong and sure.

"I didn't choose to let him live, either. I let him go for Laney's sake. If God had left it up to me, the asshole'd be dead now, and I'd be free!" Jo's words were harsh and embittered.

"I don't believe that, Jo," Father Pat said gently. "God did leave it up to you, and he sent an angel to guide you through the maze of hate—and you followed that angel's counsel."

Jo looked at the Priest with skepticism in her eyes, but she didn't argue.

They were both quiet for several moments while Jo regained her composure. Father Pat helped her to her feet, and then guided her back to the chair. With practiced ease, he handed her a box of tissues, waiting patiently until she'd taken what she needed.

She smiled up gratefully, wiped at tear-wet eyes, and then blew her nose. When she seemed more in control, he urged her to continue. "So, what happened?"

"Well, I knew I couldn't stay," she snuffled, wiping at her nose again. "The next day we left. I just took the kids—and ran." Jo looked up and met the priest's eyes. "Devin alerted the police, reporting it as a kidnapping and theft. A close friend of mine had procured a forged driver's license for me months earlier." A small half-smile tugged at one corner of Jo's mouth, and she shrugged her shoulders dismissively. "I never thought I'd have the guts to use it, but I'm using it now."

"You haven't released the hate yet," Father Pat said matter-of-factly, surprising Jo.

"I haven't even tried!" she countered forcefully. "It's what keeps me putting one foot in front of the other, Father, day after day."

"I know that, Jo. It can be a powerful tonic for many things, but I also know its side effects are devastating. It will eat away at what is still strong and good inside you." The priest leaned forward and placed one large hand over her tightly laced ones. "It will turn you into a bitter, angry, vengeful human being over time. You will never move on in your life, or truly love another human, because as long as the hate fills your heart there's no room for anything else."

Jo shook her head in denial. She knew he was right; she just didn't want to release it—not yet! "I don't…I can't…" she whispered hoarsely.

"Yes, you can," Father Pat interrupted her.

"Ho…how?"

"Prayer," he said simply. "Talk to God. Ask him to help you. Tell him how you feel and how hard it is, but promise to try. He'll walk with you, through this Valley of the Shadow of Death. You can mark my words, Jo. Hate is a living death, there's no doubt about it." His tone was stern, but compassionate and loving.

Jo looked at him, both doubt and hope clearly visible in her eyes and on her face. She took a deep breath, and then let it out slowly though pursed lips. "I've tried to forget, Father. It just wells up inside—the pain, the anger, the hate."

"Every time those memories come, I want you to do something—not for me, but for yourself, and your children." He paused, looking at her expectantly.

"What?" she asked.

"I want you to pray an Our Father, or a Hail Mary—or both. Just pray until the thoughts go away. If you force God into that chasm of hate, He will push out everything but the Light of His great Love. You can take that to the bank and cash it, Jo."

Jo nodded assent. "I'm not sure I can even be absolved, Father," she said. "I can't stop the lies. If Hawk knew, he'd have to act—he's a cop, and he'd feel duty-bound to enforce the arrest warrant."

"You don't know that though, right?"

"Well no, but," Jo raised tormented eyes,"I just can't take that chance," she said with feeling. "I believed Devin when he said he'd kill me if I left him. I'd be going back to my death, and God alone knows what would happen to my children then." The hopelessness crept back into her voice.

"Trust is the hardest thing God asks of us, Jo. Faith is a leap. A blind leap. Across the chasms of a world, that's cloaked with the blackness of sin. You can't make that leap and survive unless God holds your hand." Father Pat paused, as if allowing Jo to absorb those words before he went on. "I'm going to absolve you of the sins you've confessed, and your penance is to do what I asked you to, whenever the anger comes, okay?"

She nodded.

"I want you to try and avoid the direct lie if you can, but if you're forced to it, say a prayer and ask forgiveness. Then come see me." He grinned at Jo's surprised expression. "That's the beauty of confession. You can go every day if you need to." His smile lit his entire face. "Now, make a sincere act of contrition," he instructed.

She responded immediately, years of practice and obedience to the directives of a priest, taking over. "O my God, I am sorry for having offended you, because I dread the loss of Heaven and the pains of hell, but most of all, because I have offended You…." she started into the prayer, amazed that she still remembered it. There was immense comfort and assurance in the familiarity of the words, and a lightening of her spirit that she'd not felt in more years than she could even bare to dwell on.

She finished, and then the priest began the words that would absolve her soul, cleanse her spirit, renew her heart. Oh God, she felt her insides quiver with stunned relief. Thank you, she sighed inwardly.

"…and I absolve you from your sins, in the name of the Father, the Son, and the Holy Spirit." Father Pat made the sign of the cross, his voice hushed and touched with a note of awe, as if the enormity of the ritual he'd just performed, never ceased to amaze and humble him.

Jo automatically made the sign of the cross at his words. Her heart felt light—as if a tremendous burden had lifted from her shoulders. Yeah, she still had the same problems to face, but she didn't feel so alone anymore. She had Father Pat—someone she could talk to, confide in. And she had God. He'd opened His arms—despite all she'd done! The incredulity and wonder she experienced at that realization, left her feeling dazed.

"Go in peace, and turn from sin," Father Pat concluded.

"Thank you, Father," Jo said from her heart. "Thank you *so* much!"

~ ~ ~

Jo made her way out of the confessional and into the church. It was early evening. She was relieved to find there was no one else there. Kneeling, she stayed for a long time after her talk with the priest, a rosary slipping slowly through her fingers and her lips moving in silent, automatic prayer.

The room was dark except for a single light shining on the Blessed Sacrament and the statue of Christ that stood on a pedestal above it. Another dim light glowed a small alcove where religious reading material was displayed. Jo knew it was there for parishioners who came to do their weekly hour of adoration, a practice she'd thought seriously about taking up. A stand with candles was nestled in the alcove too, as well as a statue of Jesus, and one of Mary.

Jo liked the statues. They were visual reminders of the saints and Blessed Family. Reminders that warmed the heart, and drew her closer to the lives and sacrifices of those that had passed before her. Their familiar, unchanging faces took on a life of their own, assuming a warm, comfortable intimacy that brought peace and hope to her heart.

Saint Francis de Sale's was a beautiful church, small but quaint. Its elaborate stained glass windows were dark now, and the scents of polish and incense created a pleasant, gentle essence that permeated the space.

Jo let her mind wander.

Suddenly an image of Eric's face slipped into her consciousness. What had she seen the other night? There it was at last, the courage to ask that question. She'd forced herself to bury the incident for long enough. It was time to sort out the images and make some sense of it all.

Who was the child? Jo closed her eyes and tried to picture the face of the girl. Sandy hair, blue eyes, freckles. She looked a good deal like Eric.

Is that the tie? A sibling? His child?

Father Pat moved quietly from the sanctuary into the church. When he saw her, he came and sat down beside her for a moment.

"You doing okay?" he inquired in a hushed voice.

She nodded, and then looked at him intently. "Father?"

"Yes?"

Jo hesitated a moment. It was a tough thing to ask outright, but she pushed ahead. "Has there been a murder in this area recently?" She watched his face, waiting.

He registered surprise at the unusual question, but answered her honestly. "A long time ago, a young girl was murdered. Is that what you're asking about?"

Jo nodded. "I think so. How long ago?"

"Oh, fifteen years, maybe a little more," Father Pat replied. "May I ask why?"

"I…I just heard something about it, and…and I was upset."

Okay, forget the absolution, Jo thought with frustrated exasperation. *You just lied to a priest*! She shuddered involuntarily, causing Father Pat to place a warm, assuring hand over her icy ones.

"I'm sorry, Father," Jo's voice, sounded small and bereft. "That was a lie."

He smiled and said, "I know,"

She returned his grin, hers more apologetic than a reflection of pleasure, and then her gaze dropped to her lap where her hands twisted nervously. "I…I have these…well, I don't know…ah, mental pictures, sometimes. I mean…ah, it's like, psychic visions, sort of." Her tongue peeked out, slipping nervously across her lips. "I was with Eric Westermann the other day and sort of, I mean, I had this vision. It was a girl being murdered." She wanted to look at the priest, desperate to see how he'd taken such a revelation, but she just couldn't force her eyes to meet his. Most people were skeptical, at the very least, but the usual reaction was revulsion and disbelief.

Father Pat expressed neither. "Are you ashamed of these visions?" he asked.

Jo thought the question a strange one, but she considered it, and then shook her head. "Not really," she said. "Just worried how people will accept it." She paused for a moment before continuing. "And afraid of revealing too much of my past, I guess. I did some work with the police before, and got a lot of publicity. It's…it's a tie I'd rather not have exposed."

Father Pat nodded, understanding her fears. "Did you see who did it?" he asked softly, meeting her eyes.

Jo shook her head.

The priest nodded again, as if expecting that response. "The child was Eric's sister—well, half-sister, actually," he said. "Eric would have been about seventeen or eighteen when she died, I guess. It was a very bad time for everyone in Humboldt. Eric was the one who found the body, raped and beaten with a blunt instrument. Several days later, the police found a ball bat in the river." The words were chilling, but Father Pat's voice was calm, helping Jo deal with what she was hearing.

"What…what was her name?" she asked tentatively, the shock of it leaving her stunned. The images were there—in her mind's eye—fading, but still vivid enough to induce terror.

"Megan. Megan Westermann."

"Who did it?"

"Don't know. They never caught anyone. Cold case now, I guess." The Priest patted Jo's hands. "It's close to Christmas, Jo. Maybe Eric was remembering her and you just picked up on it. People usually miss loved ones at this time of year, and they were pretty close, I guess. He was a mess for a long time after her death. "

"Yeah," Jo agreed. That was most likely the connection. Sometimes, if the emotion was strong enough, she could connect with a thought or memory from someone else's head.

The priest smiled his reply, standing as if ready to go on about his business.

"Ah, Father?" Jo asked with tentative unease.

"Yes."

"Do I have to go to confession again?" She looked like a forlorn child, truly contrite for an offense. "I'm sorry I lied to you."

Father Pat chuckled deep in his chest. "No, child, I think we can overlook the slip."

Jo breathed out a sigh of relief. "Thanks, Father."

The priest smiled and then left the church headed, no doubt, to the rectory, and a warm bed.

Jo remained where she was for a long time. She said another rosary for the unknown child—Megan. Right before she left, she lit a holy candle for the girl, whispering a silent prayer for the repose of her soul.

XII

The dojo was quiet. Jo liked it that way. This was her first visit back since the scene with Eric. She'd waited until later to do the cleaning, so she'd be certain to avoid another accidental meeting.

"Hey."

Jo turned abruptly, not surprised to see Hawk leaning against the doorjamb, between the dojo and the hallway that led to the back exit. He was wearing his gi.

"Hi," she responded, dropping her eyes and moving to retrieve her uniform jacket. She liked working out in a sports bra and gi pants, but it was unorthodox, and not permitted in most dojos.

Hawk moved forward with surprising quickness, his hand stopping hers. "No, it's okay. I like you half naked," he said in a husky voice that was barely more than a whisper of sound. The words teased, but his tone was serious. Jo suspected they were about to have the talk she'd known was inevitable.

She'd managed to avoid him for almost a week now, but it was time to face the issue and furnish something that would divert him. Whatever happened, Jo knew she'd lie to Hawk tonight—she'd have to go see Father Pat tomorrow. Finding a chair she sat down, waiting for him to initiate the conversation.

He surprised her. Removing his own top, he walked onto the mat, and began warming up.

She watched in silence as he moved with a fluid, well-oiled grace. His bare torso glistened with sheen of sweat, and corded Bulging pectorals and biceps attested to hours of disciplined workouts. His muscle literally rippled under the glossy flesh of his chest and back. Hawk was an impressive sight, his body perfectly proportioned and powerfully built. Jo felt her groin tighten, and then start to throb.

Holy shit! I don't need horny at a time like this.

"Come here, Little Girl." His raspy voice surprised Jo, pulling her abruptly back to the here and now. She looked up with startled eyes, not sure she'd understood his request.

"Come here," he repeated, jerking his head.

Jo moved onto the mat opposite him, her hands at her sides.

"The way of the warrior," he began, "is to use martial arts to develop the character to meet danger with courage, hardship with endurance, and to live by a code of honor and dignity." Hawk dropped into a fighting stance.

Jo's body automatically responded, assuming a similar posture, poised and ready. So, was he intending to knock the truth out of her?

"Is that a Taekwondo saying?" she asked, circling in small, shuffling steps to match Hawk's testing movements.

"Naw, Combat Karate."

Jo nodded. "Impressive."

Hawk suddenly attacked with a right, thrust kick.

Jo instinctively stepped back with her left foot, dropping into a self-defense stance and executing a downward, outside parry. Without hesitation, she shifted into a front stance and delivered a palm heel strike to Hawk's right arm, catching him close to the elbow. Rotating her right hand inside the left one, she delivered an overhead claw, barely missing his eyes. Almost simultaneously, she threw a front snap kick to the groin. The contact was minimal, but executed with enough force to double him over.

~ ~ ~

Without hesitation, and before Jo had a chance to cross out and cover, Hawk dived, catching her in a tackle around the waist and carrying her to the ground under the momentum of his weight. The impact left her winded, pinned under his body, with arms above her head and restrained at the wrists.

"What the hell was that?" she snapped, struggling to break his hold.

Hawk chuckled. "Football," he replied unabashedly. "So," he continued, "now that we're nice and cozy, let's talk."

"I'm not cozy!" she countered.

His face was only a fraction of an inch from hers. He dropped his head, nuzzling her neck, his tongue warm and moist against the exposed flesh. He felt her body shudder, responding with a passion he'd glimpsed now and again, a fervor that spoke to something deep inside him.

Jo groaned, her breath coming in short, uncontrolled gasps.

"Better?" Hawk whispered, close to her ear, allowing his tongue to caress the tender flesh at the base of her earlobe.

Shuddering again, her body trembled beneath him. "What…what do you want?" she asked in a voice that was rough with arousal.

"I want you to talk to me, Jo, and stop evading and dodging intimacy."

"I don't want to talk."

"I know, but it's time." Hawk's tone was empathetic, but firm. "Let's start with where you're really from."

"Let's not," she snapped, twisting futilely to escape, the ardor of only a moment before, apparently forgotten.

"Okay, how about your real name."

"Jo."

"Cute," Hawk whispered, his lips trailing along her jaw line again. "I was thinking more along the line of surnames." Jo gasped, her eyes opening wide as Hawk lowered his head, his teeth finding one erect nipple through the material of her sports bra, and gently teasing. "Talk to me, Jo."

"Or...or what?" She gasped, trying to sound angry, but Hawk could hear the hunger, the physical need underlying everything else. "Are you going to love me to death?" she hissed.

Hawk chuckled. "Damned good idea, Little Girl," he whispered, eliciting another shudder from the woman beneath him, as his tongue trailed up her chest and neck. "Okay, Jo," he conceded, "let's forget everything else, and talk about the other night—with Eric."

He felt her shaking in earnest now, and responded almost instinctively. Rolling to his side he pulled her into his arms, holding her close against the mass and strength of his body. "What, Jo?" He whispered the words, his voice rough with emotion. "It's okay, Baby, you can talk to me." He was stroking her hair, holding her while she trembled, though his body wanted so much more than platonic comforting right now.

~ ~ ~

"I...he..."Jo started crying, wanting to tell Hawk the truth, and knowing she couldn't—she had to lie. And worse yet, it had to be a lie he'd buy—one that would elicit compassion and tenderness, sidetrack him from the suspicions that were growing in his head. "He didn't mean to, but Eric grabbed my arm...it...I mean...I just..."

"What, Jo?" Hawk whispered close to her ear, his arms tight around her. Despite the fact that she was spinning a fabrication to deceive him, Jo felt safe and protected in Hawk's embrace. If only she'd met him *first*—before Devin!

"My husband, ex-husband, knocked me around some." She said the words coldly, with almost no inflection in her voice. "Eric grabbed me, and I just flashed back—the yelling, the anger, the..." Jo started crying again, more at the deception than the memories her words triggered. Devin *had* abused her—far more horrifically than she would ever let Hawk know. They were memories she had to learn to live with, but right now, they served another purpose.

"Did you change your name?" Hawk asked softly, "after the divorce?"

He knew Kenning wasn't right—he must have done some checking. Jo nodded. It was a simple lie—if lying could be classified as such.

"I just wanted to start over—not be around the same places, and people, and...*memories*."

Hawk held her so he could look into her eyes. Jo knew he still had questions, but he didn't voice them. Instead, he leaned forward and covered her mouth with his. She felt his tongue, and she allowed herself to respond.

She clung to him, wanting more than she could allow him to give, wanting—no! She couldn't go there—not now—not like this—not with lies on her lips and in her heart. Not tonight!

~ ~ ~

The day before Christmas dawned cold and crisp. There was very little snow on the ground, just the barest powdering, but it was enough to give the feel of the season. Jo spent most of the afternoon working on the tie quilts with the children and making homemade cards. She even talked Laney into some baking. Christmas just wasn't the same without a few decorated cookies, and it made Jenny's day.

At 11;30 PM, they bundled up and drove to church for Midnight Mass. Jo looked for Hawk, but he wasn't there. He'd probably gone at another time, she surmised. There were a surprisingly large number of parishioners present, but more impressive was the candlelight and serenity of the church. It was both comforting and inspiring. Father Pat's sermon was short, but poignant, and the children presented him with a quilt before they left for home. It was a good evening—the way life should be lived, Jo reflected on the drive home.

"Fathaw Pat liked it, Mommy," Jenny chirped from the backseat as they made their way out of town.

"Of course he did, Honey," Jo laughed at Jenny's enthusiasm. "Now, I want you all in bed, pronto, as soon as we get home. Santa can't come until you're asleep.

Jenny's tiny face took on a look of awe and wonder, and then abruptly changed to concern. "Ooooh, I hope he doesn't fawget me," she whispered.

Laney laughed at her sister's worried expression. "How could he forget a little girl who's been as good as you've been, Jen?"

Jo stayed up most of the rest of the night, finishing the last of the quilts and setting out Christmas treats. She'd purchased an outfit for each of her children, from shoes to top, including hats, mufflers, and gloves. She wrapped them all in bright paper and placed the packages under the tree.

They'll be so surprised, she thought, anxious to see their faces when they discovered they actually had presents. She filled the stockings and set them out near the fireplace, tucking pens and notepads into them all. She'd also taken time to find something special that each child would take pleasure in, and she slipped those items in the stockings as well. Jewelry and make-up for Laney, a yo-yo and sports cards for Casey, and a jump rope, crayons, and coloring book for Jenny. She'd also found Laney the CD she'd wanted, a new release video for Casey, and a large stuffed teddy bear for Jenny.

It wasn't as much as they were used to, but it was something. Probably more than they expected right now, Jo rationalized her extravagance as she topped off the stockings with gum and candy. She was surprised when the phone rang. Making a dive, she managed to snatch up the receiver before a second ring woke the children.

It's almost 2:30 AM. Who'd call at this hour?

"Hello?"

"Your light's still on." Hawk's deep, bass voice resonated over the phone line, stirring feelings in Jo's body she wasn't sure she was ready to deal with again so soon. "All good little girls are supposed to be in bed."

Almost immediately, their talk at the dojo resurfaced in Jo's brain. Hawk had accepted the brief explanation she'd given, but Jo knew he wanted more than that—he still had unanswered questions, and unresolved suspicions.

"Yeah?" Jo replied. "Well, I'm waiting to catch Santa with his pants down."

"Mmmm," Hawk's voice was low and gravelly, "I guess you're not such a good little girl after all, are you?"

The sound of his voice sent chills along her spine and fired warmth in her groin. She didn't want to acknowledge that reaction now, anymore than she'd wanted to at the dojo the other night.

"Well, I'm playing Santa, Candy Ass, what's your excuse?" she shot back.

"I'm waitin' for my present," Hawk said pathetically, "but Santa must've missed my place altogether."

"That's because bad little boys don't get presents, Big Guy." Jo smiled to herself. She could almost see his face, the bottom lip pushed out and a teasing glint of mischief in his dark eyes.

"Hey, I resent that! I'm good," he rebutted.

"Mmmm," Jo's tone turned suddenly provocative, "that's what I've heard," she all but purred.

"Oh, God, Jo, that's totally unfair, and downright cruel." Hawk groaned as if he were in real psychical anguish. "I'm in pain, *really*!"

"Come on over, Candy Ass. I'll kiss it and make it *all* better." Jo kept the laughter out of her voice, but it wasn't easy, especially with Hawk moaning on the other end of the line.

"You are a hard and cruel woman, Joanne Kenning." Hawk chuckled softly.

"Yeah, that's what they tell me," she countered, and then fell silent for several moments. When she finally spoke, her voice was hushed and tentative. "Hawk?"

"Yeah?"

"Merry Christmas."

"Merry Christmas, Little Girl," he whispered, and then hung up the phone.

~ ~ ~

"Merry Christmas!" It was nearly noon the following morning. Hawk, Nate, and Carol stood at Jo's door, a huge basket of goodies in hand, and between them, they carried three, brightly colored sleds.

"Merry Christmas," Jo replied. "Come in before you freeze to death."

She had a warm fire crackling in the fireplace and most of the wrappings picked up from the morning's frenzy. The kids had been ecstatic with the presents, and their excitement made Jo's day, increasing her delight in the annual ritual. The children had even managed to pool a few dollars of their own, buying her some scented bath salts. Jo's eyes filled with tears when she opened that gift, completely surprised, and deeply touched at their efforts.

"Mom insisted we had to be sociable, but we don't come empty-handed," Hawk grinned at Jo, rolling his expressive eyes.

"HAWK," Jenny squealed, racing across the room and throwing herself into his outstretched arms.

"Hey, little Jen-Jen," Hawk squeezed her tightly, twirling her in the air before setting her down again. "What did Santa bring you?"

"A jump wope, a sled, a teddy beawa, cwayons, and…" Jenny listed off every tiny, little thing she'd found, and Hawk listened patiently, periodically injecting appropriately awed comments.

Setting a large wicker basket on Jo's kitchen counter, Carol began pulling wrapped packages out of it, one at a time, as well as several foil-wrapped loaves of homemade breads.

"These are for you and your family, Jo," Carol said cheerfully, grinning from ear to ear. It was obvious she was thoroughly enjoying the role of Santa.

Jo hated to appear ungrateful, but the their generosity made her uncomfortable. "Carol, you really shouldn't have," she said, knowing the words sounded trite, but not sure what else to say.

"Don't argue with Grams," Nate interjected conspiratorially. Jo turned to find him standing close beside her. "We've tried for years, and it don't work."

"Oh, go on with you," Carol swatted at Nate as he laughed and disappeared with Laney into the living room. "Hawk, haul these in by the tree, will you," she ordered her son.

"Your wish is my command, Mother Dear." he winked at Jo as he did his mother's bidding.

Jo felt as if her voice box had suddenly malfunctioned. She was at a loss for words, and even if she'd known just what to say, she was certain she couldn't have managed to get it out. Why did these people go to so much effort to make them feel at home and welcome? They treated them like family, not strangers. That thought brought a lump to her throat, and mind drifted to her own parents.

How are they handling Christmas Day, without us? The unanswered question left behind a pang of guilt. I wish I could call them. It was an urge she'd wrestled with on more than one occasion, but Jo knew she couldn't dare. A phone call was traceable—and she was certain Devin would have taken measures, however illegal, to track incoming calls to her parents. Leaning against the archway between the living room and dining area, Jo watched as the children opened gifts and squealed in delight. It was a bittersweet moment.

"You're looking far too down in the dumps for such a beautiful day," Hawk said from close behind her.

Starting slightly, she turned to acknowledge his words. "Sorry." Jo wasn't sure she could trust herself to say more than that without breaking into tears.

"You okay?" he asked, his expression shifting from teasing playfulness to sincere concern.

"Yeah," Jo forced a smile, "yeah, I'm fine. Just wishing I was closer to my family."

"Where do they live?"

The question was simple enough, but Jo's heart suddenly leapt into her throat and started hammering painfully. "I…they're ah…they live a long way from here," she managed to get the words out. She couldn't bring herself to look at Hawk, but she could feel his eyes on her—inquisitive, assessing, perceptive. She shivered inwardly.

Hawk changed the subject abruptly. "You're coming for dinner, you realize this don't you?" His voice was light and teasing again.

"Really, Hawk, your family has done enough for us." Jo lifted her face to meet his eyes, "I feel like we've become more than an imposition. You don't have to inclu—"

Hawk put a gentle finger over her lips, effectively stopping the rush of words. "It's not me you have to argue this with, Little Girl, it's my mother," he said, chuckling. Raising one dark brow to emphasize his meaning, he waited for her response.

Jo's eyes filled with tears. With sudden abruptness, she turned back to the distraction of presents and laughter in the living room.

"You want to talk about it?" Hawk asked gently, close to her ear.

"No," she answered his question honestly, her voice a choked whisper. "It's…nothing. Just…just feminine emotions…run rampant." She tried to sidetrack Hawk with a weak grin. His expression told her he knew there was more to it than that, but once again, he seemed to choose not to press the matter.

Jo was immensely grateful. She knew the day was coming when she'd have to make a choice to talk—or run. She just didn't want to cross that bridge right now—not on Christmas Day.

XIII

New Year's Eve day dawned warmer than Jo had expected for the last day of December. The snow everyone seemed to want hadn't materialized, not that Jo was complaining. She knew the farmers were hoping for the moisture, but she hated driving on winter roads, and especially disliked shoveling the stuff.

She'd already started her job training and liked it, very much. The paper was an interesting and lively place to be, even if the work was somewhat repetitive. Today would be her last day with Harriet as guide. Come January third she'd be on her own.

Jo reached absently for the phone on the desk beside her as it rang for the second time. "Humboldt Standard, how may I help you?"

"If I told you, I'd have to arrest myself," Hawk's voice vibrated through the phone line, his tone quite serious.

Jo laughed. "Well, a night in the slammer might do you a world of good, Big Guy."

"I called to see if I could finagle a date." Hawk's words were casual enough, but Jo's response to them wasn't. "My brothers and their spouses are going bar hopping and dancing tonight, and I'm stag, unless you take pity on me," he continued, completely unaware of Jo's ricocheting heartbeat.

"I'd love to," she answered with honest enthusiasm. The prospect of a night on the town with Hawk and his brothers was heady, and bar hopping on New Year's Eve sounded just plain—*wonderful.*

Then reality set in. She had children. How could she leave them home alone while she went out drinking? Jo amended her original response. "Ah…I'd love to Hawk, but I have kids to think of."

"I've covered all the bases, Little Girl," Hawk chuckled. "Nate's taking Laney to dinner and a movie, and Carol said all the kids could spend the night at her place. She's rented Play Station games, and videos, and even stocked up on non-alcoholic champagne so they can ring in the New Year with style. You're pretty much foot loose and fancy free—more or less."

Jo was overwhelmed. "Wow, okay, I guess."

Hawk's deep chuckle came through the phone line, igniting a now-familiar response in her gut. "*Wow*," he mimicked, "don't sound so enthusiastic and excited. I'll get a fat head or something."

"No, really," Jo rushed to explain, "I AM excited. It's just, I don't know, I wasn't expecting to get to do anything tonight."

"Well, start planning," Hawk said. "How does six-thirty sound to you?"

"Perfect."

"Okay, Little Girl, see ya later."

"See ya." Jo hung up the receiver, slightly dazed, but grinning with pleasure.

"Hot date?" Jack asked.

Jo started, completely unaware that her boss had been listening. "Yeah, I guess," she replied evasively.

Jack moved his bushy eyebrows up and down, though Jo was at a loss to know exactly what he was implying. "Gotta watch that kind," he said enigmatically, "they can leave you with nasty burns."

~ ~ ~

"Leave your hair down," Laney insisted as she fluffed out wisps of curls with her fingertips, "and not too much make-up, either."

"All right, little Miss Mary Kay," Jo laughed. "What about my outfit, too casual?"

Laney made a face. "I didn't know there was a *too casual* for bar hopping," she teased, perusing her mother's choice of blue jeans, white lace-up top, and flannel lined jean jacket. "Looks great, but that tank is a little low cut, isn't it?"

Jo stuck out her tongue, refusing to grace Laney's remark with a reply.

Hopping onto Jo's bed, Jenny plopped down beside Laney. "You look gweat, Mommy," she said with something close to awe, clutching her Christmas teddy bear in one arm.

"Thanks, Jen." Jo ruffled her daughter's curls. "Where's Casey?" she asked, realizing she hadn't seen him most of the afternoon.

"He and Nate went to the gym to play a little basketball," Laney supplied.

Jo smiled. How wonderful. How perfectly normal. Why couldn't her life really be this genuine and honest—instead of an invented existence in a real world? She sighed inwardly, pushing her sudden melancholy aside. It was New Year's Eve—a new year, a new life, a new beginning. Please God, let it be a new beginning!

"Okay," Jo forced her mind and emotions back to a neutral topic, "what about the boots? Overkill?" she asked, standing for the girl's inspection.

Assuming a dramatic pose, Jo turned her foot first one way, and then the other.

"You look gawait, Mommy. Hippan happen!" Jenny squealed, hugging her teddy bear.

Jo and Laney both giggled.

"What did you say?" Laney asked her sister.

"Hippan happen," Jenny repeated. "Casey told me that."

Giggling again Laney said, "She means hippin' happenin', and she's right, Mom," Laney gave her a thumbs-up sign, "you look *totally* awesome."

"Thanks, Sweetie." Jo smiled like a silly schoolgirl.

Glancing at the clock, she realized it was nearly time for Hawk to pick her up and suddenly, her heart started hammering wildly and her breath caught in her throat. Whoa, slow down, Jo's rational side kicked in. He's just a friend—this is just a friendly date. You cannot get anymore involved than that. PERIOD!

~ ~ ~

"You drink much, Jo?" Hawk laughed as she stumbled yet again.

"Shut up, I'm…fine. Juss a little…tired." Jo was obviously trying to keep her words comprehensible and her tone serious, but she couldn't contain the giggle that escaped.

"Okay, Little Girl, fine it is." Hawk helped her across the frosted, slippery ground toward her house. It was 2:00 AM, and the night was clear and cold as he slid his own key into the lock on the French doors that led into Jo's bedroom. He followed her inside, touching a light switch on the wall near the door. It connected to a table lamp, illuminating the bedroom with a soft, yellow glow.

Jo moved into the room, stripping off her boots and jacket, then turned and threw her arms around his neck. "Let's dancha," she said, moving against his body.

The contact ignited the physical hunger Hawk had been controlling all night. "Yes, let's," he murmured as his arms came around her, pressing her against his body.

He moved in slow turns, humming a soft, sultry tune as he looked down at Jo's upturned face. He noted her closed eyes and a blissfully content expression, and smiled. She seemed to enjoy the evening, falling in with the casual bantering, and even managing a little flirting. From what he'd observed, she took immense pleasure in the conversations, toasting, dancing, and teasing.

"You know," he whispered close to her ear, "I never did get a proper

Happy New Year's kiss."

Jo's eyes flew open, a look of consternation widening her soft, lavender-gray eyes. Her expression changed almost immediately as those eyes narrowed with suspicion. "You got a kissh," she said, then covered her mouth with the fingers of one hand and giggled.

Hawk swallowed a grin. "I got a peck," he said with mock indignation. "B.J. got a real kiss, and Bert's was damned near *passionate*."

Jo laughed at Hawk's version of the New Year's tradition they'd shared. "Your brothers are damn good kisshers."

"And I'm not?" he challenged, pulling his features into an expression of utter disbelief.

"*Soooo*," Jo cooed, "you want passhionate, too?" Her face unexpectedly took on a look of physical hunger as her eyes came to rest on his mouth.

"It's the only fair thing to do, really." Hawk's voice turned rough and gravelly with sudden desire as he watched her, his groin hard and throbbing with a lust he'd controlled for far too long.

Rising up on her toes, Jo touched her lips against his. "Like that?" she asked hoarsely, her pupils dilating with ardor.

Hawk felt a jolt of need clear to his toes. "No, Baby," he growled, pulling Jo against him, "like this." He lowered his head and claimed her mouth in a kiss that was forceful and insistent. His tongue explored and demanded—and so did his hands.

Jo responded with a fervor that surprised him. She's hungry! The thought was only peripheral, but Hawk's brain registered the fact with something close to triumph. He wanted her—desperately. Now! Right now! And he knew she wanted this as much as he did. When he pulled away, Jo clung to his shirtfront as if she were afraid her knees might buckle.

"I…God, I want you, Little Girl," Hawk whispered the words, feeling Jo's body tremble with the same desire that had dilated her pupils and quickened her breathing. She groaned. It was a desperate sound—a primal verbalization of need.

With trembling hands, she tugged at his sweater, forcing him to pull it up and over his head. Running fingertips across his warm, bare flesh, she allowed her thumbs to tease at his nipples briefly, before her mouth covered each in turn.

Hawk's sudden intake of breath sounded loud in the quiet room, and his body tensed in swift, ardent response. Oh God! He ached with craving, every cell, every nerve, every sinew of his body—hot, heady, voracious longing. Pulling Jo's top over her head with deft, sure precision, he slid the straps of her bra down, his hands finding and cupping full breasts.

Her groan seemed to vibrate through him as his thumbs teased taut nipples. Jo leaned into him, wanting more. Lowering his head he took one, and then the other, into his mouth, suckling and teasing the sensitive flesh. She whimpered, her hands clutching at his head, pulling his mouth up to meet hers with a desperation that was almost crazed.

"We…we need to stop it here, Jo," he said hoarsely, "or…" Hawk groaned as Jo's tongue found the hollow at the base of his throat and trailed up his neck. "*Judas, Woman*," he gasped against her hair, "I'm not strong enough to—"

"You gonna fuck me, or what?" she whispered deep in her throat, cutting Hawk's words off. All evidence of her earlier intoxication appeared to be gone.

"*Jesus*, Jo," Hawk lost control. In one, swift motion, he lifted her, tossing her onto the bed.

Unfastening her jeans, he pulled them off, and then effortlessly snapped the tiny bit of elastic that held her thong in place. His mouth sought and found the warm, moist apex between her legs, eliciting a cry of pleasure that energized him to his very core. Layers of taste assailed his senses, driving him to crave more—and more! Her scent was heady—intoxicating—pungent spice, rich musk! It ignited a depth of passion and need that surprised him. Lord Almighty, he thought, I'll never get enough of her!

Jo's cry of release was almost immediate, but Hawk didn't stop. He *couldn't*! He felt her tense, the second orgasm building, and his own body throbbed, quivering and burning with an obsession he couldn't remember ever feeling with any other woman—an ache so colossal, it threatened to crush him.

Nearly wild, Jo writhed and pleaded, her voice sounding desperate. "Oh God, oh *God*!" She cried the words out repeatedly, in a frenzied, gasping whisper. "Don't stop. Please, Hawk," she begged, "don't stop."

"I've absolutely no intention of it, Baby," he said huskily, then he lowered his mouth yet again, drinking in an essence that had suddenly become as dominate as his need for oxygen.

XIV

"Hello, Father." Hawk greeted the priest as he stepped into the rectory living room. He came often to visit and chat, but Hawk had more on his mind tonight than casual conversation and a beer.

"Sit down, Beau. It's been awhile since you've been by."

"Yeah, too long," Hawk agreed.

Pat walked to his refrigerator and pulled out two bottles of beer, handing one to Hawk as he returned to the living room. "What's on your mind, my friend?" he asked, eyeing him with keen perception.

"I…hell, I don't even know where to begin." Hawk hated this feeling of uncertainty.

The priest grinned. "It's okay, really, I get that a lot."

"I bet you do," Hawk replied, relaxing a little.

"Why don't you try the beginning, it usually works for me," Pat offered.

Hawk smiled wryly. "Easier said than done," he responded.

"Yeah, I know," Father Pat leaned forward, resting his elbows on his knees, a bottle of beer in one hand.

"You know Joanne Kenning?" Hawk began, feeling awkward.

Pat nodded. "She's been to see me several times, and usually makes it to daily Mass," he replied, taking a drink of beer.

"Yeah, well, she's living in the cottage on our place." Hawk wasn't particularly reassured when Pat nodded his knowledge of that fact. "I, well, ah…I…" he stumbled over the words, finding them unusually difficult.

"You like her don't you?" Pat asked shrewdly.

Hawk bowed his head. "Too much," he said in a soft, hopeless voice.

The priest chuckled, "I didn't know you could like someone too much, Beau. She's a fine woman, lots to offer."

Hawk nodded concurrence.

Father Pat raised a quizzical brow. "So, what's the problem?"

"I don't know, Father, I just have this gut instinct there's, well, she's not what she….there's just some strange shi…ah, I mean," Hawk wanted to strangle himself. Damn! How am I going to get through this?

Pat reached over and put a warm hand on his knee. "You sense she's more than what she seems?"

Hawk nodded.

"Most people are, Beau."

"I know, I just get the feeling she's hiding stuff from me. That she's not completely honest. It makes me…" Hawk paused, struggling for the right word.

"Suspicious? Scared?" the priest filled in. "Either of those come anywhere close?"

"Yeah, pick one. They both work." Hawk guzzled down several quick mouthfuls of beer.

Pat nodded understanding. He took a long swig of his own drink before responding. "You suspect there's more to her than she wants you to know, and the cop in you is nervous about it," he paraphrased.

"Bingo," Hawk grimaced at the unintentional pun. "I've tried to run down some information on her, Pat, and there's nothing. "It's as if she doesn't fuc—" he stopped abruptly. "Sorry, Father. It's like she doesn't even exist."

"Mmmm, tough one."

"You're not much help."

The priest smiled. "What kind of help do you want?"

"*Judas*, Pat," Hawk said with exasperation, standing and pacing. "What the hell am I supposed to do, just ignore my gut instincts? Pretend everything's just hunky dory? Getting to know this woman is like trying to navigate a maze!"

"Sit down, Beau," Father Pat directed, watching as his friend complied. "You know as well as I do, that most people have convoluted layers we never see or even suspect."

Hawk nodded.

"Jo has a right to keep her secrets, for now at least. This is a new place, new people. She may like you a lot, but trust is something that takes time."

"I get that, Pat, but—"

"Let me ask you something, Beau," the Priest interrupted. "If you picked up and moved to another state, would you be spilling your guts to the first person that started asking?"

"Well, I don't know about spilling my guts, but I wouldn't be defensive about telling people where I'm from, or who I am. If there's nothin' to hide, why does she act like she's hidin' somethin'?"

"I'm not sure hiding is the right descriptor here, Beau. I think it's more along the lines of just plain wanting to forget—not wanting people around here to associate her with the ugliness of her past."

"*What past*?" Hawk snapped. "She doesn't have any past, as far as I can determine."

"Does knowing who she was, and where she came from, make that big a difference to you?"

"It does to my head," Hawk flashed the priest a wan smile, "but it doesn't seem to matter to the rest of my anatomy."

"Then maybe it doesn't matter. Sometimes our heads can analyze things too much, search for answers we really don't need."

"I know that, Father," Hawk's voice sounded exasperated. "I've told myself that a million and one times, but there's just, I don't know. It's more than that. There's something I need to know, I just...*feel* it."

Pat nodded. "That gut instinct of yours is what makes you good at your job, Beau, so let me ask you one more thing."

Raising his eyebrows, Hawk, met the rector's steady gaze.

"What does your gut tell you about Jo herself, as a person?"

He looked away, his mind mulling over the question. Despite the unease and suspicion, what did his gut tell him? "She's a good person," he said at last.

"Yes, she is."

Hawk's dark eyes locked with the Priest's once again. "You say that as if you know her better than I do."

"Well, I know what you would refer to as, *her secret*. She's no threat to you, or anyone else."

Hawk raised one dark brow. "I don't suppose you're gonna tell me anything, either."

Father Pat winked. "Not a chance, my friend, not a chance."

"I wish I could feel as sure of her as you do, Pat."

"Trust your gut, Beau."

He grunted. "I don't know if it's my gut or my di—ah, groin, Father, but I'm fallin' hard for that woman. I...I don't know." Hawk's elbows rested on his spread knees, and his bent head slumped forward to rest in the palm of one hand.

"That's a rough one, my friend," the priest said, taking another drink of his beer. "Your heart trusts her enough to fall in love, but your head questions everything she does and says."

"It's not that bad—" Hawk started to defend himself.

Father Pat cut him off. "I've talked with Jo at length, Beau, and although I can't tell you what we spoke of, I believe she's a woman worthy of the feelings she's stirred in you."

Hawk looked at the priest for a long moment, contemplating those words. "Why?"

"She's loves hard, and she's been hurt hard—deeper than any of us may ever know. Everything she's doing now, the move, the struggle to make a new life, all of it, she's doing for her kids. She's trying to give them a normal life, and ensure their safety."

"*Safety*?" Hawk latched onto the word, like a cat pouncing on an unwary mouse. His eyes narrowed as his suspicions suddenly rekindled.

Pat smiled and leaned back in his chair, tipping his beer to take another swallow. "I won't say more, Beau." His voice was light, but the resolve behind the words, was dead serious. "Trust me on this call, will you?"

Hawk nodded. His eyes dropped to the floor between his feet, and he began nervously picking at the label on his beer bottle.

"There's more, I think," Father Pat smiled as if he knew exactly what Hawk needed to say.

"We…I…" Hawk stumbled over his own words again. Confession is a bitch!

"Go on Beau, I'm listening," Pat said in a gentle voice.

Hawk looked up, steeling himself and coming directly to the point. "I made love to her, Pat."

The priest wasn't in the least bit shocked, or surprised. He smiled an understanding, half smile. "Well, I'm gonna guess Jo'll be in here before long with that one, too," he said, grinning at Hawk's shocked countenance. "So," he continued, "your feelings do run pretty deep. You're not a man to take a step like that lightly."

Hawk nodded. The room was silent for several minutes. Both men seemed lost in their individual thoughts. It was a comfortable silence, a familiar pattern between the two friends.

Father Pat was the first to speak. "She won't make any kind of permanent commitment to you, not right now," he said, surprising Hawk with the comment. "She may love you as deeply as you love her, but she won't take those feelings any farther than they go right now."

"I know, she's told me that much." Hawk met the Priest's eyes. "In fact, I think she's been avoiding me ever since New Year's Eve."

Pat nodded. "I'm not surprised," he said, "my guess is her feelings for you scare her as much, or more, than your feelings for her, scare you."

Hawk didn't respond but he eyed the priest with a quizzical, raised eyebrow, waiting for him to elaborate.

"Injured animals need time to lick their wounds—inside and out—time to heal."

"You sound like my mother."

Pat chuckled. "I'll take that as a compliment," he said, sipping at his beer.

"So, you think she's wounded, inside and out?" Hawk's face looked introspective, as if he were mulling the possibility around in his head. "Is that why she holds back?"

"I don't think it, Beau, I know it. Give her the time she needs."

Hawk shook his head, and then finished off the last of his beer. "Everything about her is a mystery, a conundrum, a puzzle."

"Do you love her?"

"Yeah, I'm afraid I do."

"Then give her time and space. Trust her."

"Trust is hard come-by for a cop, Father."

"It's hard come-by for all of us, Beau, especially someone who's suffered as long and deeply as Joanne Kenning has." Pat said softly.

~ ~ ~

"Hey," Hawk said as Jo answered the phone. "I saw your bedroom light from my deck, so I figured you were still awake."

"Yeah, I was tossing and turning, so I decided to get up and find a good book," Jo responded, feeling shy for some reason. Just the sound of his deep, resonant voice made her insides quiver, igniting something in her she wasn't sure she could control. She was hungry all over again, and the voraciousness of that need was an unsettling sensation, slithering along her veins and arteries, screaming to be sated.

I don't want to get this involved! He's a cop! It was something she'd told herself repeatedly over the past two weeks, but it hadn't helped. She couldn't stop herself from responding to this man.

"Did you?" Hawk's seductively pitched voice brought back images and sensations from New Year's Eve that Jo had been trying to block from her conscious mind. She could almost feel his hands on her body—taste the salty sweetness of his skin—smell the musky aftershave. It made her gut twist into a knot of hunger and desire that ended in a throb of fire between her legs.

"Well, did you?" he asked again, after several moments of silence.

"Wh…what?" She was disconcerted. Could Hawk hear it in her voice? Had he been remembering, too?

He chuckled low in his chest. "Find a good book?" he clarified his question.

Jo cleared her throat. "Well, I…I found a book. I won't go so far as to say it's good," she replied, relaxing a little. "Actually, it's pretty damned boring."

"I could come over and read it to you. Maybe with the right inflections, in the proper places, it would take on new life," he offered, his voice honey sweet with innocence.

"Yeah, that ought to help me sleep," Jo said with a sarcastic inflection.

"Any other bright ideas, Big Guy?"

"How about a back rub?" Hawk offered.

The throb was back—full force—licking like fire all the way up to her brain. "I...*damn*! That sounds so good." Jo wasn't sure if she said those words aloud or not. Her eyes closed as images flooded her mind—remembered sensations igniting a desperate hunger she'd tried to deny.

"What're you wearin', Little Girl?" Hawk asked, catching her by surprise.

"Wh...why do you always ask that?" she whispered.

"Curiosity," Hawk replied innocently.

"Well, I'm not telling you," Jo teased.

"Okay, I'll tell you," Hawk said, his tone seductive again. "You've got on a dark blue satin nightie with spaghetti straps, and it barely covers your ass."

Jo gasped. "How'd you know that?"

"Ex-ray vision," Hawk whispered. "But the best part is your underwear."

"I'm not wearing any," Jo shot back triumphantly, giggling.

"I know," Hawk, drawled, the hunger in his voice igniting a primitive response in Jo, that left her gasping for air. She could feel the thrumming now, in her head, in her stomach, and clear down to her toes.

"Oh...Lord." It was all she could manage to squeak out at the moment.

~ ~ ~

"Good Morning, The Humboldt Standard," Jo said, picking up a pencil and pulling a notepad close in case she needed to take a message. "Can I help you?"

"Yeah, Little Girl, you can," Hawk drawled lazily on the other end of the line.

Jo felt her heart leap to her throat. Crap! Why do you affect me like this? Why can't I keep my damned heart from careening at the sound of your voice? "*Well*?" she said after a moment or two of silence.

"Well what?" Hawk teased.

"Well, how can I help you, Candy Ass?" Jo retorted,

"Mmmmm, just hearing your voice is a big help," Hawk replied, "but I do have something to ask you."

"The answer's no," Jo shot back, knowing perfectly well Hawk wouldn't let it go at that.

"NO? You don't even know the request yet."

"Okay, what's the request?"

"I need a date," Hawk said.

"Check out the supermarket. They come chopped, whole, and sugared." Jo's reply sounded composed, considering the fact that her heart had quickened its pace tenfold, and breathing was almost agony.

"Oh, very funny, Little Girl," Hawk's sounded aggrieved, "*very* funny!"

"You don't sound like you're laughing to me." Jo used the bantering to help control her corporeal response to the sound of his voice. Knowing he was as close as the other end of the phone line left her insides quivering with a desperate need to see him—to touch him—to taste him.

"*Ha! Ha!*" Hawk shot back.

"Okay, Big Guy, what are you beggin' a date for?"

"Nate has a basketball game tonight. It's a home game. I thought you and the kids might enjoy going. I'm pretty sure Laney will be there."

"She did mention something about some friends picking her up for the game." Jo was excited. She knew nothing about basketball. Football was the only sport she really followed, but watching Nate play would be fun—and with Hawk beside her, it would be heady.

"Junior varsity boys play at five, and then the girl's varsity play at six-thirty. Boy's varsity should start about eight. I thought we'd catch the two varsity games."

Jo swallowed hard several times. "Sounds great," she responded, feeling as silly as an adolescent schoolgirl at the prospect of an evening with Hawk.

"I'll be over about six."

"We'll be ready." Jo hung up the phone, feeling like a dreamy schoolgirl.

"It's just a ball game," Jack's's sarcastic words shattered her euphoric mood.

"Yeah, I know." She forced herself back down to earth. He's right, she chastised herself mentally. It's just a casual date—a basketball game, for Pete's sake. You're *married*! You can't let this infatuation get out of hand.

Jack eyed Jo with a steady, evaluative look on his face that made her edgy. "You're jumping into this relationship pretty fast, Jo. You get this hot over every guy who gets a hard-on for you?"

Jack had rough edges, and he seldom minced words, Jo knew that. She'd developed a casual, joking relationship with him over the weeks she'd filled in at the paper. In fact, she really rather liked the old fart, but sometimes he carried things a little too far. She knew it was just his way. He was blunt, seeing no need to sugarcoat words or put on airs.

Jo tried to keep anger from coloring her response. "No, and I don't see that it's any of your business, Jack."

The editor shook his head from side to side, his eyes holding hers. "Be careful, Jo," he said with what appeared to be heartfelt concern.

Jo narrowed her eyes, assessing the gruff man. "I'm always careful, Jack," she said with a hint of levity, "but thanks for the concern.

"Yeah, whatever." He pulled on his jacket as he opened the front door, seemingly embarrassed by their little tête-à-tête. "I'm goin' home for lunch," he said gruffly. "I'll be back in an hour or so."

Despite bright sunshine, the wind chill cut clear to the bone. Jo watched Jack through the front window as he made his way across the slick, packed snow toward his vehicle. Lowering his head, he turned his coat collar up, doggedly enduring the buffeting wind. Jo looked past him to the barren trees of the park across the street. Their near-black bark looked stark and sinister against the brilliant white of the snow-covered ground, like dark, ill-omened skeletons.

She felt a shiver touch her spine as she watched Jack's car back out onto the street and drive away. Are you digging for skeletons, Jack? The question flashed through her mind, leaving her cold inside. She had a few she didn't want dug up! Sometimes, she had the distinct impression Jack knew more about her past than he should—it made her nervous and uneasy.

What is it you think you know, Jack?

XV

The boys came loping onto the court to the cheers of the hometown fans. Jo felt her pulse quicken at the sight of Nate in his silver and blue basketball uniform—number 15. She watched attentively as the warm-ups began, noticing Nate handled the ball well. He seldom missed a bucket.

"Come on, Little Girl, let's get something to eat." Hawk grinned at Jo's enthusiasm as he stood, holding out a hand to help her down the bleachers.

"We'll miss the game," she protested.

Hawk chuckled. "Darlin', they won't start for another twenty minutes."

Jenny bounced up the bleachers, her face flushed from running and playing with some classmates she'd found. "Mom, I'm hungway," she hollered.

Hawk laughed, rumpling Jenny's hair when the child threw her arms around his waist for a hug. "See," he raised dark brows at Jo. "We're hungry."

Jo smiled. "Sounds like I'm out-voted," she said, following Hawk out of the gym and into the cafeteria.

"Where's Casey?" Hawk asked Jenny, looking down at her bouncing little body as she clung to his hand.

She smiled up at him adoringly. "Gettin' in twouble, pwobably," she replied, completely serious.

Hawk threw back his head and laughed, swinging Jenny up into his arms for a bear hug. "Jenny, you're my kind of woman."

"You silly biwad," Jenny responded, planting a loud, wet, smack of a kiss on his cheek.

"Here we go," Hawk said, guiding Jo into line, Jenny riding on his hip.

Jo marveled at the efficiency of the mothers and fathers that staffed the food line, and the meal was nothing short of amazing. There were three choices of homemade soups, and the variety of desserts was, in itself, overwhelming.

Hawk paid for their food and led them to a cafeteria table. At least half a dozen people spoke to him in passing, joking and teasing, or just acknowledging him with a friendly greeting. Hawk made a point of introducing Jo to them all.

"Wow," she commented as they sat down. "You're a popular kinda guy."

Hawk grinned at her. "It doesn't take long to get to know everyone in a town this size."

"Hey, Hawk," Bert slapped his brother on the back, pulling up a chair beside Jo. Sarah sat down next to Hawk.

"Well, you enjoying yourself so far?" Sarah asked Jo. She had a hot dog and a container of water with her, and promptly began munching away. "Sorry," she apologized, a little embarrassed as she wiped catsup from her mouth. "I'm eating for two, and can't seem to keep filled up these days."

"No, don't apologize," Jo laughed. "It doesn't bother me."

"Me neither, Honey," Bert smiled at his wife, deep affection clearly visible on his handsome face. "You just keep feedin' my youngun'."

"When are you due?" Jo asked. "I know you've told me before, but I can't remember."

Sarah smiled. "End of March, I hope," she replied. "I'm feeling like an inflated cow right now. It'll be wonderful to have it over with."

Jo smiled, nodding her understanding. "I remember," she murmured.

"Is it a boy or a giwal?" Jenny asked with the utmost gravity, slurping another bite of chicken noodle soup into her mouth.

"We don't know, Jen-Jen, but I hope it's a little girl, just like you," Bert ruffled the child's auburn curls, drawing a huge, adoring smile.

"Me too," Jenny declared.

"Seen Beejah?" Hawk asked his brother.

"Naw, but they'll be here. He had chores to finish up." Bert stuffed half a hot dog into his mouth, and then followed it with a swig of soda. "You like basketball, Jo?" he asked, wiping at his mouth with the back of one hand.

Jo shrugged. "I don't know, I didn't do basketball in school, and never followed it much on TV," she admitted, somewhat sheepishly.

"She's been askin' a zillion questions about every little thing," Hawk rolled his eyes, feigning exasperation. "She'll be an expert by the end of the game."

"I didn't even know what HTRS meant when the cheerleaders started up one of the cheers," Jo admitted.

Sarah chuckled. "Yeah, Humboldt-Tablerock-Steinauer School District. It's a mouthful, but the consolidation of schools has kept our rural systems alive and kickin', and that's a big plus in my book."

"So, like, you aren't into basketball, Jo?" Bert asked, looking wounded when she shook her head. "Damn, that's almost anti-American, Girl."

Jo laughed. "I take it basketball was your sport?"

"Look at us, sugar, we were born to play. Well, *I* was born to play, anyway," Bert boasted. "Hawk was way better at knockin' the shit outta' people on the football field."

"Whoa, I can out-play your ass on a court any day of the week, Little Bro," Hawk defended his honor, looking properly insulted.

"And so can I," B.J. said, coming up behind Bert and slapping him on the back, none-too-gently.

Ellie was right behind her husband. "Hey, Jo, Sarah," she said cheerfully.

B.J. pulled up a stray chair next to Jenny, and turning it backwards, straddled it. "Hey, Jen-Jen," he teased, "that pie you're eatin' is bigger than you are."

Ellie leaned over and helped Jenny wipe whipped cream off her face. "Just stick your tongue out at him, Sweetie," she advised, giggling. "It's what I do to shut him up."

Jenny grinned from ear to ear. "Chairwee is my favowite," she sighed, shoveling another huge forkful into her mouth and leaving half the whipped cream on her face.

The adults burst into laughter.

"Hey, game's 'bout ready to start," B.J. informed them. "Let's get some front row seats, if they're not already taken."

Jo sighed inwardly as she watched the family's good-natured camaraderie. This is what life should be like, she thought to herself. Husbands that love and care for their spouses, children that are happy and loved, families doing things together and supporting one another. It was what she'd had as a child, and it was what she'd wanted for her own children—but things hadn't worked out that way.

Why didn't I find this? Why was my world so ugly?

~ ~ ~

"How about drinks at my place after the kids are in bed?" Hawk asked as he pulled his truck into the barn and turned off the ignition. Casey and Jenny were in the extended cab seats, both sound asleep.

NO, Jo cautioned herself, you're getting too close, too involved. It's too risky.

She'd slipped up before, allowing a mildly intoxicated state to serve as an excuse for their intimacy—but it wasn't. She wasn't free to make love to this man. It was the worst kind of lie—she could never give Hawk what her body promised him.

"I…I don't think so." She suddenly felt shy and uncertain of what to say or do. Jo wanted to accept, but she knew what that drink would lead to, and the mere thought of Hawk's hands on her body sent her temperature skyrocketing. Instinctively, she knew she wasn't strong enough to resist him.

Her marriage to Devin had been over, emotionally, long before she'd actually made the decision to run. For all intents and purposes, she'd been alone and afraid for most of her married life—cut off from normal human love and emotion, as if she'd been lost in a bitter cold, barren, wilderness. The promised warmth of Hawk's love, the fire that burned between them, was as essential to life as oxygen or a beating heart. Jo knew she couldn't refuse what he offered her. How could she turn away from what it promised? And yet—she HAD to. For *his* sake, as well as her own/

"Okay, I'll help you get the kids into bed." Hawk didn't seem upset by her rejection of his offer.

She couldn't tell what thoughts moved behind his dark eyes as he gently lifted Jenny into his arms. She woke Casey up and urged him from the truck, helping him stumble across the lawn toward the cottage.

When they had tucked the children into bed, Hawk followed Jo down the stairs, pulling her into his arms as they reached the bottom step. His mouth closed hungrily around hers, finding an instant and eager response.

Lifting his head to look into her face and whispered, "You act like you're scared sometimes, Jo. What are you frightened of? Why do you fight intimacy so fervently?" He spoke the words into her hair as he pulled her against his body.

She could feel his swollen need. It triggered a powerful response, a craving so deep and integral, it was a part of her very fabric. She ached for this man—the feel of him inside her. The fresh smell of soap on his skin mingled with the musky scent of his aftershave, creating an intoxicating aroma. *God,* she *wanted* him—she could *taste* it! Even her skin quivered with need.

Her voice grew husky with arousal. "I'm not scared," she denied.

"You act scared to me, Little Girl," Hawk said softly, his mouth teasing an ear lobe. He trailed a warm tongue down her neck, eliciting a strangled groan.

Jo's knees suddenly felt like someone had just stripped the bones away, leaving nothing but weak, limp flesh. She clung to him for support, her hands literally digging into his back. She was breathing like she'd just finished running the mile.

"You scared of me?" Hawk's voice was the barest of whispers as his hands slid under her shirt and eased her bra down. His hands burned her skin as they found and teased a response from taut nipples.

Jo gasped, closing her eyes and relishing the sensations her body had been screaming for. Her head rolled back as erotic vibrations tingled along her nerve endings. The throb in her groin was almost unbearable. She couldn't think straight enough to form an intelligent answer. She'd been starving for this for—oh Lord, *too long*.

Hawk's deep voice penetrated the fog in her brain. "Are you afraid of me, Jo?" There was an almost desperate *I need-to-know* sound to the question. His hands were on her shoulders now, holding her away from him so he could look into her eyes when she answered him.

Opening her eyes, she tried to form an appropriately vague answer. It was a futile attempt. She couldn't lie. Her mind was numb, her body thrumming, her senses overloaded, and—*hell*, she couldn't look him in the eye and lie—not right now. "Maybe," she whispered.

"Why?" Hawk pulled her into his arms, pressing her head against his shoulder. The single word sounded agonized.

"It's…it's just that everything has been so…so fast, I guess." she stumbled over the words.

The rational part of her brain warned her to push him away—keep her distance—but she was overwhelmed with the depth of her feelings for the man. It wasn't just physical need. Jo knew that, beyond questioning. *Oh yeah*, that was a significant part of the overall package, but her emotional connection was as strong—if not stronger—than the physical craving, and yet they were intrinsically and irrevocably interwoven.

She felt emotionally torn to shreds. She'd been back and forth over this battleground too many times of late, and it always ended the same way—in stalemate. What could they ever have together? *Nothing!* Technically, she was still married. And yet, when he held her in his arms, that didn't seem to matter in the least.

"You want me to stop?" His eyes dilated and his voice grew thick with arousal. He lifted Jo to sit on the kitchen counter, his mouth warm and wet as it caressed her throat.

NO, don't ever stop!

The denial leapt to her mind so quickly, Jo wasn't sure if she'd spoken the words aloud or not. She moaned, her hands tightening convulsively as she pulled him closer.

~ ~ ~

"Yes, I do," she whispered, her voice quivering on the edge of tears.

Hawk pulled away abruptly, looking up at her, his body responding violently to the look on her face. Her lips were swollen from the pressure of his mouth, and a deep flush colored her cheeks. She watched him through half closed eyes, and—*oh God*—those eyes!

He stared, feeling a thrumming awareness start at his toes and move in waves up the length of his body, intensifying with every pulse of his heart. He was mesmerized! Dilated pupils left her eyes almost completely black. Only the barest rim of violet remained visible—a deep, vibrant purplish hue, like a swirling storm cloud, pregnant with the promise of ferocity.

Jo continued, her hands digging into the flesh of his shoulders and her voice guttural, "But if you do, Hawk, I *swear to God*, I'll hurt you."

He was lost! Caught up in the flash of tornado winds whipping out of that storm cloud in her eyes, and tearing away every shred of control he had left. Growling, Hawk's mouth found Jo's in a hard, demanding kiss. He wasn't about to argue. With one fluid motion he swung her into his arms, his mouth still devouring hers as he started toward the bedroom.

He'd given Nate and Laney a 1:00 AM curfew. He didn't intend wasting one precious minute of the time they had left. Two hours! He was going to use every minute of it to drive Jo crazy. Hawk wanted her to need him with the same obsession he felt, whenever he saw her, or heard her name. He wanted her blood to fire to boiling, her bones to melt at the sound of his voice—just the way his did.

God, he just—*wanted her*!

She was right. It was happening too fast. Hawk knew that. The sane half of his brain pointed that detail out every chance it got. The depth of his feelings for this woman scared the hell out of him, but he wasn't going to let that stop either one of them—not if he could help it.

"*Oooohhhh*," Jo moaned, gasping out his name. "Hawk," she cried, tears choking her voice. "Please, please, please," she pleaded with fierce desperation, her body writhing and twisting with a frenzied need for climax. "Don't stop."

"Don't worry, Little Girl," Hawk whispered, his words muffled against her skin. "I ain't goin' nowhere. That's a promise."

~ ~ ~

"Mom," Laney gushed at the breakfast table the next morning. "Did you see that shot?"

Jo knew she referred to Nate's final three-point goal in the basketball game the previous evening. It propelled his team to the 65-64 victory over their opponents.

Casey leaned forward, his face animated. "*Dude*!" he exclaimed. That was like, totally awesome, and Nate said he'd teach me how to play like that." Casey scooped up a second helping of oatmeal and grabbed two more slices of toast.

"I saw." Jo smiled, remembering the closing bucket. She'd been on her feet with everyone else, yelling and cheering with joyous enthusiasm. Hawk told her Nate was a guard, and a good one. When he managed to get open he seldom missed a three point shot, and he had quick hands. He was a strong defensive player as well. Hawk had spoken nonchalantly, but Jo sensed the pride.

Nate had been impressive. He'd been one of the starters, playing almost the entire game. Jo could hardly believe the coaches hadn't relieve him more often. She'd been on the edge of her seat most of the game, thoroughly enjoying every minute. She remembered launching question after question at Hawk, learning the ins and outs of every call, every play, and every turnover. Hawk patiently explained, seeming to enjoy sharing his knowledge and watching her enthusiastic responses.

"Hawk let me wide on his shouldaws," Jenny giggled, scooping a large spoonful of oatmeal into her mouth. "It washa faw upsh," she mumbled around the food. "I washa almoch toushin da skish."

Casey and Laney laughed at their sister.

"Well, that made perfect sense to me," Jo winked and smiled at Jenny, earning a bright answering grin.

"So, where'd you and Nate go after the game?" Casey teased.

"None of your business," Laney snapped, taking her bowl and glass to the sink and washing them.

Jenny chimed in, supporting her sister,"None of yowa bizwax!"

"Man, *girls*!" Casey pushed his chair back and headed to the living room for cartoons.

"Whoa there, Skippy," Jo called after him. "You got some dishes to wash."

"*Ah, Mom*," Casey protested, but he complied.

Jo had to force herself not to think past the basketball game. The mere thought of Hawk sent her blood pressure out of the atmosphere, and she almost started gasping from the lack of oxygen to her brain. Her groin tingled, and then ignited with remembered feelings and rekindled desires, overloading her senses, not to mention renewing the guilt.

He's a damned good lover, the thought slipped through her guard. NO! No, no, no. Don't go there, Jo reprimanded her wayward mind. The relationship was developing too fast. It scared the hell out of her. Jo's mind drifted back to another time—another liaison. It had been fast too, swift and passionate. No, it didn't just scare her—it *terrified* her! Hawk wasn't anything like Devin. They were *worlds* apart, but dark memories raised warning flags she couldn't ignore.

It would take time heal, Jo knew that. It would be a *long* time before she could believe and trust, again. I need to believe, she told herself. I *want* to trust. So, why couldn't she? Would she ever work her way past the defensive walls she'd spent the past decade building? Did it matter now, anyway?

You can't have Hawk, Jo, even if you're desperately in love with him—even if everything else works out, you can't have the man! The thought was cruel and mocking—maliciously, agonizingly, brutal. It left her heart raw, ripped open and bleeding profusely from a thousand inconsolable wounds, that held no hope of healing.

You're a married woman!

~ ~ ~

"Hello?" Jo answered the phone, her voice rough with sleep.

"Hey," Hawk's deep voice greeted her, "you asleep?"

Jo glanced at her bedside clock. "Hawk, it's one-eighteen," she muttered, rubbing her eyes with the fist of one hand.

"I know, I couldn't sleep." Hawk didn't bother apologizing.

"Yeah? Well *I* could. Hell, I WAS!" Jo snapped, but there was no anger in her voice. Didn't people around here sleep? This was supposed to be a quiet, peaceful little town.

Jo could hear laughter in Hawk's voice. "Feel like talkin'?"

"No," she said with blunt honesty.

"*Good*!" Hawk sounded undaunted. "It occurred to me, I still know very little about you, Jo."

Oh God. Oh God. Oh God. Sudden panic brought her wide-awake. Here we go!

"Hawk, not now. Not tonight," she tried evading.

Damn! She'd known the crossing of this bridge was inevitable. She wasn't ready—wasn't strong enough emotionally yet.

~ ~ ~

"Yeah, I know it's late," Hawk's voice was soft, "but I thought I'd catch you with your guard down. You never want to talk, Little Girl. Why is that?"

Hawk knew Jo had secrets she was loath to disclose, but he still had questions that needed answering. Questions about who she was, and where she'd come from. This woman had no past! He'd found no trace—no evidence that she or her children even existed.

Father Pat urged him to leave well enough alone, but Hawk couldn't do that. Maybe it was the cop in him, or maybe just morbid curiosity, but he couldn't jump into this relationship blind. Burns left scars—and he'd been badly burned, once. It was too painful an experience to willingly repeat.

"Hawk…I…my previous life was…pretty rough. I really don't want to drag those demons into this time and place." Jo's voice trembled.

"Yeah, you told me your husband was abusive, but I think there's more to it than that." Actually, he thought she'd lied to sidetrack him.

"Why does it matter so much to you?" she asked.

"Call it gut instinct, if that helps."

"No, Hawk, it doesn't help. I left to start over—and that's what I intend to do." There was finality in her voice, and it defied argument. "Can we…can we just leave it there?"

"No, but I'll let it go, for now," Hawk conceded. "So, why have you been avoiding me this past week?"

"I…things…I mean," Jo stopped abruptly.

"Yes?" Hawk prompted after several moments of silence.

"It's just too fast, Hawk. I…I feel like we've gone too fast."

"Scared?" Hawk asked softly.

What are you scared of, Little Girl? What are you running from? Every instinct he had was shooting up red flags. Why couldn't he step back? Why couldn't he let her have her space, and start evaluating her situation with unemotional detachment?

Naw, it ain't gonna happen. He knew that with a certainty that petrified him—he more than understood the fear. *Shit,* even now he could feel the silky texture of her skin, smell the soft, floral scent of her hair and the pungent spice of her—*oh God,* he couldn't go there and stay sane—not now. He was hard and hungry, with no relief in sight—save the ministrations of his own hands.

"Yeah, I am, Hawk. It went fast with my husband…my, ex-husband, too." Jo's voice trembled, as if on the brink of tears. "That…that was a disaster. Yeah, Hawk, I'm scared. I'm really, really, scared."

"I understand the fear, Jo." His voice was soft and sympathetic. "I'm afraid too. It was a fast and passionate courtship for me as well, and a marriage that didn't last." He sighed heavily, not sure he could talk about Allison, but hoping his openness would encourage Jo to relax a little of that guard she clung to so adamantly.

"Tell me about her," Jo prompted.

Hawk recognized the ploy to redirect the spotlight from her past to his. He'd give her that.

"Not much to tell, really," he replied. "Allison was a beauty. She was homecoming queen, and very popular. Every guy in school was pantin' after her. She was tall, with blond-hair and blue eyes, and damn, she had legs that wouldn't quit."

"Oh," Jo sounded as if this were more information than she'd wanted.

Hawk smiled to himself, going on. "We were both seniors. Allison was a cheerleader, and I was a sports jock—football, basketball, track, all of it. We got together one night after a basketball game, and I asked her to go drivin' with me." Hawk paused as the memories flooded back. They were difficult to sort through—painful, with a kind of dull, aching regret.

"Did she go?" Jo asked.

"Yeah. She went. And of course, I tried to get in her pants."

"Did...did you?" Jo didn't sound as if she really wanted to know.

Hawk paused a moment, a knowing half-smile pulling at his mouth. She's jealous. That knowledge came with sudden, dawning insight.

"Yeah, I did." He waited a moment, letting the confession sink in.

She didn't say anything.

He picked up the thread of story and continued. "I was hooked from that moment on. She had me wrapped so tight around that finger of hers, I'd have done anything she wanted."

"I know that feeling," Jo whispered.

Hawk nodded to himself. I bet you do, he thought.

With a heavy sigh he picked up the storyline, "Well, one day shortly after that she told me she was pregnant, and I jumped at the chance to legally make her mine. We were married two weeks after graduation."

"So, you got married, and Nate was born," Jo filled in.

"No," Hawk replied, his voice sounding hard, even to his own ears. "She wasn't pregnant. It was a lie, the first of many."

"Oh," Jo gasped.

"I got a football scholarship to the University," Hawk continued.

"University?"

"University of Nebraska, at Lincoln," Hawk clarified. "I played football for them for four years, which kept Allison relatively happy."

"What do you mean?"

"Allison was never content in Humboldt. Too small—too confining for her. She liked Lincoln better, and because I was a football player, she got a lot of attention. She liked that, too. That's when Nate came along."

"Did you come back to Humboldt after you graduated?"

Hawk sighed. "Naw, she kept tryin' to talk me into moving to a big city somewhere. I knew that kind of life wasn't for me, but I compromised, and enlisted in the Navy. My first duty station was San Diego. She liked it there. Those years were good, I guess."

"So...so, what happened, Hawk?"

"My six year stint ended, and I wanted to come home. I wanted to farm and be close to the folks." Hawk sighed, finding a strange kind of comfort in finally sharing his past with someone. "We moved back."

"But...but it didn't work, did it?"

Hawk laughed mirthlessly. "Naw. Allison never forgave me. She just went...I don't know, *wild* or somethin'. She was sleepin' around, partying with friends from Lincoln and Omaha, gone most of the time. One day she came home, after a weekend in Kansas City, and told me she was leavin'—movin' to California. Later I found out it was with one of those... *friends*." There was no emotion in Hawk's voice. It was over—the pain and humiliation, the sense of betrayal, the hopelessness of it all. He had to let it go.

"She left her child?" Jo sounded incredulous.

"She never wanted a kid, Jo. The boy was a burden. A constant reminder, every day, that she was gettin' older, I guess. Yeah, she left Nate, too."

"I'm...I'm so sorry, Hawk. It must have been a nightmare."

Hawk laughed again, with a little more feeling. "At the time I believed it was. Looking back, the nightmare was the marriage, not the divorce. We were better off without her and the emotional turmoil she kept constantly stirred up."

"Does she ever try and see Nate?" Jo asked. "Does she ever call?" She sounded as if she couldn't fathom a mother willingly abandoning her only child, without even a backward glance.

Hawk contemplated that. He knew Jo was the kind of mother who'd die rather than risk separation from her children. He loved that quality in her.

"No, not once," he answered her question.

Hawk could hear Jo's gasp of disbelief. "How has Nate taken it?"

"We talked about it, and then closed the subject," Hawk replied stoically. The pain of that final betrayal—the hurt she'd caused their son—was still there. The disillusionment of failure still burned. The intensity of it had faded, but he had to admit, it still stung.

"Do you hate her, Hawk?" Jo asked softly.

He was silent for a long time, thinking.

Jo waited.

"No," he said at last. "No, I guess I don't. I actually feel sorry for her. She's missed so much, not seeing Nate grow up. He's a great kid, and talented, too. She'd have been proud of him." Hawk seemed almost surprised at the truth he'd just unearthed within himself.

"He's a great kid, Hawk," Jo said softly. "Look who he's got for a father."

Hawk was surprised at the depth of sincerity he could hear in her voice.

"Thanks," he responded, his physical need of her suddenly flaming to life again. "And Laney thinks so, too." Jo giggled.

Hawk chuckled. "Yeah? Well, if he's anything like I was, I'm gonna have to keep a tight reign on that boy."

"If he's anything like you," Jo rebutted with spirit, "I'll kick his cute little ass!"

Hawk laughed.

They both fell silent again.

~ ~ ~

As the minutes ticked away, Jo tried to visualize Hawk.

Is he in bed? Does he have anything on?

The image that formed in her mind was of a freshly showered Hawk, a towel still wrapped around his waist, reclining on his bed with a phone to his ear.

She couldn't resist asking, "You just get out of the shower?"

"Yeah," Hawk sounded a little surprised. "How'd you know?"

"Lucky guess. What are you wearing?"

"A very damp towel." There was amusement in his voice, and something more. It stirred a powerful physical response in Jo. How does he DO that to me?

"What about you, Little Girl?" Hawk drawled. "What are you wearin'?"

"Nothin'," Jo said softly.

God Almighty, I want him. She could feel her body aching—needing—yearning. It terrified her to death! The more she needed, and the closer she came—the more likely it was she'd give something vital away.

What would he do if he knew the truth?

He'd hate me. Jo knew the answer, and it was physically painful. He'd hate me because I was a lying, deceiving bitch—just like Allison!

"I gotta go, Hawk," Jo said quickly—too quickly.

"You're scared again, aren't you?"

Damn his perception! He knows too much, picks up too much.

"You want me to come over there and make love to you, don't you?" Hawk answered his own question with those words.

She knew he was right on target, and she knew, he knew it.

"Yeah, Hawk, I do," she answered honestly. "I want you so bad I can taste it, and that's what scares me. How I feel about you scares me to death. I...I need some space," she finished on a whisper, her voice breaking as the tears started.

I don't want space! Her brain screamed the words. I want you to grab me, and hold me, and tell me it's going to work out. I want you *inside* me, connecting me to something strong, and clean, and…and *right*!

"Okay, Little Girl, I'll give you your space, for now," Hawk said, and then hung up the phone.

Jo felt suddenly and inexplicably bereft—cold and lost, as if a part of her soul had just disconnected itself and disappeared. She carefully replaced the receiver, and then rolled over. Clutching a pillow tightly against her body, she cried with the heart-wrenching anguish of utter hopelessness.

XVI

"Jo?" Carol stuck her head in the back door.

"Yeah, come in, Carol," Jo called from the living room. She'd spent the morning cleaning, and looked a mess, but she was glad for the diversion. Her morose thoughts had been hard to live with lately. They were nothing but a source of anger, grief, and frustration.

"I've brought you some Valentine cookies," Carol grinned, "fresh from the oven." She set them on Jo's counter, pulling up a chair at the kitchen table and sitting down.

"Mmmmmm," Jo snatched up one and broke off a piece, stuffing it into her mouth hungrily. "I didn't eat breakfast. This is great."

"Do you have a minute to talk?" Carol asked, her face going serious.

Jo felt a stab of apprehension. She'd sensed it. The minute Carol had walked into the room, she'd known. Oh hell, she sighed inwardly, this was inevitable.

"Sure," Jo replied, pouring Hawk's mother some coffee and sitting down opposite her.

Carol came right to the point. "There's turmoil between you and Beau. I can feel it, though you both try and pretend it's not there."

"Yes, there is," Jo confirmed, but said no more.

"Beau won't talk to me, Jo. That's not like him. It makes me worry." Carol was wringing her hands in her lap. "The only other time in his life he wouldn't talk to me, was when he and Allison went through their divorce. It was...it was a rough time."

Jo nodded her understanding, but still said nothing.

"Can you tell me anything, Jo?" Carol looked at her beseechingly. "*Will* you tell me anything?"

Jo took a deep breath. What could she say? I love your son, and can't keep my hands off him. So, I've decided to keep my distance, because I'm really a married woman, and it's legally and morally wrong.

Yeah, that oughta fly.

Clearing her throat, Jo started in, praying she'd find the right words.

"Hawk senses I'm not completely open with him…about my past." She paused, not sure how to phrase what needed saying. She had to give Carol something—but not too much.

"I believe he's felt that from the start, but I thought he'd gotten past it," Carol remarked.

"Yeah, well, the closer we got, the more it seemed to bother him, I guess. Being burned once tends to make a heart cautious." Jo understood that instinct far too well.

Carol nodded.

"Well, he's right. I'm…I haven't told him anything at all. It bothers him." Jo was thinking frantically. She swallowed hard several times, knowing she had to give Carol part of the truth. Maybe, just maybe, if she tossed one bone, they'd leave the other one buried. Surely, Hawk couldn't connect her to her past without all the facts!

"Is there something you don't want him to know, Jo?" Carol's question, like her personality, was straightforward and blunt.

Jo liked that about the woman. As much as she wanted to tell Carol everything, she held back, feeding her line out a little at a time. When Jo gave her an answer, she wanted Carol to believe she'd shared all there was to share.

"His feelings….our feelings for one another have escalated beyond what either of us could have predicted," Jo said, her eyes downcast. "We're both running a little scared." Her voice was raw with emotion—honest emotion. At least she didn't have to be deceitful about everything. At this moment, she almost hated herself.

Carol nodded, sipping her coffee. "So, what are you running from, Jo?" she asked gently.

Jo's countenance transformed. She could literally feel her face freeze and her insides turned cold and empty. Getting up, she walked into the kitchen, trying to buy some time to compose herself, but when she turned back around to face Carol, she knew her features were still hard and forbidding.

"My husband." Jo's voice matched her expression. It was flat and empty.

"Your…husband?" There was shock on Carol's face—and dawning comprehension.

This was harder than Jo had ever expected it would be. She'd only shared her story with one other person—Father Pat. The memories were still too brutal. They ripped through her with a force that left her trembling from head to foot. She leaned against the counter, her arms straight and her head hanging between her shoulders, unable to meet Carol's dark, assessing eyes.

She had to try several times before the words could make it past the lump in her throat. "He…he was abusive." Jo could feel Carol's eyes on her.

"So you...divorced him? Left him?" she asked.

Here it was. The truth that would shatter whatever hope of a normal relationship she had with Hawk, and yet Jo knew she would tell Carol. "No," Jo raised her head, looking at the woman with unflinching courage, unsure just where that nerve came from. "I just took the kids, and ran." Jo wanted to cry, but she forced her features into a mask of indifference. She hated having to admit even this much of her past to anyone, especially Hawk's mother.

What is she thinking? She'll hate me—I know it. Oh God, HAWK will hate me!

Carol sat in stunned silence for a moment. "Why, Jo?" She asked at last. "Divorce is so...so easy these days. Why run?" The enormity of Jo's choice seemed to leave Carol at a loss.

How did Jo explain the unexplainable? It all seemed so easy to a normal world—funny, she reflected. I thought that once, too. There'd been a time when she'd believed in fidelity, and loyalty, and unending love. She hadn't been prepared for the harsh reality of her world—but she'd learned fast enough.

"He...my husband, was...is, very powerful, and very violent," Jo's voice was a husky whisper. "I wanted a divorce, but...he wouldn't give me one."

"Jo," Carol's voice was soft and earnest. There was no reproach in the tone, only compassion. "Honey, in this day and age, you could have gotten a divorce without his cooperation."

"No, you don't understand," Jo, said with some spirit. Determinedly, she pushed herself away from the counter and walked toward the kitchen table, stopping in front of Carol. Unbuttoning her cotton blouse, she let it drop unheeded to the floor, and then turned so Carol could see her back.

The coffee cup Carol held in one hand, fell to the floor and shattered. Jo could hear her shocked gasp.

"Oh, my God," she cried on an exhalation of breath. "What...oh, my God, Jo!" Carol's hands were over her mouth, her eyes filled with tears.

Jo understood Carol's reaction, but it didn't lessen the hurt and humiliation of having it expressed. Silent tears slipped down her cheeks as she reached for her blouse, and put it back on.

Both women bent over the broken glass and spilled coffee, cleaning it up in silence, as if the normalcy of such an act could somehow lessen the glimpse of horror Jo had just shared. It didn't.

"He...your husband did that?" Carol asked at last, as she dumped a dustpan full of broken glass into the trashcan.

Jo nodded, waiting for Carol to get another mug and pour herself a fresh cup of coffee. When the woman had seated herself at the kitchen table again, Jo explained. "He just got so violent, I couldn't stay." She walked back to the counter and leaned against it once again, more for support than anything else.

"When I..." Jo's voice broke. She had to swallow hard before she could find the courage to go on. Running a distracted hand across her brow, she said, "When I asked for a divorce, he...he nearly killed me." Her voice dropped to an agonized whisper, and she squeezed her eyes shut. "I was in the hospital for a really long time." Jo shook her head slightly, the memory still brutal and terrifying. She hadn't meant to tell Carol this much—hadn't meant to relive the horror.

Carol remained in her chair. She looked as if she didn't trust herself to stand. Her ruddy face had paled, and her bottom lip trembled with emotion.

"He threatened my children," Jo continued, "and threatened to kill me, too. So I ran. I took as much savings and checking money as I could get my hands on. Devin comes from a very wealthy family, the money would mean little to him, but he's the kind that doesn't like to lose what he believes is his. He went to the police and reported me as a kidnapper and a thief." Jo looked at Carol with unflinching determination. "I'm a...a fugitive, I guess." Fresh tears were slipping down her cheeks.

Shaking her head in disbelief, Carol looked down at the coffee in her mug. "Couldn't the police help you, Jo?" she asked, her face and voice still registering shock.

Jo took a deep breath. "I tried that, Carol. Devin is a powerful man—too powerful. He has his hand in so many pots, I had no idea whom I could trust and who would betray me." How did she make someone like Carol—or Hawk—understand? They lived in a safe, comfortable world, where things —and people—were relatively normal.

Carol sat silently, waiting.

"Devin has never had to do his own dirty work." Jo continued, cupping her hands around her mug of coffee and taking a sip before she continued. "He's very adept at hiring it out, and I was fast becoming a problem he wanted eliminated. I..." Jo's voice broke as the memories she'd so carefully buried, resurfaced. No, she didn't need to tell Carol of the narrow escapes she'd had—of her suspicions. She didn't need to tell about nearly killing her husband, either—it was still something that spawned deep shame and guilt in her. Regardless of how much Devin had deserved to die—he was still the father of her children. And she'd come so close to...murder. Jo shuddered.

"I couldn't stay," she whispered. "I had to try and give my kids a chance at some kind of life—give myself that chance, too."

Rising, Carol came around the counter and wrapped her arms around Jo, holding her close for several long moments. "Beau could help you, Jo," she said at last, her voice trembling.

Jo just shook her head in denial. "If Hawk knew, he'd be duty-bound to turn me in, Carol. He'd be sending me back to my death. I believed my husband's threat. He'll kill me." Jo's tone was hard and flat once again. The certainty in her voice was almost as chilling as the words she'd just spoken. "Besides," Jo continued, the enormity of her situation dawning with gut-wrenching clarity, "I've lied to Hawk. I'm not sure he can ever forgive that."

"Sweetheart, it's going to be okay. I'm not sure what to do yet, but it'll be okay." Carol looked as if she were processing a plan of action as she spoke.

Jo felt the barest flutter of hope. Maybe she could still work this out. Her only other option was to pack and run again! The mere thought of that left her feeling, literally, sick to her stomach.

"Hawk is a good man," Carol continued, "and he cares deeply for you. Hold on to that, for now. Don't throw the friendship you've built out the window, because you're afraid to trust—afraid to love." Her passionate expression craved lines between Carol's brows.

"When Hawk learns the truth, Carol, there won't be any love...or friendship, left." Fresh tears welled up in Jo's eyes at that realization, spilling down her face. "I'm not sure we can ever be just friends."

"Joanne Kenning!" Carol's voice was sharp with reproach. "I don't know about people where you come from, but out here, a friend is a friend. Through good times and bad. Hawk may be angry, but he'll stand by you. You can count on that!" Carol looked as if she'd make sure that very thing happened—just in case Hawk wasn't willing to comply.

Jo looked up at Carol, a watery, humorless smile on her face. "I...I'm in love with your son, Carol, and I think he loves me," she said in an agonized voice. "But I'm still married...and I let him make love to—" Jo stopped abruptly, suddenly aware of what she'd just admitted to. She could feel the heat of embarrassment suffuse her face.

Carol raised one dark brow, reminding Jo of Hawk. "I'm old and fat, Jo, but I'm not stupid, and I ain't blind. Like I said before, Hawk may be angry but he loves you, and he'll stand by you, or I'll personally kick him a new asshole!"

~ ~ ~

"Hey, Jo!"

Jo turned, pulling the front door to The Humboldt Standard closed behind her. She was surprised to see Eric and Dave walking toward her down the sidewalk.

Must've just come from working out, she surmised. Jo hadn't seen Eric since the night she'd had her vision and left the dojo abruptly. It made her feel uncomfortable now, but she greeted him with a warm smile.

"Hey," she called back, waving.

She started to turn away, but Dave's words stopped her. "Wait up."

Pulling her muffler more tightly around her throat, Jo hunched her shoulders against the bite of the wind as she waited for the two men to reach her. "Hi, Guys," she smiled at them both as they approached. "Nice day for a stroll downtown."

"Nice day to be under wraps, care to join me at my place?" Dave countered, returning Jo's grin.

"Anytime, Handsome," Jo rejoined, earning a laugh from the darkly handsome man.

Eric was blowing on his hands, and then rubbing them together briskly, in an attempt at generating warmth. "Headed to lunch, Sweetcakes?" he asked, pleasantly.

"Yeah. Jack's given me five or ten minutes to catch a bite," Jo answered, winking.

"Well, we're buyin'," Dave announced, taking Jo's elbow and guiding her across the snow-slick street toward the park, and the Main Menu Café.

"Oh, well, I guess…thanks," Jo stammered, allowing herself to be led, unsure what else to do or say.

"Hey, Marge," Eric called as they bustled through the door, stomping snow from their shoes, "coffee and menus."

Dave helped Jo out of her coat, and then hung it beside his on a wooden coat rack before guiding her to a table. Marge had three large mugs of coffee waiting, almost before they'd settled themselves.

"Howdy, Boys," she grinned at Dave and Eric as she handed them their menus. "Ms. Kenning." Marge nodded a greeting at Jo.

Jo was a little surprised Marge knew her name, though she'd come in several times over the past few weeks. She returned the nod, noting the woman's face was round and pleasant. She seemed genuinely glad to see them. Her body matched her plump face, though she moved with more energy than Jo felt most days.

"Fried chicken's the special," Marge informed them. "Comes with mashed potatoes, gravy, vegetable, and roll. Your choice of coffee or tea," she said, rolling off the items from memory.

"I'll have a small chef salad, and a glass of water," Jo said softly, not even bothering to open the menu, "with Ranch dressing, please."

"Oh no," Eric moaned. "Don't tell me you're part bird, like my wife."

"Okay, I won't tell you that," Jo quipped, grinning as she handed Marge her menu.

"Specials for you bird-watchers, I'm guessin'," Marge asked rhetorically, returning Jo's grin with a wink.

"You got it, Marggie." Dave grabbed Eric's menu and handed them both to the proprietress. "And lots of coffee, pretty please."

Marge just laughed, shaking her head. "You got it, David," she mimicked. "You know I can never resist your sweet-talkin'."

"Well, this is a pleasant surprise," Jo started, as Marge bustled away to take another order. "What's up?"

"Not much," Dave replied. "We worked out this morning, and were just leavin' the dojo when we saw you escaping from Jack's dungeon. Figured you could use some stimulating company. Jack can be a bit over-bearing at times, if you know what I mean."

Jo laughed, not acknowledging Dave's words with a comment but heartily agreeing with his summation. She studied the two men more closely as they bantered with one another good-naturedly.

Eric was the taller of the two., and his mustache made him look more serious than he probably was. Slightly uneven, overlapping teeth, and a sprinkling of freckles gave him an impish, little boy look that was unexpectedly appealing. He had a comfortable, easy nature about him. Despite the episode at the dojo the other night, Jo decided she rather liked Eric Westermann.

Dave was a complete opposite in the looks department. Jo liked what she saw when she looked at the man. He wasn't tall. Probably not more than five-nine or ten Jo guessed, but his build resembled that of a professional football player. A broad, powerful chest tapered into narrow hips and heavily muscled legs. His near-black hair was short enough to gel into spiked disarray, and black brows capped the most amazing turquoise-green eyes Jo had ever seen. They were startling, framed by thick, black brows and lashes that accentuated their unusual color. His square jaw, darkened with a day or two's growth of beard, made him look almost rakish. He needs to be in Hollywood, Jo thought, not Humboldt, Nebraska. Whatever woman snatched this man up, would be damned lucky.

"Do I pass?" Dave asked, grinning mischievously at Jo's startled response.

"Pass?" she said, flustered and embarrassed.

Dave winked at her, still grinning, "The inspection?"

"Oh, I'm sorry," Jo blushed, lowering her eyes.

Laughing, Dave said, "Hey, keep lookin', Beautiful. Maybe you'll see somethin' you like."

"Maybe," Jo replied, meeting Dave's eyes and returning his smile.

The talking ended when Marge brought their order, setting large plates of steaming food in front of the two men, and a salad for Jo.

"Hey, Jo," Eric started in after Marge bustled away. "I wanted to talk about the other night at the dojo, but with the holidays and all..." He shrugged, letting his words trail off as if he wasn't sure how Jo would receive the topic of conversation. A nervous tongue tip slipped out to wet his lips.

She wasn't surprised he'd brought it up. It was equivalent to a dangling conversation—something important left unfinished between them. Inevitably, they were destined to conclude it, sometime.

Jo decided it was probably better to clear the air and get it over with, so she took the initiative. "I owe you an apology, Eric. I acted pretty weird. I wasn't feelin' very well. I'm sorry."

"No, no you don't need to apologize. I…I guess I thought I needed to." Eric seemed uneasy. "I wasn't sure if I'd done somethin' to offend you or what," he continued as he stuffed a bite of potato into his mouth, his pale blue eyes on Jo's face.

"No, you didn't offend me." She lowered her gaze, picking at her salad gingerly. How do I explain? What do I say that he'll buy? "It wasn't you, it was me. Just a flashback memory. I'm…I never meant to upset you."

"Wow," Eric sighed, "that's a relief, and it's okay. I wasn't upset, just worried about you."

"I…I sometimes use workout time to chase those memories—those demons—away. I didn't know the dojo was needed, or I'd never have stuck around. It was one of those nights that I just needed to be alone. It had nothing to do with you," Jo said, her face and voice convincingly earnest, considering the fact that she was damned near lying through her teeth.

Eric nodded.

I think he bought it, Jo assured herself. She hated the deceit, but what else could she do at this point. *Oh what wicked webs we weave,* she thought as she swallowed a bite of salad.

"Next time," Eric said softly, "just ask me to leave. It'll be okay. I'll understand."

Jo felt tears well up behind her eyes, and she swallowed hard several times, grabbing up her water glass and draining half of it.

"Hey, Jo, you're welcome to work out any time, whether we're there or not," Dave interjected, tearing at a chicken leg with even, white teeth. "Really, it don't bother us none."

"Yeah, I second that, Sweetcakes," Eric added. "You're welcome anytime, just as long as you don't humiliate us too much in front of Hawk. We got him thinkin' we're pretty damned good martial artists."

They were turning the intensity down for her—giving her back some semblance of emotional equilibrium. "Thanks, Guys," she smiled at the men, her voice trembling only slightly. She was regaining her composure, finding sanctuary in the casual bantering they'd struck up. "And trust me," she quipped, grinning, "I'd never dream of makin' you two look bad in front of

Hawk, I promise." she smiled sweetly as she picked up a slice of cucumber with her fingers and munched on it,.

"Damn! I could fall for you, Lady," Dave said, pointing his empty fork in Jo's direction, "*real* hard."

"Well, at least until I decide to kick your ass, right?" Jo rebutted, pointing her fork at Dave.

Both men broke into laughter.

"Uh-oh," Eric warned in a loud whisper. "Dave, quit hittin' on Jo, Hawk's here!" His voice was loud enough to carry easily to where Hawk stood, hanging up his jacket. Dark, intense eyes met Jo's across the room.

She felt her heart flutter wildly and knew her cheeks had suddenly flushed.

What's he thinking? she wondered as he walked toward them. He was obviously on duty. God he looks good in that uniform. *Judas*! Don't look *THERE*! Her body seemed to implode into oxygen-sucking flames. Generic thoughts, generic thoughts. Jo tried desperately to keep her face expressionless, and her hands from trembling, praying her debauched, wayward thoughts didn't show.

"Thanks for saving me a seat," Hawk greeted the group casually as he pulled up the empty forth chair and sat down.

"We didn't. You're intruding," Eric said bluntly, though the grin on his face negated his rude comment.

"I know," Hawk rebutted matching Eric's smirk. His dark, intense eyes sought out Jo's, capturing and holding her gaze for several moments.

"Well, gentlemen," Jo said, standing to leave. "I hate to miss this titillating conversation, but duty calls." The men started to rise as well, but she motioned them to stay put.

She was fishing in her purse for her wallet when Dave caught her arm. "My treat, Beautiful, remember?" He smiled up at her, winking.

Jo knew he was flirting deliberately, with every intention of provoking Hawk. Leaning over, she gave him a quick peck on the cheek, returning his wink. I could learn to enjoy this game, she though. The thought was unfair, she knew that, but she couldn't seem to help herself. It was just too perfect an opportunity to let slid and besides—Hawk hadn't even called her! It had been weeks—and nothing, not a word from him. Only a casual hello, or nod of the head in passing. Her heart ached, even though she knew she was the one responsible!

"Thank you both for a wonderful lunch," she said warmly, forcefully setting her raging thoughts aside. "See ya, Hawk."

All three men watched her walk toward the coat rack and slide into her wrap.

~ ~ ~

"Damn, that's a slice of dessert I'd love to taste," Eric breathed out on a sigh as Jo left the Café.

"You're a married man, Eric, my boy. That means you're dieting." Dave brought his friend back to reality with a blunt truth. "Me, on the other hand, well, I'm free as fly shit." He grinned at Hawk's scowl. "And damn, if that lady ain't melt-in-your-mouth good. What cha' think, Hawk? What would somethin' like that taste like?"

"Too damned rich for you, Sinclair," Hawk shot back, his scowl deepening. He'd exchanged many similar conversations with these two friends, on numerous other occasions. So, why was his dander up now? Hawk didn't want to investigate the reason behind his ire.

"Ooooo, I think Hawk's stakin' a claim," Eric teased. "Or maybe you've already tasted the pastry?"

"She as sweet as she looks, Buddy?" Dave grinned at Hawk's discomfiture.

"None of your damn business," Hawk growled.

"Come on, Hawk. Give, Buddy! You gotta be getting' some." Dave obviously didn't intend to let his friend off the hook.

The teasing usually centered on Dave or Eric, Hawk knew that, and he wasn't one to go lightly on anyone's ego, either. It was a damned rare occasion when he was the one snagged and squirming. He knew his friends were relishing the chance to taunt him a little. Yet, for reasons Hawk refused to investigate, their good-natured ribbing was more than he could handle right now.

"Yeah, Hawk, give," Eric goaded. "Wild and crazy's the way you like 'em. Is she wild and crazy in the sack, Buddy?" Eric grinned wickedly, eliciting a chortle from Dave.

There was a look of ominous warning on Hawk's face. "Guys?" His voice was soft—too soft.

Eric and Dave exchanged a knowing glance.

"Yeah, Buddy?" Eric answered.

"Shut the fuck up, or I'll kick your asses into next month," Hawk hissed.

XVII

"No!" The word escaped unnoticed as Jo tossed from side to side, thrashing in her sleep. "Hawk, behind you," she cried out, watching a scene from hell unfold.

It was dark—late at night. Jo could see Hawk's truck with its flashing lights. He pulled someone over—somewhere. The highway, yes, that's where he was! She could see it happening as if she were right there beside him—the lights and dials inside his pick-up, the clock on the dashboard that told her it was one forty-two, the squawking static of the two-way radio. So vivid—so real!

Hawk's vehicle pulled in front of the speeding car, forcing them to stop, and then circled back around to park behind them. Getting out slowly, his tall, powerfully built form moved to stand at the driver's window of the car he'd stopped. Jo couldn't see his face, but she recognized the scene playing out before her. Hawk asked the driver for his license and registration.

There was no way he could have seen the passenger door slip open as the car rolled to a stop. He didn't know a man moved stealthily, maneuvering to come up on him from behind.

Oh God, Hawk!

Panic coursed through Jo, leaving her heart thundering wildly and her blood ice-cold.

"LOOK UP!" She screamed the warning, beside herself that he couldn't hear—that he didn't see.

He has a tire iron!

Hawk never saw the blow coming.

Jo watched in helpless horror as he staggered under the impact, a bloody gash opening on his forehead. His hand went instinctively to his gun, but it was too late. With significant force, the driver shoved his door open, slamming it into Hawk's body. The move caught him off-guard, knocking him to the ground.

Hawk tried to unholster his weapon with one hand, as he pressed his shoulder mic with the other. "Officer down..."

It was all he got out before the first shot shattered the night.

Hawk cried out in agony, clutching his thigh.

The driver leveled a smoking 44-magnum at Hawk's heart, laughing. "Damn right you're down, Pig, down and out." The man's tone was cold as ice—a hoarse, grating sound that sent shivers down Jo's spine.

"*HAWK*!" She shrieked his name as the man in her dream squeezed the trigger.

Jo watched the bullet leave the gun.

It moved with painfully slowed progress toward its target. When it finally struck, it seemed to explode into Hawk's flesh. The entry hole it left, instantly spurted dark, red blood. And then, suddenly, the bullet ripped through Hawk's back with amazing speed and devastation, leaving behind a gaping, bloody hole.

Shock and disbelief crossed Hawk's face as the certainty of death dawned on him. His eyes closed, and he slumped to the ground, his body limp and unresponsive on the dark, bloodstained pavement.

"HAWK! Oh God, *Hawk*!" There was an immeasurable depth of pain and loss in Jo's cries. She knew, beyond any possible doubt, Hawk was dead. Jo didn't know she was screaming those words aloud until Laney slapped her face, waking her.

"Mom!" she cried, tears running down her cheeks. "What's wrong?"

Jo knew Laney was familiar enough with her visions to recognize this nightmare as one. They'd been through similar scenarios a time or two over the years, but this was different. Jo knew it. Laney knew it. Jo could see dawning comprehension in her daughter's eyes.

"Hawk," Jo was still sobbing his name. She couldn't blot out the scene she'd just witnessed. "Hawk's in trouble," she told her daughter, her voice shaking uncontrollably.

Jo pushed Laney away as she struggled to disengage herself from the twisted bedding and get up. She noticed, for the first time, Casey huddled in the doorway, clutching Jenny close. Their eyes were wide with fear.

"It'll be okay," she said automatically, looking at her bedside clock radio. "I've got time to help him." It was almost one. She had time, but not much!

"Is Hawk huwat?" Jenny asked, in a wobbly voice.

"He's okay, Jen," Jo said softly, kneeling beside her children. Laney had moved behind the other two, putting her arms around them protectively. "But he could get hurt if I don't warn him what's going to happen." It took every ounce of self-control Jo had to keep her voice level and her body from shaking.

"But, he'll know then," Casey sniffed. He was clearly torn between the need to help Hawk, and the chance her secrets would be disclosed.

Jo nodded, the same thought had occurred to her, but she had no choices here—and not much time!

"I'll deal with that later, Casey. Right now, I have to help him. You three crawl into my bed. I'll be home before you know it, and everything will be okay, I promise." She hugged them tightly before rising and rushing into her bathroom. With quick, panicked movements, Jo splashed cold water on her face, and then washed out her mouth to get rid of the bitter taste of bile and fear.

She'd left a pair of faded jeans and a t-shirt on the clothes hamper. Pulling them on absently, she slid her bare feet into the closest pair of shoes she could find—her boots.

Smiling reassurance at her children, Jo slipped from of the bedroom, and then out the front door. A sixth sense was pushing her—she was running out of time!

~ ~ ~

"9-1-9, Falls City," Hawk radioed in to the county dispatcher, giving them his call number identification.

"Go ahead, 9-1-9."

"10-39 on a Kansas license plate number N-W-T-2-3-9. Repeat: Nora, William, Tom, 2-3-9." Hawk went on to inform the dispatcher of the car's make and model, and then waited for her to run the requested check. Following the erratic vehicle from a safe distance, he managed to stay close enough to pull it over, if he needed to.

The dispatcher's scratchy voice broke the silence. "Falls City, 9-1-9. That vehicle is 10-7-5."

Stolen! Why wasn't he surprised?

"10-4, I'm going to stop them," Hawk replied, turning on his lights. "Send back up. I'm on State Highway four, approximately six miles east of Airport Road."

"Be advised 9-1-9, I've alerted 9-1-9-2, and 9-1-9-3. Closest back-up is thirty minutes out, copy?"

"Ten-four, Falls City, 9-1-9, out."

Son-of-a-Bitch, Hawk thought to himself as the car ahead of him sped up. He turned on the sirens, staying close on the tail of the swerving vehicle.

~ ~ ~

Jo drove recklessly fast! She'd recognized the highway—the red and white water tower. It was the main road on the north side of Humboldt—but where on that road would he be now? How far out of town, and in which direction? Just be the right place. *PLEASE*, be right, Jo prayed ardently—and then suddenly—there he was! She could see the flashing lights up ahead.

Please, please, please, the litany repeated itself in her head as she raced toward Hawk's pick-up. He was already at the driver's window!

Pulling to a screeching halt, Jo slammed her vehicle into park as she jumped out. She didn't bother closing the door.

The man she'd seen in her dream, moved stealthily, slipping out from behind Hawk's truck, tire-iron in hand. At the sound of Jo's vehicle, he turned, but it was too late—Jo was already on top of him.

He swung his weapon.

Easily dodging the blow, Jo grabbed onto his wrist as his arm swung out. She retaliated with a hard palm heel to the face, yanking her opponent into the strike. She immediately followed the palm heel with a lightening fast kick to the groin, the toe of her boot meeting soft, unprotected flesh. The man's scream seemed to echo in the still night air as he doubled over, clutching himself. Jo felt no mercy. The only image in her mind was of Hawk's face, looking shocked and uncertain, as he gasped his last breath.

Grabbing the back of the man's head, Jo propelled him into her knee, bringing it up against the exposed tissue of his face. Crossing over and covering, she stepped back, assessing the damage. The fight was over. The man was on his knees, whimpering, one hand still clutching his groin and the other holding his bloody nose.

Jo started to leave and then thought better of it. As long as an opponent was conscious, he was a viable threat—her father had drilled that lesson into her head, quite painfully at times. The spinning crescent kick was probably an over-kill, but she threw it in for good measure. It effectively flat-backed the man. He wasn't going anywhere for a long time!

~ ~ ~

"What the fuc…" Hawk started to say, turning as he saw Jo's SUV screech to a halt. He'd barely had time to register the commotion when the driver shoved his door open, catching Hawk off-guard and knocking him several steps away. Hawk sensed the weapon before he saw it. He didn't bother going for his own—he'd never have time to draw it.

With a speed and agility that always amazed an opponent, Hawk's leg flew out, catching the man's gun hand and sending the weapon flying. It wasn't much of a battle. In only moments, he had the man on the ground, handcuffs in place.

Hauling him to his feet, he dragged the guy back toward his truck, yelling at Jo, "What the hell are you doing here?" Hawk's voice was harsh with concern, his features twisted with fury.

"Saving your ungrateful candy ass!" Jo threw back.

Without another word, she left her unconscious victim for Hawk to take care of, and stomped back to her SUV. Throwing her vehicle into reverse, she squealed a U-turn in the middle of the road with a brazenness that should have earned her an expensive ticket. A shower of dirt and gravel billowed into the air as she sped off into the night.

~ ~ ~

Somewhere inside her, Jo knew Hawk's furious reaction was normal, and something to be expected, but his anger stung none-the-less.

She was shaking from head to toe. Even her insides were quivering!

God help me when he gets home, she thought as logic and sanity broke through the adrenalin still coursing through her veins.

Judas! How do I explain this one?

XVIII

"Don't you dare," Jo said evenly.

Her voice was soft, but carried enough for Hawk to hear the words clearly. It took him by surprise. This was the last place he'd expected to find her, sitting on the steps that led to his loft above the barn.

"Excuse me?" he said through clenched teeth, still seething.

"Don't you dare go storming over to that house, banging on the door at three in the morning, and scaring my kids to death." Jo sounded calm—looked calm.

Hawk found himself wondering if she was as unruffled as she appeared. Somehow, he sensed her insides were as chaotic as his were. "I had no intention of scaring your children, but I have every intention of tearin' into you, Little Girl," Hawk moved to stand in front of her, his brows furrowed and a harsh, angry expression on his face. He knew he looked menacing. His mother was constantly chastising him for his hardhearted, intimidating glare, but he did not intend to remedy it right now.

He registered the fact that Jo had showered. There was the faint scent of soap about her, and her hair hung in damp ringlets. She'd had at least an hour while he'd hauled in his catch and booked them. She'd obviously composed herself, in preparation for this confrontation.

Jo was wearing a clean pair of jeans and a long-sleeved white blouse, looking too damned good, Hawk noted, before he heatedly forced his mind away from that train of thought.

"Your kids okay?" He asked, knowing this would take some time.

"I woke Laney up and told her everything was fine, but that you and I needed to talk."

Hawk nodded. "You look pretty damned cool, calm, and collected, Jo, considering what just happened."

"I'm not, if that makes you feel any better." Jo's detached tone of voice seemed to contradict those words.

"Why?" Hawk wanted to hear her response. What in the hell just happened? His brain was in turmoil—and so was his gut. How did anyone explain something like that?

"The way you look right now would scare the quills off a porcupine," Jo shot back, showing emotion for the first time.

"Good, I want you scared of me, Jo, real scared."

"I'm not scared of YOU, Hawk," Jo's tone was unemotional again. "I'm apprehensive about the outcome of this little chat, and I'm terrified of the future, but I'm not scared of you." Jo's face remained expressionless. "I just want to get this over with and go home."

"That's too bad, Baby. That's just too, damned bad. 'Cause you ain't leavin' here 'til I get some straight answers. It just might help if you WERE a little scared of me."

"I'm through being scared by the men in my life," Jo shot back, anger in her face and tone.

"Is that so?" Hawk countered, her words stirring curiosity as he reached out to take her arm.

A lightening block caught him off guard. "*Don't touch me*," she hissed, rising and backing up several steps. Her words, and the defensive posture her body assumed, startled Hawk enough that he forgot his anger for a moment.

"God, Jo, I wasn't going to hurt you."

She didn't respond.

He could see it in her face. She wasn't sure she believed him. She *was* scared—of *him*!

"Good, God Almighty. He really did knock you around, didn't he?" Jo told him she'd been abused, but he hadn't believed her at the time. He'd thought it a ploy to divert his attention—and it had. She was a damned good martial artist. Why would she let some asshole beat her up?

"Who?" Jo asked, still wary though obviously relaxing a little.

"Your ex," Hawk growled.

~ ~ ~

"You're quite the clever one, aren't you?" Jo was angry now. "I TOLD you I was abused. *What*? Didn't you *believe* me?" Who was he anyway, to force himself into her life, and then berate her for who and what she was?

Did she ask him to come snooping around her camper? NO!

Did she ask to move here? NO!

All she'd wanted was privacy and obscurity. Would he leave it go? NO!

Did she ask him to make love to her, and stir up emotions she wanted dead and buried? Well, okay, maybe she HAD—*but she hadn't meant to*! She didn't want to care—and she didn't want to talk.

"Don't evade, Jo. It's time to end this charade once and for all," Hawk, said the words quietly, his anger apparently diffused.

"You can end whatever you want to end, Candy Ass, I'm going to bed." Jo pushed past him, intent on walking out of the barn. It was a brazen move, but it just might work, she found herself hoping.

"Not so fast." Hawk's hand shot out, grabbing Jo's arm and turning her to face him.

She instinctively started struggling, and then, suddenly, went still.

"Judas priest, Girl, I'm not gonna hurt you." Hawk leaned forward, ducking slightly to come eye to eye with her. "*Look* at me, Jo! I'm not going to hurt you," he said the words slowly and distinctly, his tone soft and gentle. It reminded her of the way you'd talk to a frightened animal, soothing, reassuring, and calming.

"I...know," Jo's voice was heavy with unshed tears as the emotions and trauma of the night started to take their toll. She slumped forward, resting her head against Hawk's broad chest.

"I need answers, Jo. I don't want to hunt them up for myself, but I will if I have to. I'd rather you tell me." He whispered the words next to her ear, his arms holding her body close to his.

"What answers do you need?" she asked in a dead, leaden voice. She felt as if she'd run herself into a corner and there was no chance now of escaping a horrendous fate.

Can I give him some—and still hold onto the rest? She wasn't sure how to do that. If Hawk knew of her physic powers, he'd have all the clues he needed to link the puzzle pieces together—and the picture he'd create would destroy any hopes she might have for a new life here. It would most certainly destroy whatever they had between them.

"How did you...know? How...."

Jo cut Hawk's words off with a forefinger on his lips. Without a word, she took his hand and led him up the stairs to his apartment. He unlocked the door and let them both in, pulling her toward his bedroom with a finger over his mouth, warning her that Nate was sleeping.

Once in his room, he motioned to an overstuffed chair. "Sit down. I'll get some hot tea."

He looks haggard, Jo thought as she watched him leave the room.

When he came back, he held two steaming cups in his hands. Proffering one, he set the other on the dresser, and then took off his shirt. Jo felt ardor stir at the sight of Hawk in nothing but an undershirt her brother used to call a wife-beater, and his uniform pants.

"So, where do we begin?" he asked softly, sitting on the bed opposite her, cupping his tea and waiting. Several silent moments slipped by.

Jo looked at Hawk, wondering how the hell she was going to start, and how the evening would end. Would he ever speak to her again? Could she hold the lies together—just a little longer?

"I don't want to talk about this, Hawk. I CAN'T tell you." There was raw agony in her tone.

"*Jo*, don't do this to me," Hawk said forcefully, steel lacing his tone. "Don't play me for a fool, 'cause I won't dance to that tune!"

"I know, Hawk, I wouldn't, I…I just have things I'm not ready to trust you with yet." Jo whispered the words, her head down. She couldn't bring herself to look at him.

"You have to trust somebody, Jo, sometime," he sighed wearily. "I've already told you, I'll find out one way or the other."

"Please, Hawk, don't!" Jo rose to her feet and started pacing.

Hawk stayed where he was, saying nothing.

"For God's sake, Hawk, just leave it alone, please," Jo pleaded, turning brimming eyes his way, "at least for a little while."

Hawk watched Jo in silence for several long moments, a narrow-eyed, evaluative expression on his face. "Okay, Jo. Let's forget you knew where I was, and that I'd be in danger. Hell, I'll even forget for a moment, you knew exactly what was goin' down." he raised one dark brow as he watched Jo, making her drop her eyes and flush. "Let's start with who Joanne Kenning is. Why are you and your kids running? 'Cause we both know you are, Jo," Hawk said softly.

"Yeah, I'm running," Jo, admitted, moving to the sliding door in Hawk's room and looking out at the night. There was nothing to see, only darkness, and an eerie, slightly distorted reflection of the room behind her.

"From your ex?"

"Yeah."

"Why, Jo? If you're divorced, it's over."

"It's never over with De—, ah, my ex." Jo sighed. "He wants what's his."

"The children?"

"Yeah, among other things."

"Did you get custody?"

Jo turned to look at Hawk, hating herself as the lie rolled off her lips. "Yes. Yes, I did." She dropped her eyes, unable to face him.

"He wouldn't let it go at that?"

"No," she whispered.

"What about restraining orders, Jo? The law has ways of helping."

She looked up at that, a bitter, sardonic smile twisting her full lips. "Oh really?" Her tone was embittered and sarcastic. "You ever see a piece of paper that could keep a man from doing what he wanted to do, Hawk? Do you have any idea how easy it is to walk right through a fuckin' restraining order?" She was unreasonably angry, but her anger was with the system—the corruptibility of the people she'd turned to for help—the Catch 22 that had trapped her all those years. Hawk was just the closest target she could find at the moment.

~ ~ ~

"He came after you?" Hawk was guessing, hoping he could keep her talking—keep the doors open.

Jo didn't answer right away, and when she did, it was something Hawk could never have anticipated. With slow, mechanical movements, she began unbuttoning her blouse, and then she let it slide to the floor at her feet. She wasn't wearing anything underneath it. Hawk felt himself respond physically to the sight of her bared chest, fire licking along his veins, blood surging between his legs. Her breasts were full, their dark nipples taut from the slight chill in the room. Without a word, she turned, exposing her back to him.

"Holy shit!" Hawk could only stare in horrified shock. He wasn't even aware he was on his feet until he saw his fingers tracing the layers of overlapping scar tissue. "Good, God in Heaven," he said on a whisper of breath, as if to himself.

Why hadn't he detected this before? He'd held her, *loved* her, for Christ's sake! Memories flooded back. She'd never turned her back to him—always made sure the lights were out. His fingers moved over the scars again, noting the smoothness of the healed flesh. These were old wounds—time had erased all but a muted, visual evidence. Still, Hawk fumed at himself, he should have *seen*!

He followed the overlapping configurations, noting where the thrashings had licked out, rending the tender flesh of her ribs. Tugging at the waist of her jeans, he yanked them down as soon as she loosed the zipper, and his finger traced fine, nearly invisible scars onto her hips and buttocks. He hadn't noticed!

He had to take several deep breaths. His stomach was twisting uncomfortably. How in the hell did a human body get this way? He felt overwhelming rage at the man who'd done this, giving him a flash of insight into why some humans were driven to murder.

With anguish he felt to his very soul, Hawk grabbed Jo's shoulders and turned her to look at him. "Your ex did this to you?" He bit out the words through clenched teeth.

Jo nodded, as if she found speech impossible. There was a hopeless, lethargic look about her. It was almost as if she'd stopped caring—stopped trying to do anything but survive.

Hawk had never experienced such cold, focused hatred in his entire life. He knew Jo could see it on his face, hear it in his voice, read it in his eyes.

"How could you let him, Jo?" Incredulity infused Hawk's expression and voice. "I mean…God, Almighty woman! Something like this takes…years of abuse."

Jo bent over and retrieved her top, slipping into it and moving to stand, once again, in front of the sliding door that led to the deck. She stared into the night at nothing. Her face mirrored that view—empty, impenetrable, and dead.

"There's the hundred-thousand dollar question," she said with obvious self-loathing. "There were lots of reasons," her words were so soft, Hawk had to strain to hear them, "and the reasons for staying kept changing. First, he begged forgiveness, promised it wouldn't happen again. Then I was pregnant, and trying to keep a family together. Then he'd change for awhile, be loving and attentive, making me believe we could work it out." Jo's voice had gone flat and cold. It was as if all emotion had drained out of her, leaving an empty husk, devoid of feeling.

"When I…when I finally realized it would never stop—that he would never stop—it was too late. His violence was out of control, and so was his ability to reason logically."

"Jo, you're not helpless. You're a black belt, for Christ's sake."

Jo turned to look at Hawk for a moment or two, and then turned back to stare out the sliding glass door, before she responded to his statement. "You know, Hawk, the thing about karate that scares me the most?"

Hawk shook his head, realizing belatedly, that she couldn't see that response.

She didn't seem to need an answer from him as she continued. "I can kill a man," Jo said dispassionately. "It's damned easy, too." Her total lack of feeling was unnerving, but no less so than the words coming out of her mouth.

Hawk found himself wishing he could see the expression on her face. "Did you?" He hated to ask the question, but he had to know. Was that why she was running?

Jo turned around then, a bitter, sardonic smile twisting her mouth. "No, Hawk, I didn't."

Thank God! He knew she could be lying, but he believed her.

"No, I was terrified of killing him, though," Jo's voice was introspective, her eyes staring off into the blackness beyond the window once again. "I knew if I even once allowed myself to respond, the hate and anger would take over, and I wouldn't be able to control it anymore." Jo's demeanor changed suddenly. "I'd have killed the son-of-a-bitch!" she exclaimed with vehemence.

There it was, at last. The passion that had been eerily lacking before. The hate. Hawk remained silent and still. He wanted to go to her, take her in his arms, but he didn't. She needed to talk, and he needed to hear what she had to say.

"I finally found the courage to leave him. I just want to start over, make a new life." Jo turned back to Hawk now, her face and eyes beseeching him to understand.

He had a fleeting impression of being expertly manipulated, but he discarded it as paranoia and over-reaction.

~ ~ ~

"I don't want to drag who and what I was, into this life, Hawk, not yet—not until I'm sure of what I can be." Jo was amazed—she wasn't lying! Father Pat would be proud of her—okay, maybe not exactly *proud*, proud. One truth in a hundred lies wasn't something to brag about, after all.

"Why won't you trust me, Jo?"

She lifted agonized eyes to meet Hawk's dark, intense gaze. "I…can't, Hawk. I…just…can't!" She flung her arms out, moving about the room with aggravated, nervous energy. "I don't trust anyone anymore. I want to…I'm trying to…I…I can't!" Jo's tirade had started wild and angry, but ended with an agonized whisper.

"Jo—" Hawk wanted to plead his case, reason with her, but Jo cut him off.

"No, Hawk. NO!" Her face and voice were passionate again. "I loved once—trusted once! I can't take that leap of faith again—not yet." Jo turned tortured eyes toward Hawk. "I want to. I try, but…it's not in me. I don't have the courage to trust yet. I'm sorry, Hawk," her voice broke, the tears she'd been fighting, coming at last. She wasn't lying. Somehow, that realization filtered through the raging emotions inside her. She did want to trust Hawk—tell him everything, but she couldn't. The words just wouldn't come out.

Hawk didn't say anything. He covered the distance between them in two steps, pulling her against his body, his mouth finding and claiming hers in a passionate, demanding kiss.

Oddly enough, Jo found her body firing with an ardor she wouldn't have anticipated, under these circumstances.

"Let me love those memories away," Hawk whispered. His hand slipped under her shirt to cup one bare breast. "Let me…*inside* you, Little Girl."

Jo knew he referred to her secrets and past, but she was also well aware he'd intended the double meaning.

It didn't matter.

With an effort that was nearly painful, Jo pushed Hawk away. She couldn't do this! She couldn't lead him on with the promise of a life they'd never be able to have together—and that's what this man wanted. He wasn't the kind who could settle for less than total commitment.

"I can't give you what you want, Hawk. I can't make any commitments or ties—not, now." Jo was crying again. "I want to. I want to, so much. I just…can't!" Jo felt as if she were cutting her own heart out of her chest and offering it as a sacrifice. The pain seemed to suck the breath from her lungs.

Hawk raised one hand, cupping her chin and wiping at a stray teardrop with his thumb. "Then give me what you can, Joanne Kenning. Just give me what you can of yourself—here and now—no tomorrow, no future, and no past," he spoke the words with passion against her hair. His hands gently moved up and down her back.

Jo wanted to believe it was a possibility, even if only for a few precious hours.

"Day by day, Jo, just give me what you're willing to give me." Hawk spoke the words with precise distinction, as if he wanted to be sure she heard and understood every word.

Jo's answer was to slip her arms around his neck, and pull his head down so her mouth could claim his with a fierce and desperate need. She felt like the condemned criminal—given one last meal.

Dawn would come. She'd march out to face the firing squad—and certain death. But right now, this precious moment in time, was hers.

No one could take that from her!

XIX

"I don't know what to do, Mom," Hawk said quietly, toying with his scrambled eggs.

"I can see that. I've never known you to lose your appetite unless there's something terribly wrong," Carol replied, concern evident on her expressive face.

"She knew, Mom! You should've seen her. She just tore up there, jumped out of her SUV, and went right for this guy. He was sneakin' up on me from behind. I'd never have seen him in time." Hawk shook his head back and forth in disbelief. "She knew he was there. She came for him!"

"Then I have a lot to thank that girl for," Carol said with emotion, tears filling her eyes. She turned away abruptly to keep Hawk from noticing, but she should have known better. He was beside her instantly, pulling her into his arms and rubbing her back.

"I love you, Mom, and I'm fine," he said tenderly.

"Yeah, yeah." Carol refused to get mushy on him. "I love you too, and I'll give you about thirty minutes to quit massaging my back." They both chuckled as Hawk sat down again, though he didn't touch his food, just cupped a mug of coffee as he resumed his musings.

"You think she has premonitions or somethin'? Is that possible?" he asked.

"Could be, but I really don't know much about that kinda thing, Beau." Carol felt somewhat torn. Would helping Beau, harm Jo? And just *what*, in the name of God, happened? Did Jo have a forewarning of some kind?

"I'm so damned torn I don't know which way to turn," Hawk said finally, his head dropping into his palms.

"You fallin' for her, Beau?" Carol's tone was serious.

"I don't know. My heart wants to, Ma, but my head keeps askin' questions she can't, or won't, answer. I'm not sure a relationship can be built on anything less than total honesty." Hawk's face had gone suddenly dark and angry. Carol knew he was thinking about Allison.

"You'd be surprised what a relationship can withstand if it's glued with the right stuff. Your troubles with Allison aren't any part of this, Beau. Don't you go mixing the two together in that little pea brain of yours."

~ ~ ~

Hawk looked up at his mother with surprise.

"Jo is nothin' like Allison was, and she never will be," Carol continued, "that girl's got moxie! She works hard and loves hard, and she's takin' on the world to do for those kids of hers." Carol's defense of Jo was adamant, which both surprised and impressed Hawk. Carol had never said anything against Allison, but in all the years she'd known her, she'd never said one thing positive, either.

"God, Mom, you should've seen her back!" The words were out before he realized what they implied.

His mother raised a dark eyebrow, but said nothing.

Taking her silence as a cue, he went on. "Not just a beating, Mom, it had to be years of abuse." He shook his head again, clearly unable to come to grips with it. "Why would she stay with him for so long?"

"We seldom ever know why people make the choices they do, Beau, but knowing Jo, there was probably a good reason. She had this man's kids, she's Catholic, and she's terrified of something—probably him. Could be a lot of things that made her choose to stay."

"But she's adept at self-defense. She could have stopped him," Hawk met his mother's gaze with his intense, black eyes, his expression hard and unyielding.

"Really? And what would you do, Beau, if you were a man intent on knocking the shit out of a woman, and she tried to stop you using force?"

Hawk was silent for a long time before he answered her question, with one of his own. "You think she was afraid he'd kill her?"

"Or that she'd kill him," Carol said quietly, sipping her coffee.

"That's what Jo said, but there are so many ways to get help these days, Mom. Why didn't she get the hell out of that situation, right away?"

Hawk realized all of a sudden, that was what he couldn't accept. She'd allowed it to happen. "Even if she didn't wanna fight back, what about the police? Why didn't she go to the police? Get a restraining order? Something!" They were questions he'd asked himself a hundred and one times—questions that had no answers he could accept.

~ ~ ~

Carol drew a ragged breath. She wanted to tell her son what Jo had confided to her—help him see and understand some of the woman's reasoning and motives, but she couldn't. It was something they needed to work out between the two of them. When Jo was ready to tell him, she would.

"Beau, you can't judge someone else by your personal code, or by the choices you would have made. You weren't there. You don't know all the concerns she had to weigh, or the factors that she was forced to contend with, at that point in time. You can't possibly know what motivated her to stick it out, and you can't judge her by what you would have done."

Hawk listened, and seemed to be pondering her words, but Carol knew he still wrestled with the horror of a woman, willingly submitting to years of physical abuse, the way Jo had.

"Think about it, Son," Carol pointed out, "you know her. She's not the kind to cow and accept something like that because she's afraid for herself."

Hawk's expression changed to one of narrow-eyed, deliberation. "You think she was afraid for the kids?"

Carol nodded.

Hawk was silent for several minutes before he responded. "She should have killed the son-of-a-bitch!" he said vehemently. "She could have claimed self-defense. No one would hold her accountable for tryin' to protect herself."

Carol's eyes met Hawk's. "She'd hold herself responsible, Beau."

"What the hell does that mean?" Hawk's tone was angry, but Carol instinctively understood it was directed at the situation, not at her. "She can't have any feelings for the asshole!"

"No, but she has feelings for his kids. He's the father of her children, Beau." Carol watched as comprehension dawned on her son's face. "If she had killed him, in a blind rage, how would she explain it to those kids of hers? How would she ever tell them that she'd killed their father?" Carol stood by the counter, supporting her weight with both hands. "They may understand his brutality and want to protect their mother, but the man is still their father. Regardless of what he's done, they'll always hold onto their love of him, even if it's tucked away in some remote corner of their heart."

Hawk didn't respond, but Carol could practically see his mind wrestling with her words.

"You gonna push this?" she asked quietly, her dark eyes meeting his.

"I don't know, Mom. I want to."

"You may discover something you can't live with, Son—something that will come between you two permanently. She'll come 'round in her own good time. You'll get your answers, soon enough."

~~~
~~~

Hawk looked at his mother. He knew his emotional struggles were clearly etched on his face, in his eyes. He didn't bother trying to hide them from her. She could always see through those attempts, anyway. "I wish she'd trust me, just a little," he whispered.

"You made love to her, didn't you?" Carol asked bluntly.

Hawk's mouth fell open. "Damn it to hell, that ain't somethin' I'm gonna discuss with my *mother*!" Hawk could feel the heat of a blush rush to his face.

"Don't discuss it then, just shut the hell up and listen," Carol snapped, as if exasperated with her son's obtuseness. "When a woman who's been beaten like that, lets you close enough to touch her, she trusts you. When she let's you caress her body intimately, she trusts you. When she allows you to slide your willy winky inside her—you can bet the farm, she *trusts* you!"

"God Almighty, Ma," Hawk gasped, standing abruptly, too embarrassed to look at her.

"Don't go gettin' all prim and prissy on me, Boy! I wiped your skinny little ass more'n I care to remember, and I kissed your scrapes, and dried your tears, and listened to your broken hearts. I know what makes you tick better'n you know yourself, but I also know what makes a woman tick—way better'n *you* ever will!"

Once the initial shock abated, Hawk found himself hard put to hide a smile. "And just what's tickin' here, Ma?"

"Most women don't love with their bodies first, Beau, they love with their hearts and minds long before they give themselves physically to a man."

"And that makes about as much sense, as I've ever been able to figure from any woman," Hawk said sarcastically, draining his mug of brew.

"Just shut up and listen, Mr. Wise-Cracker." Carol refilled his coffee as she spoke. "It does make sense, in a strange sort of feminine way. When a woman opens her body to you willingly, with passion and desire, it means she's already opened her heart. By giving herself to you, she's made an emotional commitment that leaves her painfully vulnerable, and if that's not trust, nothin' is." Carol held Hawk's dark, intense gaze with her own.

"You think, given time, she'll come around, don't you?" Hawk asked.

"Maybe yes, maybe no."

"Oh thank you, Miss Ambiguous." Hawk rolled his eyes.

"Beau, take some old Indian advice. All things worth having are worth working for—and waiting for," Carol said gently, "just like I worked with, and waited for you."

Hawk pulled her into his arms, holding her close for several moments. His mother never ceased to amaze him, and warm his heart.

What a woman—God help me!

~~~

"WILLY WINKY?" Bert and B.J. gasped together.

"*Please* tell me you're joking," Bert groaned, covering his eyes with one hand. B.J. just threw back his head and roared.

"Well, I've never known Mom to mince words to get a point across, but I have to admit, there's a limit to what a man should hear from his mother." Hawk grinned, finding it amusing now, though at the time he'd been mortified.

"So, what'd Jo tell you?" Bert asked.

"Not a damned thing I didn't already know." Hawk shook his head. "Shit, you should have seen it. She came flyin' up in that SUV, and was damned near out the door before she slammed it into park. That son-of-a-bitch she nailed never had a fuckin' chance."

"Damn, it's hard to believe. Of all the places you could've been—and the exact moment you needed help." B.J. eyed Hawk speculatively. "That's one spooky broad, Bro."

"You let her go without findin' out anything?" Bert couldn't quite believe Hawk would let this slide. Patience was not one of his virtues.

"Well, I found out her ex-husband beat the livin' shit out of her on a regular basis." Hawk growled, his temper flaring again as he recalled the chaos that should have been a human back.

"What're you talkin' about?" B.J. asked, looking confused.

"She showed me her back." Hawk rubbed his eyes as if he could erase the picture in his mind of torn and mended flesh. "Judas Priest! You should've seen it. Hell, it nearly made me sick to my stomach—not with revulsion, but with fury. My God, it had to be years of abuse to make scars like that."

Bert's eyes narrowed. "Are you shitin' us, Hawk?" He seemed incredulous until Hawk shook his head. "How does a man do that to his wife and live with himself?" he asked, his his lips compressed into a thin, white line.

"He better pray to God I never get my hands on him," Hawk snarled low in his throat, making Bert and B.J. raise their brows at one another in speculation.

"So, what you gonna do?" B.J. asked. "Have you tried to trace her steps? Track reported missing persons?"

"That's the whole point, isn't it?" Bert asked Hawk quietly, his expression grim.

"What?" B.J. barked, obviously clueless.

"You don't wanna know, do you?" Bert continued, addressing Hawk.

Hawk didn't answer. He dropped his head into his hands.
~~~

Bert explained aloud to B.J. "If he finds the police are lookin' for her, he'd be obligated to turn her in."

B.J. finally caught on. "You'd be handin' her over to the bastard she's runnin' from." His countenance turned fierce.

"There are just so many loose ends," Hawk whispered. "So many things that don't connect, don't fuckin' add up right—and yet, my gut tells me I should be fightin' on her side, and coverin' her back," Hawk finished passionately.

"Your gut or your *willy winky*?" Bert snickered, sending B.J. into a fit of laughter.

Hawk glowered at his younger brother. "Shut the *fuck* up!" he snarled.

~ ~ ~

The phone rang shrilly, waking Jo immediately. Her heart jumped into her throat as she saw the time on the clock radio beside her bed. Three forty-nine? Who would call at this hour?

"Hello?" She mumbled into the receiver.

"JO!" It was Carol. "I'm so sorry to wake you."

Jo sat up in bed, wide-awake. What would make Carol call at this hour? It couldn't be *Hawk*! Please God, don't let him be hurt.

"It's okay, what's wrong?" Jo asked, forcing her voice to remain calm.

"It's Sarah and the baby," Carol exclaimed, her voice rising a little with panic. "She fell and started bleeding. Bert's taken her to Community Memorial, and they're flying her to Lincoln."

"Is she okay?" Jo asked, a cold calm settling over her.

"I don't know." Carol's voice broke. "She's lost two other babies, Jo. She just can't lose this one."

"Are you going to Lincoln?" Jo asked, talking in an even, calm voice, seeking to give Carol something solid and steady to cling to.

"As soon as Hawk gets back. He took Bert and Sarah to the hospital here. I thought you'd like to go with us."

"I'll be at your place in fifteen minutes, Carol. Don't worry. They'll be fine." Jo sounded more confident than she was, as she hung up the phone and went to tell Laney what was happening. It was going to be a long night.

~ ~ ~

March twenty-third dawned warmer than normal for early spring. The glorious rising sun brought with it the birth of Sarah and Bert's first child, Faith Marie Hawkins. Jo stood at the nursery window, marveling at the perfection of the tiny infant.

"Looks like they both pulled through with flyin' colors," Hawk said from close behind her.

Turning, Jo perused his tired features. That he'd had little—if any—sleep, was evident in the dark circles beneath his eyes and the pallor of his skin.

"Isn't she beautiful?" Jo breathed, turning back to the nursery window.

"Yes, she is. First girl born into the Hawkins's family in three generations," he said, a tired grin touching his lips.

"Wow, I bet your mom's proud," Jo replied, wondering where Carol had gotten off to. "How's Bert holding up?"

"He's with Sarah. A very proud papa, I'd say."

"Are B.J. and Ellie here yet?" Jo asked.

"No, but they will be soon. Ellie just called on her cell. They're about half an hour away yet." Hawk yawned and stretched. "Man, could I use a twenty-four hour nap, or what?"

"When can they come home?"

"Two days. Bert'll stay up here with some friends I think, and then drive them both home, either Thursday or Friday, whenever the doctors give the thumbs up."

Hawk looked around for a chair. Finding one close to hand, he slumped down in it, stretching out his long legs and resting his head against the wall. "Wake me if there's an emergency." He grinned at her skeptical expression, and then closed his eyes.

~ ~ ~

"*Right*!" Jo replied sarcastically. She watched as Hawk settled awkwardly in the unyielding chair, unable to resist moving close and running her fingers along his cheekbone.

His near-black eyes opened immediately, locking gazes with hers.

"Hawk?" she whispered.

"Yeah, Little Girl, I'm here," he said huskily.

What had she been going to say? Why did the birth of this child make her feel emotional and weak inside? She wanted Hawk's arms around her, needed the touch of his hands on her skin. The craving to feel him inside her was overwhelming. Jo just shook her head, unable to say anything at all.

Hawk's hands came up and grabbed Jo's hips, pulling her close.

"I'm hungry, too," he said, his voice deep and hoarse with a passion that fired a burning response in Jo's gut. "Starving, actually," he grinned at her wickedly.

"Me, too," Jo whispered.

"You like polish sausage?" Hawk asked. His voice was soft as his hands kneaded her backside and thighs. "I've got some at my place."

"It's my favorite," Jo leaned over to whisper in Hawk's ear, "but it looks like you brought it with you." She giggled softly, her eyes moving suggestively to his crotch, and then back to meet his dark, simmering gaze.

"I always carry one with me, for emergencies," he drawled. His smile was languid as his eyes held hers.

Jo felt a tremor of craving shoot through her. The longing was strong enough to leave her short of breath, her nerve endings thrumming. Why did he affect her like this? It was an instinctive reaction—something she had no defense against, and no way of controlling!

God help me, she prayed silently.

XX

"MOM," Laney called as she rushed into the house.

Jo's heart thumped wildly, "What's wrong?" she asked nervously, wondering if her daughter was bringing unpleasant news about Sarah and the baby. It was Thursday afternoon. Bert and Sarah should be coming home.

Were there complications? Was the baby okay?

"Nothing," Laney's face dispelled Jo's initial concerns. It was positively glowing. "Nate asked me to go to the Prom!" Laney grabbed Jo's hands and skipped around the kitchen.

"Well, I'm glad you're taking it so casually. I would hate to see you all worked up over something so trivial," Jo teased, hugging Laney tightly.

"Mom," Laney sighed, "my first prom."

"So, when is the big gig, anyway?"

"April seventeenth." Laney twirled around the dining room, grinning from ear to ear.

"Well, that should give us time to hit all the Goodwill stores for a dress and shoes," Jo said matter-of-factly, going back to the cookies she'd been baking.

"MOM," Laney giggled, "we're going to Lincoln. This weekend!"

"We'll see," Jo promised.

My little girl going to a prom. It was a double-edged sword, both thrilling and painful, at one and the same time.

~ ~ ~

"You're invited to Easter Dinner," Hawk said casually as Jo got into the passenger side of his truck.

"Oh, thanks. Tell your mom I'll think about it," Jo responded, not sure how comfortable she'd feel around everyone, after all that had recently occurred.

"*No way*, huh-uh!" Hawk shook his head. "Not THIS boy! YOU tell her.

I ain't goin' there." He grinned impishly at her.

Jo laughed.

"So, where are we headed tonight, Big Guy?" she asked. It had been awhile since the two of them had been on anything that remotely resembled a date. Her pulse quickened perceptibly at the mere thought of it, all day long. A gentle breeze stirred along the ground, and the world around her looked fresh and clean. Spring was in the air. Tulips and crocus were everywhere, and an incredible variety of birds chirped with exuberant enthusiasm.

The night was warm. Jo's khaki slacks and white sweater were lightweight, but seemed to fit the evening well.

"We're going to Pawnee City for barbecue and beer," Hawk informed her. "A friend of mine, Pete Flanders, is having a barn dance at his place. Sound like fun?"

Jo nodded, feeling a little giddy.

"Pete and I graduated high school a year apart," Hawk explained as he maneuvered his truck out of the driveway. "Later, we ended up going through training together. He's got acreage up by Pawnee City. He and his wife are celebrating twenty years of wedded bliss," Hawk elaborated.

"Twenty years? How old is he?" Jo asked.

"A year older 'n me," Hawk answered Jo's question. "He married his high school sweetheart the year after they graduated."

"Oh," Jo responded. How simple. How perfect, she thought. Why couldn't my life have been that ordinary? Jo suddenly felt the ever-present prick of melancholy. Why had fate twisted everything into such ugly knots? She wished with all her heart she'd never lied to Hawk about who she was and where she'd come from—but that was spilled milk now. Jo shook herself mentally, inhaling deeply and letting it slip out on a sigh.

The spring air smelled of rich, dark soil, and budding life. This was a new beginning—she had to hold onto that—it had to be enough, and it had to work.

Please, Lord, let things work out. Just let me stay here, and forget Devin and everything tied to him!

~ ~ ~

"Oh, Laney," Jo breathed out on a sigh of pure joy. "You're gorgeous!" Tears filled her eyes as Laney twirled in front of her. The iridescent lavender gown shimmered, and seemed to change colors with every movement. A beauty shop Ellie recommended, had styled Laney's hair, and the upsweep of curling tendrils made her look grown up—too grown up for her sixteen years, Jo thought with a stab of regret.

"Laney, yow'a pwincess," Jenny clapped her hands as she bounced up and down, dancing around her sister.

"You think Nate will approve?" Laney asked expectantly.

"Oh, Honey, if he doesn't, I'll personally horsewhip the boy," Jo laughed, hugging her daughter close.

"It's just a stupid dance. I don't know what's got everyone so worked up," Casey snapped, flopping on the couch with a Harry Potter book.

"Meanie!" Jenny hollered, glaring at her brother.

Casey made a face and stuck out his tongue.

"Kids! Don't spoil Laney's big night," Jo admonished, adjusting a few of her daughter's wayward curls.

A rap on the back door caused Laney to tense, and then rush up the stairs to her room. "Tell him I'm almost ready," she called over her shoulder. "I just have to put on some lip gloss."

"Come on in, Nate," Jo said as she answered the door. She was somewhat surprised to find Hawk standing behind his son.

"Sorry for the intrusion, Jo. Just thought I'd capture a few lasting memories," he explained.

"No, it's great," Jo, said, her eyes lighting on the camera Hawk held in one hand, and the camcorder bag slung over his shoulder. "I didn't think to pick up a disposable," she said, holding the door open for Nate and Hawk.

"I'll give you a copy. I always get doubles." Hawk winked as he passed her, heading for the living room.

"Hawk!" Jenny rushed forward to give him a hug. "Laney's a pwencess," she gushed, looking up at him with adoring eyes.

"I bet she...*whoa*," Hawk stopped mid-sentence, looking at the stairs.

"*Holy shit*!" Jo heard Nate's exclamation as she followed them into the living room and saw Laney descending the steps.

Jo's eyes filled with tears again as she watched the graceful young lady, her baby girl had grown into, walk down those stairs and into a new stage of her life. Laney literally glowed. Twinkling studs sparkled at her ears, and a thin, silver chain held a single, glistening stone at her throat. The low neckline and backless style of the dress emphasized Laney's figure. Jo realized, all of a sudden, what a beautiful woman she'd become.

When did that happen? Jo felt dazed. She was just a little girl yesterday.

"You look great, Laney," Nate said as he walked toward her.

"Thanks." Jo heard her daughter's soft reply. "You look pretty impressive yourself."

Laney was right. Nate's black tuxedo made him appear taller than his six-foot-one frame. He was a damn, good-looking young man—a younger, slenderer Hawk.

"Nate, you're one handsome dude," Jo grinned at the boy, noting how grown up he looked. What emotions were going through Hawk right now? Was this as hard for him as it was for her?

"Thanks, Jo," Nate said, "and thanks for lettin' Laney go with me." His eyes were glued on Laney, all but eating her alive. A slightly bemused expression clouded his handsome face.

"Just behave yourself, Young Man," Jo warned in a tone that was light and teasing. "Then I won't have to hurt you."

Nate winked at her. "Yeah, I'll keep that in mind," he said.

"Okay, kids, stand together by the stairs," Hawk said. "Nice," he approved, grinning as he snapped several shots. "Okay, I'm gonna precede you outside," he directed, pulling the camcorder out of its case. "All you have to do is smile and wave to your adoring fans."

Jo watched Nate slide a wrist corsage on Laney's arm, and then he held the door of a dark blue Mustang open for her.

"Is that Nate's car?" Jo leaned over to ask Hawk.

"It's Bert's, on loan for the evening."

"Awesome," Jo approved.

"Awesome price tag, too," Hawk replied, rolling his eyes and flashing her a broad grin.

Jo waved as Nate backed out. "Have fun," she called. She didn't realize she was crying until Hawk put a hand on her face and wiped at a tear with his thumb.

"It's just the prom, Jo. They'll be home and back to normal in a few hours," he said, grinning.

"No, Hawk, it's not just a prom. It's…it's that it IS just a prom."

"*Ooooh*," Hawk teased, "now I get it!"

Jo smiled. "It's just that it's normal, and healthy, and safe, and…good, Hawk. All the things I wanted my child to have. All the things we didn't have in our lives before." She turned away, fresh tears starting down her cheeks. She didn't imagine Hawk could understand what she was trying to say, but he seemed to grasp the essence of it.

"It's Small Town, U.S.A., Jo. There are a few drawbacks, but the pluses more than make up for them."

Jo nodded.

"So, what else is it?" Hawk was as perceptive as ever. Somehow, he managed to see right through her—perceive and understand things that no one else ever did.

Jo met his eyes. "She's changed, Hawk," her voice broke slightly. "She's so beautiful, and so grown up. My little girl is…she's grown up!" Jo knew she was reacting like an emotional mother, but tonight, that's exactly what she was.

"Come here, Little Girl," Hawk said gently, setting down his camera bag and pulling her into his arms.

The feel of his strength surrounding her was wonderful. Jo leaned into the embrace, resting her head against his shoulder.

"How 'bout a beer at my place? I rented a couple DVD's for the evening. I have every intention of waiting up for our fairytale couple."

"Waiting up?"

"You realize there'll be prom, then post-prom, and then breakfast at someone's house. It'll be a long night."

"Oh!" Jo hadn't realized that. "I still have Jenny and Casey, and they're probably fighting over the channel changer as we speak."

"Mom volunteered to take them to the movies tonight, in case you and I wanted to do something," Hawk offered, looking down at Jo's face. "And I think you definitely need to do something."

"Yeah, me too," Jo's eyes were glued to Hawk's mouth as she spoke. The desires she tried to keep in check, seemed to ignite so easily when she was near this man. A shiver of delight slid up her spin as he covered her lips with his own, in a long, demanding kiss.

~ ~ ~

"When you gonna talk to me, Jo?" Hawk's voice was low and rumbling.

Jo lifted her head from his bare shoulder, raising herself up on one arm to look down at him. She knew her hair fell in tussled disarray around her face, and her skin would be flushed with the aftermath of their lovemaking, but somehow, it didn't seem to matter.

"What…what do you want me to say?" she asked.

"Don't do that, Jo," Hawk said, sitting up in bed and pulling her into his arms. "Don't close up on me like that. I can see it in your face—in your eyes." He stroked her hair and ran his hands across her back.

"I don't mean to," Jo's voice sounded muffled against his shoulder as her arms slipped around his neck. "I just live with…with…" Jo couldn't finish. Did she want him to know her daily companion was always the fear? Afraid he would discover who she was, and what she'd done. Terrified Devin would find her, and scared for her children's futures with their father—without her!

"What do you live with, Jo?" Hawk asked gently, holding her away from him a little to look down into her face.

She just dropped her gaze and shook her head, unable to say the words.

"What are you afraid of?" he asked, still pushing.

Jo looked up suddenly, startled at his perception.

"It's written all over you, Honey. Why won't you tell me? Why can't you trust me?"

Jo could hear the plea in his voice, and it hurt not to respond the way he wanted.

"That's not the point, Hawk. I can't compromise your integrity, and telling you what you want to know, could put your safety in jeopardy," Jo said flatly, dropping her head back on Hawk's shoulder. "I simply won't take that chance."

"Oh, *right*! Like THAT'S not gonna whet my curiosity even more?" Hawk's tone was sardonic.

Jo smiled sheepishly, wishing with all her heart that she could offer him the truths he wanted from her.

He opened his mouth to say more, but the phone rang suddenly. They looked at each other with the barest hint of concern. It was almost four AM. The kids should still be at the post-prom party.

Who would be calling at this hour? Please let the kids be okay, Jo prayed.

Hawk answered on the second ring. "Yo," his deep voice barked.

Jo couldn't hear who the caller was, but she felt Hawk's body stiffen.

His voice sounded hoarse as he asked, "Any idea who she is?"

Jo felt a prickle of premonition touch her spine.

"No, don't bother. I'll be there in about forty-five minutes, Pete. Thanks." Hawk hung up the phone, and then turned to Jo. "Sorry, Baby, I gotta go."

Worry made Jo's voice rough, "Is...what's wrong, Hawk?"

"Looks like a possible homicide. That was Pete Flanders," Hawk nodded toward the phone. He was already up and pulling on his clothes as he spoke.

Homicide? Jo was shocked. Murder, here? In Smalltown, U.S.A.? Jo remembered Pete from the barbecue they'd gone to in Pawnee City a few weeks ago. He'd been a tall, good-looking man, with a plump blonde at his side. He'd lovingly introduced the woman as his 'bride'.

Hawk leaned over and touched Jo's face gently. "Let's finish this conversation, soon."

Jo made a pathetic, half-hearted attempt at a smile. She had an unpleasant churning in the pit of her stomach. It was a feeling she'd had too many times in the past to ignore.

God, don't let me get drawn into this, please. Don't let me *KNOW* anything!

XXI

"Holy shit!" Hawk muttered under his breath as he knelt beside the mutilated body. The girl was no more than nineteen or twenty, if his guess was correct. The naked corpse lay sprawled beside a remote dirt road.

"Yeah, same thing I said," Pete growled, shaking his head from side to side.

"Who is she?" Hawk asked, carefully moving a bloody strand of dark brown hair away from the girl's unseeing eyes. He ached to reach out and close the eyelids, but he resisted that urge. It would compromise the crime scene investigation. He knew the photographers had already taken the pictures they needed, but there would be others here soon enough, going over the place with a fine-toothed comb. Still, the blank, lifeless stare of those blue eyes was something he knew would haunt him for a long time.

"Not sure, Hawk. Might be a runaway named Stephanie Moore," Pete informed him. "We're still checkin' it out."

Pete was a tall man, close to Hawk's own height, but there was nothing flashy about him. Even features, hazel eyes, and light brown hair, seldom drew a second glance, yet Hawk knew from personal experience, the man's appearance was deceptive. He was an exceptionally shrewd detective.

"So, why were you called in?" Hawk asked, coughing as the odors of blood, human excrement, and deteriorating flesh, assaulted his nostrils. "This is my territory."

"Pawnee dispatcher took the call," Pete explained, looking into the distance as if he had to find something neutral to focus on. "A local farmer found her."

Hawk nodded. This part of the country was hard to divide into compact territories. One farmer's land rolled into someone else's—county lines slipped unobtrusively into one another, as well. They were damn close to Pawnee County.

Pete continued. "Do you remember that murder near Steinaur last summer?"

Once again, Hawk nodded. “Like anyone could forget?”

Pete grimaced. “It had a similar M.O.” His voice sounded flat, and his hazel eyes watched Hawk’s face closely.

Hawk felt the prickle of premonition on the back of his neck. “You’re thinkin’ it’s the same offender?” His eyes narrowed as he digested the implication of that possibility.

“Yeah, we’re pretty sure it is,” Pete’s face looked grim.

Hawk stood, dusting his hands on his pants. “You’ve established a signature?” he asked in a hoarse voice, finding it hard to believe what he was hearing. A serial killer, HERE? He watched Pete kneel beside the body. The detective’s gloved finger hovered just above the woman’s chest, following the path of a bloody outline. He looked up meeting Hawk’s eyes.

“Right here,” Pete said softly, still watching Hawk. His forefinger once again followed a pattern on the girl’s chest, though he did not touch her.

“What the hell,” Hawk said, kneeling beside his friend and slipping on the latex glove Pete handed him. Pulling a clean handkerchief from his pocket, Hawk dabbed at the blood until he could see the pattern Pete was showing him. Painstakingly, and very carefully, someone had carved three letters into the girl’s flesh.

“R-I-P,” Hawk whispered as he met Pete’s eyes. “Rest in peace? Judas, what a sadistic S.O.B.,” he growled as he continued to examine the corpse more closely.

“I’m not sure that’s what it means, but yeah, R-I-P.” Pete pointed toward the feet. “Ankles were bound, but not together, and the wrists the same way.” He cleared his throat, standing.

Hawk noted the bruised and torn flesh at both sites. She struggled hard against whatever held her, he thought to himself, sickened at the thought of this child fighting to live.

“Hey, Bev,” Pete called out, as a tall, slender woman walked toward them, carrying a clipboard. “Bev, you remember meetin’ Beau Hawkins at the party, don’t you?” Pete reintroduced them. “Hawk, this is Bev Skinner. She works outta our office.”

Hawk did remember Bev. She was a bony woman with a sharp tongue and critical eye, but she looked efficient. “Hi, Bev,” Hawk shook her outstretched hand, giving no hint of his uncomplimentary thoughts. “It’s good to see you again.”

Bev nodded. “Hello, Mr. Hawkins.”

“Ah, Hawk, just Hawk will do fine.”

Smiling, Bev nodded again. “Okay, Hawk.”

Hawk found himself thinking that even the smile on her face did little to relieve the harshness of her features. Her brown eyes were set too close together. Devoid of make-up as they were, they tended to be all but non-descript. A beak-like nose was narrow and too large for her face, and thin lips were little more than a line of color against her pale flesh.

Forcing his mind down a different avenue of thought, Hawk returned abruptly to the case at hand. "Has cause of death been determined for certain?" he asked, swallowing hard to control a sudden urge to vomit as his gaze rested, once again, on the mutilated body.

"Well, nothing in writing 'til the pathologist does his thing," Bev replied, kneeling down next to the victim. "There's ligature marks on the wrists and ankles, so I'd say she was restrained while the perp raped her, and most likely during his artsy thing." She traced over the carved flesh, her finger a hair's breath above the gaping wounds. "Probably still alive at that point."

Bev moved to hover near the woman's head as she spoke. Gently she placed her hands on both sides of the face and moved the head a little from right to left. "Broken neck," she said, looking up at Hawk, her tone aloof and professional.

He couldn't help wondering what thoughts moved behind her dull brown eyes. "Looks clean. He knew what he was doing," Hawk commented, kneeling beside Bev and examining the victim's face and neck more carefully. "No sign of extensive bruising here, just a quick, clean break." Hawk looked thoughtful. "Could he have just snapped it? Like that?" He snapped his fingers. "No struggle?"

"Anything's possible these days," Pete said, standing behind Hawk and Bev.

Bev moved down the body, kneeling at the woman's side. Pulling gently at one of the victim's thighs, she said, "Looks like probable rape."

"Probable, my ass!" Pete snapped. "She's torn all to hell and back!"

"Probable rape," Bev repeated, rolling her eyes expressively as she jotted something down on her clipboard.

Pete looked disgusted.

"Lucky enough for semen?" Hawk asked, standing slowly and pulling off his glove.

Bev shrugged. They hadn't done any testing yet, but most rapists were smart enough to avoid that telltale link to an identity.

"What do YOU think?" Pete growled, removing his own glove.

Hawk just shook his head, exhaling slowly through pursed lips. "So what else ties the murders to the same perp?" he asked.

"Plenty," Pete motioned with his head toward a parked police vehicle. Bev and Hawk followed him as he continued talking. "Wrists and ankles were bound separately, tortured, brutal rape, and the RIP carving. Since we didn't print the existence of that little tattoo, I'm pretty sure we aren't lookin' at a copy cat."

"Our girl was a student at Peru College," Bev added, referring to the first murder near the town of Steinaur. "She was found on a remote country roadside about twenty miles from town, like this one."

"That's pretty tight," Hawk acknowledged, his gut twisting as the significance and magnitude of such a crime sifted through the shock. "What was her name? Where was she from?" He suddenly needed to know. "Your vic, I mean." Hawk clarified, as Pete and Bev sent slightly startled looks his way.

"Nichole Umbridge," Pete said softly, looking as if he suddenly comprehended Hawk's motivation. "Twenty-one year old junior at Peru, originally from Omaha."

Even during their training, Hawk had always looked at a crime from the victim's perspective. He'd read a quote, which claimed it was too easy to become distracted by the criminal's profile and forget the value of understanding the victim. It was something that had impressed him enough to study it in more depth.

"I'll send over details and crime scene photos," Pete added.

"Yeah, you do that," Hawk said, suddenly weary to his very bones. "Man, these kinda things just don't happen round here, Pete."

"No shit, Sherlock! We got an ugly one on our hands, I'm afraid."

~ ~ ~

"So, what's this about a murder?" B.J. didn't even let Hawk sit down before he was drilling him for information.

"B.J.!" Carol was quick to reprimand her son. "You know Hawk can't discuss a murder case with us," she chided, sliding a stack of pancakes onto B.J.'s plate.

"Mom, I've never had a murder case before," Hawk reminded her as he poured himself a cup of coffee, "but you're right, I can't talk about details."

"Anyone we know?" Bert asked.

"Possible runaway," Hawk replied, not bothering to look up from his food. He saw no need to tie in the first murder. It was something they'd all shaken their heads over at the time. After all, murders in this part of the country were rare, and tended to draw a lot of speculation and attention for miles around. His stomach suddenly turned over at the memory of the victim he'd seen last night, threatening to reject breakfast. Taking several deep breaths, he forced himself to continue eating as normally as possible.

"Funny how no one ever sees anything." Bert looked thoughtful. "Just left beside the road, and nobody knows squat?"

"Looks that way right now, but they're canvassing the area. Could be someone saw something," Hawk said, noncommittally.

"Where'd this happen?" Bert asked.

Hawk didn't see much use withholding that information. The media was already running with it. "Off Highway 105. She was dumped on a country road, between two corn fields, in the middle of nowhere."

"Damn," B.J. shook his head, "too close to home."

"Tough way to go," Bert lowered his gaze, staring intently at his coffee.

"How old was she, Hawk?" Carol asked.

"Eighteen, nineteen, I'm guessin'. Too young to die like that," he said, pushing his half-empty plate away and rising. "Sorry Mom, I gotta go in early this mornin'." Hawk pulled his mother into a strong embrace for a moment or two before kissing her cheek. "Later," he called over his shoulder as he left.

~ ~ ~

"You can't give me anything?" Jack asked, somewhat put out.

"Really, Jack, how would I know anything more than you do? It's police business. Why would you think I'd be able to give you information?" Jo found Jack's assumption somewhat disturbing. What did he think Hawk would say to her that would be printable?

"You were with him when he got the call, weren't you? Anything slip there?" Jack pushed.

"How'd you know that?" Jo found herself feeling defensive, and very uncomfortable. "That's really none of your business."

"As soon as the news came on my scanner, I called your place to see if you could catch Hawk for a few questions. There was no answer, but you said this mornin', you were home all last night," Jack shrugged, grinning knowingly. "Just puttin' two and two together, Jo."

"Yeah? Well, maybe you had better rethink your math, Jack. Assumptions make bad press!" Jo was angry. "Besides, I wouldn't presume to give out unauthorized information, to you or anyone else, even if I did know something."

"I wasn't thinkin' about unauthorized info, Jo. I was curious about what you know." The look on Jack's face made Jo shudder inwardly. He looked like a cat that had eaten the family canary, and knew he couldn't be punished for it.

She studied his round face and pale blue eyes. He wasn't much taller than she was, but his build made him look like a large man. He was stocky, though he moved with an easy grace that bespoke conditioning.

"What are you getting at, Jack," Jo asked, her voice amazingly calm, considering the chaos in her gut.

"You know somethin', Jo? I've been in the paper business awhile, and I got a pretty good eye for detail, and a very long memory."

Jo said nothing, sitting perfectly still as she raised her eyes to meet his.

"I thought you looked familiar when we first met, and the sketchy info on your application was puzzling." He paused for several moments, his gaze locked with hers.

"And?" she said, at last.

You know, don't you, she thought as she watched his face. Just get on with it, you son-of-a-bitch!

"Well, it seems you're a rather well-know celebrity, *Mrs. Parrish*."

Jo could see triumph in his eyes, a kind of gloating in his smile. He obviously imagined himself to be quite the reporter, digging up her background the way he had.

"What are you intending to do with this information, Jack?" Jo asked in an emotionless voice.

"I'm not sure yet, but I'm wonderin' just how long you'll be able to keep it under wraps, with this murder an' all. From what I've pulled together, you've got a very impressive history with the police in L.A."

"Yeah, impressive." Jo suddenly felt tired, dog-tired. So, the fight was over—there was no escaping now, no more second chances. It was an effort to draw breath.

Jack continued speaking, obviously pleased with himself. "Having a full-fledged, documented psychic right here in Humboldt, working on this murder—now, there's a story worth printin'."

Jo tried to concentrate on what he was saying.

"It appears these freaky cases were your particular specialty, Jo," Jack pointed out, looking like a puffed up rooster. "You even brought down a serial rapist, Samuel Hoekkendale?"

Jo could barely suppress the involuntary shudder she felt, at the very mention of that name. Those years of her life were particularly black memories—the crime scenes, the police questionings, the repulsion and fury her gift stirred in Devin—and the nightmares! Oh God, those dreams! The never-ending, bloody, visions!

"I'm not helping the police on this, Jack. You're the only one who knows who I really am. I'd prefer to keep it that way," Jo said quietly, meeting his pale gaze.

"I bet you would," he replied. "It won't take Hawk long to figure it out."

Jo wasn't so sure Jack was off base on that prediction. Hawk had all the puzzle pieces. He'd just been too preoccupied to fit them together.

"Yeah, you're probably right, but he hasn't yet," Jo said, exhaustion in her face and voice clearly apparent. "*Please*, Jack,"

He perused Jo for a moment or two before he spoke. "Okay, I'll hold it for now, but I won't let this story go for long, Jo. The murder is big news. *You're* big news. And I don't need a physic to tell me that.

~ ~ ~

Hawk sat at his desk mulling over the pictures delivered to his office. The crime scene of any murder was gruesome, but the brutal, senseless deaths of two young women was callous and inhuman—utterly impossible to come to grips with. He thumb tacked the eight by tens to the corkboard over his desk, and then leaned back in his swivel chair to scrutinize them again.

Talk to me, Hawk thought as he examined first one picture, and then another. What am I missing? What can you tell me? Very little bruising on either neck. That seemed odd to him. Why didn't you fight? Hawk silently asked the lifeless, bloodied face of Stephanie Moore, staring at him from the photograph. "Talk to me," he muttered out loud.

They were all single. He'd spent hours upon hours sifting through lifestyles and family histories—their friends, occupations, employers, medical histories, criminal histories—everything. Detailed timelines of their last known activities and contacts were carefully sketched out—all of it turning up a brick wall. Nothing!

Hawk pulled down a picture of the co-ed, Nichole Umbridge. She was sprawled naked on the side of a dirt road, just as Stephanie had been.

"Who did this to you, Nichole?" Hawk asked, his voice a hoarse whisper that sounded oddly out of place in the silent, empty room. He went over several other pictures, examining every detail he could see.

Did either of you know the son-of-a-bitch? Relative? Lover? Classmate? What significance do the carvings have? Was the physco trying to tell the cops something? What?

R-I-P. What in the hell are those letters spelling for this sick bastard?

XXII

"You look like you're a million miles away, Hawk," Jo said, picking out a quiet melody on her guitar. She sat on the patio outside her bedroom, playing softly, enjoying the warm April evening. Jo needed to clear her mind, and she definitely had to come up with a plan of action—soon.

Seeing her from his deck, Hawk had waved, and then walked over. He looked tired and haggard. Jo found herself wondering what horrors he'd been dealing with over the past week. She'd barely seen hide-nor-hair of the man, let alone had a private word with him.

"Yeah, I have been." He smiled half-heartedly, leaning against one of the support beams that held the vine-covered arbor above their heads. Honeysuckle and climbing rose were greening out, and the myriad of spring bulbs and perennials someone had painstakingly planted around the cottage, were budding, starting to bloom.

"Wanna talk?" Jo asked, setting her guitar aside. She doubted he could, but she offered anyway.

"They…she was young, Jo. A runaway," Hawk said, closing his eyes and rubbing the bridge of his nose as if he could erase the tension that obviously filled his every waking hour.

Jo swallowed hard. I don't want to know this, she thought with mild alarm. Dear God, don't draw me into this. Her days of aiding the police and using her cursed gift were over. The nightmares and visions that gave her a birds-eye-view—and occasionally a first-person reliving—no, no more! Never again! That was another lifetime, another person—dead and buried like her past.

And then there was Jack. How long would he give her? It wouldn't take much to spur him into a full-blown write-up, with her picture and name plastered all over the front page. The mere thought made her heart race painfully. Was her life in Humboldt over so soon? The very real possibility of that outcome caused Jo's chest to constrict painfully.

She watched Hawk's face. He was worried—really worried. It ate at him.

She could see it—*sense* it.

"It's close, isn't it?" Jo asked, suddenly feeling apprehension over more than the possibility her gift would resurface, or that she would have to pick up stakes and run again.

"Too damned close for comfort," Hawk whispered hoarsely, stuffing his hands deep into the pockets of his jeans.

"You've got to separate yourself from it, Hawk," Jo said, recognizing the single-minded frenzy she'd seen on other faces, with other cases. "You're not giving yourself time and space to put this into perspective."

Hawk nodded. "Where're the kids?" he asked, as if suddenly registering the quietness of the house.

"Laney's at Carmen Deitter's for an overnighter, and Ellie asked Casey to stay over."

Hawk's eyes widened with sudden consternation. "Oh, *man*," he exclaimed. "Mark's birthday was today, wasn't it?" He rolled his eyes in exasperation with himself. "I can't *believe* I forgot."

Jo wasn't surprised he'd failed to remember his nephew's birthday. "Small wonder," she smiled at him. "Anyway, Jenny was feeling left out, so Carol invited her to stay the night at her place. It seems she's acquired a new kitten, and Jenny's ecstatic." Jo laughed softly, shaking her head in amazement. The little things that make life so ordinary, are the ones to be cherished, she realized with a pang of regret. Her children had never had those little things.

And now, she thought, just when I've found that simple, ordinary, wonderful life—it's being ripped away. Why?

"A rare evening alone then," Hawk observed.

"It's a nice break," she admitted, and then her attention shifted to a black Taurus, pulling into the driveway and coming to a stop near Hawk's pickup.

"Wish I could say the same," Hawk said, pushing himself resignedly away from the post he'd been leaning against, as a tall, middle-aged man emerged from the vehicle.

"Pete," Hawk raised his voice.

Jo recognized the man immediately. She'd met him at the barbecue, but he looked different now, aloof and professional. An uneasy twinge raced up her spine as the lanky man approached. He was every inch the cop—and she was still a wanted fugitive.

"Pete, this is my neighbor, Joanne Kenning. She was with me at your shindig." Hawk reintroduced them. "Jo, you remember Pete Flanders?"

"Jo," Pete acknowledged politely, shaking her hand as she stood up.

"Nice to see you again, Pete," Jo lied. She didn't feel comfortable around this man.

"Well, Pete and I have some work to do. I'll see ya." Hawk turned and led

Pete toward the stairway that would take them to his deck.

Jo watched them ascend the stairs, slowly lowering herself back onto the lawn chair, but she didn't reach for her guitar. Somehow, the pleasure she'd found in the early evening and the gentle sound of her music, had been snuffed out.

Trepidation settled inside her, refusing to listen to any of the silent arguments she hurled against it. She felt cold and terribly frightened. Her past was catching up to her! What in the world had made her think she could pull this off? How in God's name was she going to avoid Devin's clutches, and keep her children safe? How could she ever hope to run from the curse within herself? She would never be free of her visions—never! And they would always tie her to Jocelyn Parrish!

~ ~ ~

"It doesn't fuckin' add up," Hawk hissed, looking out over the cottage and the tree line behind it. The moon was nearly full, bathing everything in its soft, silvery glow.

He'd changed out of his uniform into jeans and a sleeveless undershirt, and sprawled now on a deck chair, nursing a beer. Pete sat quietly beside him, holding a Bud Light in one hand and a glowing cigarette in the other.

"It never does, Hawk," Pete, said quietly. "It never does."

"This has got to be one sick son-of-a-bitch," Hawk muttered, wondering idly if Jo were still awake. It was well past midnight, and the light from her bedroom had been off all evening.

"Somehow I doubt he's sick—at least not as in mentally deranged," Pete mused. "All the evidence points to premeditation. He planned these attacks, right down to the drop site."

"Well, hell, Pete," Hawk glowered at his friend, "who the hell does somethin' like that if they're sane? He may have planned it, and he's undoubtedly brighter than most, but he's sick all right. Sick to the bone!"

Pete nodded, snuffing out his cigarette. "Don't let it eat away at you, Hawk."

Hawk just laughed. It was a cold, humorless sound.

Both men were silent for a long time. They'd discussed what facts they had, gone over Hawk's findings on the girl's backgrounds, families, lives, and activities. Every aspect of both crimes had been diced and sliced so many times, it was barely recognizable anymore, and they had absolutely nothing. Then again, Hawk had barely started on the victim profiles. It would be a long, tedious job, but an essential one.

"Hey," Hawk said at last, "I don't know about you, Pete, but I'm burned out. Let's call it a night." He pushed himself to his feet.

"You'll think about what I said?" Pete asked as he, too, rose. "If we can establish context and connection, we'll have a jump on an investigative direction."

"Yeah, I'll work on the victim profiles," Hawk replied, following Pete down the steps and over to his vehicle. "Keep me posted on the investigation from your end."

"You got it," Pete said as he shook Hawk's hand.

Hawk watched as the Taurus pulled out of the driveway and headed down the road. It's going to be a long summer, he thought, turning to head back. He noticed Jo's French doors were open, and decided she was probably taking advantage of the cool evening breeze.

He'd love nothing better than to slip inside her room and slide into bed with her. He needed to lose his thoughts in their lovemaking, drown his depression in Jo's cries of pleasure, and feel the release that seemed to wash away everything but the fire of their passion. With firm resolve, Hawk squelched the yearning. Long day, late night, and 5:00 AM will be here too damned early!

~ ~ ~

When he reached his deck, Hawk plopped down on a lounge chair, unable to face the empty house. Nate was at Ellie's, helping entertain his cousins and their company for the night. Hawk reached into the cooler he'd brought out earlier, and fished out another bottle of beer. Maybe he could drink himself into a stupor strong enough to deaden his raging thoughts, and give him a good night's sleep for a change.

The scream ripped through the stillness of the night, sending Hawk's heart into his throat. Sliding out of his hand, the beer clunked onto the deck and rolled, the frothy brew spewing around his feet. Hawk was already racing down the steps by the time the second scream slashed through the darkness.

It's coming from Jo's bedroom!

"No, please." Jo's cry was a pleading whimper as Hawk slid the screen door open with a vicious jerk. His eyes had adjusted to the darkness of the night, and the moon's light filled the bedroom. Hawk could see Jo thrashing wildly in bed, the sheets wrapping themselves about her legs and arms.

"I don't understand why," she moaned. Another scream of pure anguish followed.

"JO!" Hawk was beside her on the bed grasping her shoulders and shaking her. "Wake up. It's a nightmare." His words fell on deaf ears. Jo began struggling weakly.

"*Noooo*!" Her cry cut through him like a knife. "Oh God! Oh God!" she kept repeating the words, sobbing uncontrollably.

Raising his hand, Hawk slapped Jo's face hard enough to hear the crack of palm contacting cheek. She screamed in response, her eyes flying open, but the look in them sent a chill down Hawk's spine. They were wild with fear and horror, not registering who he was or even where she was.

"Why?" She asked, still struggling in his grasp, though her movements were weak and unfocused. "Stop him!" Jo looked up at Hawk, but there was still no recognition in her face. "He's going to kill her," she cried out, becoming frantic that he wasn't doing anything.

"It's okay, Jo. It's just a nightmare." She's more upset by the murder than I realized—that has to be it, he reasoned. "It's okay, Baby," Hawk said huskily, pulling her into his strong embrace.

"He's tied her up, I can see it!" she cried, her voice muffled against Hawk's shoulder. "He's raping her, why won't you stop him?"

Jo was nearly hysterical, struggling again as if she could reach the woman she saw in her mind's eye and help her. "*Do* something! He's going to kill her!" Hawk felt a chill of apprehension start at the base of his spine. He held Jo away from him, looking into her eyes.

"What are you talking about, Jo?" he demanded in a harsh voice.

"He…he has a knife. It hurts, it hurts," She whimpered now, swatting blindly at her own chest. "He's…he's writing something on her, with the knife." Jo wrenched herself free of Hawk's grasp, flinging herself onto the floor. She was up in an instant trying to run, but Hawk was just as quick. His strong hands grabbed her shoulders shaking her hard.

"Snap out of it, Jo! It's a dream, a nightmare." He said the words evenly, but his voice was forceful, unrelentingly harsh.

"Oh, God," Jo suddenly buckled, nearly carrying Hawk to the floor with her. "She's dead. We're too late." She looked up at him with horror etched in every line of her face. "He…he just…he just snapped her neck. Just like that. One, quick, easy…oh, *God*!" she wailed, fighting weakly against Hawk's vice-like grip.

"Look at me, Jo, it's me, Hawk. We're in your bedroom. There's no one else here." He kept his tone level and firm.

Jo looked into his face with recognition for the first time, her eyes still wide with the terror of the dream. "Oh, my God," she whispered, clearly in shock. "What did I see?"

"It's over, Jo," Hawk soothed. "It was just a nightmare."

Jo tried to break away, but Hawk didn't loosen his hold. "I'm gonna be sick, Hawk," she whimpered.

"It's okay, I'm here, Jo." Hawk held her close, half carrying her through the doors.

Her knees gave out almost immediately. Hawk held her as she vomited repeatedly, until there was nothing but dry heaves.

What in the hell, he thought as he held her. The words she'd cried out were racing through his mind, making connections he didn't want made. How could she possibly know? It was as if she'd been at the murder scene!

Hawk eased Jo onto a chair.

"Wait here, I'll be right back," he said. He hurried inside the house, but was back in less than a minute with a cold, wet washcloth in one hand, and a glass of water in the other. "Here," he said, holding the water close to Jo's lips. "Swish it around in your mouth, and then spit it out," he instructed firmly, wiping her face and neck with the cloth after she'd followed his directive.

~ ~ ~

Jo didn't say anything, she couldn't. Her mind was numb with shock and horror, and the incessant pounding inside her brain. She lowered her head into her hands, rubbing futilely at her temples. It was always like this after one of her visions—the nausea, the vomiting, the weakness, and the throbbing headaches.

"We need to talk, Jo," Hawk said softly, as if he hated having to bring it up, but desperately needed to do so.

"I…" Jo looked up at Hawk with wide, frightened eyes. He was right. They would have to talk—she knew with unquestionable certainty, that what she'd seen was the murder Hawk was working on. She'd seen it happening! The binding, a brutally vicious rape, the knife carving into innocent flesh, and the cold, calculated snapping of a neck, that ended a young girl's life!

"Oh, God," Jo lowered her face into her hands, sobbing uncontrollably. "Oh, my God, Hawk, what have I seen?" she cried, her voice muffled in her hands.

Hawk wrapped his arms around her, unable to resist giving the comfort she so desperately needed. "I wish I knew, Baby," he said softly, "I wish to hell I knew."

~ ~ ~

"I need to talk with you, Mom," Hawk said.

Carol felt a chill clear to her toes at the look on her son's face. He made no move at all toward the plate of food she'd sat on the counter in front of him, a sure sign something was wrong. His face was haggard. Dark circles marred the flesh under his eyes, and his complexion looked peaked under the normally healthy glow of his copper-hued skin.

"You didn't sleep much last night, did you?" she asked quietly, pouring them both a cup of coffee, and then sitting next to him, waiting for him to speak.

"I didn't get any sleep last night," Hawk emphasized, and then fell silent again.

"Go on," Carol prompted after a few minutes.

Hawk looked at her with a steady, evaluative gaze for a few more moments before he spoke. "What we discuss here goes no further than this room," he said evenly.

"It never does, Son," Carol assured him, meeting his dark gaze with her own.

He nodded, a sardonic smile twisting his lips. "The case I'm working on," Hawk paused, not sure, how to phrase what needed explaining.

"The murders?" Carol supplied.

Hawk looked up, surprised. "How'd you know there were two, that they were connected?" he asked.

"I may be old and fat, Beau, but I'm not stupid, and I have a very good memory. Besides, a murder around these parts isn't something one tends to forget easily. The one you're on now is tied to that other one from last summer, isn't it." She was stating a fact, not asking a question.

"Yeah, yeah, it is," Hawk, replied, sipping at his coffee, his eyes meeting hers over the rim of his cup. "They're bad, Mom, real bad. We've got a very sadistic killer running loose, and not much to go on for clues." Hawk set his cup down slowly.

"And?" She knew he'd not yet come close to what he needed to tell her.

"I was on my deck last night, after Pete left. It was late—or early, whatever," he paused, and then forced himself to go on. "The doors to Jo's patio were open and she was sleeping, when I heard her scream. I raced over and tried to wake her but…" He paused again, running a distracted hand through his hair. "I don't know, it was like she was in a trance or somethin'. She was cryin' and talkin' about a man murdering a woman—and she was seeing it!" Hawk met Carol's eyes, anguish clearly readable in his dark gaze.

Her heart suddenly stopped, and then race wildly in her breast. "She saw your *murder*?" Carol's sharp mind connected the dots Hawk had left for her.

"Yeah, with all the gruesome details," he said softly.

"Did you discuss it with her at all?" she asked, leaning forward to place a warm hand over Hawk's, where it rested on the table.

He turned his hand so he could grasp her fingers, holding on tightly. "No. She wasn't in any condition to talk when she finally came 'round." he shook his head from side to side, as he remembered. "She was weak, and sick, and scared to death. I finally got her to bed with some aspirin in her, and sat beside her the rest of the night while she slept," Hawk explained, his voice sounding exhausted and drained.

"You need to talk with her, Beau," Carol said evenly. "You owe her the chance to explain."

~ ~ ~

"You still believe in her, don't you?" Hawk asked, his voice holding an edge of incredulity.

"Do you?" Carol countered. Hawk looked at her for several long moments, than lowered his head quickly so she wouldn't see his eyes filling with tears. He should have known better than to try to hide his feelings from her. She had mother-ESP or something. She'd always known what went on inside him—he'd seldom needed speech to explain it to her.

Carol got up and moved close to her son, pulling his bent head to rest against her breast and holding him close for several moments.

"I love her, Mom. How can I separate myself from those feelings and look at this situation rationally? I don't see how she can know the details like that, and not be involved!" Hawk held onto Carol, finding strength and comfort in the feel of her arms around him.

"What does your gut tell you, Love?" Carol asked softly, close to his ear.

"I can't accept that she's involved. No, I know she's not involved in this," he said firmly, raising his head and looking his mother in the eye.

"No, she's not involved with the murders," Carol confirmed with a certainty that defied argument, "but she is involved."

Hawk's grip tightened as he met her gaze head on. "Meaning?" he whispered hoarsely.

"That's what you have to find out, Beau, but think it through, Son. What is the one thing you've questioned about her for some time, aside from her past?" Carol prompted. The wheels were turning. He was remembering the incidents of precognition, the eerie way Jo had known things she couldn't—shouldn't have known.

"Psychic?" he asked, disbelief warring with dawning comprehension.

"Most likely,"

"But why try to hide it?" Hawk was baffled.

"A lot of people are frightened by such a thing—put off. She's trying to start a new life, make friends, and build trust," Carol said matter-of-factly. "She probably perceives this gift as a hindrance to those goals. Where there's fear, there's distrust, and often hatred. I wouldn't want to fight those battles on top of a struggle to survive, would you?"

"What makes you such an expert all of a sudden?" Hawk asked, grinning warmly at his mother.

She returned his smile. "Your great grandmother, my grandmother Eloise Bowles, was known as a wise-woman among the Cherokee. She had many such visions—knew things that were happening, or had happened. Sometimes, she could even see things that were going to happen—like Jo did with those thugs that almost killed you," Carol said, cupping Hawk's face with one hand.

"Don't go cryin' on me, Ma. I can't take much more today." He smiled down at his mother as he pulled her back into his embrace.

"Yeah? Well, for your information, Young Man, I was not gettin' blubbery on you," Carol snapped, pushing at Hawk's chest.

He just laughed as she bustled away to refill their coffee cups.

"You think Jo is psychic?" Hawk asked bluntly, sobering again.

"Yes, I do," Carol, replied, equally serious. "Talk to her, Beau."

XXIII

"He knows," Jo said softly, holding her daughter's hands. "It's only a matter of time before he connects all the dots, Laney."

"Mom, we can't move again!" The realization of what Jo was saying seemed to dawn on Laney as she studied her mother's face.

"I'm having visions—about this murder, Laney. Hawk knows it, and I can only avoid him for so long before he corners me into talking. I can't lie anymore, I just can't."

"If you help him, Mom, that newspaper guy will know all about it," Casey interjected. "It'll get on all the news—just like before."

"That newspaper guy already knows who I am. He confronted me about it the other day." Jo hated to tell them that.

"If it's in the news, Dad will find us," Laney whispered, her eyes filling with tears.

Jo nodded, not trying to hide the seriousness of the situation from her children. It was late, after ten. Jenny was in bed asleep. Jo had waited until now to discuss the situation with Laney and Casey. They had a right to know exactly how things stood.

"Are we gonna leave here?" Casey asked, fear and uncertainty creeping into his voice as he scooted close to his mother.

"No, Mamma, I don't want to leave," Laney pleaded, her voice breaking as tears trickled down her cheeks. "I like it here, so much."

Jo closed her eyes for a moment, experiencing a similar anguish. Nate held Laney's heart here, just as securely as Hawk held hers. That, however, didn't alter the facts.

"Maybe they could keep it out of the news?" Casey supplied hopefully. "You could just ask Jack not to say anything."

"*Yeah*, I can see *that* working," Jo said sarcastically. "It's a small town, Honey, nothing gets by for long undetected," she whispered, brushing Casey's hair into place with the fingers of one hand. "If it's not Jack, it'll be someone else."

"What…what are we going to do?" Laney asked in a voice that was barely more than a squeak.

"I don't know, Honey. I need to think about it a little more," Jo replied honestly, pulling both children into her embrace. They sat that way for several, long minutes before Jo shooed them both up to bed. "We'll talk more tomorrow," she promised.

Can I avoid Hawk that long? Will he push? Will I run again?

Jo didn't know. She just didn't know! What she did know was that the fear she'd lived with for so long was back—a bitter, acidic taste that permeated her whole being.

~ ~ ~

Jo moved across the mat with a focus and determination that betrayed her riotous emotions, and the anger that gnawed at the edges of her self-control every waking hour these days. It was nearly dark out—she'd waited until now to come in and clean the dojo, bent on evading anyone who might be of a mind to drop by for a practice session. Learning that lesson once had been more than sufficient for her.

She'd spent the better part of the past hour on rote drills, finding some reassurance in the familiarity of the Kihon. Using weighted bags and padded boards for kicking and punching drills, Jo took her frustration and anger out on the inanimate, unresponsive apparatus. She'd spent another hour going through every Kata she could remember, again and again—every step, every stance, every move—until her legs and arms felt as if they'd been cast from lead.

Pushing past pain and fatigue, she resumed the Kihon drills, moving up and down the mat with the semi-circular crescent step she'd had drilled into her from her first days on a dojo mat. Overhead block, inside block, downward block, repeatedly, up and down the mat. Forward kick, sidekick, roundhouse kick, a continuous repetition—constant movement, constant focus, until she could barely lift her arms or move her legs.

With slow, dragging steps, she forced herself toward the punching bags again, going through a combination of strikes and kicks, using the bag as an imaginary opponent. The creak of the chains that held the bag, sounded unusually loud. Besides the groaning chains, the only sounds in the nearly dark room were an occasional kiai, and the subdued shuffle of her feet against the mat.

She hadn't seen Hawk since the dream, three long nights ago. He hadn't attempted to call or come by. Jo found she was both relieved and worried—and angry. The confrontation was coming—not knowing when, was almost as bad as knowing it was inevitable. It was small wonder that sleep had been evasive the past several nights.

I had damned well better sleep tonight. The thought slipped in and out without any real conscious acknowledgement. Jo was exhausted—past awareness, past feeling, past fighting. Every muscle, every joint, and every fiber of her being ached with intensity that screamed for attention.

"Who you bent on killing, the bag, or yourself?" Hawk's deep, resonate voice startled Jo, sending her heart into her throat, where it beat wildly for several painful moments.

She whipped around, instinctively dropping into a fighting stance, but spent muscles refused to answer to what she demanded. In a single, fluid motion, she crumpled to the floor. Crawling to her hands and knees, her head hanging low between her shoulders, Jo tried to find the strength to stand, but it was a feat beyond her present capabilities.

"You need somethin'?" she asked sarcastically, her tone rough with pain, weariness, and apprehension.

"You," Hawk whispered hoarsely, not moving from where he stood in the darkened hallway that led to the back door. He was leaning against the doorjamb.

Jo wondered how long he'd been standing there watching, before making his presence known. "Well, I ain't goin' nowhere, Candy Ass," she hissed, anger bringing her head up to glare at him.

Damn you! Why can't you just leave me alone? Why did he insert himself so intimately into her life—into her heart? How could she tell him the truth and stay? I can't stay! Jo wanted to scream in anger and frustration, with futile, impotent rage.

"You look like you're wantin' to kick the shit out of me," Hawk observed, his voice almost seductive.

"I do!" Jo snapped. She was still breathing hard, struggling for every labored breath. Nausea was making her stomach roll and pitch—forcing her to acknowledge she hadn't eaten since the single piece of toast she'd consumed at breakfast. Slumping to the mat, she rested her head on her folded arms and started laughing, slowly at first, and then building until she rolled over holding her sides, unable to control the urge—unable to stop.

"You planning on laughing me outta here?" Hawk asked, looking as if he were trying to control an inclination to laugh with her.

"Ahhh," Jo sighed as the laughter subsided, "whatever works, I guess." On her back now, with knees bent and one arm thrown across her face, she challenged, "Go ahead and come in, Candy Ass, it's your damned dojo." Her voice was dull and lifeless. Jo knew this dialogue was as inevitable as the sunrise—it was time to face it and move on.

Hawk didn't say anything. He moved onto the mat and sat down cross-legged beside her.

"Well?" Jo pushed after several minutes of silence elapsed.

"Well what?" he responded.

Jo sat up and looked at him. "Don't fuckin' beat round the bush, Hawk!"

"Ah, much better," he teased, as their eyes met.

"Go to hell," Jo snapped trying to push herself to her feet.

Hawk made no move to stop her, but he didn't have to. Her legs refused to function properly.

"Son of a bitch," she hissed as she dropped back on the mat. Rolling onto her back again, Jo flopped one arm across her eyes.

Hawk did laugh this time, a deep, honest sound that only served to escalate Jo's frustrated agitation.

"Why are you so angry, Jo?" he asked softly, leaning over and looking down into her face.

"I—" she shot back, then stopped abruptly as she met his gaze, directly above her.

His face was haggard, tired. Jo could see the pain in his eyes—but there was more than just pain. There was—what? Trust? Love? How could there be? Suddenly the wind behind her sails died—her anger completely spent. The strength it had imparted ebbed away, leaving behind an exhausted husk—raw emotions took over.

"God, Hawk," Jo cried. Reaching up, she wrapped her arms around his neck, as uncontrollable tears started spilling down her cheeks.

His arms encircled her. Pulling her into his strong, sure embrace. Hawk said nothing, just held her close, letting her cry.

When the tears were spent she pulled her head away from his shoulder and met his eyes.

He looked at her for a long time, saying nothing, just studying her features. One hand came up to trace the same path his eyes followed, his fingers light and gentle against her skin. He seemed to be perusing every part of her face, sealing it in his memory as his eyes roved from one feature to the next, until they met her eyes, and held her gaze.

"I..." Jo started again, but Hawk stopped her words as his mouth covered hers. The fire he always ignited in her flared as his tongue demanded a response. Her hands pulled his head close, and grasped at his back.

"Do you love me, Jo?" Hawk asked, his voice a hoarse whisper.

"*Yes!*" Her answer was immediate and emphatic. It surprised her. I DO love him! With every fiber of her soul, she felt that emotion.

"Show me," he whispered as he unbelted her gi and slid the sports bra down, exposing her breasts.

His mouth found and suckled first one, and then the other, eliciting a groan of pure, unfeigned need. Fire ignited, consuming all reason. Jo didn't even realize her hands were tearing at Hawk's clothing, and she was never certain, afterward, how they came together unclothed on that dojo mat. She was only cognizant of the moment he entered her, the sensation of completeness—two halves of a whole, united and strong again—*one soul*!

~ ~ ~

"I'm not sure I've ever slept in a dojo before," Jo said, feeling somewhat shy as she sat across from Hawk at her own kitchen table the next morning.

"I don't remember too much sleeping," he said huskily.

Jo's only response was to lower her eyes, as a dull red blush colored her cheeks. She could not have said with certainty, when Hawk woke her, or how she got home. She only remembered waking in her own bed, Hawk's arms around her.

"You up to a talk?" he asked in a gentle tone of voice.

"Yes." She met his eyes squarely. "After I get the kids off to school and take a shower."

"Deal," Hawk agreed. "I'll go home and do the same. Why don't we meet at my place in about an hour?"

Jo didn't answer, but she nodded concurrence.

Oh God, it's time. Please don't let him hate me too much. *Please*!

~ ~ ~

"You're not going to like this, Hawk," Jo said, her voice hesitant and nervous.

"Probably not," he agreed.

Great! Let me off the damn hook! Make it a little easier why don't you.

Jo tried to curb her rebellious thoughts. She owed him this much—but telling him the truth was going to be the hardest thing she'd ever forced herself to do.

With a deep, shaking breath, she plunged in. "I'm not Joanne Kenning from Florida. My name is Jocelyn Parrish, and I'm from California," she said softly, pacing. "I…I'm not divorced." Her voice broke as she twisted her hands helplessly, unable to meet his eyes.

Jo could feel the tension in the room build, but Hawk said nothing, just waited for her to continue. When she chanced a look in his direction, he was leaning on one hand against the doorframe between the kitchen and dining room. His head was lowered and his face a mask, hard and uncompromising.

She could see his jaw clenching and unclenching.

Help me get through this, God, please!

Walking to the glass door that looked from Hawk's dining room onto the deck, Jo paused for a moment. The door was open. An early morning breeze wafted in through the screen. It smelled fresh and clean as it lifted a tendril or two of hair and caressed her hot face.

The world outside that screen seemed so calm and complacent—so beautiful. The grass was green now, and spring buds dotted trees with white and varying shades of pink and lavender. Lilac bloomed, and daffodils and tulips bobbed bright heads. It was a fairytale world—so close, and yet so far away. A magical kingdom just beyond her grasping fingertips, and here she was, trapped in a nightmare that seemed to have no ending!

Jo leaned her head against the screen. When she finally continued, she kept her eyes glued to a fixed object on the deck, knowing instinctively, that if she looked at Hawk again, she'd break down.

"My husband was abusive, excessively so, as you've already seen. I tried for years to work things out—to be what he wanted. There were times I thought we might make it, but they never lasted long. I finally had to leave," Jo finished on a whisper.

The room was quiet a long time before Hawk finally broke the silence. "*THE* Jocelyn Parrish?" He asked evenly, giving no indication of what thoughts moved behind his features. "The Jocelyn Parrish whose name has been in and out of newspapers over the past decade?"

"I…yeah," Jo was unable to find words to defend herself—what was there to say? She knew a chasm was opening between them, she could feel it in her bones.

Will I ever reach him again? Will he ever really trust me now?

If their roles suddenly reversed, she wasn't sure she'd want to reconcile. It took every bit of determination Jo had to stand there, when every instinct was screaming, 'RUN'!

"What in the hell were you *doing* here, Jo?" The dam broke.

she could feel the torrents of cold, frigid water crash through. Everything in the path of that raging flood was doomed for annihilation.

"What did you want from us?" There was raw pain in Hawk's voice. It cut through her heart like a razor sharp knife. She knew she was mortally wounded, knew there would be more blood than she'd ever be able to deal with, but right now she was numb—the real pain hadn't even started yet.

"I wanted to start over, to give my children a chance for a life that was safe and normal." Jo had no real defense, at least not one a man would understand.

"There are ways to go about that—*legal* ways. Most people don't just pick up and run." Hawk's voice rose as he turned to glare at her.

"I asked once—for a divorce, I mean. He refused." She paused, remembering Devin's contorted face, the pure rage that seized him. She believed she was going to die that night! She only vaguely remembered the beating now. He'd grabbed at anything he could use—a lamp, a golf club, a chair, a booted foot, and his fists. Jo shuddered as the images flashed through her mind.

Was it worth explaining that to Hawk? Would he—could he—fathom the hell she'd lived through, or understand the unreasoning terror? He would see the lawman's side—call the police, get a restraining order, file for divorce. Had she tried all those things, would her life have taken a different course—or would she be dead?

"So you ran?" Hawk asked, his voice harsh with the effort it cost him to control his reaction to her words. "What, wouldn't he cough up enough alimony to keep you comfortable? He wanted his kids?" There was blatant hostility laced through those words, bitter acrimony, and terrible anger!

"No," Jo whispered, turning back to the view from the screen. "I...didn't want...I," Jo's initial reaction to his words was an anguish she'd not known before, agony that tore at her heart. She could feel a psychical reaction to that rending. It made her want to double over and cry out.

"*What*, Jo? *WHAT*? How could you just leave? Why come here? Why the lies?"

Suddenly the emotional endorphins kicked in—Jo found relief in anger. "You know nothing!" she cried out. "You sit in your safe, easy world, and don't know a God-damned thing about real life—or real pain!" Jo turned around to face Hawk, leaning into her words, the rage carrying her and giving her momentum.

"What I do know, is that you're someone I don't know, Jo—or Jocelyn—or whatever you're calling yourself today. I know you're some big fuckin' psychic from Los Angeles who gets her kicks out of dabbling in police business, solving the unsolvable crime. I know you ran away from your husband, and kidnapped his children. I know you lied to me, and my family—never gave us a chance to understand or help. I know you've betrayed my trust in you. Anything else I need to know, Little Girl?" Hawk's question came out on a hiss of breath that sent a chill of bitter awareness down Jo's spine.

He hates me!

Even the vilest of criminals had the right to a fair trial.

The indignation set in then. He had no clue what she'd lived through—the beatings, the intimidation, the threats, and the all-consuming, ever-present fear. It had permeated her entire existence! She'd done what she had to do to survive, and she'd accept the consequences of her actions on that count. She had finally been compelled to act. Not for herself, but because she'd been terrified for her children's safety. No man on this earth would force her to cower and apologize for that decision. Not even Beau Hawkins!

"No, I think that about covers it," Jo said, her voice as cold and hard as his had been raging and passionate. She opened the screen door. It was time to end this conversation, but Jo turned for one parting comment. "I'll help you with your murder, if you want the help of a big fuckin' psychic."

Walking as normally as she could force her body to move, Jo headed down the deck stairs and across the lawn. There was no choice left now, she had to leave—and very, very soon.

~ ~ ~

"Carol?" Jo called softly from the kitchen doorway. It was early afternoon. The kids would be home from school soon.

"Yeah, come on in, Jo," Carol called from the bedroom.

Jo walked in and stood nervously by the kitchen counter.

"Get yourself some coffee and sit down," Carol grinned as she bustled into the room. She paused almost immediately as Jo's tenseness and demeanor registered. "What's wrong?"

"I'm…I'll be leaving, Carol, in a day or two," Jo said, unable to meet Carol's eyes.

"Sit down," Carol commanded, motioning to the kitchen table. "Tell me what's goin' on."

Following that directive, Jo slumped into a padded swivel chair wearily. "I have to…ah, I mean, I'm…damn!" Jo cleared her throat and started again, coming straight to the point. "My real name is Jocelyn Parrish," she said in a monotone voice. "I'm a married woman. My…husband…Devin Parrish," Jo nearly choked on the name, "is a prominent, powerful attorney in Los Angeles. He's also a violent man, as I've told you before—that wasn't a lie." She took a deep breath, and then continued. "I tried for years to make the marriage work, but it never did, so finally I just left—and ended up here."

"You told me once, you tried to ask for a divorce, but it didn't work?" Carol said, but there was no condemnation or anger in her voice.

Jo laughed at Carol's reminder. It was a cold, harsh, bitter sound. "Yeah, divorce. I spent two weeks in ICU when I asked for one." Jo covered her eyes with one hand. "He threatened the kids—and said he'd kill me if I even tried to leave him." Jo looked at Carol with sad, tormented eyes, "I believed him," she ended in a tortured whisper.

"But you left anyway?" Carol prompted.

"I would have stayed indefinitely, even with the abuse and adultery," Jo said, her voice changing from impassioned to coldly unemotional.

"So, what changed that?"

"I came home one day and found Devin beating Laney." Jo could hear Carol's inhalation of surprised shock, but she forged ahead, needing to finish quickly. "I nearly killed him. I...I lost it, and...attacked him. I had his head in my arms with every intention of snapping his neck. I would have, if Laney hadn't stopped me." Jo's voice was still detached, but her face reflected the horror she was describing, as if she were reliving it as she spoke.

"It scared me into action," she continued, "so I cleaned out every account we had, took a forged license a friend had given me months earlier, and left."

Jo got up and went to stand beside the opened door, leaning her head against the cool wood frame. Her eyes stared out at the beautiful spring day, but all she saw was her own inner anguish. "We kept moving," she continued, "constantly, one town, and then another. I traded in and bought half a dozen different vehicles. I just wanted to get lost, find an obscure, unlikely destination and make a new life for us."

"Good plan," Carol said gently after a long pause. "Jocelyn Parrish...that name is familiar."

"Jocelyn Parrish, Police Psychic?" Jo swallowed hard, hating the very sound of the words she'd seen in far too many headlines. "I was inadvertently drawn into a police investigation on a violent murder once. I get visions sometimes. I offered to help the police, and publicity followed," she sighed.

Carol just nodded as if a few wayward puzzle pieces slipped into their proper places. "So, why leave now, Jo? You've found your obscure, unlikely town."

"I'm having the visions again...I saw...I," Jo stumbled, unsure how to tell Carol.

"Hawk told me about the dream," the woman supplied.

Jo nodded. "And Jack knows. He confronted me the other day—wants to make a name for himself at my expense." Jo's tone was bitter, but she knew it was inevitable. The media would snatch this thing and run with it, one way or another.

"Jack's a good reporter and loves sniffing out a story, but he's not cruel, Jo. He wouldn't jeopardize your safety for a headline."

Jo met Carol's eyes for a moment, assessing those words. "No, probably not, but if it's not Jack, it'll be someone else. Things like...what I do, aren't easy to keep under wraps, and they generate a lot of curiosity and publicity."

Carol nodded understanding.

"As soon as it hits a newspaper anywhere, Devin will track us down. If it were just me I wouldn't care, but I have to protect my children—I have to!"

"Hawk is a cop, Jo. You're safe here."

Carol wasn't seeing the whole picture.

"You don't get it, Carol!" Jo was almost angry at the woman's lack of comprehension. "Devin has a reputation for eliminating problems—and I've become a big problem. He practically owns half the police force—and his family probably owns the other half. Hell, he even has his hands in state and local government. There's nowhere I can go that he can't reach, and there's no one I can turn to he can't hurt. If he finds me—I'm a dead woman. And if Hawk stands in his way—he'll end up in a body bag, too. I can't take that chance—I WON'T take that chance!" Jo's hand was at her forehead, rubbing at temples that were suddenly throbbing.

Moving to stand beside her, Carol put her arms around Jo's shoulders. "So, what are you planning?" she asked, her hand stroking the top of Jo's bent head.

Haunted eyes turned to meet Carol's unflinching gaze. "I told Hawk I'd help him—if he wants me to. I'll go to the murder scene and try to sense whatever I can. Then we have to get lost again." Jo extricated herself from Carol's embrace and walked back to stare out the screen door. "Hawk hates me, Carol. I've hurt him so much," the words were a grief-stricken whisper.

"Did you explain?" Carol sounded surprised Hawk would react that way. "Male pride is always a factor to be dealt with, but Hawk is a compassionate, empathetic man, and he loves you desperately."

Jo felt a heart-rending pang at those words, but she forcefully pushed them from her head. It was over! Hawk didn't love her now. He felt betrayed, and rightfully so.

"He really didn't want an explanation. He'd come up with his own," she said in a tired voice. "I let him have that. The anger will carry him through the…harder times ahead."

Carol said nothing, but she looked as if her mind were racing a million miles an hour. There was definitely an *oh he DID, did he*, look on her face.

XXIV

Jo could see the shape of a man—a big man. He moved through the darkness with deadly purpose. The woman was completely unaware he was anywhere close to her. She stumbled toward her car, laughing and giggling as a second man, close to her, whispered something erotic. Jo could see a small tavern behind the couple—Lucky's Bar. She had no idea what that was, or where.

The dark man watched—and waited. Jo could feel the waiting. There was determination behind the menace. Purpose-driven loathing. She could feel it emanate from him an intense, overwhelming hatred for the woman—for *all* women. They were powerful, too powerful. They used men. HE would never be used, though. He did the using now, and he could dominate and control any woman he wanted to.

And the pain! He loved the pain they suffered. It made him hard, aroused, and ready to impale them on his sword of justice. Jo could feel his thoughts and emotions as though they were her own, and it made her ill, sick to her stomach. She wanted to scream her protest, but she didn't exist in this place.

Run! Hurry! She heard her own voice, but she was the only one who did. The man and woman were parting. They were kissing, feeling one another's bodies, making promises of where they'd meet, and what they'd do to each other.

The dark shape watched—and fantasized—and waited.

~ ~ ~

Jo came awake with a cry, sitting up in bed. The aftermath of the dream haunted her. She could feel the malevolence and peril as if it permeated the very room.

Oh, No! Her hand was at her throat and she was swallowing hard, trying to keep the bile down. Think! She commanded her brain. Think. Think. Think! Where? When? Who? What should I do? I have to stop him.

Jo glanced at the bedside clock, 4:20 AM—it's over. Whatever she'd seen had already happened—she suddenly knew that with a certainty that made her stomach lurch. Jumping from her bed, she raced to the open French door and pushed aside the screen. She barely made the edge of the grass before her stomach began heaving what little she'd managed to consume at supper that night. Her sobs mingled with the sounds of retching.

Dead. She's dead! That poor girl—just like the other one.

Hawk wouldn't need to describe the crime scene. It would be eerily familiar—a tortured body dumped on a remote roadside. Ankles and wrists would show rope burns, and the body would be bruised and cut—the dark shadow loved the torture best. He needed the pain of his victims as much as others needed oxygen. He would carve his signature: R-I-P. It described what he was doing—his mission.

Eventually he'd rape her, hard and fast, tearing the vagina with a metallic covering he strapped to himself. The girl would scream, begging and pleading—but he wouldn't stop, not for a long time. When he did, his victim would be near death. And the blood—so much blood! He would kneel at her head and casually snap her neck between his two huge hands.

Jo put a trembling hand over her eyes, trying to shut out the images. "Oh God, I don't want to KNOW this. I don't want to SEE this. Please!"

"Another dream?" The words came out of the shadows beside her.

Screaming, Jo lashed out with a sidekick. She caught him hard in the upper thigh, and heard a muffled curse as the man staggered backwards. Almost immediately, she propelled herself in the opposite direction.

"For the love of God, Jo, it's me." Hawk swore under his breath as he picked up a small wooden table he'd upended.

"You...I...*you son-of-a-bitch*!" Jo was furious. Her mind was still wrapped around the nightmare, and he'd damn near walked out of it!

"Sorry." Hawk seemed to realize his indiscretion. "I was awake sitting on my deck with a cup of coffee, when you came barreling out of your room and puked your guts out."

Jo glared at him for several moments, breathing hard and trying to still her thundering heart. Unexpectedly she crumpled to the ground, her face in her hands.

~ ~ ~

"God, Jo." Hawk was instantly beside her, lifting her into his arms and holding her close. "I'm so sorry." He couldn't stay mad, though he was struggling to maintain some aloofness—some dignity.

"It...he...another girl is dead." Jo stumbled over the words, not sure what Hawk's reaction would be.

He held her at arms length, his grasp on her shoulders hard and demanding. "What are you talking about?" he said, his voice deceptively soft. The words sent a cold chill through him, suddenly reminding him that this woman was no longer Joanne Kenning. She was Jocelyn Parrish—a married woman. A fugitive wanted for kidnapping and theft. A stranger!

"Your killer…he's struck again." Jo's voice was a hoarse whisper as her liquid gray eyes met Hawk's cold, dark gaze.

~ ~ ~

"What do you mean you don't know?" Hawk demanded brutally. The young man sitting at the table across from him cringed at the venom in his tone.

"*Man*, I didn't do nothin'! We just met. I bought her a couple drinks and we were…leavin'." The young man stumbled over the words, obviously not sure how much to say and how much to leave unsaid.

"What, she wouldn't put out, Jake? That it? Decided to get even, didn't you?"

"No, Dude! She said she'd meet me at the—" the boy stopped abruptly, unsure if he'd be digging himself in deeper by admitting they'd planned to get it on at a nearby motel.

"A little roll in the hay, Jake? At the Roadside Inn?" It was the closest motel. Hawk made a logical guess that brought a look of surprise to Jake Kramer's face.

"She never showed. *Really*," Jake whined.

"I think you're lyin' through your teeth, so how 'bout this one, Jake." Hawk said, dropping his hands onto the table close to the kid, and leaning into his face. "She showed. You got rough. She balked. You got mad. She tried to run. You tortured and raped her!" Hawk's voice was a hiss of accusation, his expression cold and frightening.

"Noooo! No, man, I swear. You *gotta* believe me!" Jake was hysterical, obviously terrified to death.

"No, Jake, I don't *gotta*," Hawk said very softly, an undertone of deadly intent lacing every word.

"Hawk!" Pete stepped into the room. Jerking his head toward the door, he motioned Hawk to join him outside the tiny meeting room they were using to interrogate Jake Kramer.

"The boy's attorney is here." Pete nodded to a middle-aged, stocky woman sitting at his desk.

"Judas, Pete." Hawk shook his head from side to side, rubbing the bridge of his nose. "I believe the bastard." He was exhausted, dead on his feet. We have nothing, he thought with a weariness that permeated his very bones.

"Every damn lead's as cold as a whore's tits!" Hawk growled.

"Looks that way, Buddy. The kid's alibi checks out. He went back to his apartment and watched some porno flicks with his roommates until three that morning. 'Sides, he wasn't anywhere near the other two victims. Solid alibis there as well."

"Son-of-a-bitch," Hawk snapped. "We back to square one?"

Pete nodded despondently. "I'll tell him the good news," he volunteered. "You'd better go home and take a couple sleeping pills. When was the last time you got any?"

"Too damned long!" Hawk snapped.

"I was talkin' about sleep, Hawk, not ass."

"Pete?" Hawk growled.

"Yeah?" Pete replied, grinning from ear to ear.

"Shut the fuck up!"

~ ~ ~

"Will you agree to go to the scene? Do your...*thing*?" Hawk's tone was remote and cold.

Jo knew he worked at keeping his anger stoked against her—and maybe he should. He had to be hurting, at least as badly as she was, and what hope was there? None. Not only was she a fugitive, but she was also a married woman! It was better, all the way around, for Hawk to stay harsh and angry.

Huddled in a huge chair in his office, Jo hoped she didn't look as fragile as she felt. She knew she was very near her own psychical and emotional breaking point—with no relief in sight. Hawk stood leaning against a wall on the other side of the room, as though he were trying to stay as far from her as possible. Pete sat propped on the desk beside her, a curiously evaluative expression on his face.

"Not now," Jo protested.

I need time, she thought with mild panic. Jack was remorselessly dogging her steps: '*Was it true? Another vision? Had she seen the killer's face? What could she tell him? Who was this mystery victim?*' She knew the evening paper would break the story.

It would take Devin less than twenty-four hours to locate her. Jo knew she had to get her children to some semblance of safety first, then she would help these men track their killer.

"When would be a convenient time for you, Mrs. Parrish?" Hawk's words oozed bitter sarcasm. Jo didn't look up. She kept her eyes on her hands. Her jaw worked hard, clenching and unclenching, to control the retort on the tip of her tongue.

"Give me a few hours," she said in a surprisingly even tone of voice.

It was nearly 1:30 PM. Hawk rushed her down here as soon as she'd showered and gotten the kids off to school, and Pete met them at the door. It had been a grueling morning, but they'd been able to pinpoint the bar Jo had seen in her dream. It took a little while, but searchers managed to find the mutilated body. Jo was aware they'd already pulled in the boyfriend for questioning. Now it was her turn.

"A few hours? Hell, why worry about a dead girl and a lunatic killer." Hawk's tone was vicious and unrelenting. "We'll just put all that on hold while you rush home to make plans to skip town, shall we?"

Jo knew he was fueling his anger at her expense, keeping his heart hard and angry so he'd be able to see this thing through to the end. Still, understanding the motivation didn't lessen the pain she felt at his bitterly sarcastic words. She didn't trust herself with a retort, so she looked away, saying nothing.

"Let's go over the details again," Pete said on a sigh of weariness. Standing, he moved behind Jo. She didn't bother to watch him. She'd given the man everything she could remember over the past hour and a half. "Describe this woman," he ordered.

Jo didn't argue, she just closed her eyes and remembered—again! "Young, twenty-one or two. Slender, maybe my height. Blonde hair, long, almost to her waist."

"What was she wearing, Mrs. Parrish?" Pete prodded.

Jo shuddered at the use of her married title. Even the sound of the name sent a chill of dread down her spine. "Jo, please," she insisted.

"Okay then, Jo. What was our vic wearing?" Pete asked again.

Jo sat in stunned silence for a moment, unable to believe what she'd just heard. "Vic?" she said at last. "VIC?" Her tone was incredulous. She turned and glared at Pete Flanders. "Is she just a piece of meat to you? She was a beautiful young woman—someone's daughter. And she was brutally murdered!" Jo was almost screaming.

She felt Hawk's hand on her shoulder, but knocked it away hard, and then lurched out of the chair.

"What the hell difference does it make what she was wearing?" she challenged, fury giving her strength. "You won't find her clothes! Your VIC was naked when you found her, wasn't she? Or did she still have her shoes on, denim clogs?

"She'll have knife wounds running up and down her thighs and arms and across her abdomen, and cigarette burns, too. He loves that part!" Jo leaned into her tirade, her face and posture aggressive. All the uncertainty, fear, and anguish seemed to find vent in righteous anger, directed at Pete for a simple slip of the tongue.

"Your VIC," she continued, "will have been raped. The guy wore some metal covering on his penis that had spikes, or barbed wire, or something like that. Nice touch, don't you think? He wanted her to feel him slide inside her—to beg for release. And she did. She screamed and pleaded, but he just laughed. It made him hard—turned him on. You gettin' *turned on*, Pete?" Jo leaned forward, spitting the words at both men, her arms wrapped around herself as if she were freezing, though the temperature in the room was warm enough to make sweat bead on her forehead and upper lip.

"Jo," Hawk took a step toward her.

"NO!" She shouted at him, holding up a restraining hand. "No, I'll tell you what you want to hear, and I'll go to your damn crime scene, too. You can use me however you want—but I'm gettin' my kids outta here first."

"We can't let you do that, Jo. There are criminal charges against you for kidnapping and—"Pete tried to explain.

Jo interrupted his objection. "No shit, Sherlock!" she hissed at him. "If I don't get my kids to safety, you don't get my help." She didn't look at Hawk, but she was aware he stood with his hands shoved deep in his pockets, an expression of torn loyalties on his face.

"You're really not in a position to bargain here, Mrs. Parrish," Pete pressed, his face and voice remaining conversationally calm. "We have the authority to keep you here indefinitely."

"You and what fuckin' army?" Jo's voice had dropped to a deadly cold monotone. With clear intent, she started walking to the door.

~ ~ ~

Pete stepped into her path, reaching an arm across the doorjamb to block her exit.

Jo reacted with a quickness that surprised even Hawk, who'd been expecting something.

Her right hand flew out to grasp Pete's wrist, yanking him toward her as she slammed a hammer fist into his groin. Almost instantaneously she grabbed the back of his shirt, yanking his body toward the impact as her knee came up, slamming into vulnerable ribs. Her hand moved in a lightening quick palm heel toward Pete's face. If she'd finished the maneuver, she'd have smashed his nose, followed through with an elbow, and raked the eyes on the return stroke.

Hawk managed to grab her wrist and stop the strike, barely in time. He pulled her hard from behind, slamming her against him, with her back pressed to his chest and his arms encircling her.

Pete crumpled to the ground holding his side, and gasping for breath.

Without even a moment's thought, Jo slammed her elbow into Hawk's ribs. Dropping into a horse stance, she brought her heel down with intemperate force on the top of his foot, and in one fluid motion, her clenched fist came down in a brutal hammerfist strike, catching Hawk in the groin. Grasping his arm, Jo propelled him over her shoulder, slamming him to the ground with enough force to drive the wind from his lungs.

She didn't wait for the men to come to their senses and agree to her request. In less time than it takes to draw breath, she snatched up her purse, leaped over the prone bodies, and escaped out the door.

Hawk groaned, rolling to his hands and knees, breathing in deeply.

"You gonna…put out…the…A.P.B. or…am I?" Pete gasped as he pushed himself to his feet, struggling for breath.

"Neither." Hawk laughed weakly, his hand to his crotch as he, too, regained his feet. "Damn, she's got…a hell-of-a-wallop, don't she?" He took some deep breaths, trying to ease the fire that was cramping his groin.

Pete scowled. "Shit, Hawk, she's a fugitive," he pointed out caustically.

"She'll keep her promise," Hawk said with confidence. "She'll be back to help with the case."

Pete was obviously seething, though he managed to keep his voice level. "Yeah? Your little Miss Bruce Lee just clobbered two cops, and made a clean get away. Why the hell come back?"

"I know Jo," Hawk said firmly. "She'll keep her word." His tone implied that further argument was useless.

Pete made his way to one of the padded chairs and sat down heavily. "Yeah, right!" he snapped. "You know Joanne Kenning. OH! *Excuuuuse me*, I meant Jocelyn Parrish."

"Pete?" Hawk growled.

"Yeah, Buddy?"

"Shut the fuck up!"

XXV

"Jo, wait!" Carol's words stopped her in her tracks. "Let's talk."

Jo had just jumped out of her vehicle, headed toward the house. She only needed a few necessities—she'd grab them, get the kids from school, and be long gone before Hawk could rally the troops.

"Not now, Carol," Jo put her off.

Carol stepped into her path, "Right now, Honey," she said. "Hawk just called."

Jo froze, waiting. "And?" she asked warily.

"He told me to help you get your kids somewhere safe."

Shocked, Jo said, "He…he did?"

Carol nodded.

Jo's heart swelled, loving Hawk more than she'd ever thought possible, but the sentiment only lasted a moment. Then reality set in. She knew Devin would find her—and very soon. She also knew exactly what he was capable of doing. He'd think nothing of hurting Carol and her family if he thought they knew anything.

"No, Carol," she said stoically, "you can't. You don't know Devin. He's not above hurting you, or Hawk, or your grandkids, to get the information he wants. You can't help—you can't know where we are."

"You're underestimating my family, Jo." Carol replied.

Jo shook her head as she watched a car pull into the driveway, a look of panic distorting her features.

"It's just Bert and B.J.," Carol assured her. "They'll help."

"No!" Jo felt panic rise in her stomach. She knew Devin. His thugs would beat it out of them, or burn their homes, or both! She knew it could happen —had happened—to other people. Sticking her head in the sand and telling herself repeatedly, that it couldn't be true, hadn't made the atrocities Devin was involved with, any less appalling. These people just had no frame of reference on this. Jo knew she couldn't allow them to become involved. She'd already upended their lives enough.

"Go home," she called to Hawk's brothers. "Stay out of this." Turning to Carol, Jo pleaded, "Carol, I'm so sorry you're involved. I never meant anyone to be drawn into my life like this, but you don't understand. Devin is a cold and ruthless man. He's tortured, swindled, terrorized, and killed! He does whatever he has to do, to get what he wants. I can't let you folks put yourselves in his path." Jo was speaking as much to B.J. and Bert as she was to Carol.

"Family covers each other's back, Jo." B.J. grinned at her, winking.

"You're not my family!" she snapped, frustration and panic making her tone harsher than she'd intended. She tried to explain, scaling her voice to a controlled, even level. "My brother tried to step in once. Devin had him beaten so severely, he nearly died." She was crying now, remembering. He'd nearly died—trying to help her. She couldn't risk that again!

"Jo—"Carol began.

"Please," Jo cut her off. "I've done enough damage here, don't make it worse."

"We're not afraid of your husband, Jo," B.J. growled.

"Neither was Mark, till Devin's thugs broke his legs and smashed in his face with a tire iron!" Jo's fear was channeling itself into anger now. She had to make them understand, one way or another.

"Give it up, Jo," Bert said gently. We aren't backin' down, and you are not leavin' here with those kids, to fend all alone again. It just ain't happenin', Girl."

Jo shook her head with exasperation, watching with impotent helplessness as a second car pulled into the driveway. Father Pat got out and walked toward her.

"Please," Jo turned to look at each of them in turn, her eyes and voice beseeching, "please don't. Don't get involved any deeper. Just let me go, we'll be okay. I'm not your concern—not part of your family." She had to try—one more time.

"Maybe not," Bert said gently, wrapping an arm around her shoulders and pulling her against him, "but close enough, Honey."

"Jo." Father Pat greeted her warmly.

"What...what's going on?" she asked, her voice shaking.

"Carol talked to me last night, Jo." Father Pat said gently, leading her inside the cottage. "She explained the situation. I suggested your children would be safe at the retreat house in Geneva, and Carol agreed."

Bert continued when Father Pat paused. "B.J.'s gonna drive Mom and your children there tomorrow morning."

Jo looked up at Bert, her eyes wide with wonder. "Why? Why are you helping me?" she asked, putting her thoughts into words. Why indeed? She'd lied to them, deceived them, and put them in harm's way. They owed her nothing.

"Hawk promised me you'd finish your towel dance if I helped." Bert shrugged. "I'm a sucker for a good-looking woman in a towel. Ask Sarah! That's what she was wearin' the night Faith was conceived."

"Bertram Jacob!" Carol snapped.

Bert had the decency to blush, but the grin he flashed Jo was unrepentant.

~ ~ ~

"Did you ask her any questions? Do you know why she finally ran?" Carol demanded.

Hawk looked at his mother over the breakfast plate in front of him. She'd fixed fried eggs, ham, and homemade biscuits—a particular favorite of his—but Hawk hadn't been able to dredge up a desire for food lately. B.J. and Bert, however, were making up for his lack of appetite. They were already on their second plate.

An unreasoning flash of irritation surged through Hawk, at his mother's words and tone. What could Jo possibly say, that would change what she'd done? "She took his kids and his money, and split. What else do I need to know?"

Carol began slamming pots and pans into cupboards, madder than a wet hen. When she finally turned to face him, she stood with fisted hands on her hips and a look of fury on her face. "She found him beating Laney with a belt, Tough Guy. Did you know THAT?"

Hawk felt the blood drain from his face, followed almost immediately by a rage so potent, it literally made his stomach pitch. Both Bert and B.J.'s faces registered shock and horror, but Hawk was certain that whatever they were feeling couldn't hold a candle to the fury slicing through him. He pushed his chair away from the table and walked to the door, staring blindly, his fists clenching and unclenching.

"That son-of-a-bitch better not show up 'round here," B.J. growled.

"He's lucky she didn't kill him before she took off," Bert interjected.

Hawk turned to look at his brothers, finally understanding the comment Jo made once, about her fear of losing control of the rage in the moment, and killing her husband. Hawk knew, with a certainty that left him shaking inside, that if he'd been there Jo's husband would be dead right now.

Carol's expression changed suddenly from anger to grief. "She said she nearly did. Laney had to pull her off," she whispered, her eyes filling with tears.

"Well, I can *definitely* see *that*," Hawk said, his expression hard and grim.

"So, why not pursue a divorce, Ma? There's legal ways to handle scum like that."

Carol's features hardened—the anger was back. "Because he put her in ICU for two weeks the first time she asked, and threatened her and the kids if she ever left him, Mr. *I Got All the Answers*! She was too damned afraid to risk it again."

"Judas Priest!" Bert exclaimed, looking as if he might lose his breakfast. "Two weeks in intensive care? What the hell did he do to her?"

Hawk closed his eyes, remembering Jo's back and realizing it had probably been a small thing compared to what she'd lived through with that bastard.

"I didn't ask," Carol responded, moving to the sink and washing dishes with a little more aggression than they probably deserved. "She believed her husband when he said he'd hunt her down and kill her if she left, so she stayed."

B.J.'s face was dark with leashed fury, his jaw clenching and unclenching. "Until he got off on beatin' Laney," he hissed.

Carol turned and met Hawk's eyes as she replied. "Yeah, that's what finally made her leave." One hand came up to cover her mouth as tears filled her eyes again.

Bert went to his mother, pulling her into a strong embrace. "It's okay, Ma," he soothed. "We'll make sure she's safe now."

"I just can't even imagine what that girl has lived with—so many years of pain…and fear," Carol said on a sob.

"She's got family, and what about the police, Mom? Why didn't she get help? Lock that bastard up?" Hawk fumed.

"She told me her husband is wealthy and powerful, and has his hand in government and law enforcement alike. It sounded as if he's into some pretty nasty stuff. She mentioned hired guns, and a reputation for eliminating problems and people that got in his way." Carol answered Hawk's questions, her voice suddenly sounding tired and drained. "Jo was even afraid for us, Hawk. She didn't want us mixed up in this. She's afraid we might get hurt."

"She said her brother tried to help once," B.J. interjected.

Bert nodded. "Evidently, her husband had some hired thugs beat the shit outta him with a tire iron. I guess he almost died."

"You think that bastard will come after her?" B.J. asked. "Here?" He sounded as if he almost hoped the man would try it.

Carol nodded. "She's certain he'll come, and she believes he'll kill her. She told me he sees defiance as a challenge to his power and reputation. He'll want to make an example of her." Carol shook her head. "She should be goin' with us into hiding, not stayin' here to help you with that murder!" She glared up at Hawk.

"She's a wanted fugitive. If I let her go, I'm breakin' the fuckin' law," Hawk snarled, torn between his need to protect Jo, and his duty.

"Well," Bert said softly, "I'd say you hit it smack dab on the head, Big Bro."

"What're you talkin' about?" Hawk snapped.

"It IS the fuckin' law, if you turn her in. You'll be handin' her over to that bastard, Hawk." Bert's eyes narrowed as he continued. "You might as well beat the shit outta her yourself, and save him the trouble."

Hawk's scowl deepened. Turning to Carol he asked, "When are you guys leavin'?"

Carol drew a deep breath, letting it out on a sigh. "This morning, about eight. Father Pat'll be here soon. Jo's getting the kids ready to go."

Hawk nodded, feeling as if his insides were shredded and raw. He was almost too numb to feel anything else.

"It's gonna kill her, seein' those kids of hers leave without her," Bert commented, his voice and expression pensive.

"It's the best chance of protectin' them," Hawk said stoically. "She'll deal with it." His face was dark with suppressed frustration. He wanted to stay angry—needed the anger to help him through this.

Carol looked at her son, her eyes tear-filled, but her voice hard and cold. "Yes, she'll deal with it, Hawk. It'll tear her heart out, but she'll deal with it. That woman's got more strength and courage than most people I know. I just hope to God, that she's wrong about her husband being able to find her, 'cause if she's not..." her words trailed off, the implied consequence of Jo remaining behind, left unsaid.

"I need to hit somethin'," B.J. growled, standing and pacing like a caged bull. He looked as if he wanted to put his fist through the wall—or somebody's face.

Hawk didn't say anything, but he was feeling the same urge, so intensely it was a physical pain.

~ ~ ~

"He takes them to his place," Jo said, her voice hushed and ragged with strain as she moved around the ground where they'd found the latest victim. She wasn't sure what she was seeing in her mind's eye—an older style farm home, a wooden structure of some sort. She tried to describe it.

"That's where the torture and rape occurs?" Hawk asked.

Jo nodded.

"How close?" Pete asked, keeping his distance from her.

"Close enough." She closed her eyes, trying to see more. "He lives... relatively close to all the murder sites. He's from this area of Nebraska."

"Who is HE?" Hawk asked, hoping against hope Jo had some insight to offer.

"HE is a serial rapist," Jo said with assurance.

"Well, that's beginning to be quite evident," Bev Skinner said, a little sarcastically. It was obvious she'd never held much stock in psychics, especially those that involved themselves in police work. Glory seeker. Attention monger. That's all you psychos are. Jo could almost read the woman's thoughts on her face.

"There are different kinds of serial rapists," Bev's tone held a biting edge to it.

Jo knew the policewoman was challenging her—testing her. It didn't matter. They would either believe her—or reject what she had to offer. It was that simple.

"He's a classic example of anger-excitation, a sexual sadist," Jo said calmly, meeting Bev's eyes. She wasn't sure she liked this woman, with her tall, lanky form and caustic tongue. She looked awkward in the uniform she was wearing, and her short, cropped hair was too masculine a style for the angularity of her face. Bev's temperament and demeanor were angular too—full of sharp turns and rough edges.

"Only about seven to ten percent of sexual crimes fall into that category," Pete commented. "What makes you think you've got this one pegged, Jo?"

"I just know," Jo, replied, unperturbed by the negativism she felt from these law enforcement officials. She'd dealt with it before. "Look at the facts," she continued. "*Listen* to what I'm telling you about him. This isn't about sex. It's about power. He enjoys their pain. He needs to be in control. There is no conscience, and no remorse with this man. You're lookin' for someone who's probably white, mid-twenties to mid-thirties. He's educated and probably looks like a regular Joe, with a higher than average intelligence."

"How do you know that?" Bev challenged.

"That's the standard statistics for a serial rapist. Nine out of ten will fall into that category." Jo's voice sounded bone-weary, even to her own ears.

Bev's expression was confrontational, at the very least. "That's right, you've done this a few times haven't you, Mrs. Parrish?" she snapped cynically. "Got all the stats down, do ya?"

She didn't bother acknowledging Bev's comments. It didn't matter whether they believed her or not—they could use what she gave them or discard it and fly on their own. Yet somehow, Jo knew they'd never crack this one, without the kind of help she could provide. The more she worked with the case—the more in-tune she'd become with the killer. The closer she got—the more she could give them.

Jo shuddered, remembering other killers—other cases—other visions. She wasn't sure she was strong enough to sink that deeply into another killer's psyche, and then her conscience kicked in.

Okay, give it one more try.

She forced herself to push onward as a sudden vision of Brandi Cambridge's face formed in her head. No one should have to die the way she did—no one!

"He has all the classic signs," Jo continued. "He relates to people in terms of power. He's callous, without remorse or empathy. The pain is his ticket—he gets off on it. He rehearses every detail and masturbates while he fantasizes about it. He has a mission." Jo turned to watch Pete intently as she spoke. "He's cleansing the world, ridding it of the evil of women, eliminating all the bitches, whores, and sluts that contaminate it."

"Sounds like a sadist to me," Pete agreed, shaking his head at the mutilated body of one of the victims, captured forever in the photograph he was holding.

"Sexual sadism?" Hawk looked as though he could be ill. "Yeah, I'm afraid I'm buyin' it. This asshole sounds like a real winner."

"He's a winner all right," Pete ground out. He was looking slightly sick himself. Things like this just didn't happen around this part of the country. When they did—it left everyone feeling exposed and vulnerable.

"Well, if it *is* a sadist, we'll have our hands full," Bev said matter-of-factly. "It's the great white shark of sexual crimes, and it could get a lot uglier before it's all over with."

Her words made Jo shudder inwardly. A great white shark indeed, she thought. The image those words conjured up in her mind seemed all too appropriate. They were hunting a premier predator—and gut instincts warned her, he was toying with them.

~ ~ ~

Jo sat stiffly in the passenger seat of Hawk's pickup, too tired and heartsick to care if they ever exchanged a civil word again. Sighing wearily to herself, she stared blindly out the window at the passing countryside. It was close to dusk now, but Jo knew the night would bring little relief. Unless she consumed several potent pills, there was no way she'd be able to sleep.

It had been a long day—a tortuous couple of days to be exact. Spending the day at the crime scenes and answering question after hostile question, had taken a toll, but it couldn't even come close to the anguish that still burned in her heart from the events of the morning.

Closing her eyes, Jo found herself remembering how Jenny had clung to her, sobbing and begging her to come with them. And she vividly remembered the moment when Carol and Father Pat had left with her children. The mere recollection tore a stifled sob from her lungs. The back of one hand came up instinctively to cover her mouth.

"You okay?" Hawk looked over at her.

Jo nodded, not bothering to look at him. She kept her face pressed to the cold glass of the window, and her eyes on the landscape. Hawk hadn't been there—he hadn't seen that parting—hadn't said good-bye to Jenny. Somehow, *that*, more than anything else he'd said or done, told Jo just how angry he was with her, and just how much she'd hurt him.

It was probably better Hawk didn't shown up, Jo assured herself. If he'd been there she'd have thrown herself into his arms and cried her heart out—and she'd hate herself even more right now. Still, even that awareness didn't mitigate the hurt, or soothe the ache in her heart.

"Jo…I," Hawk started to say.

Jo put up her hand in a mute plea for him to stop. "No, Hawk, not now. I can't handle any more." Her voice was cold and dead—it sounded as lifeless as she felt inside.

Whatever Hawk had to say, could wait. She'd tried to talk to him, but he'd met every attempt with barely suppressed hostility. Jo knew what she'd done was wrong, but she also knew Hawk hadn't given her even half a chance to explain. He'd reacted with disgust and anger, shutting her out. All that talk of trust and love—it was all just lip service until things got rough. That's when real love came through—but Hawk hadn't come through, he'd turned away from her.

It didn't matter anymore. It was over. Jo dashed at a tear that slipped down her cheek. Her kids were safe now—as safe as she could make them. That was the only thing that carried any significance for her. She'd help Hawk and the police—and then face the consequences for running. Devin would have her—but he'd never get his hands on her children. Never!

Jo sighed as her mind slipped back to the events of the afternoon. Oddly enough, Hawk hadn't seemed quite as standoffish toward her today, but tensions between them were still high—possibly insurmountable. He'd been pleasant enough, but it was an aloof cordiality, one reserved for strangers.

Spending the day at the sight where they'd found Brandi Cambridge's body had been grueling for Jo. She hadn't given the police much to go on—not yet, but it would come. She knew that from experience. The images that were flashing through her head right now were disjointed—a screaming mouth, a bloody knife, a fist wrapping itself in a woman's long, blonde hair.

Closing her eyes, Jo tried to blot those pictures from her mind. Sometimes she truly hated her gift—she hated the dreams, the images, and the horror of it all—but at other times, she knew what she had to offer was important. The authorities had a chance with her help, a chance to rid the world of one more piece of garbage. With any luck, no other little girl would have to suffer what Brandi Cambridge had suffered!

Hawk pulled up in front of the barn, not bothering to turn off his engine. "I've got to meet my brothers at Bert's place, I'll see you later," he said stoically.

"Yeah." It wasn't the most intelligent response, but it was all Jo could think of to say.

~ ~ ~

"I'm sorry, Jo, this has been rough," Hawk said, unsure what thoughts he wanted to verbalize—what he should say.

Watching her as she'd helped them these past couple of days, had been hard. He'd tried to be angry—to hate—but it wasn't in him. All he'd really wanted to do was take her in his arms, love away the hurt and pain on her face—in her eyes.

He watched now, as her hands nervously smoothed out the skirt of her striped, knit sundress. She was only holding on by a thread, Hawk knew that. She couldn't take much more, but then again, neither could any of them. This case had the potential to rip out the heart, suck it dry, and then shred it to pieces.

"Life's rough," Jo snapped out the retort, and then got out. She headed toward the cottage without a second glance his way.

Hawk had to fight an urge to call her back, to iron things out, to tell her he'd talked to Carol that morning and received a well-deserved ass chewing. He knew why she'd been driven to the choices she'd made—but they were both too exhausted to have any kind of rational conversation at this moment. He let her go. There was strength in anger, and right now, she needed that.

As he backed out of the driveway and turned toward Bert's place, Hawk wondered how he'd ever reach her—how he'd win her heart back. She had withdrawn from him—from everything. It was as if she'd stopped living, stopped feeling, and stopped caring. Would she ever trust him again? Could he reach her behind the defensive walls she'd erected? He wasn't sure, but he'd try—tomorrow. There was time enough for apologies and making up—tomorrow.

XXVI

Jo sensed something was wrong the minute she entered the house, but exhaustion and preoccupation with the emotional turmoil of the past two days, dulled her reflexes. She was too slow to react when the attack came.

Muscled arms slid around her neck and waist in the same instant she saw a second man pointing a Magnum at her head. As her eyes adjusted to the dusky light in the living room, she noticed Devin sitting calmly on her couch, drinking a beer he'd obviously pilfered from her refrigerator.

"Hello, Sweetheart," he said calmly. "Long time no see."

"Not long enough," Jo rejoined. Her reward was a painful tightening of the arm around her throat.

"Be nice," the man holding her hissed in her ear. She could feel the hand around her waist groping her body. "Just checkin' to see if you're holdin'," he laughed maliciously.

"Since when do you check bras for weapons?" Jo snapped.

"Since now," he reached for her breast again, squeezing painfully. Jo instinctively struggled, and then fell still as the second man moved his revolver closer to her face.

"Vince is right, Jo. You need to learn to be a little nicer," Devin said, standing and moving toward her. Jo watched her husband with cold dread, trying to keep her expression neutral.

Devin was tall and well built, though more wiry than bulky. He wore his long, dark brown hair, slicked back away from his face and tied at the nape of his neck. Straight, thick, black brows met at the bridge of his nose, practically hiding pale, icy blue eyes. High cheekbones, and a straight, aristocratic nose, complimented a thin, delicately carved mouth. He'd grown a goatee since she'd last seen him. Somehow, it seemed to suit him.

The blow took Jo by surprise.

Devin's hand flashed out, backhanding her across the face and mouth. She felt the sting, and then tasted blood. Without thought, she tried to retaliate, struggling in Vince's grip as anger surged through her.

"*Wild* thing, you make my *heart* sing," Vince murmured close to her ear, perfectly imitating the song lyric. He growled low in his throat, and his tongue left a warm, wet trail around her earlobe. "You this crazy in bed?"

"She can be," Devin grinned wickedly, winking at Jo. "I warned you once, Jocey. You don't listen too good, do you?" His even, conversational tone was almost as chilling as the feral look in his pale eyes. Jo glanced around the room trying to assess her chances of escape. Devin had five other men with him, not counting Vince or the man with the gun. She'd never get past them all.

Suddenly, another blow slammed across her face, followed by one to the stomach. Jo buckled, doubling over and gasping for air. Before she could even draw breath, Vince grabbed her, dragging her toward the kitchen table. A third man snatched her wrists and wrapped a cord around them, then pulled her down hard, slamming the small of her back into the table's edge. Vince stood behind her, his crotch pressed against her backside.

Jo's frantic struggles drew sniggers and laughs from Devin's men, but gained her little else. She gasped as the tension on her wrists suddenly increased, cutting off circulation, and slicing into her flesh.

"We're gonna get some play time, *Wild* Thing," Vince purred, leaning across her body to whisper the words in her ear. "All of us."

The men guffawed and made lewd comments at Jo's sudden reaction. Panic seized her—God Almighty, she believed the man! She fought with panic-driven energy, screaming and kicking, only going still when the gunman set the barrel of his weapon against her temple.

"Don't make Carl mad, Joecy. He's got an itchy trigger finger," Devin teased.

Out of the corner of her eye, Jo saw Devin give Vince a signal. Almost immediately she felt the bindings on her wrists yanked hard, and cried out as the unforgiving table edge slammed against her backbone again.

"If I remember right, Joecy, you always loved the foreplay best," Devin leered, leaning over her and pulling her knit sundress over her head. He worked it up her arms until it twisted around her already pinned wrists. A switchblade flashed open in his hand, and he cut her bra up the middle, leaving a long scratch that oozed red. Devin's free hand closed painfully around one full breast, and he bent his mouth to the other, his teeth breaking the flesh around her nipple.

Jo screamed, unable to hold it back.

"Where are my kids?" Devin asked, his voice a cold, emotionless monotone close to her ear.

"Go to hell!" Jo ground out between clenched teeth. She gasped as the rope yanked again.

"Tsk, tsk." The sounds were so casual, so conversational. Devin looked as though they were having a pleasant, Sunday afternoon get together. "I've told my friends here," he motioned to the men around him with one hand, "how much you love rough sex. They're all eager to taste a little." Leaning over her face again, Devin covered her mouth roughly with his.

Jo fought. She tried to wrench her head away from him, but his hand caught her face and held it while he forced his tongue between her lips.

Oh God, she thought wildly. If he was planning to turn her over for a gang rape, he was going to murder her. Devin never shared his possessions! If he'd intended to drag her back to L.A., he'd beat the shit out of her, but he'd never let his thugs touch her.

"I've warned the guys you're quite the little Karate Kid. They're intrigued. Imagine that. They'd all like a chance to knock you around, Joecy—well, after they've tasted your treasures, that is." Devin spoke calmly as he walked toward the French door and stood looking out.

Vince leaned over and took one of Jo's breasts into his mouth, drawing first a gasp, and then a groan as his hand found its way between her legs. She kicked out, trying to make contact with something, inflict some damage. The only thing her struggles accomplished was another eruption of laughter and taunting from the men watching. Vince leaned over so she could clearly see his face, leering at her and running his tongue suggestively across his lips.

"See gentlemen, she likes it brutal," Devin mocked, a sadistic grin twisting his thin lips.

"Don't do this Devin, *please*." Jo hated herself for begging, but she had to try. She couldn't fight, and there was no running.

"Where are my children, Sweetheart?" Devin asked again, pushing his face close to hers.

Jo didn't answer. She pressed her lips together and began focusing her mindset. The realization that she was going to die, slowly and painfully, sank in. She had to be strong—stay strong. This was going to be a living nightmare, Jo knew that with a certainty that made her insides go suddenly cold and still. She'd die like this a thousand times over, she told herself, before she'd give Devin the information he wanted. That resolve was all she had to cling to for courage. She started praying that it would be enough.

"Well, Baby, it looks like we're just beginning." Devin winked at her, sitting back in one of her kitchen chairs as he watched Vince unzip his pants, exposing himself.

The man made sure Jo had a clear view of his anatomy as he began massaging himself, taunting her with the promise of what was to come. "Impressive, ain't it?" Vince hissed. The gesture was a deliberate taunt, designed to enhance Jo's dread.

It worked.

She felt instinctive panic surge through her, blind and unreasoning. She wasn't sure if she cried out, but breathing suddenly became a struggle as she gasped in breath too fast, hyperventilating. She couldn't think or focus—only react. Growling, she struggled violently against what she knew was coming, silent tears running down her face.

Vince leaned over her, running his hands down her belly.

"No!" The word escaped almost unnoticed. *No*, this *can't* be happening!

Gasping involuntarily, she thrashed her head from side to side, struggling again. Twisting her body, Jo tried to pull her knees up and strike something, but it was a futile fight. The man holding her bound wrists increased the tension on that binding yet again, wrenching a scream of pain from her lungs.

"Where are my kids, Jocey?" Devin said evenly. "Tell me, and this ends." He leaned back in his chair, fingers steepled in front of him.

Jo knew exactly what he was doing. First came the helplessness and humiliation, but that would inevitably be followed by brutality and pain. He wouldn't stop—regardless of what she said or did. Jo knew that from horrific experience. She was dead, whether she gave him the information he wanted, or not.

She went suddenly still, no longer fighting. It was over.

Vaguely, Jo was aware of the leers and laughter of the men, but she forced her mind to slip away, trying to shut out the inevitability of what was coming. It doesn't matter, she told herself resolutely. It'll be finished soon enough, and then nothing will matter. Her kids were safe. Somehow, despite all that had transpired between them to drive them apat, she knew beyond any doubt that Hawk would protect her children for her. Closing her eyes, Jo found strength in that knowledge. Strength to clamp her jaws together, and mutely accept her fate.

"Talk to me, Jocey." Devin was there again, whispering in her ear.

Her eyes flew open and she locked gazes with him. I'll be damned if I'm gonna betray my babies, you piece of pig shit, Jo thought, knowing that sentiment would be clearly readable on her face.

The barest flick of Devin's fingers brought immediate results.

Rough hands grabbed at her, throwing her face down on the table. She felt the probing fingers first, and then, only moments later, Jo felt Vince drive himself inside her body. Her scream was involuntary.

Closing her eyes, Jo refused to acknowledge the torture that ripped through her with each violent thrust. She clenched her teeth together, refusing to allow herself to cry out again. *Survive, just survive*, her brain was clamoring. You can live through this.

"Where are they, Jocey?" Devin was leaning over her again grabbing her hair and yanking her head back painfully, his face only inches from hers.

The weight of Vince's body, forced Jo's hips to slam into the edge of the table with every thrust. Her eyes glazed with pain and hate, but she said nothing, just bared her teeth and growled, forcing her mind and body to endure. The fury that surged through her was, in a way, a Godsend. It gave her the impetus she needed to focus her mind on something other than the rape—it whetted a thirst for revenge—gave her a reason to endure.

The backhanded slap was hard enough to jar her teeth. Jo felt a biting sting along her cheekbone as a large diamond ring on Devin's hand, cut into her flesh. She was only vaguely aware of Vince's muffled cry of release, and the cessation of the pounding. Devin grabbed her hair again, pulling her up and off the table. With a violent thrust of his arm, he threw her roughly toward the living room.

Jo stumbled over a small, wooden table, crashing to the floor. She tried to get up, but Devin was already on top of her. His shoe came up hard against her unprotected ribs, literally lifting her off her hands and knees, and propelling her farther in the general direction of the couch.

"How long were we married, Jocey? Fifteen years?" Devin hissed. His voice was a soft, ominous sound in the nearly silent room. "You're butt dumb if you thought I'd let you get away with something like this!" Grabbing her hair again, he dragged her to her feet.

She tried to ward off the blow with her bound hands, but her reflexive action was too slow. The backhand slammed into the side of her head, knocking her to the ground again. Jo knew she was hurt, and hurt bad. She could barely breathe, and foaming blood choked her nose and mouth.

It's better to die on your feet than live on your knees.

The thought formed in her head. It was a saying her father had painted, in bold, dark letters, across the front of his dojo. A quote she'd read every day of her years in training.

Funny I should remember that now, she thought disjointedly, when I need to live it. It gave her courage, and the strength for defiance.

"You're…butt dumb…" Jo paused to spit blood from her mouth, "if you think…I'm afraid of…a piss ant, like you," she gasped out, pulling herself to her feet against the edge of the couch.

Suddenly, she felt hands grab her from behind, and Devin flashed his switchblade a second time, holding it close to her eyes. "You've got about two seconds to tell me where my kids are, before I start slicing your face to ribbons!" he hissed, his mouth a bare inch from hers. Jo could feel his breath on her cheek, and smell the pungent stench of the beer he'd consumed earlier.

Just get it over with, her mind implored. *Please*, God, let it end soon. She started praying the only prayer she could think of, one she'd repeated thousands upon thousands of times in her life. Yet, suddenly, the words seemed to hold a new and poignant significance.

"*Hail Mary full of Grace, the Lord is with thee. Blessed art thou among women, and blessed is the fruit of thy womb, Jesus. Holy Mary, Mother of God, pray for us sinners now, and at the hour of our death.*"

She wasn't aware she'd mumbled the words aloud until Devin's face contorted with utter hate and rage. "By the time I'm through with you, Sweetie, you'll be singing a different tune."

Jo didn't bother opening her eyes. *Just DO it*! she pleaded silently.

The sound of shattering wood was like a gunshot in the quiet that followed Devin's words.

"By the time I'm finished with YOU, you'll be *dead*!"

HAWK!

Jo was delirious with fear and pain, but she recognized the sound of that voice. She was only peripherally aware that he wasn't alone, but she was too far-gone to register who, or how many others there were.

The man that had grabbed her was reaching to pull his weapon. Jo whirled, catching him by surprise, her elbow smashing into his face. He staggered back, but Jo couldn't pursue the fight. The blow rocked her with agony. Crying out, she doubled over, clutching ribs she was certain were broken.

Unexpectedly, Devin yanked her up, dragging her toward the doors in the kitchen. She tried to resist, but the knife he held at her throat subdued the struggle before it even began. Sounds of fighting filled the room, grunts and cursing, the crashing of furniture and shattering of glass. Above it all, Jo heard Hawk's voice again.

"Stop, Devin, or I'll shoot! Raise your hands above your head where I can see them." His voice carried across the room.

Devin pressed the blade more securely against Jo's throat, drawing a strangled gasp as it cut into flesh. She knew Devin's free hand fumbled at the lock on the door, but she couldn't stop him.

Suddenly, gunshots shattered the air!

Jo watched, bemused, as Devin lurched back against the glass of the door, and then fell forward. The weight of his body carried her with him to the floor.

Devin's face was wild with hate as he pushed himself up. All Jo could see was the blood—on his chest, running from his mouth—and then she saw the weapon. His right hand rose above her breast, the knife glinting with ominous purpose.

"You're still a dead woman," he hissed.

Jo watched the blade descending, as if in slow motion. It was like an eerily surreal dream. Then, all of a sudden, time slipped back into full speed. The knife slammed into her chest, drawing a strangled scream.

She wasn't aware of the weight of Devin's lifeless body, or that the battle in the living room was all but over. The only thing that registered was the piercing, searing pain shooting through her, tearing a cry of agony from her lungs. Then everything went dark.

~ ~ ~

"JO!" Hawk screamed her name. He'd seen the knife flash, heard the scream. "God, *NO!*" The simultaneous plea and denial reverberated in his brain, escaping from his mouth in a cry of utter disbelief.

Bert and B.J. had come with Hawk when he returned to his house. They'd taken the back road from Bert's place, and B.J. had noticed the dark, unfamiliar vehicles, parked on the edge of the road. A copse of trees provided cover, insuring no one at the cottage would see them. That very fact sent a thrill of alarm through all three men. The looks on his brother's faces told Hawk they'd jumped to the same assumption he had—Devin!

They reached the porch in a matter of minutes, but to Hawk it had seemed to take an eternity. Despite all that Jo had told him about her husband, he wasn't prepared for the brutality of the scene he'd witnessed through the front window. His blood turned to ice with a cold, implacable fury. Hawk's brothers held him back, pleading for caution and the need to keep a level head.

"It's too late to stop it, Hawk," Bert whispered hoarsely in his ear. "We have to make what we do count—so we can keep her alive!"

Hawk nodded then, clenching his teeth. He'd never experienced a rage so deadly and consuming before.

Motioning to B.J. and Bert to take the side door, he forced himself to inhale several deep breaths. He didn't dare look through that window again—his brothers needed time to reach their destination.

The wait was agony. Hawk could hear dialogue, and the sounds of a struggle. He tried to count to ten, but only made it to four, and then he smashed in the front door with a booted foot.

The first man he encountered was the one he'd seen raping Jo. Hawk's fist smashed into his face. Grabbing him off the floor, he hit him again and again, as hard as he could, seeking to inflict painful and lasting damage. When the man's knees buckled and he crumpled in a heap to the ground, Hawk would have continued pounding the son of a bitch into hamburger, but a second opponent grabbed his arm, spinning him around.

Ducking instinctively, Hawk barely missed a haymaker. His foot shot out in a sidekick, making contact with the man's shin. He heard the snap at almost the same instant the man screamed.

Out of the corner of his eye, Hawk saw B.J. duck a punch and then come up hard, striking an unprotected ribcage. As Hawk spun away from a rushing adversary, he caught a glimpse of Jo, buckled over clutching her ribs.

Bert saw her, too. He tried to reach her, but one of Devin's thugs waylaid him, grabbing a lamp and swinging it at his head. Bert's sidestep enabled him to escape the full force of the impact, but he staggered as the lamp caught him a glancing blow across his shoulder and back. With lightening speed and agility Bert spun, throwing a solid roundhouse kick that caught his antagonist off guard.

Hawk's opponent dropped a shoulder and charged, intending to take him to the ground. Hawk came up from a slight crouch, his arm extended in a clothesline that dropped the man to his knees, making his face an easy target for Hawk's booted foot.

He glanced toward Jo again. Devin grabbed her from behind and began dragging her toward the kitchen, holding a knife against her throat.

"*Son of a bitch*," Hawk spat, pulling his weapon and trying to get an open shot. He'd wanted to avoid gunplay. The room was too crowded.

Jo's face and neck were covered with so much blood, he wasn't sure if Devin's blade cut into her flesh or not, but Hawk knew instinctively he couldn't let the man drag her out of that room.

"Stop, Devin, or I'll shoot!" Hawk leveled his weapon, grasping it in a firm, two-handed grip. "Raise your hands above your head where I can see them."

Devin didn't even pause. He looked up with an, I dare you, sneer on his face.

Hawk fired twice. Both bullets thudded home in Devin's body. The man slammed into the door, shattering glass, and then lurched forward, taking Jo to the ground with him. Hawk saw Devin raise his knife above his head, and knew what the man intended. Leaping over prone bodies, he tried desperately to reach them in time, but he was too far away. Devin drove the knife home in Jo's chest, and then collapsed on top of her.

"JO!" The scream ripped through Hawk's gut. He leapt over upended furniture and unconscious bodies. "*CALL FOR HELP*!" he screamed at Bert over his shoulder.

Tossing Devin's corpse callously aside, Hawk knelt down. "Jo," he whispered hoarsely, running experienced hands down her body, feeling first for a pulse, and then injuries.

Gray eyes fluttered open as his hands encountered her ribs. Jo moaned, her eyes rolling back in her head, before closing again.

Broken ribs, Hawk registered. Punctured lung. He recognized the telltale sign as blood bubbled from her open mouth. The flesh on her face was already turning mottled purple and blue where she'd obviously sustained several blows. A ragged, bloody cut gaped open along her cheekbone, and her bottom lip was cut and swollen.

"Stay with me, Baby," Hawk pleaded, his eyes filling with tears. Christ, he thought as he examined her. She was a bloody mess from head to foot. Blood was running down the inside of her legs and covered her face and chest. The knife handle protruded just below her left collarbone, but Hawk didn't touch it. He knew if he tried to remove it, he'd never be able to staunch the blood flow.

A phone cord still secured her wrists, and Jo's sundress twisted into the knots. Sliding his belt knife from a sheath at his waist, Hawk carefully cut away those bonds, rubbing feeling back into her hands and arms. She made no indication she felt anything.

"God, Almighty," Bert choked out, leaning over Hawk, a blanket in his hands.

"Help me turn her on her side," Hawk commanded in a voice rough with emotion.

"Hawk, you'll kill her," Bert protested, tucking the blanket around Jo's exposed body.

"Her ribs are broken," Hawk gritted out. "She's got a punctured lung." He pointed to the frothy red liquid around Jo's nose and mouth. "Blood from the injured lung will fill her good lung if we don't do somethin'."

Bert wasn't convinced, but he did what Hawk directed him to do, cringing as Jo groaned and cried out in pain.

"Ambulance is on the way," B.J. said from close behind them. "I called Wendy. Nolan and Cramer are on their way, too." He motioned behind him. "I've got that pile of shit tied up—or what's left of 'em." The intensity of the fury that poured through him, at the sight of Jo's tortured body, was clearly readable in every line of his face.

"Will she make it?" Bert whispered, dabbing at the blood on Jo's face with a damp cloth.

Hawk's voice was a gruff whisper of anguish. "I don't know, Bert," he choked. "God, *I don't know*!" Hawk knew tears were spilling down his face, but he didn't care. And then he felt two hands, one on each shoulder.

His brothers were there.

He drew on that strength as he cradled Jo in his arms, stroking her hair, and waiting for the ambulance to arrive.

XXVII

"Take it easy, Girl," Bert said, laughing at Jo's enthusiasm. "They're not goin' anywhere." He kept a firm hold on her as he eased her from the car, helping her to stand. Two weeks in a hospital had been an agony of endurance for Jo, especially once she knew Carol was bringing her children home.

The May afternoon was warm, but a cool breeze touched her face. Flowers around the cottage were in full bloom, and the extensive assortment of colors and varieties, sent a thrill of pleasure through her. Home! It feels like home.

Carol stood with Laney and Casey on the front porch as Jenny came racing toward her.

Bert laughed, scooping Jenny into his arms. "Whoa, Little Tiger," he teased. "Mama's not up to a running jump just yet." He gave the child a hug, and then set her down beside Jo.

Jenny clutched Jo's leg, looking up at her with teary eyes. "Mommy! Mommy!" she cried.

Jo knelt, controlling an urge to grimace at the still tender twinge in her ribcage, and pulled Jenny into her arms. Her own tears went unnoticed as she clutched her child tightly.

"Oh, Baby, I love you so much!" she whispered with fervent emotion.

Jenny patted Jo's head as she spoke, "Don't cwy, Mommy. It's okay now."

When Jo looked up, she saw Casey and Laney. Bert helped her stand, and she pulled her older children close for a hug. They didn't say a word, almost as if it were enough just to be together again.

Nate was close behind Laney, and he reached out to pull Jo into a light embrace. "It's good to have you back with us, Jo."

"Thanks, Nate," she whispered, feeling teary-eyed again. "It's good to be back."

Carol met Jo at the top of the stairs, pulling her into another hug before holding her at arm's length. "Hawk's inside, Jo," she said softly. "You two need to talk. The kids…know." She paused, as if unsure how to finish her sentence. "About their dad, I mean." Carol said the words in a hushed whisper, meant for Jo's ears alone.

Her heart fluttered painfully, and then stilled. She nodded, grateful for that, at least.

"They're coming to my place for cookies and milk," Carol continued. "Ellie and Sarah are there now, getting supper ready. We'll all be there when you two are done." She winked, squeezing Jo's arm affectionately, and then moved down the steps. Jo turned to see Jenny in B.J.'s arms, and Bert with an arm around Casey's shoulders. Laney walked between Nate and Carol as they started toward Carol's house.

"Don't look so apprehensive," Bert laughed up at her. "You've scared all the piss and vinegar outta that big lug. He's got just a little bark left, and I know you can handle that," he teased, grinning at her.

Jo returned the smile, feeling more confident, but she inhaled a deep breath of fortification before opening the screen door and stepping inside.

The living room was dark. It took her eyes a moment to adjust before she saw Hawk's large form. He was standing beside the fireplace, one hand resting on the mantle to support his weight, his head slightly bent. He didn't move, but his head turned, and his eyes met hers.

Standing transfixed, no more than half a dozen steps away, Jo's hands moved to rest on the back of an over-stuffed chair for support. "Hey, Big Guy," she said softly, offering a tentative smile.

Hawk didn't respond, he just watched her with his dark, intense eyes.

Jo could read nothing in them. What are you thinking?

Seconds ticked by with slow agony as she stood watching his pokerfaced features. His eyes moved from her face, to her throat, to her breasts. Slowly and tantalizingly, they progressed to her feet, and then back again to meet her gaze.

"Don't…don't hate me, Hawk," Jo's words were an angst-ridden whisper, her voice breaking as emotion took over.

In two steps, he was beside her, pulling her into his arms. One hand cupped her head against his chest, and the other was strong and sure at her back. "I could never hate you, Jo. I'm crazy about you, Little Girl," he said tenderly, close to her ear.

Sliding her arms around Hawk's neck, Jo pulled his head toward her hungry lips. She needed to taste that love, feel it sing through her body, igniting her soul. The room was quiet for a long time as their mouths met. They kissed as though they were new lovers—searching, needing, assuring, pledging.

"If you ever scare me like that again…" Hawk's words drifted into silence as he struggled with the tears that filled his eyes.

"You'll what?" Jo whispered, reaching with her forefinger to catch a single drop that escaped down his cheek.

"God, Jo!" Hawk pulled her hard against him, wrapping his arms around her.

Biting back the cry of discomfort that sprang to her lips, Jo responded, holding Hawk tightly against her, savoring the feel of him.

"It's over," she said simply, amazed at her own lack of emotion to that reality. She'd prayed for this freedom for so long, and yet, there had always been the agony of knowing it was impossible. Now, suddenly, a new world was opened before her. Jo's mind couldn't grasped it yet.

"Yeah, Baby, it's over," Hawk said, kissing her face and hair as if he couldn't get enough of her.

"Make love to me, Hawk," Jo pleaded, needing this man to fill her with his clean, wholesome essence. She needed his love. And she needed it to wipe away the ugliness that still haunted her—and probably would for a long time to come.

His hands slid her blouse off and pulled her bra down, exposing full breasts to the warmth of his mouth. Jo's mind registered surprise. Her shirt had been unfastened without her awareness.

How'd he do that?

The thought was only peripheral, and then she lost herself in the sensations Hawk's mouth was educing. She felt his arms lift her, and she leaned her head against his shoulder as he carried her into the bedroom.

He chuckled. "Even with busted ribs and a knife wound that's barely stable, you're horny?"

Jo sighed, resting her head against his shoulder. "I can't help myself," she said in a husky voice. "You turn me on."

Hawk set her gently on the edge of the bed, kneeling beside her. His dark eyes looked up, meeting Jo's. "How are you…handling it all, Jo?" he asked, concern etched in every line of his face.

"You gonna fuck me, or what, Candy Ass?" Jo whispered the words, her eyes dilating as they locked on his mouth. She heard the gasp of an inhaled breath, but he showed no other reaction to her question.

~~~

Hawk felt the jolt of her words clear to his toes. The fire that had licked along his veins, at the very sight of her, ignited now into a raging inferno. His hands trembled to tear at her clothing. He needed the taste of her in his mouth, the feel of her body—hot, moist, closing around him. He ached to feel her arms
~~~

holding him close, assuring him she was alive and whole again, but he refused to allow that urge to govern his actions now.

"You're not in any condition for a roll in the hay, Little Girl," he grinned up at her.

Jo's eyes filled with tears. "Yes I am, *try* me," she pleaded. He could feel her body trembling.

"Oh, God, Jo." Hawk pulled her into his arms, pressing her head against his shoulder and stroking her hair. "Give it time, Honey. We got all the time in the world."

"Hawk," Jo said, pulling away and taking his face between her hands. "It's okay. I'm okay. A little sore and tender, but I'm okay."

Hawk looked into her eyes for several moments before asking, "What about emotionally, Jo?" He, of all people, knew there was severe trauma with something like what she'd just lived through. Despite how deeply a victim buried it, the nightmare had to be dealt with, sooner or later.

"No," Jo whispered, looking away. "No, I'm okay. I'll be okay."

Hawk's hand came up, brushing a stray curl from her eyes and caressing her cheek. God! His brave, defiant, little Jo! Always fighting, always so sure she could handle everything. An amazing combination—so incredibly fragile and vulnerable on the surface—and yet within, there was pure, fire-tested, steel. His thumb traced a still raw scar along her cheekbone, and then moved to gently run across the surface of the cut on her lip. The physical wounds were healing—the emotional wounds would take time.

"I saw, Jo," Hawk's words were whispered agony as his eyes filled with tears. "I saw what that bastard did—well, some of it anyway. I…I couldn't stop it! *I'm so sorry.* I couldn't stop it," he said on a hiss of breath filled with tortured guilt.

Jo's arms tightened around him, pulling him close for a moment before she sat back and looked him in the eye. "Hawk, my life with Devin was… hard." her voice was steady, as if she'd thought this through and come to terms with it. "It was harder than you can possibly imagine. Harder than I'll ever be able to express or convey to anyone," she said hesitantly, running her tongue over dry lips before continuing. "Being raped is…emotionally and physically traumatic…but for me, maybe less so than for someone else." Jo paused, as if she struggled to find the right words to explain.

Hawk's gut twisted and his heart felt ripped to shreds, but this was ultimately Jo's battle, *her* war—not his, though he had his own demons to come to terms with. Watching the play of emotions on her face, Hawk waited quietly, letting her get it out in her own time, and at her own pace.

"It wasn't the first time I…I mean…I've been forced to…to have sex against my will before." Her voice was agonized as she stumbled over the words, struggling for control. "I've endured...*worse* things...than being raped." Memories flooded back—it was written all over her face—old wounds, and new ones.

"My lovemaking must make it so...I mean, does it bring..." Hawk groped for the right words.

Jo turned her head to meet his gaze. "Bring back painful memories?" she supplied, summing up what he was trying to ask.

He nodded.

"No, Hawk," she said softly. "It helps erase them. It expunges them, in a weird kinda way." Jo smiled at his skeptical expression. "Father Pat told me once, if I stopped the hating, and allowed God's love to permeate the part of me that was filled with that hate, the ugliness would be forced out—replaced with His Love. That's kind of what it's like."

Hawk pulled her close, covering her mouth with his. Jo responded the way she always did in his arms. He could feel her need—the desperate hunger. With gentle hands he pushed her down on the bed and slid her jeans off. As his fingers lightly caressed her skin, he noticed the mottled remains of fading bruises, and squeezed his eyes shut for a moment, struggling against the rush of emotion.

As he resumed his lovemaking, Hawk watched Jo's face for any telltale sign of negative reaction, but her eyes closed, and a blissful smile tugged at the corners of her mouth, awakening one tiny dimple in her cheek. Her body stirred, responding to his touch with passion as Hawk's mouth moved across her skin, his lips brushing the flesh, his tongue leaving a warm, moist trail.

Jo shuddered, her hands gripping the bedding as she arched toward him. "Make love to me, Hawk," she pleaded. Please! *Please*." The last word was a whimpered plea.

He didn't answer, but his mouth did.

Almost immediately, Jo's cry of release filled the room, her body trembling with the violent orgasm.

She grabbed his face between her palms, her eyes locking on his. "More," she pleaded. "Please, Hawk. I need you inside me!"

Hw grinned, a slow, seductive half-smile. "I think supper will be stone cold by the time we get there," he drawled.

"*I hope so*!" She said fervently, her eyes closing as Hawk's mouth once again brought her body to the brink of climax.

~ ~ ~

It was a week of unqualified bliss. Nothing penetrated Jo's safe, comfortable world. The children were winding down their school year, and the spring weather was idyllic. Jo planted flowers, and had coffee with Hawk on her patio, or his deck, each morning. She even managed to read a light romance novel, curling up in a lounge chair every afternoon.

She explored Carol's gardens and orchard, and learned that Hawk's mother ran a produce stand from late spring to mid-fall. She spent most mornings helping Carol harvest the early spring crops of asparagus and strawberries, and clean the roadside stand, which was located on the back edge of the property. Though Jo didn't feel she needed it, Hawk insisted she take a nap every afternoon. She didn't argue.

In the evenings after supper, she looked forward to her walks with Hawk and the kids. The orchard was close to the end of its blooming season, but the delicate pink and white flowers still emitted a softly sweet scent that filled the air around them. Walking beneath the canopy of blossoms, Jo could almost believe she'd indeed died—and gone to Heaven.

And the nights! Jo's body thrummed with desire whenever she allowed her mind to remember the feel of Hawk's hands and mouth on her body. Their lovemaking was tender, but passionate. She could loose the pain and horror of the past in the beauty of it.

Hawk was always close-to-hand when she needed him. Enmeshed though he was in the murder investigations, he somehow managed to keep it from intruding into her world. It was a reprieve, but not a long one. She knew that it couldn't last.

Jo had to deal with the reality of Devin's death—their home, the insurance, his family, their possessions—all of it. She hadn't even contacted her own family, though she was now free to do so. The murders she'd so vividly seen in her visions were waiting, as well. Somewhere, in the back of her mind, Jo knew she'd have to face the world of Humboldt again, too—the questions, the gossip, the unwelcome notoriety, the speculations.

~ ~ ~

"Hey," Hawk touched Jo's cheek.

She was lying on a reclining chair on his deck. The late afternoon sun was warm, but Jo didn't seem to mind. Hawk had cleaned up the cottage and repaired the damage, but Jo still had trouble being inside for long periods. Hawk knew it would take time to come to terms with the memories that still haunted her.

"What's going on behind those pretty eyes of yours?" he whispered. Jo suddenly looked anguished—frightened and sad. It tore at his heart, but he knew he couldn't protect her from the outside world much longer. Pete had been badgering him incessantly the past several days to get Jo back into the investigation, before someone else ended up in a body bag.

"Reality," Jo replied, her eyes still looking distant and troubled.

"Yeah, it's waitin', Little Girl," Hawk said, choosing not to patronize.

"Tomorrow?" she offered.

The look on her face told Hawk that she was aware of his divided loyalties. He'd found himself torn, between needing her to be truly back, and wanting to protect her from the pain of coming back.

"Tomorrow's soon enough," Hawk agreed.

They sat quietly for several long minutes, Jo sipping a cup of coffee and Hawk with a bottle of beer. He inhaled deeply. The scent of lilac drifted up from a hedge below his deck, and he could smell fresh soil—new life was stirring. Birds were singing everywhere, darting back and forth from their nests to the half dozen feeders his mother kept stocked. His particular favorites were the gold finches. Jo seemed to be enjoying them as well.

In the few short months they'd known one another, the world around them had changed so much, Hawk mused. His mind drifted back to the first day he'd seen Jo—at Lake Park, huddled next to a chiminea, strumming a guitar.

He'd run with his intuition then—his own intuition. So, was Jo's really all that different? Her sixth sense was just more highly defined, more attuned to the world around her, than his was.

~ ~ ~

"Tell me about this…this thing you do, Jo," Hawk said. "How does it work?"

Jo went very still.

She had never wanted the talent, and certainly didn't like it. At first, she'd been afraid because it had horrified her—she hadn't understood what was happening. Later, she'd feared it because others—society in general—didn't understand. Hard, painful experience taught her to be evasive, not admitting or exposing too much.

"There's lots of different research about psychic abilities," Jo began tentatively. "I read someplace, that everyone has a psychic intuitive center. It's called the Chakra, or Mind of Christ. A physicist named Gerald Feinberg invented a proof for the existence of a faster-than-light particle that he called a tachyon," Jo looked up at Hawk. His eyes were on the horizon, but he was nodding, as if he'd heard of the term.

She continued. "Many scientists now believe the tachyon does indeed, exist, and that it's probably the physical basis for ESP," she paused again, taking several sips of coffee.

This felt good! She'd never discussed her gift with anyone before. She'd read books and explored the Internet. Researched everything she could find—

but there'd never been anyone she could discuss it with—no one to listen and understand.

"I've heard about Feinberg's research," Hawk commented, "but I wasn't aware it had been linked to ESP. Is that what you have, ESP?" Hawk seemed genuinely interested. There was no hint of criticism or derisiveness in his face, or in his tone.

Jo took a deep breath. "ESP, or parapsychology, is now being called the 'orphan science'," she said. "ESP is simply a general term that refers to information received through telepathy, clairvoyance, or psychokinetics."

"So, what is all that stuff?" Hawk took a long swig of beer as he leaned back in his deck chair, propping his feet on an end table.

"Well, telepathy is communication of impressions of one kind or another, from one mind to another, and usually over some distance. You know, like I might be at Carol's, and you would focus on me and picture something in your mind, and I'd see that object in my head?" It was a rhetorical question, but Hawk nodded.

"The Soviets did a lot of research and experimentation in that area, I think," Hawk said, taking another drink.

Jo nodded. "Clairvoyance is seeing with the third eye," she explained. "In the body, there's something called a pineal gland, located in the back of the brain. It's in the middle of your head. and used to be about the size of a ping-pong ball, but because of centuries of disuse, it shrank to about the size of a pea. It's kinda like an eye. You know, round, with an opening in one part that has a lens for focusing light. It's hollow, and has color receptors. Just like the eyes on your face, it can move up to ninety degrees away from the direction its set in." Jo had her eyes closed now, her head resting on the back of the chair. It was apparent, she simply regurgitated information she'd researched and stored in her brain.

"Is that what you are, clairvoyant?" Hawk asked.

"Sometimes," Jo replied, looking at him. "Some psychometrics too, I guess."

Hawk looked puzzled, which prompted her to explain. "That's when you can take an object that someone else has touched, or be where someone else has been, and receive images. It's kind of like you become a part of them, or their experiences."

"So, how did you get this way?"

"Well, some people become clairvoyant after a traumatic experience, like almost dying. Sometimes a high fever, serious accident, or even a blow to the head can trigger episodes of clairvoyance." Jo paused for several moments, and then forced herself to go on. "Mine began soon after Devin started beating me," she said stoically, her voice going suddenly flat.

Hawk said nothing.

Jo could feel his eyes on her, but she couldn't meet that gaze at the moment. She took refuge in continuing her explanation. "Mostly though," she said, "I experience what scientists call, psychokinetic psychic phenomenon."

"Which is?"

"Well, it's when you perceive information about future events, or things that are currently happening—or have just happened. For me, it's usually visions experienced with dreams." Jo stopped, suddenly feeling self-conscious.

Hawk didn't respond immediately. He looked at her speculatively for several minutes, which felt like hours. When he did speak, it wasn't what Jo expected from him.

"What did you dream about me, that night you came flying out to the highway like Joan of Arc?" he asked, leaning forward, his elbows on his knees.

Jo debated evading, but decided against it. He had a right to know. "I saw you die," she said evenly, no emotion coloring her voice. "The man I knocked out, came at you from behind and stunned you. Then the driver pulled out a gun and shot you through the heart."

Hawk's expression didn't change. He looked thoughtful.

Jo swallowed several times, as the memory of that vision chilled her anew with its horror. "You just…looked surprised, and then…slumped over, dead." Tears filled her eyes, choking her voice. "There was blood everywhere, and I was…so helpless. I just watched it happen." There was pain and disbelief in Jo's voice, the agony she'd endured while caught up in the vision, evident.

Hawk moved quickly, kneeling beside her and taking her in his arms. "It didn't happen like that, Jo, and it was because of that vision, I didn't die," he said firmly. "Your gift has advantages, too. You help people."

"Hawk, it doesn't negate the horror of seeing what will be, or could be!" Jo said with feeling. "It's the ultimate nightmare, because you know it could be a reality if you don't make the right choice, or get there in time. And sometimes," Jo paused, wetting her lips, "there is no *in time*. It's just a vision of what has already occurred—ugly and unchangeable." She shivered as the nightmares of the murders resurfaced in her mind's eye.

Hawk was still kneeling beside her, rubbing his hands up and down her bare arms. "Did you know that in 1994, the CIS started a Stargate Project?" he asked, obviously trying to redirect Jo's train of thought.

She shook her head.

"Well, it was managed by the Defense Intelligence Agency, and was created to explore para-psychological phenomenon," Hawk continued.

Jo was surprised. "How did you know that?"

"Mom suggested you might be psychic, so I did a little research on it," Hawk said casually.

Jo wondered if she should feel angry or indignant, because she was neither. "So, what did they use it for?" she asked.

"Well they had hard targets, like locations of military weapons, research facilities, submarines, and things of nature. Then there were the soft targets, like the minds of military or political figures."

"Did it work?"

"I guess they had some success with it, but obviously not enough to continue its use, unless it's so super secret now we don't know it's going on." Hawk grinned.

Jo nodded, sipping her coffee and falling silent for several minutes, lost in thought. "There are rules, you know," she said unexpectedly, her voice and face quite serious.

"With psychics? You have to follow rules?"

"Yeah, ancient rules. If you break them you risk consequences, because every cause has an effect, or so it's claimed. You can't use your gift to accumulate wealth, status, or power. You can't read the future, and you can't use your ability for demonstrations or experiments. It has to be a genuine need or quest."

"Wow, that's heavy shit."

"A lot of experts think everyone is capable of ESP."

"It doesn't surprise me," Hawk commented. "I've had hundreds of instances of foreknowledge and premonitions. You know, just plain knowing something is wrong, or sensing something's going to happen." Hawk replied seriously, as if really thinking about it for the first time.

Jo nodded. Yeah, she knew.

"Even Sigmund Freud believed man had, locked away in his mind, the powers of the paranormal, among other things." Jo grinned impishly, running her hand along Hawk's chest and up his neck.

Sarcasm permeated every word of his reply, "Yeah, Freud is someone I'd put my money on," he chuckled. "Will you tell me something else?"

Jo looked up and nodded.

"That night at the dojo, with Eric?" He paused, but when she nodded, he continued. "What happened? Did you have a vision or somethin'?"

Jo looked into the distance for several moments, remembering, and then turned back to meet Hawk's gaze. "Yeah," she said. "I saw…" she stopped to swallow. A tongue tip swiped across her lips before she managed to go on. "I saw a young girl raped and beaten to death." Closing her eyes, Jo rested her head on the back of her chair. The horror of that vision still had the ability to haunt her. When she finally opened her eyes, she saw Hawk staring off into the distance. Even his voice sounded remote when he finally spoke.

"Yeah, I remember that time. It was Eric's half-sister."

Jo nodded, remembering what Father Pat had told her.

"It was...pretty ugly." Hawk grimaced as his eyes moved to lock with Jo's. "Eric was devastated for a long time afterward. He found her, you know."

"Yeah, I know," Jo said. At Hawk's surprised look, she qualified, "Father Pat told me."

Hawk looked into the distance for a moment, and then started up again. "I remember the Sheriff talking to everyone in town and interviewing all the guys at school, but nobody knew anything, I guess."

"They never solved it." Jo stated the fact she'd learned from Father Pat.

"No," Hawk confirmed. "No, they never did. I'm not sure Eric's ever really gotten over it."

"What do you mean?"

"I don't know," Hawk's mouth pulled up on one side, but there was no humor in the half-grin. "He broods a lot, and can be damned moody."

"You think he's still mad at whoever killed his sister?"

"Yeah, maybe. I think he's never come to terms with the anger stage of grieving." Hawk smiled at Jo. "Sometimes, when he's working out, it's like he's trying to kill the punching bags."

Jo grinned, nodding. She was more than familiar with that urge. She'd certainly been there a time or two. "What about Dave?" she asked.

"What do you mean?"

"Was he around then, too?"

"Yeah," Hawk replied. "We all hung out together most of the time."

"You guys have been good friends, Hawk."

He shrugged. "Small towns are like that."

They were both quiet for a long time. Hawk scooted onto Jo's reclining chair, pulling her half on top of him. They lay in companionable silence, watching the sun set along the western horizon. The sky was clear, except for a few whips of low-lying clouds, and Jo was amazed at the intensity of the colors as iridescent oranges, pinks, and gold, blazed across the horizon.

"How are you handling it, Jo? I mean, really?" Hawk asked at length, voicing a concern that had obviously eaten at him for a long time.

Jo sighed. "It's hard, late at night, sometimes. I wake up in a panic and can't get it off my mind. But most of the time I'm okay," she replied honestly.

"Shit, Jo, I was so scared! I thought..." Hawk choked on the words, he couldn't finish his sentence.

Jo reached out a tender hand, touching his cheek. "I was expecting to die, Hawk," she said seriously, almost reflectively, as though she were thinking it through for the first time. "There was no way I was going to tell Devin where the kids were, and he'd have killed me anyway. I had worked myself into a state of mind, to accept whatever happened. To endure a painful and humiliating death." Jo paused to draw a deep, shaky breath. "I think…the reprieve of life, has been harder for me to deal with than the rape." She smiled a cynical, half-smile, "How weird is that? I'm upset I didn't die."

Hawk understood what Jo was expressing. It was something a good many cops experienced as well—being snatched from the jaws of death could leave you reeling and numb, unable to connect to the everyday world until your brain reworked itself into a new mindset.

"You're alive, Jo, very much alive. And you're mine. I'm going to spend the rest of my life making sure you know that—and love that," Hawk said huskily.

"So," Jo challenged, her eyes narrowing provocatively, "you're waiting for…*what*, an invitation?"

Hawk chuckled deep in his chest as his hands slid under her clothing.

~ ~ ~

"It's fow me? Jenny jumped up and down, clapping her hands.

"It's for everyone," Hawk pointed out patiently. He stood beside Nate, who was squatting down near the front porch of Jo's cottage, a nine-week-old Golden Retriever held firmly in his arms. The fluffy, golden-brown body wiggled ferociously, its tongue wetting anything that got within licking distance.

"DUDE!" Casey breathed out on a sigh of pure delight. "Can we keep him, Mom?" he pleaded. "Pleeeease!"

"Oh, Hawk," Jo squatted down beside Nate. "He's beautiful! Where'd you get it?"

"A friend of mine, Steve Vicars, breeds 'em. His bitch had seven. Five male and two female." Hawk grinned at their expressions of delight.

"He's so cute," Laney exclaimed, taking the puppy from Nate and giggling as he bathed her face. "Oh, Mom, please. We've never had a pet."

Jo looked up at Hawk. "He had to be expensive. I'll pay for him, Hawk," she offered. There was no way she could tell her children 'no'.

"Yeah, they cost a few bucks, but Steve owed me a favor. I got the pup cheap, and you're not repayin' me," Hawk said firmly. "He's my gift to you and your family." Hawk's face and tone were set. Jo knew that look. It wouldn't do any good to argue with him right now.

"What 'cha gonna name him?" Nate asked Jenny, who was holding the puppy on her lap with Laney and Nate's help.

"King," Laney said, stroking the puppy's back.

"Naw, that's dumb," Casey objected. "He needs a name like Zeus or Brutus."

"Well, that sounds pretty dumb to me," Laney protested, wrinkling her nose at Casey's choices.

"I like Lestaw," Jenny piped in, grinning from ear to ear.

"LESTER!" Laney and Casey responded at the same time.

"You can't even say it right," Casey teased.

"Yes, I can! Lestaw's a booteful name. He looks like a Lestaw to me," Jenny insisted defensively, her bottom lip trembling.

"Lester sounds like a perfect name," Hawk laughed. "Here, Lester, come on, Les," He knelt and patted one thigh, talking to the puppy. Immediately the animal's ears perked up. He trotted over to Hawk, wagging his tail.

"See!" Jenny clapped her hands with delight. "He alweady knows his name. He's a Lestaw!"

"He's a Lester, all right," Jo, laughed.

Hawk rose to stand by Jo as the children ran and played with the puppy. "How are they handling…everything?" he asked.

"Okay, most of the time, but it's hard."

Hawk nodded understanding. "Do they know what happened?"

"Yeah," Jo said in a soft, pained voice, "most of it—well, at least Casey and Laney do." She ran a tongue tip over her lips before continuing. "I tried to spare them the baser details though."

"They don't look like they're grieving," he said softly.

"They are, Hawk." Jo's voice shook slightly. "He…he was their dad. They knew he was violent and could be cruel, and they agreed to come with me willingly when we ran. Still, I think somewhere in the back of their minds, they thought Devin would change—be more like he used to be. Like the dad they loved."

Hawk nodded his understanding. "Keep them busy, Jo," he advised. His face was serious as he watched the children. "Keep them too busy to brood, too busy to dwell on the loss."

"I'm tryin'."

"The puppy will help," he continued. "Make sure they have chores. Get them busy helping Mom at the fruit stand—anything will do."

Jo nodded, instinctively knowing Hawk was right. They'd heal, but it would take time. As cruel as he'd become, Devin was still their father—they needed to mourn that loss.

"I love you, Little Girl," Hawk said gently.

Jo looked up to see his dark eyes studying her face. "I love you too, Big Guy."

XXVIII

"He's not a complete loner, but close," Jo said, her eyes almost closed as she knelt beside the road, at the site where they'd found the first victim. Flashes of events, images of horror, hammered at her awareness. They would come full force if she allowed them to, but it was hard letting them in. Jo wanted to run, to escape. She steeled herself and laid her hand against the soil, opening her mind's eye.

A shudder shook her body. She warned Hawk what might happen—told him not to interfere. He had to let the visions run their course. The deeper she delved into them, the more details she'd see and feel.

"It's dark, and it's late. She has to hurry because she doesn't like the dark much," Jo said, swaying with the rhythm of the images. "Someone's behind her. She feels it." Jo whispered, as though talking to herself. There was no sign of emotion on her face as she continued. "She's running now, past darkened buildings on the campus, trying to get to a car. "It's cold out—no, it's hot, but she's cold—she's afraid. *Arghh*!" The strangled scream was unexpected. Jo's face contorted with fear and horror.

~ ~ ~

"He has her. His hands are big, strong. One covers her mouth—one's around her waist. He has something on a cloth that makes her…sleep." Jo's voice was agonized. Hawk saw tears slipping silently down her cheeks. He had to bite his lip hard to keep from stopping this whole damned thing.

"Oh God, O God, where am I?" There was terror in her voice now, desperation etched on her face. The eerie way she slipped from third to first person made Hawk's skin crawl. He wondered what emotions Jo felt—was she aware of herself as a separate entity, or had she completely assumed the victim's identity? It was an unnerving possibility.

Suddenly, she was the observer again. "The house is dark. Only one bare bulb hangs from the ceiling. There's a bed—sort of. It has posts on one end.

He ties her hands—one to each post. Her legs hang over the edge, and he ties her ankles—apart."

Jo shuddered and slipped into first person. "It *hurts*. It's cutting me," she whimpered, her head rolling a little as the vision moved forward. "He has... toys, but his toys hurt." She gasped as though she felt the pain.

"He likes his toys." She was just observing now. "They cut and tear. They make the girls cry out, and then they tell him things he wants to hear. He's naked when he plays with his toys," Jo said, her brows furrowed as though she struggled to see clearly, or to understand what she was seeing. "He likes to feel himself get hard while he...plays.

"Their pain is erotic. Can't you *feel* it? It's powerful! It's *stimulating*!" For a moment, it was as if Jo had slipped into the killer's brain—even her facial expression changed. Hawk felt a chill run down his spine, and his stomach turned over.

And then, as suddenly as it had come on her, it was past. Jo was narrating again, but Hawk could see the struggle for control on her face. Whatever she was witnessing, it was obviously agonizing. "He loves the fear, and hearing the cries," she whispered. "He cuts, and pinches, and burns her with cigarettes. He's creating a work of art. Every masterpiece is different—he has to decide which tools to use, which toys to play with." Jo groaned, trying to cover her eyes as though unaware they were already closed.

Hawk knew Jo couldn't escape whatever it was she saw. His jaw and hands clenched as he watched her struggle. She was rocking back and forth now, huddling into herself.

"He tells her he'll let her go free soon. He just wants to play awhile. He wants her to feel pleasure, too. He..." Jo whimpered, pushing at her breasts and groin. "He's trying to excite her, make her have an orgasm, but she's too scared." Jo gasped, her voice rising. "It makes him mad. He feels impotent—used! He's putting something on himself—another toy. It straps on his penis. It has sharp wires sticking out. He...*Noooo*!"

Jo screamed then.

Hawk couldn't take any more. He grabbed her, shaking her hard, pulling her out of the trance that had enveloped her.

"No more! Not now," he spat, glaring at Pete.

Jo huddled in his arms, breathing hard and trembling from head to foot, her eyes screwed tightly shut. "I feel...sick," she whispered, swallowing convulsively several times, as if she were trying to control a rebellious stomach.

"Give her a few minutes then, Hawk, but we need whatever she has to give us." Pete was frustrated, Hawk was well aware of that fact. They knew most of what Jo had just told them—not all the gory details, but certainly enough to piece this picture together.

Bev knelt beside Hawk, holding a Styrofoam cup of water close to Jo's mouth and helping her drink. There was an uncharacteristic look of compassion on her homely face.

"Not now," Hawk snarled. "No more today, Pete."

Pete looked like he was prepared to argue the point.

"It's okay," Jo, volunteered. "I need to get through this as much as Pete needs to hear it." With an obvious effort of will, she forced herself up and away from Hawk. Once again, she knelt and laid a hand where Nichole Umbridge's tortured body had been sprawled.

She was trembling. What she'd just lived through was still too real—too vivid. The expression on her face said as much. She took a few deep, unsteady breaths, as if struggling with herself to continue. It took several long, tension-filled minutes before the images resurfaced.

"He…drives himself inside her. She screams and screams, but he just laughs. Her cries excite him—he has an orgasm. He talks to her, boasting, but she's not aware of anything anymore," Jo paused long enough to draw a ragged breath. "He doesn't feel anything anymore either. He feels empty and emotionless." Her voice became matter of fact, as if she were watching from afar, aloof and removed.

"He's writing on her, using a pointed tool of some kind. He has a mission. He has to restrain them, impale them, and purge the world of their filth. Teach them a lesson. He's in control, he's in charge."

Jo's head dropped into her hands, and she began sobbing softly. "I'm going to die. He's killing me, why? I don't understand why. I want my mama."

Hawk had to turn away. He felt his own stomach twist and heave. Were they hearing that girl's last thoughts—her final plea? It tore at his heart, and made him want to pound something, or someone, to a pulp. The urge was so overpowering, he was shaking with the effort required to control it.

~~~

"He walks up behind the bed and takes her head in his hands," Jo continued. "One arm is wrapped under her chin, the other pressed on the side of her face. He just…snaps." She swayed, feeling sickened by the coldness she could sense emanating from her vision-killer.

"What does he look like?" Bev asked softly, hoping to prod Jo to a response.

"Tall and dark, no," Jo paused, her face reflecting an effort to focus and find the details Bev asked for. "The dark comes from within, but his skin is
~~~

light—pale. He hides his face. I can't see his face. He's wearing a cowl snapped under the chin, but I can see his mouth." Jo's had her eyes squeezed tightly shut, but one hand reached to her own mouth. The fingers trembled as she touched her lips. "The lips are thin and the teeth a little crooked. He licks his lips a lot—all the time. He likes the taste of her on his lips. He likes the taste of the blood, too."

Jo's brows furrowed as she continued. "I can see lighter colored hair on his body, blonde, maybe. He's strong, a predator. I can feel his hate and anger. It…it consumes him, eats away at him, constantly."

Jo slumped forward.

Immediately, Hawk was beside her, supporting her body weight.

There was nothing left to give, Jo realized. Every ounce of energy felt sucked out. She could barely keep her hold on Hawk's shirt as he eased her to a sitting position.

"Just rest, Jo." Hawk rose and walked to where Pete stood.

"You happy, you son-of-a-bitch," he ground the words out through clenched teeth.

"It's not enough," Pete shot back. "We got a sadistic bastard, with thin lips, that likes the taste of blood, God damn it, Hawk! How the hell do you put an A.P.B. out on that?" he snapped in a low, intense voice.

"No more today, Pete," Hawk insisted, anger tingeing the words with a harsh sharpness.

"Damn it to hell, Hawk. Every day we wait, we risk some other little girl dying like that. Shit, Man, I hate this almost as much as you do," Pete continued. "I *like* Jo, I really do, but I've got a little girl at home. I know how I'd feel if someone told me she'd died like this."

Pete was obsessed. Jo knew Hawk was aware of that fact, and empathized. His objections were personal, not professional, and Jo couldn't let that stand in the way of his investigation.

"We can't stop now, Hawk, not when we're this close!" Pete's face was intense and determined.

"He's right, Hawk," Jo said weakly. She was standing behind him, feeling like she might collapse if a strong breeze stirred. "Every day, we risk another…" Jo shuddered so violently Hawk had to grab her to keep her from falling. "Let's go to the second place. Maybe I'll see more. Maybe there's a clue I can pick up."

"Jo, you can barely stand," Hawk tried to reason with her.

"Hawk," Jo put her hands on his arms, her eyes meeting his. "The more I put myself into those visions, the longer I'm close to…him," she shuddered, "the closer I'll get." It was hard to explain what she wanted him to understand. "I'm getting impressions all the time now, from his thoughts and feelings. I'm starting to see from inside his head, instead of just viewing the scene."

Hawk was clearly torn. "That sounds...bad, Jo, dangerous." His eyes were agonized, his features rigid with what it was costing him to control his emotions.

Jo shrugged. "I...I've done it...once before." She couldn't altogether suppress the tremor that shook her at the memory. She'd become so enmeshed in Samuel Hoekkendale's head, she'd felt as if she were drowning in the insanity—indelibly tainting herself with its vileness. It had left her shaken and haunted for months afterwards.

"You slip into the victim's head, too, Jo. That can't be easy," Hawk said, in a low, intense voice.

Jo closed her eyes momentarily, and then nodded. "Yeah," she whispered. "Sometimes." She lifted her gaze to meet and lock with his, saying nothing more. Hawk's jaw clenched and unclenched several times, but he nodded his acceptance. She knew if he were in Pete's shoes, he'd be pushing just as hard, demanding just as much.

Closing her eyes, she nodded acceptance of what was to come. Now that Hawk had agreed, Jo realized she wasn't sure she had the courage to live that nightmare again—but she had to try.

They had to find this bastard, and fast. He was going to strike again—very, very soon. Jo could feel it—hell, she could damn near taste it! The need to stalk, torture, and kill, was as dominate an impression as the images she had forced herself to witness. The craving was strong. So stimulating and exhilarating, it was addictive.

Yeah, that's it! The power is addictive—the killer's hooked on the high.

~ ~ ~

"Restrain them, impale them on his penis? Purge the world of what, women?" Bev asked, lifting a puzzled face to look at Pete, and then Hawk.

Hawk shrugged. "Sounds about as plausible as anything else we've come up with."

"What's he thinkin'?" Bev said, almost to herself. It just didn't add up. Every vision that Jo had today, had ended with the same line—the same mission. Bev paced, a photo of Stephanie Moore clutched in one hand. The R-I-P, carved into the girl's chest was clearly visible in this picture.

Bev hadn't liked Jo when they'd first met. She was everything Bev wasn't. The fact that she claimed psychic powers had only added to Bev's disgust—until she'd seen the woman in action.

Judas, Bev thought, it was like...freakin' eerie shit! Jo could see and feel things that had happened—as if she actually slipped inside the killer's head, and was thinkin' his friggin' thoughts!

Bev shuddered inwardly at the memory of Jo's face distorting with those shifts of awareness. She'd uttered words that could only be the ramblings of a deranged mind. It hadn't brought them any closer to knowing who he was, but they knew he wasn't finished yet. He was still hungry—still angry—still lethal!

The visions made Jo sick to her stomach. She'd retched and retched, until there was nothing but bile—and still she'd struggled to curb the nausea. It was more than obvious she grew weaker with every excursion into that haunted mind-world. At the last crime sight, Jo finally collapsed, nearly sending Hawk over the edge of control.

The tension between Pete and Hawk was almost palpable now, but somehow, they were holdin' it together. No, Bev didn't doubt any longer—no one could fake like that. Shit, who'd want to?

"This son of a bitch is vicious, and damn illusive," Hawk muttered, almost to himself.

"Another Jack the Ripper," Pete threw out.

"Somebody the RIP-murderer," Bev supplied.

"Well, Jack has taken a fancy to that handle," Hawk growled.

Pete scowled at him, his eyes heavy-lidded and red-rimmed. "What the hell you talkin' about, Hawk?" he snapped, pulling out a cigarette and lighting it from the butt of the one he'd just finished.

"Jack Hollings, the editor of our local paper." Hawk tossed a newspaper at Pete. The headline jumped out in bold, black letters: '*MYSTERY R-I-P MURDERER! Where Will He Strike Next?*'

"Judas Priest," Pete sucked hard on his cigarette before continuing. "He's gonna have the whole damned southeastern part of the state in a frenzied panic."

"Yeah, but it's good press," Hawk spat. He sat on the edge of his desk, rubbing the bridge of his nose. "Maybe our killer's read somethin' somewhere that he's copycatting," he offered, looking exhausted.

It was well past midnight. Hawk had taken Jo home hours ago. Bev knew Hawk's brother and sister-in-law were staying with her, and that his mother was helping look after the kids. They would probably be at it again tomorrow, bright and early, if Pete had anything to say about it.

"Been there," Pete groaned. "We've checked and cross-checked everything we could get our hands on."

"Yeah," Bev yawned, "a big, fat, zero. Zip, zilch, nada, nothing!" She moved to the darkened window of Hawk's office, wondering if the motel they were staying at had a massaging bed. She really needed something more than a hard, flat mattress tonight.

They'd hit one dead end after another. The trail wasn't cold, but it was damn close to it. If nothing else, Jo's visions had brought home the chilling viciousness of the mind behind these atrocities. Bev desperately needed something to warm her up again.

Come to think of it, she just might get lucky. She'd met a nice young man the other night, at the local bar. He'd been uncommonly attentive, and even handed her his cell number. Bev's hand reached into her pant's pocket, feeling the small slip of paper the man had given her. Maybe he'd be around tonight—after they wrapped things up here.

Hawk stood up. "Okay, with every victim, Jo said this sick-o had to restrain them, impale them, and then purge the world." He wrote the words in black on a dry erase board across from his desk.

Suddenly, Bev stopped in the middle of her pacing, the picture in her hand shaking slightly as she looked up at Hawk, and then Pete.

"What?" Pete snarled, exhaustion finding expression in anger.

"That's *IT*," Bev whispered, her eyes wide. It really didn't get them any closer, but she had his signature!

"What?" Hawk asked as his eyes narrowed.

Walking to the board and picking up a red marker, Bev drew a box around the first letter of each of the three words Hawk had written there. Restrain, Impale, Purge.

"I'll be God-damned!" Pete hissed, smoke from his cigarette floating into the room on his exhalation of breath.

"Shit," Hawk muttered.

"What does the victim profile look like, Hawk?" Pete asked standing and pacing as he puffed on his cigarette.

"Well, the first girl last summer, Nichole Umbridge, was a twenty-one year old coed at Peru College, majoring in business. Victim two was the runaway, Stephanie Moore. A twenty-year-old that dropped out of Peru in September. Vic three, was Brandi Cambridge. Twenty-three years old and never went to Peru, but roomed with someone who did. Hawk shook his head miserably. "*Damn*, what a waste!"

"They're all young, college aged," Bev commented.

Pete scowled. "Too damned young to die like that."

Bev ignored Pete's temper tantrum, continuing her line of reasoning. "They all seem to have some tie to the college," she observed. "You checked that out?"

Hawk nodded. "Yeah, but you're welcome to go over that territory again, if you've a yearnin' to," he replied. "I've run everything, from hobbies to medical histories, and boyfriends to high school affiliations. The only thing that remotely ties them together is that they all lived around this general vicinity, and they've all been on the Peru college campus at some time in the recent past."

"Okay," Bev pursued her original train of thought, "maybe our killer used the college to scout for victims. You know, stalking, and deciding which one to go after."

Hawk nodded. "It's possible."

"Not enough, though, is it?" Bev sighed.

Hawk shook his head.

"Crap, we ain't got jack-shit," Pete fumed. "We're looking for a needle in a fuckin' haystack!"

Hawk closed his eyes and massaged the bridge of his nose again. He looked as if he'd had the exact same thought more than once tonight. "Have you checked other campuses?" he asked in a weary voice. "Any missing girls or murders that might be remotely similar?"

Pete was pacing, an angry, frustrated expression on his face. "Like we need to dig up more corpses?"

"I'd be curious to know if there's any kind of pattern, anywhere. Is he just now startin' this killing spree, or has he been at it awhile?"

"I'll do some checkin', Hawk," Bev offered. She walked to the window again and stared out. One hand, shoved into a pant's pocket, idly fingered the small slip of paper.

Please God, let him be awake and horny. I need a healthy distraction right now.

She'd had enough of this dark, ugly case. She needed something—someone—who could drive it from her head, even if only for a few hours. A small, knowing smile played about her mouth.

The man had been flattering and attentive, promising her things she'd never had before—things that had left her panties wet and her gut twisted in knots. Just remembering made her groin throb with wanting.

Yeah, she was gonna have to look up…what was his name? She suddenly realized—she had no idea.

~ ~ ~

Bev stretched lazily, her body still thrumming with the intensity of the physical release. The man next to her on the motel bed stretched, too, toying with one of her bared breasts. "You're a little wild cat in bed, Bev. I like that." He winked at her.

It made her insides ignite again. She wanted more!

Short hair stuck out at odd angles, hopelessly mussed from the frantic lovemaking, and her face was flushed. Leaning over, Bev started suckling at one of her partner's nipples, her tongue darting in and out.

The man groaned. Lying back on the bed, he relaxed, allowing Bev to tease his skin with her mouth and fingertips. She continually glanced up, curious to see his reactions, enjoying his pleasure.

He was so handsome! Men with his kind of looks seldom gave her a second glance, let alone wanted to make love to her. The things he'd done! The places he'd touched! Bev wanted to please him—to make him hungry for her again and again, all night long. Her mouth moved slowly down his slightly paunchy belly, intent on firing him for another go-around.

"Damn," he whispered, his hands splayed through her hair. "I love horny bitches!"

"Does it feel good?" she asked, allowing her tongue and mouth to stimulate his still flaccid penis.

"Yeah, Sweetcakes, it feels damned good," he replied, his head back and his eyes closed.

Bev growled.

"You don't look like a wild cat, you know that?" the man whispered.

"Looks can be deceiving," she purred.

"Yeah," he said hoarsely, holding her head down as he savored the sensations her mouth was stirring. "Looks are very deceiving."

~ ~ ~

"Jo lay quietly on the mat, her energy spent, but feeling good. It had been her first workout since…her mind still shied away from even the sound of his name! How long would it be before she'd be able to hear it without shuddering?

Devin was dead! She'd lived with the fear so long—the reality of his death was hard to accept. Sometimes, she found herself reacting as though he were still alive—still a threat. She turned her head so she could look out the huge plate glass window at the front of the dojo, setting those thoughts aside.

It was late—past ten—and from what she could see of the sky, it was a clear night. A crescent moon rode low on the horizon and the sky was brimming, full of twinkling stars. She was still amazed at how many stars she could see, and how bright they appeared here. She'd turned out all the lights except one, enjoying the peacefulness of the quiet, empty dojo. A Yanni CD played softly. It was relaxing, serene. Her ribs were still tender, but she was feeling stronger every day.

"You sure pick odd times to work out," Eric said softly from the hallway that led to the back door.

Jo started, sitting up self-consciously. "Sorry, Eric," she smiled at Hawk's friend. "I'm done, just winding down." She was surprised he was already wearing his gi.

"You looked lost in thought."

"Not really," Jo confessed. "Just enjoying the peace and quiet for a moment."

"Feel like a little friendly sparring?" He offered casually, bowing and moving onto the mat. He sat down cross-legged beside her.

Jo was tired and ready to call it a night. She didn't want to appear rude, but being alone with Eric in a darkened dojo, made her a little uncomfortable. "Not tonight," she said honestly. "I've had about all I can handle for one workout." She could only hope he'd understand and not take offense.

"Sure?" He asked, his voice dropping to a husky, seductive pitch as he moved toward her, leaning across her body.

Jo rolled down onto the mat in an attempt to evade the physical contact, but it left an opening for Eric to straddle her, one hand beside each of her shoulders. "There are all kinds of workouts, Jo."

She knew exactly what Eric was implying. Her heart beat wildly as she tried to roll away from under him. Don't do this, she pleaded silently. Please!

"Eric, I…I want to go home," Jo said, controlling the pitch of her voice with difficulty. Her heart was pounding frantically.

"What, no good-bye kisses?" he teased.

Jo was past the point of politeness. "Get off me!"

"Whoa, or what?" he countered.

"Or I'll kick your ass." Jo didn't recognize the male voice that answered that question, but Eric obviously did.

He immediately rolled off Jo, allowing her to scramble to her feet unhindered. "Shit, Dave, I was just having a little fun," he defended himself.

"Your idea of fun is damned warped," Dave snapped. "Come here, Jo," he said gently, one hand extended toward her. She obeyed the directive without question, taking Dave's hand and allowing him to pull her behind the protective mass of his body.

Eric was on his feet now, one hand reaching out in supplication. "Come on, Dave, you know that didn't mean jack-shit."

Dave's face was hard and cold. "Considering what this woman has been through, I'd say it does mean shit, Buddy. Apologize," he commanded, his hands clenching and unclenching as he glared at his friend.

Eric ducked his head, his face crimsoning. "Sorry, Jo, I was just teasin'. I didn't mean nothin' by it."

I almost feel sorry for you, you son-of-a-bitch, Jo thought, softening a little. "It's okay. Just, don't go there again, please."

"How about I escort you home?" Dave volunteered, his eyes still holding Eric's gaze.

"My…my car's outside, I'll be okay." Jo was feeling weak with relief as reaction began setting in, but she could manage to drive herself home. Just for a moment, she'd slipped back to another place and time—feeling trapped and helpless. She clung to Dave's shoulder for a minute more, still feeling weak-kneed.

"You sure?" Dave glanced over at her, and then reached out and covered her hands with one of his. "Want me to call Hawk?" he asked gently. "He's on duty tonight, but he'd come in a heartbeat."

Jo shook her head, then reached to grab up her belongings. "No, I'm fine. Thanks, Dave," she said softly.

Dave walked her to the door, and then stepped outside with her. "He really didn't mean nothin', Jo." he said in defense of his friend.

"Yeah, I know," she replied, still shaking a little inside. "It's okay. I'm okay."

"Eric just feels driven to prove himself in strange ways, sometimes."

"It's okay, Dave. I get it." Jo was ready to let the whole thing drop. She didn't know why Eric had come on like that, but it had resurrected memories she wanted dead and buried. Jo closed her eyes, shaking her head slightly to rid herself of the thoughts that were pounding incessantly, demanding acknowledgement.

She didn't want to remember.

~ ~ ~

"Why didn't you tell me?" Hawk ground out, finding Jo on her knees planting a small garden behind the cottage. Lester was bouncing around her, tugging at her shirt when he could get a hold of it.

"What?" Jo asked, dusting dirt from her hands and wiping her forehead with the back of her wrist. "You look like you're ready to bust something into its collective parts," she teased in a light voice.

"Damned straight, Little Girl." Hawk grabbed Jo's shoulders and pulled her to her feet. "Why didn't you say something?"

"Hawk, what the hell are you talking about?" Jo asked evenly, obviously making an effort to control an angry response.

"I just had a little chat with Dave?" Hawk raised a single dark brow, looking at her expectantly.

"Oh."

"Oh. *OH?*" His anger was on the upswing again. "That's not something that just slips your mind!" He was feeling impotent rage.

"It happened a week ago, Hawk, it's past being important. Let it be over, okay? Eric got a little out of line, he apologized, end of story." Jo picked up her garden tools and tossed them into a work bucket, and then reached for the puppy.

"I'm gonna kick his ass into a new time zone!" Hawk spat. His hands balled into fists at his sides as he fought to control the fury.

Jo looked up at him. "Hawk, it was nothing, let it be over." She went up on her tiptoes and drew his head close for a tongue-teasing kiss, one arm still clutching Lester.

His arms were around her immediately, his mouth hungry and demanding, until Lester squeaked a protest. "Damn," he said with passion, "I'd like to continue this in your bedroom, but I'm on a mission." He smiled down at Jo, his anger suddenly dissipating as he ruffled Lester's head with gentle affection.

"Mmmmm, sounds important, Sheriff." Jo set Lester down, and then moved closer to Hawk, her tongue following the curve of his neck and finding the hollow at the base of his throat.

He growled low in his chest, his mouth claiming hers in a long, ardent kiss.

Unexpectedly he pulled away, putting distance between them.

"Stop that," he admonished, shaking a finger in her face. "Mom says to round up the kids and make sure everyone's wearing old clothes. We're going fishin'."

"Really?" Jo clapped her hands in delight. Lester bounced at her feet, barking his high-pitched puppy bark. Jo smiled at Lester's antics, wiping at suddenly teary eyes.

"Jo, it's just fishin'. What the hell you cryin' for?"

"I love fishing," she replied in a soft, pensive voice.

"Well, hell, I like fishin' too, but I ain't cryin' about it," Hawk said, grinning.

"It's something I used to do with my Dad—a lifetime ago," Jo tried to explain.

"Yeah, me too." Hawk pulled her close for an exploratory kiss. Instantly the passion flared between them. "Shit," he swore, more at himself than at Jo. He was hard with need for her, and wondered absently if they'd have time for just a little…No! His mother would kill him—painfully!

"Hey," he said, his mind latching onto the significance of Jo's words. "You called your folks yet?" He watched Jo's face intently, noting the tic near one eye and the clenching of muscles along her jaw line. He hated to take her thoughts anywhere close to Devin and the nightmare she'd just lived through, but he knew dealing with it was part of the healing process.

"Yeah," she whispered, "yeah, I have."

"They comin' out to see you?"

"Probably, but not right away. I'm gonna fly home later and, well…" Jo's voice trailed off. She was picking at a frayed spot on her work gloves, giving it her undivided attention.

"You heard from Devin's family?" Hawk hated pressing but somehow, he felt he needed to.

"No," Jo replied, still absorbed with her glove. "Mom called and said his funeral was last week. I…" Jo raised agonized eyes to meet Hawk's gaze. "Maybe the kids should have…gone. He is…was…their dad."

Hawk nodded. "Yeah, but you can take them to the grave site later, once they've had a chance to deal with it all and accept what's happened."

Jo didn't say anything. She just nodded.

"Dealing with the legal shit's gonna be tough," Hawk continued, taking the gloves from Jo's hands and tossing them into her work bucket, "but I'll go with you, if you want."

Jo looked up, hope lifting the shadows that had clouded her eyes. "Really?"

A half-smile tugged at the corner of his mouth as he replied, "Yeah, Little Girl, really."

Jo threw herself at him, wrapping her arms around his neck, and finding his mouth once again. Hawk pulled her close, savoring the feel of her body against his, and the taste of her kiss.

Forcing himself to release her and step away, he said, "Come on, let's get hoppin'. Mom's making a picnic lunch, and I've got the poles and bait. Bert's comin', and Beejah is bringin' his boys. We'll even take Lester along, and make it a regular family affair."

Jo smiled, clapping her hands together at the remembered prospect of an outing, and then suddenly looked distraught. "I…I don't have a license."

Hawk laughed. "Well, I do have some pull with local law enforcement, but we'll stop at the liquor store downtown for licenses, just to play it safe."

Grinning from ear to ear, Jo sighed. "A whole day of laying in the shade, splashing in the water, and hauling in supper." She threw her arms around Hawk's neck again, holding him in a tight hug for several seconds. "Did I tell you today, how much I love you?" she whispered.

Hawk growled. "Yeah, but you can tell me again, Little Girl." he said huskily. His heart filled to near bursting at the look of expectancy and elation on her face. She'd needed this—a day away from the constant stress, and from endless absorption with death, victims, and killers. He needed the break, too. They were getting nowhere fast, and it was eating away at all of them.

It was only one day—but it would have to be enough, for now.

XXIX

"You taste good, did you know that?" The man licked his lips, his voice hoarse as though he seldom used it, or had used it too much recently.

The woman's cries and whimpers went unacknowledged. She struggled against the rope that secured her wrists and ankles, but the bindings only became tighter, cutting painfully into her flesh.

"Now, here's a toy you'll like." The man grinned, showing uneven, overlapping teeth. He ran a tongue across his lips again, as he held it up for her to see.

Only a single, bare bulb glowed in the room, suspended from the ceiling on a long, black cord. It wasn't much light, but it was more than enough to allow the woman to see what he held. It looked like a small animal trap—two half-moon shaped pieces of metal hinged on the flat end. The rounded jaws were smooth, but inset with straight pins that looked as if he'd painstakingly welded them in place.

"You open it like this." He demonstrated. "Then you can put it wherever you want. On a buttocks," he slapped her backside, "or a thigh." His hand strayed up high on the woman's inner leg, callously pinching her flesh.

She bit back the cry of pain, squeezing her eyes shut.

"Maybe right here," he teased, his hand toying with her genitals. He enjoyed watching her eyes fly open, wide with dread at the mere anticipation of such a thing. He laughed at her look of sheer horror.

"Please," she whispered. "*Please*, don't hurt me."

The man ignored her words, continuing as if she hadn't even spoken. His tone was conversational. "Actually," he drawled, "I have two. One for each," he paused, drawing out the moment, and relishing his victim's frantic struggles. "Breast," he hissed, leaning close to her ear. As he finished speaking, he snapped one, and then the other, into place.

The woman did scream then.

A long, tortured, cry of anguish and utter hopelessness.

Jo saw her face.

She knew that face!

The woman's scream became her own.

~~~

The wind howled through the trees, tossing leaves and broken branches everywhere. It grasped up anything in its path, whipping debris before it with untamed abandon.

"What in the…" Hawk muttered, struggling to pull himself out of a deep sleep. Instinctively he glanced at his bedside clock. It was 2:50 AM. He hadn't crawled into bed until 12:52 that morning! One hand came up to rub sleep-drugged eyes as he struggled to orient himself.

What had he heard?

Has to be the wind, he reasoned to himself, looking over at his patio doors. He'd left them open. Normally, he liked the feel of a breeze at night, but obviously, a storm was brewing. Better check the windows, the thought moved Hawk to roll up to a sitting position on the side of his bed, his head in his hands.

Crap, he hadn't had a decent night's sleep in…God only knows how long.

The scream seemed to spring from the very heart of the storm—like a ghostly banshee blown in from hell, shrieking out in fury. It shattered Hawk's grogginess, bringing him fully awake.

Jo! It was coming from her place!

Pulling on jeans to cover his nakedness, Hawk sprinted down his deck stairs, an eerie sense of deja`vu enveloping him.

God, don't let it be another girl, please!

"He's got her. He's going to kill her," Jo cried, frantically fighting the bedclothes. She tumbled onto the floor as Hawk threw open the screen.

"Jo," he called out, "what's wrong?"

"Hurry, Hawk. Hurry!" she pleaded, tears drenching her face and choking her words. "He's got another one. She's not dead yet!"

"Where? Can you give me a location?"

It had been almost three weeks since the last murder—a long, silent, fruitless stretch of frustration and dead ends. Hawk grasped Jo's shoulders harder than he meant to, though she didn't appear to notice.

She closed her eyes, trying to concentrate. "Yes," she whispered. "I can take you there."

"NO!" Hawk's rebuttal was adamant. No way was he going to let her walk into even a remote chance of danger. "Tell me where," he demanded.

"I…I can't, Hawk, I don't know how to tell you. I just have to…*feel* it,"
~~~

Jo sobbed, clutching at his chest with trembling hands. “We have to hurry, please!”

“Okay, Baby, okay,” Hawk soothed in a calm voice, though his insides were anything but steady. He helped Jo to her feet, grabbing up jeans and a t-shirt she’d left draped over a reading chair.

She pulled them on frantically while Hawk dialed Pete’s cell phone.

“Meet me outside my office,” Hawk barked after he’d given Pete a succinct accounting. He listened for a moment more. “Okay, thirty minutes, tops.” There was another short pause. “Call Bev, have her notify them.”

Jo was staring at Hawk with wide, terror-filled eyes as he hung up. “What?” he asked, the look on her face giving him a nauseous feeling in the pit of his stomach.

“She…she can’t, Hawk,” Jo whispered, her voice raw with despair.

“What are you talkin’ about, Jo?” Every muscle in Hawk’s body tensed—waiting.

“Bev.” Jo was shaking from head to foot. “She can’t call anyone, he… *HE*…has her.”

~ ~ ~

“*Here*!” Jo’s cry was sudden, causing Hawk to whip the wheel hard and fast. His vehicle swerved dangerously on the loose dirt of the country road, eliciting a curse from Pete.

“Keep going.” Jo closed her eyes, opening her mind to the tug she felt. Her hands clutched a uniform shirt of Bev’s that Pete had given her. He’d seemed incredulous and skeptical at the request, but hadn’t argued.

“A long way, down this road,” Jo whispered, and then opened her eyes to see where they were.

Clouds scuttled across the sky. The moon was half-full. It hovered close to the western horizon, bathing the landscape with intermittent silver-white light. Jo could see trees blowing frantically about them, and an eerie howl shrieked around the car from time to time.

“We got weather warnings going off all over the damned place,” Pete muttered, pulling an earphone away from one ear. “Tornado watch for this area, Hawk.”

Hawk didn’t respond, just nodded his head, as his hands tightened convulsively on the wheel.

Jo kept her eyes closed as she reestablished a tenuous hold with the woman she sought to save. She wasn’t sure when the rain started. She was only aware that it pelted against the windows, and drummed out a tempestuous tempo on the roof of the pick-up.

"Left!" she shouted suddenly. "There. THERE!" She was pointing frantically at a side road they'd just passed.

Hawk screeched to a stop and backed around, then gunned his truck down the road Jo indicated.

No one spoke for several, long minutes, and then Jo whispered, pointing to the right, "There."

One lone house stood back off the road. It looked empty. All the windows were dark, and there was no sign of life. Trees lined the drive leading up to it, and Hawk could see the dark silhouettes of several out buildings and silos. He didn't know this place—had no idea who owned it. He turned off his headlights and stopped his vehicle at the end of the drive.

"You don't move, Little Girl," he commanded, his face close to Jo's. His brows furrowed ominously as he glared at her, daring her to argue. "Keep this close." He pressed a revolver into her hand.

"You know how to use it?" Pete asked, casually checking the magazine on his own firearm, and then sliding it smoothly back into the grip.

Jo didn't answer, merely nodded, and then realized neither man could see that response. "Yeah," she said shakily. "I can use it."

"Good girl." Hawk touched her cheek briefly before slipping away into the darkness, close on Pete's heels.

~~~

"I'll take the front," Pete said. "You got the back door."

"Be careful, Petey Pie," Hawk cautioned, using an old high school nickname.

"Shut up, Asshole," Pete growled, water running in runnels down his face and dripping off the end of his nose.

Hawk raised one dark brow, a reproving look on his face, then grinned and winked, as he turned to slip around the back.

Pete's hand shot out and grabbed his sleeve. "You too, Buddy," he said softly.

Hawk's teeth flashed in a bright smile, and then he slipped away, melting into the darkness and brush around the side of the house.

Unlocked? He was mildly surprised as he eased the back door open, shaking water out of his eyes. You're feelin' pretty damn safe, aren't you, Asshole?

Hawk's gun hand rested across the wrist of his left arm. His left hand clasped a flashlight, the lighted end protruding from the backside of his fist. Every muscle tensed as he eased his way through the kitchen.

He could hear muffled talking, but he couldn't pinpoint a source. Step, by
~~~

wary step, he progressed through the kitchen. It opened into a large dining room that was bare of furnishing. Hawk moved along one wall. With every measured, cautious step, his light raked the room around him and the path ahead. From the corner of his eye, he spotted another moving light. The living room, his brain acknowledged. Pete's in.

Pete apparently saw Hawk at almost the same instant.

With silent hand signals, Hawk motioned him to take the upstairs—Hawk would take the basement. He watched Pete move guardedly up the staircase, his gun braced securely on his left wrist. The flashlight he held swept back and forth, every step painstakingly precise.

Drawing a deep breath, Hawk eased the basement door open a fraction, praying it didn't need oiling. The murmur he'd heard off and on before, suddenly became a little louder.

Bingo! You're mine now, Shit Head.

Hawk could only pray he'd be in time to save Bev from the fate the other girls had suffered. He moved guardedly, one step at a time.

The scream tore through him like a bullet, sending his heart into overdrive. He didn't abandon caution all together, but moved with quicker, surer steps, his gun ready. Pete's progress was clearly audible above him, coming back from searching the upstairs.

He must have heard the scream too, Hawk surmised, the footsteps sounded hurried. Hawk waited, expecting to see Pete at the top of the stairs any minute, but he didn't show. A sudden, loud clattering, told him Pete had obviously encountered an unexpected obstacle or two.

Judas, can you make a little more noise there, Petey Pie, Hawk thought, as he made the decision to go on alone. He crept up on a partially open door.

Soft light filtered out of the room. Switching off his flashlight, Hawk stowed it, edging the door open a little wider—his gun ready. The view he had of Bev drew a gasp. He had to restrain himself from making a wild dash toward her.

Slowly, warily, he surveyed the room, checking every possible hiding place. It was empty except for Bev. Next to her sat a table covered with contraptions that would make the top ten on any torture chamber's list of dearly beloved. An open door at the other end of the room led to—only God knew where. Hawk closed it carefully. If physco-man got out this way, he ain't gettin' back in unnoticed, he thought, bracing the door with a nearby crate.

Holy shit, Hawk reeled as he cut through Bev's bonds and eased her tortured body to the ground. She's still alive, barely.

He found it hard to believe she could be. Blood covered her inner thighs and legs, and the flesh of her torso looked like strips of raw meat. The clamps on her breasts were still in place, and Hawk could see the killer had just begun his infamous tattoo.

Hawk's tone was gentle but insistent. "Come on, Bev, we're gonna get you outta here."

She was barely conscious, but one hand grabbed at his sleeve, demanding attention. "He'll...be...back," she gritted out, whimpering with anguish as Hawk tried to lift her. "Leave me...get..."

"No way, Girl! Not today." Hawk forced his voice to sound strong and sure, though he seriously doubted the woman had much time left, if the pool of blood on the floor was all hers. Gently, he eased her tormented body to the floor. She'd never walk out of here, and he couldn't carry her without causing further injury. He needed to get to his truck and radio for an ambulance. "Hang on, Bev."

"Sweet, isn't it?" The words hissed out from behind him.

Hawk spun around, dropping into a defensive posture, weapon in hand—and then froze.

His quarry stood in the doorway, Jo held tightly in his grasp.

She looked groggy and dazed, and water plastered her hair against her head. Bloody runnels ran down her face, dripping off her chin. The man pressed a Ruger against her ribs.

Hawk couldn't risk a shot. The chances of a finger convulsing on the trigger, were too great.

"Just lay it down, Buddy," the man said.

I know that voice!

Hawk couldn't see a face. Jo had been right-on when she'd said he wore a cowl. It obscured everything but a mouth, and the man was naked except for a bloody, metal covering over his genitals. The sight of it made Hawk want to gag. He could see pieces of flesh still imbedded on the tiny points of metal that protruded out at odd angles.

XXX

"No, Hawk," Jo groaned, struggling. "Don't do it. Kill him, now!"

"We both know he ain't goin' there."

Jo shuddered. She knew that voice! The shock of that realization petrified her with a suffocating dread.

"Who are you?" Hawk hissed, slowly lowering his weapon.

"Jo knows, don't you, Sweetcakes?"

Jo's eyes were wide as she met Hawk's dark gaze.

How could you know this man your entire life, and not have a clue? You never saw beneath the façade of, friend? The thoughts raced through her mind, but she said nothing.

"Now, step back toward that wall over there." The man motioned with his semiautomatic, directing Hawk away from the torture bed and Bev's crumpled body.

Suddenly, his gun came down toward Jo's head.

She tried to dodge the blow, but it clipped her, dropping her to her knees, half-conscious.

Hawk leapt toward them, coming up short as the man casually leveled the 9mm at Jo's head.

"You know I'll do it, Hawk. Don't go pissin' me off! Sit down, Buddy, you ain't goin' nowhere." He motioned to a chair against the wall, tossing Hawk a pair of handcuffs. "You probably got a pretty good idea how to work those," he sniggered.

Hawk glowered as he fastened the cuffs. He snapped one end around his left wrist, and the other on the chair arm, only complying after the man pressed his weapon against Jo's temple as incentive.

"You stinkin' bastard!" Hawk seethed, the words an ominous hiss of sound.

"A little torked off, are we?" The killer grinned. "Wait 'til you see the floor show." He reached for Jo, dragging her toward the bloodied bed.

She tried to fight, but her movements were disoriented and ineffective.

Her head throbbed, and she knew blood from the gash he'd opened on her scalp, covered half her face.

Hawk was on his feet immediately, chair and all, but the man turned and fired a single shot, hitting him mid-thigh. Crying out, Hawk dropped hard onto one knee, clutching the wound. Blood spurted out between his fingers.

With sheer effort of wil, he forced himself to stand.

"*HAWK*!" Jo screamed, trying to run toward him.

The killer grabbed her arm, spinning her around, and his open palm smacked hard against her face. "Ain't this a slice of heaven." He was obviously in his element as he turned and taunted Hawk, "Just sit back and let yourself get entertained, Macho Man. You ain't in control here!" Pulling off his cowl, he tossed it aside, before looking down at Jo with utter contempt.

She was on her hands and knees, shaking her head slowly from side to side, trying to clear her brain.

HAWK! Her mind reeled. Oh God, please be okay. *Please*!

~ ~ ~

"Don't do this, Eric. For God's sake, Man, why?" Hawk couldn't wrap his brain around it yet. "What about your wife and son? Don't do this to them."

Not Eric! They'd been friends since high school. He was married, and had a kid near Nate's age. Keep him talking. Keep him distracted. Get up, Jo, he pleaded silently.

"That bitch I'm married to deserves this more'n any of the whores I done." Eric's face suddenly contorted, his inner rage changing its lines into a mask Hawk didn't recognize. "But it's more fun watchin' her cringe and grovel, then it would be to snuff her out," Eric sneered.

"Why Eric? Why the torture…the murders…all of a sudden?" Hawk tried to keep Eric focused on him. "What the hell happened?"

Get up, Jo. Get away from here.

He refused to look at her, but Hawk was aware she was struggling to stay conscious, to gain her feet.

"Not so sudden." Eric looked pleased with himself as he bragged. "I been playing games all my life. Just none 'round these parts, or at least not too close."

"What the hell you talkin' about, Westermann?" Hawk spat, disgusted by the braggadocio.

"Oh, I get around. There's lots of whores needin' a lesson on respect!" Eric's free hand reached down to cradle his penis as his mouth twisted into a leer.

"You God-damned son of a bitch!" Hawk spat. "How many?" He hissed the question.

"More 'n you'll ever find, Mr. Macho Sheriff-man!"

Hawk suddenly had a flash of insight. Eric had applied once, for a Deputy Sheriff position, but Hawk had turned him down. He was too volatile, and far too hotheaded. It hadn't set well with Eric—strained their relationship for a while.

"This stem back to that job you didn't get, Eric?" Hawk asked, keeping his voice steady.

"Oh, come on, Hawk, you disappoint me," Eric ridiculed. "I thought you'd be quicker on the uptake than that. I been at this awhile, now. One, even pretty close to home."

Hawk racked his brain. Murder? Close to home?

Suddenly the puzzle pieces clicked into place.

Oh, my God. Oh no, it couldn't be! Hawk's knees buckled, forcing him to sit down as he asked, "Megan? You raped and killed your *sister*?"

Eric nodded, grinning.

"Why Eric? For the love of God, *why*?" Hawk felt as if his whole world had unexpectedly turned upside down and inside out. It just wasn't possible!

This is a dream. A fuckin' nightmare. It has to be! Things like this just didn't happen—not here! Not with people he knew and cared for!

"The little *whore*!" Eric slipped into his memories. "She was as bad as any other woman. Leadin' me on, teasing me with lookin' but never touchin'. She didn't want no part of me," Eric said, his hand touching his penis again, as he spoke.

"She was just a little girl," Hawk growled, his face contorted with loathing.

Eric laughed. "Sure she was. A little girl that liked to play doctor, now and again, a real tease." He leaned over then, grabbing Jo by the arm and dragging her toward the bed. "Kinda like you, Bitch," he hissed in her ear. "Didn't want me touchin' you, but you sent out signals sayin' you wanted it. Now, is that nice?"

Jo didn't answer. Hawk could see she struggled with the blow to her head, trying to stay conscious. He tried to adjust his own position, put less weight on his wounded leg. With a conscious effort, he put the pain out of his mind. He couldn't allow himself to acknowledge it.

"Eric, we can work this out," he said in a placating voice. "Just let Jo go. Come on, Buddy, let's talk this through." Hawk steeled his tone to an even pitch. It was the hardest thing he'd ever had to do. Every instinct in him was screaming for action—for vengeance.

"Don't *patronize* me, Hawk. You and I both know there ain't no workin' this out. They'll *fry* me, but they gotta catch me first," Eric said casually, almost lightly. His expression and tone sent a shiver of alarm and dread through Hawk's body.

Who are you? He thought incredulously. Who the hell are you?

"She was my first, you know."

Hawk's mind reeled. Eric was boasting, in a casual, conversational tone. There was no remorse, no self-recrimination. Not even the remotest semblance of accountability for what he'd done.

"I ended her pain too fast. I didn't get nothin' outta it." Eric grinned at the look on Hawk's face.

"You're a sick bastard," Hawk spat between clenched teeth, tearing a strip of material from his shirt to tie around the wound on his thigh.

"No, not sick, really. I prefer to call it…eccentric. Look!" Eric turned and swept his hand above the table laden with metallic horrors, some of them still bloody. "I've perfected things since Megan, see?" He fixed his eyes on Jo. "Looks like I'm gonna get a little of this ass, after all." Eric's gaze moved slowly back to Hawk, with a cold and triumphant grin distorting his handsome face.

His wink was goading and disdainful as he reached over and grabbed one of Jo's wrists. Yanking her toward the head of the bed, he securely bound it to one of the posts of the headboard. Jo wrestled against his superior strength, but it was a futile battle. She could barely hold her head up.

Hawk gritted his teeth, afraid to act irrationally. Eric still held the gun.

"How'd you get Bev, she's a seasoned cop?" he asked, grasping at anything to keep Eric talking, keep his attention focused away from Jo.

"She was the easiest one of all," Eric crowed. "Just a man-starved, homely bitch, needin' a good fuck," Eric taunted. "I kept her serviced, and wormed information outta her. I milked her pretty good these past few weeks. Pretty slick, hey?"

"God, I can't believe I never saw this side of you," Hawk spat, pain making his voice harsh and raspy.

Eric just laughed, ignoring Hawk's words as he grabbed Jo by the hair again. She yelped, struggling, her feet kicking out as she desperately tried to make contact with some part of his anatomy.

"This one's a fighter," Eric licked his lips maliciously. "Maybe she'll help me work up an appetite," he said in a conversational voice, setting down the Ruger on the tray of torture tools. He picked up a small hand rake with large, razor sharp points fanning out from its handle.

Jo was beyond rational thought. She could only stare at the weapon in Eric's hand as terror contorted her face. Hawk could almost see it pushing out every ounce of reason.

"NO!" Hawk struggled to his feet, fighting to reach her.

"I'm gonna really enjoy this," Eric gloated as he laid the blades of the weapon against Jo's thigh and pressed down.

Jo's scream echoed through the room as the pointed prongs pierced her jeans and made contact with flesh. She thrashed wildly, grabbing at Eric's wrist with her free hand, her feet kicking out in a futile effort to inflict damage.

"I'm gonna KILL you, Westermann!" Hawk shouted. Unconcealed fury surged through him as he lunged forward, dragging the chair with him.

"Pretty brave talk for a man, cuffed to a chair, with two bullet holes in him." Eric grabbed up his weapon and fired again, hitting Hawk square in his right shoulder.

Hawk cried out as his body slammed back against the wall, propelled by the impact of the bullet. It left him sprawled on the ground.

"*NO!*" Jo screamed the denial, her foot finally making contact. She hit Eric's gun arm hard, sending the 9 mm flying from his grasp.

Eric grunted, stumbling back.

"*HAWK*!" Jo struggled desperately with the rope that held her captive.

"Okay, Bitch," Eric hissed, "now it's your turn." Clutching his hand, he stalked toward her.

~~~

Jo gave up on the bindings that refused to budge, scooting her body off the side of the bed. Standing, she felt a sudden, unexpected calm fill her as she turned to face Eric.

At least I can use my legs, she thought. Her head throbbed with an agony that made her stomach roll and pitch, but seeing Hawk shot a second time had cleared her brain and focused her energy.

After the initial, all-consuming horror, her brain honed itself to a single-minded, deadly resolution. The rage that seethed through her was detached now, implacable and merciless.

I'm sorry, God, she apologized silently, but there was no sorrow or regret. She intended to kill this man—without hesitation, without pity, and with absolutely no compunction.

"Come on, Jo. You're gonna enjoy this sliding inside you." Eric's tone was coaxing as he cradled himself, flaunting his appendage. He was hard and aroused.

It made Jo want to vomit. "I'd never feel that insignificant prick of yours," she forced herself to laugh, though the sound was humorless and harsh. She could see Eric's face distort with rage at her words.
~~~

That's it, Asshole. *React.* Get mad. Get careless.

Her hand was still working at the rope holding her.

Eric grabbed up a long knife from his table of horrors, flaunting it menacingly as he moved forward.

Jo watched his eyes. Just let me get close, and I'll kick your balls into the next galaxy.

Her mind was focused, her concentration unwavering. She didn't, at first, see Hawk force himself to a standing position. Nor was she aware he raised the chair, smashing it into the wall until it splintered and freed his arm—but Eric was.

Whipping around, Eric brandished his weapon at Hawk.

It was the opening Jo needed.

With every scrap of strength she could draw upon, she swung her body up and out, using the rope around her wrist as a pivot. She drew her legs in toward her torso as her body launched forward, and then kicked the right leg out, catching Eric square in the back. The blow sent him sprawling to the ground. Jo's bound wrist brought her to a sudden and painful stop, yanking her back hard, but it was enough—Eric was down.

~ ~ ~

Hawk was on him immediately, a booted foot making solid contact with his ribs. Eric screamed in pain, and then rolled away, one hand around his middle. Hawk stumbled to one knee, as the force of his action took its toll on his weakened body. He resolutely pushed himself to stand, and the two men circled one another warily.

"This might be more fun than the girl," Eric snarled, breathing hard. "We've done this a time or two, haven't we, Buddy?" he goaded, referring to their friendly sparring matches.

"Yeah, Eric, we have," Hawk replied, feeling blood trickling down his back and chest. His right leg was almost numb. He couldn't draw this out much longer—he knew that, and so did Eric.

Whirling suddenly, Eric's leg came around in a spinning sidekick. Hawk managed to evade the blow, catching the apendage with one hand, and yanking hard. Eric went down on one knee, but it was all Hawk needed. He landed a well-placed kick in the man's groin, driving the metal casing back against Eric's flesh.

Eric screamed, doubling over, but almost immediately rolled out of Hawk's reach.

The force of the strike drove Hawk to his knees. He grabbed out to keep from falling, his hand making contact with Eric's table of toys and pulling it down with him.

Jo saw the Ruger spin across the floor.

So did Eric!

He crawled his way toward it in a semi-fetal position, cradling his genitals with one hand.

~ ~ ~

Jo could see blood trickling through Eric's fingers, leaving a trail along the floor.

Her hand was nearly free!

There was enough blood around her wrist now to allow it to almost slide through the rope—almost, but not quite. She struggled with frantic desperation. She had to get to Eric before he reached that Rugar!

"Hawk, the gun!" she cried.

Hawk hadn't seen it. He was trying to keep from collapsing all together, fighting against the torture of movement, to get to his feet.

THERE! Jo's bloodied hand slid free—but she was too late.

Reaching for the semiautomatic, Eric grabbed it up and rolled into position to fire.

"DOWN!" Hawk yelled, propelling his body toward Jo and carrying her to the ground under him as the first shot hit the wall directly behind them.

Jo heard Hawk's grunt of agony as they slammed into the floor, rolling. "Stay down," he commanded, forcing Jo behind the edge of the bed for cover.

"You're dead, Hawk, you just don't know it yet," Eric goaded, firing several more shots that ricocheted too close for comfort. "Then your woman and me, we're gonna have us a little party."

~ ~ ~

Hawk didn't answer. He'd managed to force Jo behind the bed, but he could see Bev lying on the floor not six feet from him. She was in the open, an easy target for a stray bullet. He knew if he tried to drag her to cover, Eric could easily riddle them both.

"No," Jo whispered frantically, suddenly comprehending what Hawk was contemplating. "You're wounded, Hawk. Please!" She clutched at his shirt to hold him back, but he'd already decided against it.

They were running out of time!

Eric fired again.

The angle of the careening bullets had changed. Eric was moving toward the stairs. It would eliminate whatever protection the bed offered if he succeeded in reaching that goal.

"Comfy back there?" Eric taunted.

They had no choices left. Hawk's head rested against the wall as he sucked in air, gritting his teeth against the anguish that made each breath a battle.

Jo…listen to…me," he ground out, groaning as he eased himself into a position to move. "We've got…to take Eric, out…or we're…both dead."

She nodded, glancing toward the stairs. Even crippled as he was, he'd reach them all too soon.

"Where's Pete?" she asked, her hand cupping Hawk's face.

"Eric must've…gotten to him." It was the only logical conclusion. Pete would have been here otherwise. Hawk sealed his mind from acknowledging what that meant. "As soon…as he…comes into view…I'll charge." He closed his eyes, struggling to control his reaction to the inferno that sucked the breath from his lungs, and licked along every nerve ending in his body.

"You try…and get…to Bev's…gun."

~ ~ ~

Jo looked at Hawk with surprise

A gun? Why hadn't she noticed?

She followed Hawk's nod toward a pile of clothing, disdainfully heaped on the floor not more than a yard from Bev's body. She could see the tip of a gun holster protruding.

It's a chance!

"Say your goodbyes," Eric jeered, his voice so much closer.

Jo's eyes returned instantly to Hawk's face, and her hand came up to stroke his cheek. "I love you, Candy Ass," she whispered. "Live, for me."

Before Hawk realized her intention, Jo was up, diving in a forward roll that carried her to the edge of the discarded clothing.

Eric aimed several shots in her direction. The explosion of sound assaulted Jo's ears as bullets ricocheted around her. She groped, with wild desperation for the gun she knew was there.

"*Son-of-a…*" she heard Hawk's oath.

She was aware his body lunged, almost on her heels, but he propelled himself in the other direction, toward Eric.

God, help him! Please!

The world around her suddenly slipped into slowed motion. She could see their actions unfold as if she stood apart, watching.

Jo rolled onto her back, pulling Bev's Glock from its holster.

Hawk had a knife in his hand, probably one he'd snatched from the scattered arsenal on the floor around them.

She saw the blade fly through the air, end over end, toward Eric.

Eric ducked, easily dodging the weapon, and then he turned, aiming his Ruger at Hawk's heart.

"*NO!*" Jo screamed, pulling the trigger of her weapon.

It fired, again and again, until she could hear nothing but the impotent clicking of an empty magazine.

"Easy, Baby," Hawk said soothingly, putting his hand on the top of the gun and gently working it out of her frozen grip.

Jo looked up at him in stunned disbelief.

He was alive! She was alive!

"It's over," he whispered, swaying.

XXXI

Jo paced the length of the front porch, Lester bouncing happily at her feet. Hawk was due home any minute. She hadn't seen him in almost three weeks.

Coming to terms with the reality of the past month was something she still struggled with on a daily basis. When she allowed herself to, she could clearly remember the turmoil of that horrendous night—the blood, the flashing lights, the scurrying police, the ambulance sirens. The stench of death had permeated her clothing, and filled her nostrils.

An early morning sun peeked over the horizon when they guided her out of that house of horrors, trying to find its way from behind dark banks of storm clouds that still scuttled across the sky. She had felt surprise—the storm had raged when they'd made their way to the farmhouse—but that had been a lifetime ago!

Pete was alive.

She saw him half carried out of the house, a paramedic on one side, and a police officer on the other. He'd looked over at her and nodded, his face a bloody mess, but she didn't get a chance to speak with him. An ambulance rushed him away.

Bev, hadn't been that lucky.

They carried her out too, on a gurney—a bloody sheet pulled over her face.

That was when Jo had retched, as everything in her protested the irrevocability of that reality. The memory still made her break down, if she allowed herself to think about it.

They'd wheeled Hawk out, too.

He'd collapsed, losing consciousness.

Insane with dread, Jo screamed at the paramedics and police to help him. They had, though she'd not made their task any easier.

She'd seen Hawk only twice since then.

Once, in ICU, immediately after he'd undergone seven hours of surgery. She sat next to him for almost forty-eight hours, until Bert practically carried her out of the room, forcing her to go home and rest. The second time was about eight hours later. Hawk had been unconscious, but she'd held his hand and talked to him for a long time. She told him about Pete—and about Bev.

And then, leaning over to whisper the words close to his ear, she said, "Hawk, I'm pregnant." A trembling hand reached out to trace his eyebrow, caress the angle of his cheekbone. "Please, come back to me—to us." He didn't respond, of course, but she still believed she'd felt his fingers squeeze her hand—just a little.

The past two weeks, for Jo, was still a blur. She'd taken the children and flown to Phoenix, reuniting with her parents and siblings. Together they'd tackled the job of disbursing and selling her property in California. She'd even managed to meet with Devin's family. Though strained and uncomfortable, she lived through it.

Jo broke down at the cemetery, crying with her children. They wept with the pain of physical loss—but her tears were for something intangible. The loss of her youth and naivety—and perhaps, for the man Devin might have been.

She decided to keep nothing. The children's baby pictures and videos were all she packed to bring back to Nebraska. Jewelry, paintings, sculptures, furs, cars, clothing, and furniture—everything went. She wanted no ties to that other life. It no longer existed. Jocelyn Parrish was a non-entity—as dead as Devin, Eric, and Bev!

~ ~ ~

"You're gonna wear a hole in the boards," Nate said, picking up Lester and coming to stand beside her. Jo looked up and smiled at the boy, surprised at how calm he appeared.

He reached out and touched her cheek, smiling at her. "You looked so sad, Jo," he said. "You okay?"

She nodded. There was no way he could ever comprehend the horrors she struggled with. No way, he should ever have to.

"Yeah, just pensive," she replied. "Where's Laney?" Her daughter was seldom far from Nate's side these days. They were a handsome couple, a good match.

Nate grinned. "Getting Jenny prepared not to throw herself on Dad the instant he's out of the car."

Jo chuckled. "Good plan."

"It's okay, Jo," Nate said, his face and voice serious again. "Dad's fine." The boy whispered the words close to Jo's ear, putting an arm around her shoulders and giving her a quick hug.

"I know," Jo responded, smiling up at the handsome youth. She slipped her arm around his waist, returning the hug. Yeah, I know, she thought, but I need to witness that for myself!

"See them yet?" Casey yelled, banging the front door screen as he joined them. He plopped down on a wicker chair and started tossing a baseball into the air, catching it in a gloved hand.

"Not yet," Nate replied.

Jo could hear the clatter of activity inside the cottage. Ellie and Sarah were getting a meal ready in her kitchen. She felt a little guilty at not helping, but she—couldn't. She was a mass of jittery nerves.

After she'd dropped and broken the second plate, Ellie had shooed her out onto the porch. "Go see if you can break a chair or something." She'd swatted at Jo with her dishtowel, grinning and winking.

"I got Hawk a pwesent," Jenny cried, slamming out the screen door five seconds after Casey.

"What's that?" Jo asked, kneeling and drawing Jenny close.

"Look," Jenny held out a rounded glass globe. Its clear surface magnified the colored glass shapes inside with incredible intensity. It was a beautiful paperweight, one they'd found in a pawnshop in Tempe. It was also Jenny's prized possession. Jo knew her daughter loved the colored orb, and it brought tears to her eyes to think Jenny wanted to give it to Hawk.

"There they are!" Casey shouted, jumping up and racing down the sidewalk toward the driveway.

Laney rushed out of the house and joined Nate as he started toward the vehicle, followed closely by Ellie and Sarah. Jo watched as B.J.'s white van pulled to a stop. B.J., Carol, Bert, and Father Pat got out. Jo smiled warmly at the sight of the Priest.

The side door slid open, and Jo caught her first glimpse of Hawk. His eyes immediately sought hers, and she saw the briefest smile touch his lips before B.J. reached to help him out.

"I'm fine, Beejah," Hawk growled, rejecting his brother's offer of assistance.

"You're damned stubborn's what you are," B.J. retorted.

"Like what," Bert teased, "you thought the doctors could fix THAT?" He was grinning from ear to ear.

"You can wipe that shit-eatin' grin off your puss," Hawk snarled, though there was no anger in his face or voice.

"BOYS!" Carol chided. "Put a lid on it and act your ages, please. There's a man of the cloth present."

"Yes, Ma'am," they said, almost in unison.

Lester had already reached the van, hopping around and barking with delight. Hawk picked him up and gave him a quick hug.

"Good to see you too, Les." He ruffled the dog's head, and then set him down. His movements were slow, but he adamantly refused assistance.

"Dad," Nate greeted his father, his voice gruff as he stepped into Hawk's embrace.

"Hello, Son," Hawk said softly. "Looks like you got yourself two beauties there," he said, winking at Laney. She was standing beside Nate, holding baby Faith.

"Hi, Laney." Hawk smiled at her with genuine affection, ruffling Faith's downy curls.

"Welcome home, Hawk," Laney said, a shy blush coloring her cheeks.

Both Ellie and Sarah hugged Hawk. Jo was only peripherally aware they were exchanging pleasantries and mild bantering. She could hear the words and the laughter, but her world had centered on one predominant reality: Hawk was standing at the end of the sidewalk. Whole. Safe. Alive!

"HAWK!" Jenny's voice carried over the top of the chatter.

Oh God, Jo thought. She's running!

Jenny had shyly clung to Jo's leg, watching the reunion, but now she was scampering down the sidewalk at full speed. She came to a dead stop not more than six inches from Hawk, hanging her head as she held out her treasure.

"This is fow you," she said, her face coloring with uncharacteristic tentativeness.

Hawk immediately went down on one knee.

Jo noticed that he grimaced, ever so slightly, but refused Bert's helping hand.

Hawk took the paperweight and held it up to the light, one brow raised as he examined it carefully. "What is it?" he asked.

"It's a papaw weight," Jenny replied.

"It's just a stupid old piece of glass she begged Mom to get her," Casey said, grinning at Hawk. "She sleeps with the dumb thing."

Jenny scowled at her brother, and then promptly ignored him. "Mommy bought it fow me in Aiwazonas. It's the bestest papawweight in the whole wowld." She clapped her hands, jumping up and down in place.

"It is," Hawk said, his face and voice reflecting genuine enthusiasm. "Thank you, Jenny, I love it." He pulled the child into a tight embrace, meeting Jo's eyes above her head.

'*I love you,*' he mouthed.

Jo reached out a trembling hand toward the porch banister, suddenly needing its support as her eyes filled with tears and her knees went weak.

God, I love you too! She wanted to shout the words, but she didn't. She wasn't even aware Carol had come up beside her, until she felt an arm around her waist.

"He's gonna be fine, Jo," she said softly. "You're both gonna be just fine."

"I know," Jo whispered. "It's just...there's been so...much! So much uncertainty and turmoil."

"Argh," Carol made the guttural sound with a flippant wave of her hand. "Piece 'a cake. Especially after what you two've lived through. Give yourselves time, Jo. You got the rest of your lives, and believe me, makin' up is...well...you know!" Carol winked at Jo, grinning.

"Thanks, Carol," Jo laughed. "I needed that."

"Now, we'll get some food into him, and he'll be good as new before ya know it," Carol continued, patting one of Jo's hands. "Nothin's a better healer than food. Trust me on this one." She started to turn toward the house, and then stopped, looking back at Jo. "Okay, well, maybe sex, or at least it runs a close second. But only if it's real passionate!"

Jo stood with her mouth open, watching Carol bustle into the house. Well, there's a hell-of-a plan, she thought, grinning.

"You're my kinda woman, Carol!" Jo shouted after her, laughing at Carol's chortle.

"Jo," Hawk's voice was directly behind her.

She turned slowly, trying desperately to control the frantic beating of her heart.

Hawk's eyes were eating her alive. "God, you look good," he said in a low, throaty voice.

Jo felt her eyes well up, tears spilling down her cheeks as she walked into his warm, strong embrace.

"Hawk, oh, Hawk," she whispered his name over and over again, unable to believe she was finally in his arms. He was safe, and well, and they were together. Her mind couldn't quite grasp it all. Her heart felt as if it could explode from the intensity of her emotions. So much, she thought. They'd both been to hell and back, but it was over now.

"Hey," he whispered close to her ear, "we gotta stop meetin' like this."

Jo giggled.

"I love you, Little Girl," Hawk said gently, his mouth pressed against Jo's hair.

"I love you, too, Hawk. So very much!"

"Can the mush," B.J. interrupted their reunion, winking at Jo as she pulled away. "You got all night to get reacquainted. I'm famished."

Bert followed B.J. up the porch steps. "You're always famished," he retorted. "Look at that gut of yours. Hell, you'd think you were birthin' in a week or two!"

"What! Like you don't stuff your face all day long?" B.J. retorted. "Oh, *EXCUSE* me! I forgot. You don't eat, you're the one that's gotta have *sex* every waking hour!"

"At least you don't get fat on sex," Bert laughed.

"Fat? I am NOT fat! Pleasantly plump maybe, but definitely not fat." B.J. sounded indignant, but the wink and grin he shot Jo, belied that impression.

"BOYS!" Ellie chided. "Don't make me hurt you. You're upsetting Hawk, and embarrassing Father Pat."

Hawk laughed, raising his hands in mild protest. "Don't put me in the middle of this," he said. "Today, I'm just an innocent bystander."

"Innocent, my ass," B.J. retorted as they stepped inside the house. "I'll bet you got ideas in that head of yours that'd REALLY make Father blush."

"Well, if he does," Father Pat interjected, chuckling, "I'll be having confession tomorrow afternoon, at five."

They all laughed as Hawk lowered his head, a dull flush coloring his cheeks.

"Thanks, Father," he said. "I do believe I'll need it." Hawk grinned playfully at Jo, winking. He reached out, holding her back a little, as the others bunched around the kitchen table, talking and teasing.

The unmistakable aroma of fried chicken permeated the room, making her stomach growl. She hadn't eaten all day—too nervous to even think about food—and right now, she didn't think she *could* eat.

"Damn, I missed you," Hawk whispered, pulling her close as his mouth claimed hers in an all too brief kiss. She could feel his tongue teasing and exploring, and then he pulled away, looking at her with an expression that made her gut twist with physical need.

"Me, too," she replied, her eyes locking on Hawk's mouth. I love his mouth. I love his eyes. I love this man!

"Is it true?" Hawk whispered.

"What?" Jo asked, unable to wrench her eyes from his face.

Hawk laid a gentle hand on her belly, and lifted an eyebrow.

Jo hadn't told anyone else! "You…you heard me?" her voice quivered ever so slightly as her hand reached up to cup his cheek.

Hawk didn't say anything, just nodded, his eyes holding hers. The depth of love she saw there made her knees tremble.

Nodding she said, "Yeah, Hawk. Two months along."

His face broke into a huge, white smile, but he didn't say anything. Like Jo, he seemed to understand this was their moment. A time for the two of them to hold the knowledge of their precious secret close to their hearts, drawing strength and healing in the promise of joy and life—after so much tragedy and death.

"I love you, Little Girl," Hawk breathed on a sigh, close to Jo's ear.

"Oh God, Hawk. I love you too!" Jo nearly broke into tears, swallowing convulsively to regain some measure of control. He'd come so close!

"You gonna nurse me through the night?" He teased. "I'm feelin' pretty weak right now." His mouth moved close to Jo's ear and his breath tickled her neck, sending a shiver down her back. Jo's hands, resting lightly on his chest, wanted desperately to reach up and pull his head down for another long, passionate kiss, but she controlled the urge.

"Shit, Hawk," Bert interrupted, coming up and resting a hand on his brother's shoulder. "What's that you got tucked in your pants?"

Hawk didn't grace the remark with a reply, but he did grin and wink suggestively at Jo, a single eyebrow dancing up and down mischievously. She felt the immediate rush of fire to her cheeks, and knew they were probably crimson.

"*Damn*! I didn't know you could grow 'em *that* big," B.J. contributed, chortling at his own witticism.

"Definitely a Nebraska, corn-fed doggie, there," Bert teased, grinning mischievously at Hawk's raised eyebrow of reproof. "Don't be tryin' to stare me down, Big Bro. You ain't gonna whoop any ass for a day or two."

"SEE?" B.J. jumped in. "I ain't the only one's fat 'round here."

"That ain't fat, B.J.," Bert retorted, "that's *HORNY*!"

Embarrassed clear to her toes, Jo lowered her head, but not before catching a glimpse of Father Pat holding his side, and wiping tears of laughter from his eyes.

"BOYS!" Carol's tone was ominous, but the look on her face was even more chilling. "There are children present, not to mention a Priest!"

"Whoa," Bert sobered immediately. "Pissin' Hawk off is one thing, but I ain't tanglin' with Ma," he informed B.J. in a loud whisper.

B.J. grinned innocently at Carol. "Ain't nothin' they haven't heard before, Ma."

"*Sit down*," Carol commanded, "and let's say grace."

Everyone complied, without question.

They joined hands and began their prayer. "*Bless us, O Lord, and these thy gifts, which we are about to receive, from Thy bounty, through Christ our Lord, Amen,*" they prayed in unison.

"Hawk, after dinner, why don't you and Jo get your guitars out," Carol suggested, passing the bowl of buttered corn to Ellie.

"I'd love to, Mom. How 'bout you, Jo?" Hawk winked at her, grinning.

"Sure." She wasn't in the mood for music, but just being near Hawk was enough of an incentive.

"Hey, do you know that new Alan Jackson song, *Remember When*?" Ellie asked, picking daintily at a chicken breast.

"Yep, I believe I do." Hawk smiled at his sister-in-law, slathering butter on a warm biscuit.

"No way," Bert interjected, waving his fork in Hawk's direction. "You have to play, *Proud Mary*."

"Yeah, *Proud Mary*!" B.J. insisted, shoveling a forkful of mashed potatoes into his mouth.

"No way, I ain't playin' that song, guys. Just give it a rest."

"It's tradition!" Bert reminded him, waving a chicken leg for emphasis.

"You two always insist on that song. You know I don't like it, and it ain't happen' this time."

"*Proud Mary, Proud Mary, Proud Mary*!" Bert and B.J. chorused, pounding the ends of their forks on the table.

"YO!" Hawk shouted at last, wiping his mouth on a napkin.

"What?" His brothers said together, grinning innocently at Hawk's glowering expression.

"Shut the fuc—!"

"Beauregard James!"

Jo chuckled, not a bit surprised that Carol had the last word on the matter.

~

Dear Readers,

I have lived many places in my life, and yet I find myself immeasurably impressed by the resilience, compassion, and work ethic of people from America's Heartland. It was my hope, in some small measure, to capture this area and its people, in my work.

I hope you found Dark Secrets both exciting and entertaining. I am presently working on a second romantic suspense, Dark Dreams, to be set in Auburn, Nebraska, and I hope to see my first Young Adult novel, Emma's Choice, (set in Wymore, Nebraska), in print in the very near future.

To look for more information on Dark Secrets, and upcoming publications, please go to my website:

http://www.reedwriting.com

Thank you for purchasing and reading *Dark Secrets*. I welcome your insight and comments. My email address is:

plwallinger@hotmail.com

P.L.Reed-Wallinger

Printed in the United States
35096LVS00005B/47